"Come on, then," Nick[ ] putting her own probl[em] into the spirit of thing[ ] suspense. What exactl[y]is good news you've got for us?"

They were all looking at her. Maggie felt her heart give a funny little thump. It would be a relief to unburden herself to them, to tell them how wobbly and uncertain she felt, to tell them how much she needed their support.

Maggie took a deep breath and looked around the table, at Stella who was so sanely calm and well-balanced, Alice so maternal and protectively loving, Nicki, who had her own problems, Maggie knew, but who out of all of them would surely understand her feelings.

"I'm pregnant," she told them shakily. "Oliver and I are going to have a baby."

Penny Jordan's novels "...touch every emotion."
                                        —*Romantic Times*

*Also available from MIRA Books and
PENNY JORDAN*

POWER PLAY
THE PERFECT SINNER
A PERFECT FAMILY
TO LOVE, HONOR AND BETRAY
POWER GAMES
CRUEL LEGACY

PENNY JORDAN

Now or Never

MIRA®

ISBN 1-55166-671-5

NOW OR NEVER

Copyright © 2003 by Penny Jordan.

All rights reserved. Except for use in any review, the reproduction or
utilization of this work in whole or in part in any form by any electronic,
mechanical or other means, now known or hereafter invented, including
xerography, photocopying and recording, or in any information storage or
retrieval system, is forbidden without the written permission of the publisher,
MIRA Books, 225 Duncan Mill Road, Don Mills, Ontario, Canada M3B 3K9.

All characters in this book have no existence outside the imagination of the
author and have no relation whatsoever to anyone bearing the same name
or names. They are not even distantly inspired by any individual known or
unknown to the author, and all incidents are pure invention.

MIRA and the Star Colophon are trademarks used under license and registered
in Australia, New Zealand, Philippines, United States Patent and Trademark
Office and in other countries.

Visit us at www.mirabooks.com

Printed in U.S.A.

Now or Never

1

'You're sure? I mean, it couldn't possibly be a mistake?'

Maggic Rockford's voice trembled. She could feel Oliver's warm, protective grip of her hand tightening as she looked away from the doctor to exchange anguished glances with him. There had been so many visits here to see this highly acclaimed specialist over the months—visits prior to which she had swung perilously from hope to fear and then back again. Visits involving what had seemed like an unending raft of tests and medical procedures backed up with counselling sessions, and questions that had sometimes seemed even more invasive than the physical side of what she had been undergoing.

Crossing London this morning in their taxi, Oliver Sanders had held both her hands in his as he had told her emotionally, 'Whatever happens this morning, whatever we hear, I want you to know that it will make no difference to the way I feel about you. About the way I love you, Maggie.'

But of course it would. How could it not?

Anxiously she refocused on the doctor, who was frowning.

Maggie shivered, her eyes blurring with the tears she had sworn she would not cry.

'This mascara cost a small fortune and no way am I

going to waste it by crying,' she had insisted to Oliver when he had stood looking at her put it on.

'Stop watching me,' she had demanded uncomfortably in the early days of their relationship. Her ex-husband Dan used to lie on the bed watching her dress and put on her make-up, it was true, but things had been different then, she had been different, and in the newness of her relationship with Oliver she had felt acutely self-conscious sharing such intimacy.

'There's no need to be defensive with me,' Oliver had told her gently. 'All I want to do is love you, Maggie.'

'There is no mistake.' The specialist was assuring her soberly, his voice breaking into her thoughts. 'The blood test is totally conclusive.'

'No mistake!'

Immediately she turned towards Oliver.

His face had lost its colour, his eyes dark with emotion as he reached for her. Now she could see in his expression what secretly she had already known. Now she could see just how much this did matter to him. Her already knotted stomach tightened.

Patiently the doctor waited for his words to sink in.

After all, delivering news like this was part of his job, and he had learned just how to say the words so that they were properly absorbed and their meaning retained; words that could give hope, or totally destroy it. Words that in effect held the gift of life!

When he judged that he had given them enough time, he continued.

'The procedure has been successful.'

As she focused on him Maggie could see Oliver wiping his eyes as they brimmed over with tears.

Surely she was the one who should be crying? But somehow she felt unable to do so. The tension inside her was too great, the enormity of what lay ahead of her too big for the easy release of crying.

'There is no mistake,' the specialist repeated and this time he smiled at them both. 'Congratulations, Maggie. You are quite definitely pregnant.'

Pregnant! The innovative, hugely expensive private treatment she had undergone had worked, and she was carrying Oliver's baby!

She, who until Oliver had come into her life, believed that she had managed to come to terms with the fact that she would never have a child.

Somehow Maggie realised that they had both stood up, and that Oliver was hugging her, his voice thick with emotion as he thanked the specialist.

'Maggie you've done it. You clever, wonderful girl,' he praised her emotionally.

Just for a second Maggie felt the darkness of the familiar shadow hovering. Determinedly she pushed it away. She wasn't going to allow it to spoil this special moment.

Even so, her natural honesty forced her to point out to him quietly, 'I've had a lot of help.'

The specialist was opening the door and showing them out, reminding Maggie that she would need to make a series of appointments so that the progress of her pregnancy could be carefully monitored.

Maggie eyed him anxiously.

'There's nothing to worry about, is there?' Oliver asked the doctor, immediately reacting to her body language.

'No. But of course, in view of the circumstances of this pregnancy, Maggie will need to be careful.'

'I'll make sure that she is,' Oliver was responding fervently.

'You heard what the doctor just said,' he reminded

Maggie, two minutes later, after they had checked through her appointments and were on their way out of the clinic.

'Oliver,' Maggie told him quietly. 'There is no way I am going to do anything that might jeopardise this pregnancy. Whatever it takes for your baby to be born safely and healthily, I am going to do it.'

'My baby? This is our baby,' Oliver told her fiercely.

Their baby. Conceived with Oliver's sperm and another woman's—a fertile woman's—donated egg!

'Maggie,' Oliver challenged her insistently when she made no immediate response. 'This is our baby.'

The look in his eyes made Maggie give herself a small warning mental shake, but before she could give him the response she knew he wanted a door opened and a dark-haired, heavy-set woman burst into the corridor.

'Don't lie to me!' she was screaming at the white-coated man following her. 'I know what you've done. You've stolen my babies… You promised me…'

Wildly she turned towards Maggie, who instinctively placed her hand protectively against her still-flat tummy. Just as instinctively the woman's gaze honed in on Maggie's betraying gesture, her eyes narrowing, an angry flush of colour staining her pale skin.

'They're liars in here. Murderers,' she hissed, staring at Maggie whilst she demanded,

'Is it you they've given them to? Whoever it is I shall find out.'

Shocked, Maggie stepped back from her.

Out of the corner of her eye she saw that two nurses had quietly entered the foyer and were approaching the woman, taking a careful hold of her. As she was firmly but gently led away, still screaming and sobbing, the man who had been with her, whom Maggie recognised as one of the clinic's medics, apologised.

'I'm sorry about that.'

As he turned to follow the nurses the receptionist shook her head and whispered confidingly to Maggie and Oliver.

'Heavens knows how she got in. The commissioner has got strict instructions not to admit her. She's a bit of a crank.'

Although Maggie managed a polite smile the incident had upset her. Was this what motherhood was all about? Seeing danger everywhere and feeling fiercely determined to protect one's child from it? One's child. Oliver's child... Her child!

'Are you all right?'

Maggie could see that Oliver was frowning as he stepped protectively close to her. 'I'm fine.' She gave a small shrug. 'Being pregnant must be making me feel extra sensitive,' she told him lightly, trying to shrug off the feeling of disquiet the other woman's behaviour had caused her.

'I just wish...' She paused, her expressive eyes shadowing. 'It's silly of me, I know, but I wish that hadn't happened. She looked so...so anguished, Oliver. I know that everyone who comes here for help doesn't get to be as lucky as we have been. And the only reason we have been so lucky is because of the generosity of the woman who donated her eggs.'

Although naturally it was against the clinic's protocol for them to have met her, they had been given sufficient information to know that in build and colouring she was very similar to Maggie.

When Oliver had first told her that he wanted them to have a child, she had thought that he was joking.

'I can't,' she had reminded him.

'You were made to be a mother,' he had insisted. 'And there are ways.'

That had been over a year ago but she could still remember the fierce, thrilling jerk of emotional response her heart had given to his words. It had been as though he had uncovered a truth about herself that she had previously kept hidden, a sore place she had refused to acknowledge.

And then she had happened to read an article about the clinic and the controversial pioneering work it was doing, using eggs donated by fertile women to help women who could not possibly conceive naturally to have a child.

Right from their first visit to the clinic she had refused to allow herself to be optimistic, to hope too much.

Oliver had been the one who had been convinced she would conceive, who had carried the hope for both of them.

Watching Oliver as he hailed a taxi to take them back to their hotel, Maggie felt a resurgence of her normal self-confidence. She had booked them into the Langham, one of London's most prestigious modern designer hotels, mainly for sentimental reasons. The Langham was the hotel where they had spent their first night together. 'Remember the first time we stayed here?' she asked Oliver half an hour later as they crossed its foyer.

At six feet one he towered over her. She was only five feet two without the heels she always wore. Dan, her ex, had been even taller at six feet two, his hair so deep, dark brown it was almost black, thick, his olive-tinged skin in direct contrast to her red-gold curls and celtic paleness, where Oliver's hair was a much softer brown, bleached blond at the ends, a legacy he claimed from his days spent surfing in Australia during the year out he had taken following his degree, to heal himself emotionally from the pain of his mother's death.

'Of course.' He grinned, answering her question. 'I'd been working for you for more then twelve months, every second of which I'd spent wondering just how I was going to get you into bed, and then we came here and...'

'And you said to the receptionist behind my back that there'd been a mistake and that we only needed one room. You were lucky I didn't sack you on the spot when I found out,' she told him mock severely.

She had been suffering from a bad bout of uncharacteristic vulnerability prior to the fateful first night she had spent here with Oliver; going through a period when she had been questioning her own satisfaction with her life and secretly comparing it with the lives of her friends; envying them their secure relationships with their male partners; the closeness and intimacy they shared; the children they had together, things that she had believed were permanently going to be denied to her.

'I was lucky, full stop, the day I met you,' Oliver corrected her softly. 'You are so special, Maggie,' he told her emotionally, raising her hand to his mouth and tenderly kissing her fingers. 'So special, so perfect; so irreplaceable. So very, very much the woman I want to be the mother of my baby.'

Maggie shivered a little. It scared her sometimes when he spoke like this. No one was perfect, least of all her.

She could remember when she had first introduced him to Nicki, her best friend.

'He worships you,' Nicki had told her wryly. 'You'll have to be careful never to disillusion him, Maggie,' she had added warningly.

Thinking of Nicki reminded Maggie of the fact that she was going to have a considerable amount of grovelling and apologising to do when she broke the news of her pregnancy to her close circle of lifelong friends. They would want to know why they had not been let into her plans, allowed to share the trauma of what she had been going through with her, no question. Especially since…

'Come back.'

Ruefully she smiled at Oliver as he ushered her into the lift.

The first time they had stayed here together, they had barely left the suite, making full use of its luxurious, opulent fittings, including the private Jacuzzi. Oliver had poured champagne over her naked body, licking it ardently from her skin, touching her until they had both been high on the pleasure of the intensity of their desire for one another.

But tonight there would be no marathon sex session, and nor would there be any champagne or long soak in the Jacuzzi. But then sex wasn't high on her list of priorities right now, Maggie acknowledged as they walked into their suite.

'You do realise that we're going to have to buy a proper house now, don't you?' she challenged Oliver. 'A house with room for a nursery, and with a garden and…'

'I know,' Oliver agreed. 'The apartment will definitely have to go.'

Maggie watched him indulgently. Oliver had fallen in love with the apartment the first time they had viewed it. On the top floor of the building, it was a modern conversion designed to imitate the loft apartments so popular in New York. Privately Maggie would have preferred something a little bit more traditional, and rather more comfortable, but Oliver, with his designer's eye, had laughed at her and so she had kept to herself her no doubt old-fashioned fears about the practicality of keeping the immaculate stainless steel kitchen in its gleaming clutter-free state, and her concerns about just how the contents of her extensive designer wardrobe were going to fit into and remain crease-free in four artistically stacked woven storage trunks. In the end the conversion of the apartment's third bedroom into a dressing room with fitted wardrobes had solved the clothes storage problem, but the kitchen was not and never would be her own ideal of what a kitchen should be.

She had been living in the small cottage she had bought after the breakup of her marriage to Dan. They had sold the family home, and she had used the money she had received from her share of it to finance her expansion of the small business she and Dan had originally started together.

'Oh, Maggie…Maggie…'

As he wrapped her in his arms and kissed her Maggie could feel the emotion emanating from Oliver. Whilst not perhaps strictly good-looking in the movie-star sense, he possessed a special something that was all his own, a sweetness of nature that shone from his steady-gazed warm brown eyes, an attraction that went way, way beyond mere good looks.

A woman, any woman could look at Oliver and know immediately that he was a man who liked women, genuinely and wholeheartedly liked them. And in addition to that…!

He was gorgeous. He was sexy! He was tender and

loving and good-humoured. He possessed an almost telepathic ability to guess how she was feeling and the love he gave her flowed from him with a generosity she sometimes had to pinch herself to believe was real.

There had been a special rapport between them from the moment he had first walked into her office, even though initially Maggie had fought hard to both deny and deride it. She hadn't been in the market for a relationship. The breakup of her marriage had left her too wary, too self-protective to want one.

Oliver had told her that he had read about her company and that he hoped to persuade her to commission him to do some conceptual design work for them. Her company planned and designed office interiors, providing a highly personal and tailored environment for those fortunate enough to be able to afford their services.

The business did not make a vast profit, but it did make a very comfortable one and, more importantly so far as Maggie was concerned, she considered running it to be both challenging and satisfying.

It had amused and delighted her a great deal earlier in the year to read a newspaper article claiming that to be able to have the forward-thinkingness, the taste and the money to afford a Rockford interior for one's offices was to truly have arrived!

Maggie had looked at Oliver as he'd stood there in her office—her own design team's work, of course with just enough witty touches of feng shui, colour planning and atmospherics to whisper a discreet statement about her to those in the know. Maggie herself was not a designer, but she was an administrator *par excellence*, a woman with extraordinary 'people' skills and she had found herself thinking enviously of the woman who must inevitably share Oliver's life—

and that alone had been enough to shock and frighten her.

Even so it had taken Oliver a good many months to wear down her resistance and her objections to the point where she'd been prepared to admit how much she cared about him, and even longer for her to agree to going public on their relationship.

She suspected the turning point had been when she had finally started to open up to him about her marriage to Dan.

Unlike her, Oliver had had no hesitation in telling her about his life. She had ached for him when he had told her about his childhood, and the years spent worrying about and caring for his mother who had suffered badly from MS. From the day his father had walked out on them shortly after Oliver's sixteenth birthday, until his mother's death whilst he was at university, Oliver had virtually become her sole carer.

'What do you think we're going to have?' Oliver was whispering to her now as he took her back in his arms. 'A boy or a girl?'

'I don't mind,' she told him. And it was the truth. Right now it was enough just to know she was carrying his child. She felt as though she had successfully negotiated a gruelling obstacle course, and all she wanted to do now was enjoy the respite of having done so.

'I hope it's going to be a girl, just like you,' Oliver told her.

Immediately Maggie stiffened and pulled away from him.

'Haven't you forgotten something?' she challenged him. 'This baby isn't going to have any of my genes, Oliver.'

To her chagrin Maggie could feel her voice starting

to thicken. She had promised herself that she wouldn't do this; that she wouldn't allow herself to be tormented by what by rights should now be an old and bearable pain. She didn't want to remember now the days…the nights when she had endured the ferocious, savage agony of it, tearing at her. She had known grief in her life; many times; the deaths of her parents, the breakup of her marriage, but this grief had been like none other she had experienced. It had been terrifying in its enormity, its inescapability, its finality.

'Not your genes,' Oliver agreed softly. 'But our baby will have your love, your mothering, Maggie.'

Our Baby. Maggie could feel the yearning aching deep inside her.

'I suppose now that it's actually official you'll be wanting to tell The Club,' Oliver teased her, pulling a face.

'Don't call them that,' Maggie protested, but she was smiling too. 'They are my best and closest friends. The four of us have known one another since we were at school.'

'And you share a bond that no mere male can possibly understand,' Oliver interrupted her. 'Yes, I do know that.'

'I have never said that,' Maggie denied.

'You don't need to,' Oliver told her wryly.

'They aren't going to be very pleased with me for keeping it a secret from them,' Maggie admitted. 'Especially Nicki. After all, I was the first to know when she was pregnant with Joey. In fact I knew even before Kit! And they still haven't really forgiven me for not telling them about you sooner.'

'So the phone lines are going to be burning, once we get home?' Oliver smiled.

Maggie shook her head vigorously, her curls dancing.

'No. We're due to go out for a meal together, on Friday. I think I'll wait until then when we're all together.'

It would be a relief to tell them, to bask in their amazement and excitement. She had never let any of them know just how much she had envied them as one after the other they had given birth to their babies, partially because she hadn't wanted their pity and partially because of Dan, and by the time she had realised that they had come to assume that she simply did not want children it had been too late to correct their misconceptions.

Even in a friendship as close as theirs there were sometimes secrets, Maggie acknowledged.

'What's wrong?'

They had had dinner an hour earlier and were just preparing for bed. Maggie was more tired than she wanted to acknowledge—because of her pregnancy or because...

'I just hope that we're doing the right thing,' she answered Oliver quietly.

'Of course we are,' he reassured her robustly. 'Why shouldn't we be?'

Silently Maggie looked at him.

'You know why,' she told him. 'I'm fifty-two years old Oliver. A woman who has gone through the menopause, who without the intervention of modern science and the gift of another woman's eggs could not be carrying your child. You, on the other hand, are a young man in the prime of your life. You're in your thirties, with a whole lifetime of impregnating younger fertile women ahead of you.'

'Maggie. Stop it! The fact that we are different ages, the fact that you went through an early menopause, they mean nothing in comparison to our love.'

Maggie looked away from him. They had argued so many, many times before about this. She might not feel her age, she might not even look it—certainly Oliver had flatly refused to believe she could possibly be a day over thirty-five when they had first met, just as she had initially completely believed him when he had told her that he was in his late-thirties—but the cruel facts were that there were an inarguable, an inescapable sixteen years between them.

She had known, of course, that he was younger than her—but she had assumed the age gap was much less than it actually was. She had been in her mid-forties then, and had Oliver been speaking the truth when he had claimed to be in his late thirties she could just about have persuaded herself that the difference between them was acceptable.

Had she known then just how great it was she would never, ever have allowed a relationship to develop between them.

'He's how old?' Nicki had demanded in disbelief when Maggie had finally, at Oliver's insistence, told her friends about him.

She had to admit that once they had got over their shock her friends had been very supportive.

As she remembered that conversation a small secret smile curved Maggie's mouth. They had teased her a little, asking her if it was true what was said about the sex between an older woman and a younger man, and mock primly she had refused to either encourage or answer them.

They had laughed at her, of course, and she had laughed with them, knowing, as Nicki had openly told her, that the air of suppressed sensuality that surrounded her told its own story.

'You positively glow with it,' Nicki had remarked ruefully.

'You were the same when you first met Kit!' Maggie had reminded her friend.

Suddenly Maggie longed to be able to talk to her friends. She, Nicki, Alice and Stella had been friends since their schooldays and their regular once-a-month evening out together to share a meal, a bottle of wine and their hopes and fears was so sacrosanct that only births and deaths had been allowed to interrupt them.

Oliver had nicknamed them 'The Club' or sometimes 'The Coven', claiming that between the four of them they had both the talents and the power to make magic, and that she, his wonderful, wise, wicked Maggie, was the witchiest of all of them.

The girls, her friends, Maggie knew, would understand all the things she had not been able to bring herself to admit to them before. All those feelings and fears she had experienced when, soon after her fortieth birthday, her doctor had had to explain that the cause of the health problems she had been suffering was the onset of a premature menopause. Nothing had prepared Maggie for the realisation that nature was closing certain doors against her; that shockingly an era of her life she had somehow believed would last for ever was over; or for the despair and anguish that realisation had so unexpectedly and uncontrollably brought her.

At the time she had been too overwhelmed by her own feelings to admit them to anyone. But she could admit to them now just how awesomely miraculous it was for her that, because of Oliver, she had found a way to halt nature in its tracks. To snatch from its closing, grinding jaws that which it was relentlessly taking from her.

Motherhood. She had told herself when she and Dan had split up that it just wasn't meant to be for her, and she had believed truly that she had accepted that situation. It had taken Oliver to show her just how much she had lied to herself. And how very much a part of her still ached for that fulfilment. Why had she never realised until it had been all but too late just how important, how elemental, how essential such an experience would be to her?

Silently Oliver watched her. Why couldn't she accept that the difference in their ages meant nothing to him; that he loved her as she was and for what she was?

He truly believed that in spirit Maggie was far younger than he was himself; she had the enthusiasm for life of a young girl and a rare kind of physical beauty that would never age.

He had always been drawn to older women. He liked their emotional maturity; he felt at ease with them.

Maggie's achievements filled him with pride for her; he loved being able to claim her as his partner and he knew she was going to be a wonderful mother.

Oliver loved children. And he loved even more knowing that Maggie was going to have his child... their child.

So she was over fifty. What did that mean? Nothing as far as he was concerned! The specialist at the clinic had agreed with him that Maggie was in perfect health; he had even offered the information that had Maggie not experienced an early menopause she could have become pregnant naturally and that it was not unusual for women of her age to do so.

'Maggie,' he begged her now. 'Please don't make age an issue between us.'

'I'm old enough to be your mother, never mind this baby's!' Maggie couldn't help reminding him.

'And I'm old enough to know that you are my love, the love of my life,' Oliver told her softly.

Cupping her face in his hands, he added, 'I have waited for you a long time, Maggie. You are everything to me. You and our baby.'

The tenderness with which he kissed her made Maggie's throat ache with emotion.

She had loved Dan passionately, too passionately and too intensely perhaps, but it was Oliver who had shown her just what a generous gift love could be.

Here in the shared darkness of the bed as he drew her down against his side there was no age gap between them; here they were equals, partners, lovers.

2

'Alice, it's Nicki. I'm just ringing to check that you're still okay for tomorrow night?'

Tucking the telephone receiver into her shoulder, Alice Palmer deftly retrieved the small toy the elder of her two small grandsons was trying to push into the ear of the younger.

'Yes. I'm fine. Do you want me to ring Stella to make sure she's still going?' she volunteered.

'If you would.'

'I expect you've already spoken to Maggie?'

'Yes. Yes, I have.'

It was an accepted fact amongst the four of them that Maggie and Nicki shared an extra-special closeness, so Alice frowned as she registered the unexpected constraint in Nicki's voice.

'Nothing's wrong, is it? Maggie's okay, isn't she?' she asked in concern. 'I mean, everything's all right with her and Oliver?'

'Oh, yes, they're still totally besotted with one another,' Nicki Young answered her wryly. Alice laughed.

'Stella was saying the other day that it's not so much that Maggie is behaving as though she's still a young girl that makes her feel old, as the fact that she can actually get away with it!'

'Well, I dare say a good helping of the right kind of

genes, a size eight figure, and the kind of glow a woman gets from regular helpings of orgasmic sex have something to do with it, although in all fairness Maggie has always looked young.'

'Mmm…well, you're looking pretty good yourself,' Alice told Nicki, adding ruefully, 'I am at least ten pounds overweight, and Zoë refuses to believe that I could ever possibly have had a twenty-four inch waist. Actually what she said was, "Mother, are you sure you aren't losing your memory along with your waistline?"'

'Being slightly plump suits you, Alice,' Nicki offered comfortingly. 'It makes you look…'

'Grandmotherly?' Alice supplied dryly. On the other end of the line she could hear Nicki laughing.

'I've got to forewarn you that Maggie has some news…something she wants to tell us when we are all together. Whatever it is, she's obviously very excited about it.'

There was a note in her voice that Alice couldn't identify. Nicki had always been the calmest of all of them, careful both with her opinions and her emotions. Unlike Maggie, who was always so wildly passionate about everything.

'Perhaps she and Oliver have decided to get married,' Alice suggested, hopefully.

'I don't know. She said that there was no point in me asking her any questions because she wasn't going to say another word until we're all together. Which reminds me, I've booked us into that new place that's just opened in the high street.'

'You mean where the wet fish shop used to be? Honestly!' Alice protested. 'Since the new supermarkets opened on the outskirts of town, nearly all the old local shops have closed down and the high street now is virtually one long chain of coffee shops and restaurants.'

'Mmm. I know, but since the motorway turned the town into an up-market dormitory area for the city, eating out has become the new trendy thing to do. Not that I should be complaining. The demand for extra staff has meant that we've been so busy at the agency that I'm going to have to take on someone new full-time to deal with the increase in business.'

'I wish you'd tell me how you manage to do it,' Alice said half ruefully, and half enviously. 'You're running your own business, being a full-time mother to a nine-year-old, and a wife. Which reminds me, Stuart said he bumped into Kit at the golf club the other day, and Kit said something about Laura giving up her job in the city and coming home to live with you.'

There was a brief pause before Nicki responded with telling feeling, 'Don't remind me! I can't wait for our get-together and the chance to let off steam! Look, I'd better go, I've got to collect Joey from school in fifteen minutes.'

'Okay, I'll see you tomorrow night, then.'

As she rang off Alice reflected sympathetically on the situation that existed between Nicki and Laura, her husband Kit's daughter from his first marriage.

Ten years ago when Kit and Nicki had married, Laura had been sixteen and still at school. Right from the start Laura had made it plain that she did not want her father to remarry, and no amount of olive-branch offering on Nicki's part had softened her attitude.

'Grandma, biscuit…biscuit!'

'Biscuit—please.' Alice automatically corrected George as she went to get him and his younger brother William some of the homemade biscuits she made especially for them.

They were adorable little boys, who reminded her very much of her own twin sons at the same age, and she loved them to bits, but there was no getting away from the fact that, after a full day of looking after them, she was more than glad to hand them back to their mother, her daughter Zoë.

Thinking of Zoë caused her forehead to wrinkle in an unhappy frown. Like her, Zoë had married young. Too young? Alice was increasingly feeling that that was what she herself had done.

Zoë wasn't going to be pleased with the news Alice had to tell her. And what about Stuart? He wasn't going to be very happy about her plans, was he? He had never encouraged or wanted her to be independent or to strike out on her own, and she knew that he was not going to understand, never mind approve of, the need that was motivating her now. She was going to have to be very strong, very single-minded if she was to be successful in reaching her longed-for goal, she knew that. But she knew too that her friends would support her. After all, they had always supported one another, been there for one another. She was looking forward to the excitement of breaking her news to them as much as she was dreading revealing it to her husband and daughter.

Quickly she went to check on her grandsons before going to telephone the fourth member of their quartet.

'Stella, it's Alice,' she announced when Stella answered her call. 'Do you still want me to pick you up tomorrow night?'

'Could you? The only problem is that I don't want to get back late. Hughie's coming home from university today—just for a couple of days. Apparently there's a break in lectures he can take advantage of. He says he has run out of clean clothes, but I'm not falling for that one. No doubt the real reason he wants to come home is to see Julie.'

The energetic sound of Stella Wilson's voice reflected her personality, Alice thought. An almost frighteningly well-organised, no-nonsense person, she ran the lives of her husband and her son with streamlined efficiency. There was no agonising from Stella about a creeping band of weight transforming her body from that of a young woman to an older one; no soul-searching, or insecurities; no doubting or dithering; no hint, in fact, of any of the doubts and anxieties that so beset her, Alice recognised ruefully. But then Stella was one of those women who suited middle age.

The plainest of their foursome when they had been girls, Stella had grown from a girl whose looks, brisk manner and sensible, practical outlook on life had meant that she'd often been left in the background into a woman whose forthright manner and confidence in her own beliefs meant that she was now recognised as a valuable asset of the many committees she sat on and by those whose causes she championed. There was no sentimentality about Stella; she was not flirtatious or playful, and could when offended retreat into an awesomely dignified silence, but she was tremendously loyal and could always be relied on to offer straightforward advice and practical help. When it came to problem-solving Stella had no equal, and she was dearly loved by all of them.

'Julie's a great girl,' she pronounced. 'But she's still at school, and Hughie has only just turned nineteen. I'm having to bite on my tongue not to sound like an over-anxious mother, but the last thing either of them need right now is an intense, emotional, long-distance relationship when they should be concentrating on their studies. I haven't forgotten all the problems you went through with Zoë, when she was so determined to marry Ian that she threatened to drop out of university.'

Alice bit her lip. Stella never meant to be tactless, it was just that sometimes she forgot that others had less robust sensitivities than she possessed herself.

'Zoë doesn't know how lucky she is,' Stella was continuing affectionately. 'If anyone was born to be a wife and mother, it was you, Alice. How are the twins, by the way?'

'Still in South America, so far as we know,' Alice replied. It was far easier to talk to her friend about her twin sons than her elder daughter. 'Stuart was saying only the other night, he doesn't know which is going to prove the more expensive, financing their studies, or paying for their gap year! To be honest I think he's a little bit envious of them. I mean, in our day, "gap years" were more of a rare luxury than an accepted fact of life. Stuart went straight from university into his career. We were married two years after that and then Zoë arrived and then of course the twins.'

'Mmm. I know what you mean. Richard tends to grumble that Hughie has life far easier than he did at his age, but I suspect that really he's a little bit jealous of him. After all, he's just about to start out in life, and he's got everything ahead of him, whereas for most of our generation the best thing that lies ahead is early retirement and the worst the threat of redundancy!'

Whilst Alice was wincing inwardly at the unwittingly brutal picture Stella had just drawn, Stella added wryly, 'Unless of course you're fortunate enough to be someone like Maggie! Richard was saying only the other day that it didn't surprise him that she should end up with a younger man. He said that she's always been the sort of person who challenged the status quo; a sort of minor social revolution in her own right, and at the forefront of new trends. And of course it's true! Do you remember how she used to shock us when we were girls? How daring we thought she was, and how inside we all ached to be like her?'

'Yes,' Alice conceded. 'It hasn't all been easy for her, though, has it? She and Dan were so much in love when they got married. I never thought that they would split up.'

'Well, no, but Nicki let it slip in a moment of weakness—you know how, normally, she's always the first to leap to Maggie's defence—that she wasn't totally surprised, because she knew that Dan had always wanted children. Nicki dated him first, didn't she? And apparently he had told her then that he wanted a family. I know that Maggie has never really talked about their divorce, but she did once say to me when I asked if they were planning to have children that the business was her "baby". With her feeling like that I suppose it's not surprising that Dan left her!' Stella pointed out.

'Well, at least she's happy now with Oliver,' Alice intervened pacifically. 'I must say that when she first told us about him, I was a bit concerned. Especially when she admitted that he was much younger than she had at first realised. But you only have to see them together to see how much he loves her.'

'Alice, you are such a romantic.' Stella laughed.

Was it because she was just that little bit younger than the others that they always tended to treat her as though she were someone who was somehow not quite as up to speed as they were themselves? Alice wondered. There was a very fine line between affectionate indulgence, and patronising indulgence and sometimes she felt that her friends unwittingly crossed it. Or was she being over-sensitive?

Of course *they* had all been to university—had those life-shaping years in common—whilst she had not.

'There isn't any point, or any need,' Stuart had told her, at the time. 'I'm in love with you, Alice, and I don't want to wait three years to marry you whilst you get a degree you're never going to use. I can think of a much better way for you to occupy your time,' he had added, with the powerful sensuality that had originally swept her so easily off her feet. At nineteen she had been impressed and awed by such a macho attitude.

At nearly fifty-one, though, she was beginning to feel that it was not so much sexy and sensual as domineering and selfish. Beginning to? Or had she in reality thought it for quite a long time but pushed the thought away, burying it rather than confronting it? Guiltily Alice reminded herself that Stuart was a good husband and father who worked very hard to provide them all with financial comfort and security. And who enjoyed a career that took him all over the world, whilst she stayed at home being a dutiful wife and mother…

'Oh, I nearly forgot,' Alice told Stella, hastily dragging her thoughts back to the present. 'Apparently Maggie has told Nicki that she's got something to tell us. Wedding plans, do you think?'

'I hope not,' Stella responded forthrightly. 'I mean, I know it's all roses and romance now, but if you want my honest opinion it can't last! Of course, the press has got a lot to answer for. It's impossible to pick up a newspaper these days, even the sensible ones, without reading some hyped-up article about how our generation has still got the bit firmly between its teeth and is totally refusing to let go, and be turned out to grass gracefully as previous generations at our age would have done. The mystique we've managed to attach to ourselves is the most disgraceful propaganda really.'

'But it is true that we have pushed back an awful lot of boundaries,' Alice felt the need to point out.

'Indeed, but although we might have convinced ourselves that we can hold back time, we still can't actually turn it back,' Stella told her dryly. 'Oliver is well over a decade younger than Maggie and sooner or later that is bound to cause them problems.'

'Mmm! And how are my two special boys?'

Alice stood to one side as she watched her daughter kneel down to hug her two young sons.

'I'm afraid I'm not going to be able to collect them until eight tomorrow evening, Ma,' Zoë announced, not quite meeting Alice's eyes as she informed her, 'I've arranged to get together with some of the girls at the wine bar after work. If you could bathe these two for me, so that I can just put them straight to bed when I get them home, that would be great. They'll be good company for you with Dad away, and—'

'Zoë,' Alice interrupted her. 'I can't have them tomorrow evening.'

'What? Ma, I can't possibly cancel now, it would make me look totally unprofessional. This isn't a social thing, it's more of a networking meeting, and I could make some important contacts.'

Claiming that she was bored stuck at home with two small children whilst her husband worked a ten-hour day, Zoë had used the lever of her degree and the danger of her brain 'rotting' to pressure Alice into agreeing to look after her sons for her whilst Zoë worked part-time for a local estate agent.

'I do understand,' Alice tried to placate her. 'But surely Ian could look after the boys for once. He is their father, after all.'

'Oh, yes, that's right, pick on Ian.'

Alice's heart sank as she saw the tell-tale spots of angry red colour burning in her daughter's face.

'You've never liked him, have you? You never wanted me to marry him. And don't think I don't know why. Just because he supported me. Sided with me and told you that he could see how much you favoured my brothers above me.'

'Zoë, that isn't true,' Alice tried to protest.

The real reason she didn't much care for her daughter's husband was because she felt that, far from supporting Zoë, Ian actually secretly undermined her and subtly played on her insecurities.

Of course, there was no doubt that financially Ian was a good provider. As an investment banker he earned more than enough to keep his family in considerable comfort, which in turn meant—although Alice would never have dreamed of risking alienating her daughter even further by saying so—that if she chose to do so Zoë could quite easily have stayed at home full time with her children, as Alice herself had had to do.

'Anyway, why can't you have the boys?' Zoë was challenging her suspiciously. 'Dad's away.'

'It's my regular night out with Maggie and the others and—'

'Oh, of course, I should have known,' Zoë exploded angrily, her normally pretty face contorting into an ugly mask of temper. '"Maggie and the others,"' she mimicked, her voice rising. 'And, of course, they are far more important to you than William and George.'

The sheer unexpectedness of Zoë's attack left Alice breathless. The unexpectedness of it, and the unfairness!

'Zoë, that simply isn't true—' she began.

But Zoë refused to listen to her, immediately cutting her short as she burst out, 'If you'd rather be with your precious friends than with your grandchildren, then you go right ahead!'

'Zoë…' Alice protested, but it was too late. Zoë was already scooping up her sons and heading for the door, refusing to listen to her.

It seemed to Alice that it had always been like this between them—antagonism and misunderstanding where there should have been love and harmony. Was it all her fault, as Zoë always insisted? 'Perhaps she feels jealous of you,' Nicki had suggested, softening the words by adding, 'Sometimes it happens.'

'No,' Maggie had argued. 'I think it's her brothers she resents, and that she blames you for their unwanted presence in her life.'

'Sometimes mothers are harder on their daughters than their sons,' had been Stella's practical contribution.

Alice suspected that Maggie had come closest to recognising the cause of Zoë's behaviour. She had been six when the twins had been born, pretty, strong-willed, and perhaps a trifle spoiled, and certainly well able to articulate her angry resentment of the two babies who were taking her parents' attention away from her.

The adored only child of elderly parents herself, and with a far gentler nature than her assertive daughter, Alice felt that she had somehow failed Zoë, in not being able to satisfy her emotional hunger. Just as she herself had turned to Stuart for the security of his love and protection, his ability to take control of her and of her future, so she felt had Zoë turned to Ian to provide the intensity of emotion she sought.

'Mum, will Laura be there when we get home?'

One hand on the passenger door of her car, Nicki turned to look at her young son, Joey.

He was scuffing his new school shoes in the dust, as reluctant to meet her eyes as he obviously was to go home.

Joey was the image of his father, with Kit's wheat-gold hair and toffee-brown eyes, and Nicki's heart melted with love every time she looked at him.

Melted with love, and, increasingly lately, tensed with guilt.

'She might be,' she confirmed, forcing herself to sound jolly and unconcerned. 'After all, she is Daddy's daughter.'

'She's grown up and I don't like her. She's always cross with me,' Joey responded with the unimpeach-able logic of a nine-year-old. 'Why does she have to be with us? Why can't she go back to her own house?'

Nicki sighed.

It was impossible to explain the complexities of the situation to a child of Joey's age, and impossible too to let him see what she was really feeling. She certainly shared her son's dislike of Laura's presence in their home, although, of course, she could not voice it quite so openly.

In the early days when she and Kit had first started cautiously dating, she had been at pains to show every consideration for the feelings of his teenage daughter. The tragic death of her mother after a long-drawn-out

illness was bound to have traumatised her, and Nicki
had recognised that fact, but, no matter how slowly
and discreetly Nicki had tried to progress, Laura had
flatly refused to accept that her father could possibly
want any kind of relationship with Nicki, or allow her
into his life.

At one point Laura's hostility towards her had become so great that Nicki had declared wearily to Kit
that, for everyone's sake, she felt they ought not to see
one another any more.

That time apart from Kit had been one of the worst
periods of her life, and if anyone had told her then that
ultimately she and Kit would be together and that she
would have Joey she would have refused to believe
them.

It had been Kit who had insisted that they should
marry, and that Laura would eventually come to accept the situation, and Nicki had made a mental promise to herself that she would be the most understanding, the most caring stepmother there was, if only
Laura would allow her to be.

After all, Laura was a part of Kit, and Nicki had
been prepared to love her for that alone! She was also,
Nicki had reminded herself determinedly, a teenager
who had lost her mother at a very vulnerable time in
her life. She needed and deserved to have her feelings
recognised, and Nicki fully intended to do that and to
assure her that there was no way she wanted to deny
her mother's role in either her life or that of Kit. And
she had done her best, her very best, but Laura had
simply refused to reciprocate.

Less than four months after their marriage Laura
had walked out, announcing that she was going to live
with her godmother, and in the end it had been agreed
that she should be allowed to do so, although Kit had

told her over and over again that she must always consider the home he and Nicki shared to be her own.

She had returned briefly between leaving school and going on to university, to spend the summer with them, but if anything her hostility and resentment towards her stepmother had been even more marked in Nicki's opinion, and she had been relieved to see Laura go.

That had been seven years ago. Seven years during which Laura had grown up and made her own life, only now she was back. And just thinking about her and what she had done filled Nicki with tension and seething anger.

'Why? Why has she come here to us?' she demanded angrily, pacing the kitchen floor as Kit sat and watched her. 'It's not even as if this has ever been her home, in any real sense! You sold your family home when we got married and the money was invested for her. We bought this house together.'

And she had supplied the bulk of the down payment and paid the mortgage, Nicki could have added, but of course she did not.

'Because we're her family,' Kit answered her.

'No!' Nicki denied bitterly. '*We* are not her family, Kit. She has never wanted to be a part of this family. She has never accepted me as your wife or Joey as your son. *You* are her family. And that's why she's come here. To claim you, to cause discord between us and—'

'Nicki, you're reacting over-emotionally,' Kit protested.

'Me over-emotional?' Nicki challenged him angrily. 'The truth is that you just don't want to accept the facts about Laura and her behaviour. You'd rather blame anyone than her! You just won't see what she's doing!

She's already upset Joey. He's the one you should really be protecting, and not her,' she threw at Kit, tears burning her eyes. 'He's only a little boy and she's an adult. Why has she come here? Has she told you yet?'

The look on his face was its own answer.

All Laura had said was that she had handed in her notice at work and given up the lease on her flat and that she needed to give herself a breathing space before she decided where she wanted her life to go.

It was incomprehensible to Nicki that a young woman in her mid-twenties should behave in such an irresponsible way, and had Laura actually been her child she would have been insisting on being given some answers to some far more pertinent questions than Kit seemed disposed to ask. Not for her the slightly nervous, conciliatory attitude adopted by Alice towards her aggressively determined daughter!

But, of course, Laura was not her child.

'She'll talk to us when she's ready, Nicki, and until then we have to respect her privacy,' Kit had told her firmly. 'Right now, Laura needs our love and support just as much as Joey does, but in a different way.'

Laura was a bone of contention between them that was never going to go away, Nicki acknowledged grimly.

Where was Kit? Nicki wondered irritably five hours later. He knew she had work to do tonight and he had promised to be home early, but there was no sign of him.

Angrily, she remembered the row they had had last night. An exchange of destructive hissed whispers in the darkness of their bedroom, both of them tensely aware that they might be overheard.

The result had been an 'atmosphere', which had

been still hanging over them like a black cloud this morning.

Even before Laura's arrival they had been having problems. Kit's business as an independent insurance broker and financial adviser was suffering badly in the current economic climate—a reflection on the general situation and not on him personally, as Nicki had already pointed out to him.

Part of the trouble was that she was simply not the kind of woman who was prepared to spend her time propping up a male ego, even when that ego belonged to the man she loved. She had gone down that road with her first marriage and all she had got from it had been a bullying, violent husband, from whom she had been glad to escape through divorce.

But when she had fallen in love with Kit he had been in no need of any ego massaging. He had applauded the fact that she was a successful businesswoman in her own right, just as she had admired his uncomplaining shouldering of the responsibility of caring for his terminally ill wife and his teenage daughter.

She and Kit had originally met when he had approached her agency wanting to find a part-time housekeeper to help him with the responsibility of caring for his wife, Jennifer, and providing a home for Laura, then thirteen years old.

There had been an immediate spark of attraction between them, which they had both equally immediately and separately chosen to ignore. After all, Kit had been a married man. And she had been still bruised from her first marriage, with a young and fragile business to nurture, and no place and even less need in her life for the emotional trauma of falling in love with a man in Kit's position.

The agency was to be her life, she had insisted to Maggie.

It had been thanks to Maggie that Nicki had set up the agency in the first place. After the breakup of her first marriage and before she had met Kit, Nicki had done temping work. When the agency she had worked for had announced that it was closing down, she had been panic-stricken, knowing how much she'd needed the money she'd been earning.

'So set up your own agency,' Maggie had told her.

'I can't,' Nicki had protested. 'I could never run my own business. I don't know how.'

'Yes, you do,' Maggie had contradicted her firmly. 'You just don't realise that you do.'

And somehow or other Maggie, being Maggie, had managed to chivvy and downright bully her into taking what had then, to Nicki, seemed to be an impossibly dangerous step.

To her own surprise, what had started out as a small venture run from her own home had now become a very demanding and thankfully healthily profitable business. And what had been even more surprising had been the discovery that as the business had grown so had she; that she positively enjoyed the challenges it had brought her and that she was far more business-minded than she had ever known she could be. Or at least she had been until Joey had been born.

'You're pregnant. But you can't be. You're too old. It's disgusting. *You're* disgusting!' had been Laura's furious reaction when they had told her the news about Nicki's pregnancy. 'You're being such a typical second wife,' she had taunted Nicki when Kit had not been there. 'They always rush to get pregnant. I'd hate to be in your position. Always feeling you've got something to prove, always knowing that someone else had been there before you. It isn't my father who wants this baby, no matter what you say. It's you. After all, he already has me!'

It had been just over a week after they had broken the news of her pregnancy to Laura that she had announced that she intended to leave. By then Nicki had had enough of trying to placate her. Overwhelmed with 'morning sickness' that lasted virtually all day, beset by anxieties about her agency, and worrying herself sick about the wisdom of her actually having a child who had not been planned, she had been in no fit state to cope with Laura as well.

The peace that had descended on the household after Laura's departure had given Nicki a blissful taste of pure and absolute happiness, as within days of her stepdaughter going so had her morning sickness. But with that happiness had also come a bitter aftertaste of guilt, from knowing how badly Kit felt about Laura leaving. His anxiety for her had overshadowed Nicki's pregnancy and Joey's birth—so much so that Nicki had suffered a severe and unexpected bout of depression following the birth. Laura, predictably, had refused even to acknowledge the baby, never mind come and see him, and Joey had in fact been walking before Laura had met her new half-brother for the first time.

Nicki tensed now, collecting her thoughts as the kitchen door opened and Kit and Laura came in.

'Where's Joey?' Kit asked as he looked round the kitchen.

'In bed,' Nicki told him sharply. 'It's past his bedtime and, as I told you this morning, I have work to do this evening.'

Nicki paused deliberately before reminding him,

'You were supposed to be reading him the next chapter of his book.'

'Oh, Dad, remember when you used to read my bedtime story?' Laura smiled, interrupting Nicki, one hand on her father's arm. She threw Nicki a smugly triumphant look before adding, 'You never missed a single evening, no matter how busy you were. But of course things were different for us. With Mummy being so ill I really only had you. I expect that's why we're so especially close.'

As Nicki listened she could feel herself starting to grind her teeth. She itched to be able to tell Laura that she'd made her point and that there was no need for her to over-egg her bread, but if she did she knew that Laura would immediately turn to Kit for support. The last thing Nicki wanted right now was to be humiliated in front of her stepdaughter!

'You mustn't blame Dad for being late, Nicki,' Laura was saying mock apologetically now. 'It's my fault! I wanted to have a daddy and daughter chat with him. Private stuff…'

As Laura leaned into Kit's side Nicki tried to control the fury building up inside her. She knew that Laura was deliberately manipulating the situation, and trying to cause an argument between them.

'I loved driving the new BMW,' she added enthusiastically, ignoring Nicki to speak to her father. 'And thanks for letting me have the spare set of keys, Dad. I promise I'll check with you before I borrow it.'

Nicki had had enough.

'Actually, Laura, I am the one you should be checking with,' Nicki told her stepdaughter with icy rage. 'The BMW is actually my car.'

Nicki could feel her face burning with resentment and guilt as she saw the look Kit was giving her.

* * *

Nope, she still appeared the same, Laura acknowledged derisively half an hour later as she peered at her reflection in her bedroom mirror. She had not suddenly turned back into her pony-tailed fifteen-year-old self, even if she had just given a pretty good display of that self to her stepmother.

What was it about the relationship between oneself and one's family that somehow meant that within minutes of being with them one reverted to childhood, not to mention childish habits? Laura knew that she was not alone in experiencing this unpalatable phenomenon, just as she also knew she was not alone in being guilty of still enacting in adulthood the travails of her teenage step-parent wars!

It was a subject her generation were experts on and a powerful bonding agent. 'Show me a person who can put their hand on their heart and honestly say that they accepted and welcomed their step-parents from the word go, and I'll show you an alien. It is a universally accepted truth that a child in possession of two parents is not in need of a step-parent,' one of Laura's friends was fond of saying facetiously. But there was a certain black-humoured element of truth in her statement.

Laura wasn't exactly proud of the way being in her stepmother's presence made her revert with dizzying speed back to the mindset of her teenaged self, employing deliberately contentious tactics as only teenage girls knew how. It gave her no pleasure now she was back in her adult skin to recognise how quickly and effectively she had stoked the fires of Nicki's hostility and resentment.

As a girl she had told herself that it was her duty to show Nicki to her father in her true colours, and to show Nicki herself that there was no way she or Joey could ever match, never mind usurp, the place she and her own mother held in her father's heart.

What must it be like to always have to live with the knowledge that your husband had previously been legally committed to another woman, another family? Was there always a fear lurking on the edge of one's awareness that one might be less loved…the lesser loved?

Laura knew that her stepmother was hardly likely to give her the answer to such questions!

And as to seeking her input, her guidance, her support on the matter that had brought Laura here, running for cover, seeking safety… A mirthless smile curled her mouth, her grey eyes shadowing.

Her hair, like her father's, was wheat-gold and thick, just like Joey's. She shared other similarities with her half-brother as well, she recognised, not least a tendency to be wary of anyone trying to push their way into their family life!

She had felt very sorry for her father earlier when Nicki had made that acrid comment about the BMW. Her smile gave way to a frown. Did Nicki habitually humiliate him like that? Did he always allow her to?

Resurrecting the battle between Nicki and herself had been the last thing on her mind when she had made her decision to come here; she wasn't an insecure teenager any more, after all, terrified of losing her father as she had already done her mother, and resentful of the woman who in her eyes had been the catalyst for that loss. But listening to the way her stepmother had spoken to her father had swamped her good intentions and reawakened all her old bitterness and hostility.

A little ruefully, she reflected on the generous company car allowance she had given up when she had given up her job. With a little careful handling it would just have stretched—just—to the pretty BMW convertible she had had her eye on!

Still, with her qualifications and CV she knew she would not have too much trouble in getting another job, but not yet…not until… Instinctively she reached into her bag for her mobile, and then grimaced. She had handed it in along with her notice. Much better that way. After all, her mobile, like her job, would be easy enough to replace.

Even so, she couldn't resist working out just how long it would be before he realised what she had done… Quickly she calculated. He was still away and not due back for another couple of days, and… Stop it! she warned herself, quickly clamping down on the thought and on the sudden give-away surge of her heartbeat.

'Was that really necessary?' Kit asked Nicki grimly when he walked into their bedroom, having finished reading Joey his belated bedtime story.

'Was what really necessary?' Nicki asked him defiantly, but of course she knew what he meant.

'That dig about the car,' Kit told her. 'You were the one who insisted that I should drive it.'

'That *you* should drive it, yes,' Nicki agreed. 'But there is no way I am prepared to have Laura driving it.'

'Nicki!'

The very way he said her name was a weary sigh. Ridiculously, Nicki could feel tears pricking the backs of her eyes. She was a grown woman, for heaven's sake, and not a teenager!

'Oh, Nicki…this is crazy,' she heard Kit saying in a much warmer voice as he walked over to where she was standing, brushing her already neatly glossy nut-brown bob. Standing behind her, he wrapped his arms around her, nuzzling the exposed curve of her throat. Immediately Nicki stiffened and tried to pull away.

'What is it? What's wrong?' Kit demanded.

In the mirror their glances met. Nicki looked away first.

'I'm tired of having to cope with Laura. You know how I feel about her living here, Kit. About the way she's upsetting Joey.'

She shivered as she saw how Kit was looking at her, his voice tense as he told her, 'This isn't just about Laura, is it, Nicki? This goes back to before Laura's arrival.' He paused. 'Look, if it's because...'

'I don't want to talk about it,' Nicki denied, jerking frantically away from him. 'Just like you didn't want to talk about it when... All I want is for you to leave me alone.'

She could feel the emotions surging up inside her with frightening force. Pain; guilt; the horrible tormenting, debilitating fear that robbed her of the ability to think or function properly, and with it the full force of her anger against Kit, and against life itself.

'Nicki...'

She could hear the anxiety in his voice, but she felt too isolated and distant from him to want to respond to it. It was safer feeling like this, she recognised. Safer and easier. Let him turn to his precious daughter if he wanted someone to sympathise with him. She no doubt would fully endorse his feelings—his behaviour!

'Look, Nicki, what happened happened to both of us.'

Nicki gave him a bitter look.

'Oh, really? You can say that now, Kit, but at the

time, according to you, it was my problem…my decision.'

'Your decision, yes. But…'

They both tensed as Laura knocked on their bedroom door and called out, 'Dad, are you in there? Can I have a word?'

'You'd better go,' Nicki told him fiercely, and rejectingly. 'Laura needs you!'

'No Hughie? I thought you said he was coming home today?'

Accepting her husband's perfunctory kiss on her cheek, Stella nodded. 'I did and he has. He's gone round to see Julie,' she told Richard wryly. 'He seemed to be a bit on edge before he left, and he's lost weight.'

'Students always do,' Richard pointed out equably, 'and I shouldn't worry too much about Julie. To be honest I rather got the impression that things had cooled off somewhat between them.'

'I'm not worried,' Stella denied. 'But it has occurred to me that Hughie might have given us that impression deliberately, because he knows it's what we want to hear. He's an intelligent boy, after all. I mean, it's like I was saying to Alice earlier. It's not that I don't like Julie, I do. I just want them both to be sensible and look beyond the here and now, the immediacy of the moment, and think about the future. Hughie is far too young to even think of tying himself down to a steady relationship. Apart from anything else, with him away at university and Julie here, it just isn't practical!'

As she spoke Stella suddenly heard Maggie's voice from their own teenage years, teasing her. 'Oh, Stella! Miss Practicality, that's what I think we should call you!'

Funny the things one remembered…and why. At the time she had found nothing wrong in Maggie's comment, even preening herself a little for it, telling herself that she had more common sense than the other three put together, and that without her to put an end to some of their more outrageous exploits and sometimes too silly attitude towards life they would have been in a sorry mess indeed. They needed her to remind them of what was what—to stop them behaving foolishly. Yes, she had prided herself on her role within the quartet—the sensible one, the cool, non-flirtatious one whom boys knew better than to approach with too-familiar overtures. The one whom, in fact, the male sex tended to treat more as a pal and an honorary member of their own sex that they could confide in, rather than a mysterious and exciting object of desire and lust. And she had continued to pride herself on it, feeling both empowered and ever so slightly superior to the other three because of her foresight, her ability to rationalise and plan, her sheer sensibleness.

But just lately…

'Are you in this evening or out?'

Although Stella no longer had any paid employment, having given up her social services job after Hughie's birth, over the years she had been co-opted onto the committees of a variety of voluntary organisations, starting with the Parent-Teachers Association of Hughie's junior school, and picking up along the way a position on the Board of Governors for his senior school, an appointment as a local JP, and three local charity organisations, all responsibilities on which she had thrived, with which she dealt with her famed efficiency, and which kept her just as busy as Richard since his promotion to Chief Clerk of the Local County Council.

'In but I'm out tomorrow,' she told him pragmatically. 'Dinner with Maggie and the others. Apparently Maggie has something she wants to tell us!'

Richard shook his head. He was a hard-working, honest, but unimaginative man who found it hard to get to grips with the emotional intensity of the bond the four women shared. For a start they were all so very different. Alice, the quiet, gentle, stay-at-home mother; Nicki, the glossy, immaculate businesswoman; his own Stella with her formidable efficiency and practicality, and who—thank the Lord!—had never and would never exhibit any of the passionate intensity that was so much a part of Maggie's vibrant personality. But that was women for you. And Richard, one of the last of a dying race of a certain type of man, was quite happy to openly admit that, so far as he was concerned, the female sex was a complete enigma!

'So why couldn't Maggie tell you whatever this news is before tomorrow night?' Richard asked.

'You know Maggie,' Stella responded wryly. 'Typically, Alice is convinced that she's going to announce that she and Oliver are planning to get married.' She gave a small exasperated shrug. 'I hope she's wrong. You'd think after what she went through when she and Dan split up that Maggie would be very wary about inviting any more emotional pain—and that's what she's going to get ultimately, because, no matter what he feels about her now, sooner or later Oliver is going to want a younger woman.'

'Mmm. I always thought that was a rum business— Maggie and Dan splitting up. I mean, you never saw them apart. Whenever we went out together, they were always all over one another.'

'Well, according to Nicki, Dan wanted children and Maggie didn't, so—'

'I thought they split up because Dan had that affair,' Richard interrupted her, looking confused.

'Well, yes, they did, but we always knew that there had to be a reason *why* he had the affair. I mean, Dan just wasn't that kind of man.'

'He was a damn good-looking chap,' Richard mused.

'Very good-looking,' Stella agreed ruefully.

All of them had at one time or another been a little bit in love with Dan, even her, although she had kept her feelings determinedly to herself, firmly lecturing herself against being foolish.

People might nowadays describe her approvingly as a striking looking and confident woman, but in her youth she had quite definitely been plain. Yes, she had had regular features, healthy, clear skin, and good teeth, but what they had added up to had always fallen short of the head-turning male-attention-getting looks the other three had in their different ways possessed.

Not that she had minded. Prettiness had been in her opinion, then, a dangerously two-edged sword, in that it encouraged her sex to rely on it and, if they were weak and silly enough, to trade on it. Not that any of her friends had ever been guilty of that!

At the time she had calmly accepted her position in the foursome as the plain one, the sensible one, without resentment; it was only recently that she had begun to look back and feel resentful, to feel that somehow she had been cheated of the right to something—

a certain femininity and sensuality—that the others had openly enjoyed.

Deep down inside she knew that these feelings were somehow connected to the very obvious air of sexual and emotional happiness that surrounded Maggie. Somehow it disturbed her; made her feel that she was less of a woman than the others, especially in the sexual sense. And yet that was ridiculous, surely, because she had never once experienced those kinds of feelings when they had been young. In fact, it had been her friendship with Richard that she had prized most in their marriage, the interests they had in common—which had never included a desire to spend hours in bed indulging in sexual Olympics. If anything she had actually pitied Alice for having such an obviously highly sexed husband as Stuart, just as she had pitied Maggie when Dan had had his affair, and Nicki when she had fallen so passionately in love with Kit.

So why was she now feeling that somehow she had missed out?

And more importantly why was she wasting time brooding on it? She had always been a doer not a dweller, dealing in realities and practicalities rather than the vagueness of emotions.

Her only womanly vanity was her hair. When she was a girl it had been long and lustrous, and for years she had worn it in a neat chignon. Just recently, though, for some reason she had decided to have it cut, and she still wasn't totally used to the unfamiliar feel of it on her face, even though everyone had been extremely complimentary about it. Her good teeth and good skin had accompanied her into middle age, and she was now, according to her hair stylist, an extremely handsome woman.

No one would ever describe Maggie as 'handsome'.

No, Maggie was stunning. Sexy…vibrant…fun. The thought lingered in her head with a slightly bitter mental aftertaste.

Although Nicki had never said so, it must have been hard for her when Dan had ended their relationship and started dating Maggie.

'He went off to the States, didn't he, after the divorce?' Richard commented, breaking into her thoughts.

'Yes.'

Stella gave Richard's downbent head an exasperated look as he spoke to her without looking up from his paper. His bald patch was growing larger, she noticed absently.

'I hope that Hughie doesn't come in too late. I didn't get a chance to ask him how he's liking his course,' she commented, relieved to have a reason to dismiss her unwanted and discomforting thoughts.

'Well, he's got a long slog in front of him, especially if he goes on to take a PhD as he plans,' Richard reminded her.

'What the devil's going on?'

The acerbic note in the voice of the head of the clinic caused the security officer to wince a little.

'I'm sorry, sir, but we felt we ought to call you out. Just to be on the safe side. It's Ms Lacey.'

'Charlene Lacey?' Graham Vereham frowned.

'Yes,' the security officer confirmed. 'We found her in your secretary's office, going through some files.'

Graham Vereham sighed heavily.

Working in the field he did, he was used to emotional traumas, and at first he had simply assumed that Charlene's distress was caused by the fact that they had been unable to help her to conceive, compounded by the breakdown of her relationship under the stress of the situation, but then she had started coming to the clinic and complaining bizarrely that they had stolen her 'babies'.

Since Charlene had been the recipient of another woman's eggs, rather than a donor of her own, her claims had absolutely no basis in reality. They had tried to help her, he had even personally recommended a psychiatric colleague for her to consult, but all to no avail. Charlene had continued to haunt the clinic, making her outrageous claims.

By rights they should send for the police and have the matter dealt with by them, but they were in a very sensitive business, and the last thing he wanted was any kind of adverse press. He would have to talk to her himself.

'Where is she?' he asked the security officer wearily.

'In your secretary's office, sir.'

3

'So come on, then, what's this exciting news?' Stella demanded, once they were all sitting down and their drinks and food had been ordered.

'Not yet. You're going to have to wait,' Maggie teased them mischievously.

'I don't want to spoil your surprise—' Alice laughed '—but I think I may know what it is.'

When they all looked at her, she gave Maggie a semi-apologetic smile.

'Zoë saw you and Oliver in the estate agents. She said you were asking about some of their properties.'

Much to Alice's relief, her daughter had rung her with this news earlier in the day, their row of the previous afternoon apparently forgotten.

'You're planning to move house?' Nicki gave Maggie a wry look. She was still feeling bruised from her row with Kit, and Maggie's obvious euphoria was jarring on her slightly.

She loved Maggie, of course she did, but sometimes... Sometimes it seemed to Nicki that life wasn't always as fair to her as it was to her closest friend. Caught up in the excitement of her new love affair, Maggie hadn't even noticed the problems that she had been having!

'Is that it?' Nicki couldn't resist demanding acerbically. 'Honestly, Maggie, you...'

'Well, no, as a matter of fact it isn't,' Maggie defended herself. 'Yes, we are looking for a new house. But that's not what I wanted to tell you. Well, it's a part of it…the result of it, so to speak, though, and not the cause.'

She was glowing with happiness, positively bubbling over with it, Nicki recognised enviously, and it was perhaps no wonder that the group of business-suited men at the adjacent table were watching her in admiration.

Nicki's head was aching with tension. Laura had disappeared shortly after lunch, announcing that she was going for a walk. She had still not returned when Nicki had come out and of course Kit had been concerned.

'She's an adult, Kit,' Nicki had told him angrily. 'If it was Joey who was missing I could understand your concern, but, of course, you would never be as concerned for Joey as you are for Laura, would you?'

'That's not fair, and it isn't true either!' Kit had exploded.

You'd have thought after the trauma of her first marriage that she would deserve to have some happiness in her second, Nicki reflected angrily, and she had thought that she did have until…

Stop it, she warned herself. The feelings of despair and panic that she was suffering were indications of a lack of ability to be in control of herself and her life of which she felt ashamed. But she couldn't help the way she felt; couldn't help agonising over Joey and what would happen to him if she weren't there to love and take care of him. He wouldn't be able to rely on his father. Kit, after all, had other responsibilities…more important responsibilities…Kit had Laura to worry about…

'Nicki, is something wrong?' she could hear Maggie asking with concern.

'Laura has come home and she's moved in with them,' Alice replied for her.

'Oh, Nicki, no. When did that happen? And why?'

Brusquely Nicki gave them an abbreviated outline of what had happened.

'Laura hasn't said why she's here—at least not to me, and if she's discussed it with Kit, he isn't saying. All I do know is that she felt she needed to "take time out and reassess where she's going". It's so ridiculous!'

They could all hear the frustration and anger in her voice.

'She's twenty-six, after all, and more than old enough to already know where she wants to go, but of course Kit can't see that! She knows exactly how to press all the right buttons and make him feel guilty, about his precious little girl and the stepmother he inflicted on her, and of course she's loving every second of it! Poor Joey can't understand what's happening and why his father suddenly doesn't want to be bothered with him any more. Why he'd rather spend time with his daughter. She even had the gall last night to suggest that Kit was working too hard, and to drag up the fact that when she was younger Kit had talked about selling up here and going to live in Italy! She claimed it had been his cherished dream! And of course she was making it all too clear that Joey and I were the reasons he hadn't been able to follow it!

'Naturally, all this is music to Kit's ears, and he's revelling in having an adoring daughter to sympathise with him—instead of a nagging wife who doesn't,' she finished bitterly.

She could see that the others were watching her

with varying degrees of compassion, but, predictably, it was Maggie who reached across the table and took hold of her hand.

'Don't let her get you down,' she counselled her gently. 'And try not to blame Kit too much. He's a man, after all, and as we all know even the best of them can be emotional cowards.'

'Oh, spare me the homily, Maggie!' Nicki snapped. 'Just because you're deep in the throes of a fantasy romance, that doesn't make you an expert on human relationships, you know!'

Nicki knew that she was being unfair, but the words of apology she wanted to give were somehow stuck in her throat.

She tensed as Maggie squeezed her hand before releasing it, whilst Alice burst into animated chatter, exclaiming, 'Stella, you haven't told us how Hughie is doing. Is he enjoying his course?'

'Mmm…he says so,' Stella replied cautiously. 'But…you know what boys are like.' She gave a small shrug, but there was a little frown of anxiety between her brows. Something was worrying Hughie, she could tell, no matter how heroically he pretended that it wasn't.

Nicki's outburst had somehow cast a shadow over the evening that echoed her own inner feelings. The friendship between them all, which had trundled along so comfortably for so long, suddenly seemed to be showing signs of fracture and stress strains, of not being what it had once been. Alice's desire to please, Maggie's euphoria, Nicki's outburst—tonight all of them had irritated her.

The relationship between them that had always been so supportive suddenly felt constrictive, restrictive. It compelled each of them to play a preordained role, and somehow Stella wasn't sure she wanted to play her designated part any more. It was all right for the others—rather like certain members of the local am-dram group she helped to manage, her friends had chosen the plum roles for themselves, leaving her to play the part no one else wanted!

The thought of them all not sharing their close friendship was unthinkable, and yet wasn't there a secret, dangerous allure to it—to the thought of being free to write her own role, to finally be that person she had recently come to feel she had always been denied the chance to be?

'Tell us a bit more about this house move you're planning, Maggie,' Alice was demanding predictably pacifically. She hated arguments and upset, and felt very sorry for Nicki. 'I thought that Oliver loved the apartment?'

'Well, yes, he does,' Maggie acknowledged. 'But…'

'But you've finally convinced him that your clothes need a proper home,' Nicki interjected dryly, wanting to make amends for her show of bad temper.

All of them, including Maggie, laughed. Her weakness for designer clothes had always been the subject of good-natured teasing between them.

'Well, you're sort of on the right track,' Maggie agreed. 'Although it isn't my clothes we are going to need the extra space for. In fact…'

'Zoë said something about you wanting a property with some land attached to it,' Alice offered.

'Oh, no.' Stella groaned, stifling her own inner critical voice to follow Nicki's lead. 'Don't tell us, Maggie. You've got the "must eat organic, back to the land and grow your own" bug. Well, let me tell you, if you are thinking of dragging us into it, you can definitely count me out! I know you and your wild ideas…'

'Yes,' Alice chimed in. 'Like the time when you enrolled us all in the local theatre group, and we all ended up having to dress up as men!'

'It wasn't my fault they were doing *Seven Brides for Seven Brothers*, and they were short of male actors,' Maggie defended herself indignantly.

'And then there were the salsa classes,' Alice reminded her.

Maggie grinned. 'They were fun. Especially that weekend we spent in Barcelona!'

'Oh, yeah! Terrific fun,' Nicki agreed drolly, rolling her eyes. 'I have particularly happy memories of having to prise that ardent Spaniard off you, the one who said—'

'Yes, yes, don't remind me,' Maggie pleaded, covering her eyes, her face suddenly deep pink.

Alice looked round the table in fond happiness. For all that Nicki and Stella tended to tease Maggie, she did have a way of lifting everyone's spirits and injecting adventure and laughter into their lives.

'Come on, then,' Nicki demanded, determinedly putting her own problems to one side and entering into the spirit of things. 'Stop keeping us in suspense. What exactly is this good news you've got for us?'

They were all looking at her. Maggie felt her heart give a funny little thump, almost as though the baby knew just how important this moment was; how important these women were going to be in its life. Her closest friends and supporters, the women who had shared her life's sadnesses and joys with her, its failures and triumphs; the honorary family, she would be gifting to her child; three women who between them had enough experience to see any baby safely on its way to adulthood even if she, its mother, did not.

It would be a relief to unburden herself to them, to

tell them how wobbly and uncertain she felt, to tell them how much she needed their support.

Maggie took a deep breath and looked round the table, at Stella who was so sanely calm and well balanced, Alice so maternal and protectively loving, Nicki who had her own problems, Maggie knew, but who out of all of them would surely understand her feelings. Joey after all had been born when Nicki had been in her early forties...

'I'm pregnant,' she told them shakily. 'Oliver and I are going to have a baby.'

The silence that had seized her audience made Maggie smile.

'I'm impressed,' she laughed. 'You're speechless. I...'

'No! It isn't possible! You can't be!' White-faced, Nicki had pushed back her chair and was standing up. 'You can't be!'

Maggie's smile wavered as they all looked at Nicki. Her face was suddenly as pale as Nicki's, but where anger burned hotly in Nicki's eyes, in Maggie's the other two could quite plainly see the sheen of shocked tears.

Helplessly Alice watched them both, struggling with her own shock and discomfort. Both Maggie's disclosure and Nicki's announcement had left her lost for words, and she guessed from Stella's stiff expression that she felt the same.

'You can't be pregnant,' Nicki was continuing. 'You've been through the menopause, we all know that and—'

'I've had special treatment...special help!' Maggie interrupted her. 'And... And it's because of the baby that we need to move house.'

She was very obviously and very visibly distressed, Alice recognised.

'Nicki, please,' Maggie heard herself begging shakily. This was the last reaction she had been expecting and she was trembling with the shock of it.

She could hear herself gabbling the words a little as she hurried to fill the uncomfortable silence left by Nicki's refusal to respond to her. 'The apartment wouldn't be suitable. I think I knew just how much having a baby meant to Oliver when he agreed to give the apartment up.'

She had meant it as a joke, a means of lightening the taut, uncomfortable silence surrounding her, but instead of laughing her friends were regarding her with differing degrees of incomprehension.

Alice, she recognised, simply looked shocked. Stella was frowning, and avoiding meeting her eyes, whilst Nicki...

Her mouth suddenly dry, Maggie could feel herself flinching as she searched Nicki's stonily silent features.

'I thought you'd be pleased for me,' she told them. Like a child seeking adult approval, she recognised miserably as she heard the pleading note in her own voice.

'Well, yes, of course we are. It's just that it's such a shock.'

That was Alice typically trying to ease things and be tactful.

'It certainly is.' True to form, Stella added bluntly, 'I just can't see you as a mother, Maggie. You've never seemed the type. Are you sure...?'

'Of course she's sure, aren't you, Maggie?' Nicki cut in, her voice sharply acid. 'Maggie is always sure about what she does. At least, at the time she decides to do it she is. Of course, she doesn't always stop to think about anything other than the moment, do you, Maggie? How pregnant exactly are you?'

'It's…it's just about a month…'

'A month?' Nicki stopped. An expression Maggie couldn't recognise crossed her face. 'Four weeks! Have you any idea just how vulnerable a pregnancy is in its early stages, Maggie, especially at your age?' They could all hear the bitterness and the fury in her voice as she warned, 'You could quite easily wake up tomorrow morning and discover that your dreams of a baby are over!'

'Nicki!' Alice stopped her quickly, giving Maggie's white set face an anxious look. The open and unexpected hostility in Nicki's voice had shocked them all, especially Maggie, who started to protest shakily.

'Nicki! What are you saying? What's wrong?'

Nicki knew that she was overreacting; that she was letting the anger she felt against Kit spill over into a safer escape by venting it on Maggie, and that she should have found a kinder way of expressing her feelings. But it was too late to call back her sharp words now. And besides…

She could feel her stomach churning with a mixture of moral outrage, shock, and anger at Maggie's blind selfishness, and, worst of all, sheer, raw jealousy, streaked with a pain she had told herself she had managed to control.

Out of the corner of her eye she registered the silent looks that Stella and Alice were exchanging, whilst Maggie looked at her as though she couldn't believe her ears. Her red-gold curls were a wild halo around her head, her delicately boned face almost childishly flushed, the dark blue eyes that Nicki had secretly envied all the time they were growing up rounded with shock.

'What's wrong?' Nicki repeated, her voice brittle. 'Do I really have to tell you? Maggie, you are fifty-two years old! During the thirty-odd fertile years you had in which to become pregnant you chose not to do so. You weren't into babies, you told us all—remember? I'll bet that Dan does. He would have given anything to have a child, but you didn't want one! Then!

'But now things are different—apparently. Now, when you're in a relationship with a man who is considerably younger than you are, you've changed your mind! I don't want to be unkind, but, let's be honest, statistics prove that such relationships rarely endure. I'm not saying that Oliver doesn't love you now, we can all see that he does. But when you bring a baby into the world, if you have any forethought, any maturity, you surely want to provide it with the best emotional environment you can, and once again statistics prove that this entails a baby having two parents in its life. Yes, countless thousands of children have been brought up successfully and happily by heroically selfless and devoted single parents, but those parents often did not have a choice! You do. And not only do you have freedom of choice, Maggie, supposedly you also have wisdom and maturity as well. If you were a young girl…but you aren't, no matter how much you might be trying to behave like one.

'Which brings me to something else. Doesn't the fact that nature has declared that she no longer considers you physically able to produce a child mean anything to you?'

'What are you trying to say, Nicki?' Maggie interrupted her with quick defensiveness. 'That only naturally fertile women have the right to have children?'

'Of course I'm not, but you have to admit that there's a huge difference between a woman who is medically unable to conceive, and one who has rejected the opportunity to have children, until she is through the menopause and then decided, Oh, I've changed my mind. I want a baby after all. What do you think a baby is, Maggie? Some kind of status symbol? The fertility equivalent of a course of Botox and a face-lift? A way of gaining instant youth?'

'That's not fair,' Maggie protested. 'This has nothing to do with anything like that!'

'No? I'm sorry but I don't believe you! I think the only reason you're having this baby is because of Oliver. Because you think...'

'Because I think what?' Maggie challenged her angrily. 'Because I think that by having Oliver's baby I'm going to keep him?'

As their glances clashed it was Nicki who looked away first. A dull flush had spread up over the smooth column of her throat. As she reached out for her wineglass her fingers trembled slightly when she picked it up, the immaculate glossy darkness of her manicure reflecting the richness of the red wine.

As she took a deep swallow Alice murmured, 'When is the baby due, Maggie?'

'October. Not for another eight months. They do a blood test a fortnight after...after. I was very lucky. Some women go through several unsuccessful attempts before they actually become pregnant.'

'I've read about the procedure,' Stella commented, resorting to practicality in an attempt to lower the emotional intensity level a little. 'But what is actually involved?'

'What is involved is that a healthy, young fertile woman is tricked into believing that her voluntarily given eggs are going to be donated to another young woman,' Nicki told them angrily before Maggie could respond.

'The woman whose egg I received had made no stipulation about the age of any donee,' Maggie informed them all quietly.

'It's a very big step to take,' Alice said gently.

'I know,' Maggie agreed, with quiet dignity. 'That was why I was counting on having your support, and your help.'

There was a look in her eyes that made Alice ache for her.

'Of course we'll help you,' she assured her.

'I'm sorry, but I just don't want anything to do with this,' Nicki exclaimed, finishing her wine and putting her glass down. Beneath her immaculate make-up her face looked strained.

'Nicki,' Alice intervened softly, 'I'm sure that Maggie has considered everything.'

'Has she?' Nicki's voice was cynical. 'Or is she simply following another trend? What is it exactly that you want to prove, Maggie? Or can we guess? First a young lover, and then a baby. It's all so easy for you, isn't it? You just decide what you want and then you go out and buy it, whether it's a new car, a new man, or a new life!

'Has it occurred to you to wonder how this baby is going to feel when he or she gets laughed at and taunted at school for having such an old mother? Has it even occurred to you that you might not be there when he or she most needs you, when they reach their teens?'

Alice couldn't bear to look at either Maggie or Nicki. The silence between them was bad enough, armed with spikily dangerous emotions. Stella, she could see, was frowning, and looking as though she was about to give them both a lecture.

Desperate to avert the disaster she could see looming Alice burst out frantically, 'I've got some news to tell you all as well!'

'Don't tell us that you're pregnant too!' Stella demanded, giving her a wry look. 'Mind you somehow in your case it wouldn't be that surprising, Alice. You've always had that earth mother look about you, and as we all know your Stuart is very highly sexed!'

Whilst Alice blushed, Maggie made a brave attempt at a slightly crooked smile, but Nicki's face still looked as though it had been turned to stone.

'We always used to have to ring you before coming round, in case Stuart had slipped home and taken you to bed,' Stella reminded her dryly.

'Yes, he put a lock on the inside of the bedroom door to keep the children out,' Maggie agreed.

'Remember that water bed he wanted to buy?'

'Stop it, all of you,' Alice protested, but she was smiling now as well. 'That was years ago, when we were young,' she reproved them all mock primly. 'Anyway, I'm not pregnant! It's nothing like that. I've applied for and been accepted on an Open University course.'

There was a small silence whilst they all looked at her with varying degrees of amused kindness.

Because they thought her news wasn't important, or because they thought that she simply did not have what it took to carry her plans through?

Why, when they were her friends, did she sometimes feel as though secretly, inwardly, they felt that she was inferior to them; that they treated her more as a junior member of their group than an equal? Why was it that people just never seemed to show respect for her and for her needs?

'Goodness, Alice, if I'd known you'd got that kind of spare time I'd have co-opted you onto one of my committees,' Stella was saying briskly.

'What good news. I'm so pleased for you,' Maggie offered warmly.

'You're a lot braver than I am,' was Nicki's slightly terse contribution. 'I find it hard enough keeping up with Joey's homework—just one of the pleasures of motherhood that's going to come as quite a culture shock to you, Maggie,' she added grimly.

'Well, it's something I've wanted to do for a long time,' Alice admitted, valiantly trying to ignore Nicki's barbed comment. 'More for my own satisfaction than anything else.'

Her own satisfaction; those years and that sense of self she had suddenly started feeling that her early marriage had robbed her of? Once she would have immediately expressed those feelings to the others, but now somehow she felt reticent about doing so, and about revealing her small dreams for their probably critical inspection. After all, they had hardly greeted her news with any degree of awe or admiration, had they? If anything, it had fallen rather flat.

'I need the loo,' Maggie announced, pink-faced, as she stood up. As she made her way across the restaurant she refused to allow herself to mourn the little daydreams she had been entertaining of having her friends reminisce about their pregnancies, bonding with her in her joy and excitement; teasing her for her shy uncertainty about things they were experts on.

Tensely Nicki watched her go.

'Don't look at me like that,' she said grimly to Alice and Stella. 'You know I'm right! If Maggie had wanted

to be a mother she had ample opportunity to do so
when she was married to Dan. Look, I'm going to go.
Here's enough to cover my share of the bill,' she told
Stella, pushing some money towards her.

'Nicki…' Alice protested unhappily, but Nicki simply shook her head and got up.

'Oh, dear,' Alice sighed, watching her leave.

'I can understand how she feels, but she did go a little bit over the top,' Stella pronounced judicially.
When Alice looked uncertainly at her, she explained,
'The probabilities are that Maggie is having this baby
for all the wrong reasons. She has always been inclined to be impetuous, we all know that. She should
be acting her age.'

Alice frowned as she caught the note of angry bitterness in Stella's voice. What was wrong with them
all tonight? Why did they seem to be so at odds with
one another?

'It would be awful if Maggie and Nicki quarrelled,'
she said, searching Stella's face for signs that she
shared her anxiety and disquiet. 'She and Maggie
have always been so close. We've all always been so
close. Our friendship is a very important part of all our
lives, isn't it?' she pressed.

In the ladies' room, Maggie ran cool water over her
wrists and tried to compose herself.

Her face was burning with pain and anger. This was
not how she had envisaged her news being received.
There was no laughter or sense of closeness bonding
the others to her now, Maggie recognised. And for
Nicki, Nicki of all people, to react in the way that she
had!

As she returned to their table Alice told her awkwardly, 'Nicki said to say goodbye. She had to go. I

think she was worried about Joey. He doesn't like Laura, apparently.'

Alice was lying to her, Maggie knew. Nicki had left because of her! Because of her baby!

As though she sensed what she was feeling Alice told her, 'Don't be upset by what Nicki said, Maggie. You've given us all a shock and Nicki…'

'And Nicki is the same age as me and the mother of a nine-year-old son, but, of course, it's different for her. After all, we all know how much Nicki wanted to have children; she even stayed with that rat of a husband of hers long after she should have left because she wanted to conceive so much. Now there's irresponsibility for you, if you like. Nicki was being physically abused by Carl, and we all suspected it, but she lied to protect him, and she would have had his child, even though the statistics she's so fond of quoting prove that physically abusive men often abuse their children as well as their wives!'

'Come on, Maggie. We understand how upset you are, but that's not—' Stella began.

'It's not what?' Maggie demanded. 'It's not fair of me to criticise Nicki, but it's perfectly acceptable for her to criticise me?'

'Oh, Maggie,' Alice begged unhappily. 'That wasn't what Stella was trying to say… We've been friends for so long, we can't let a little thing like this—'

'A little thing? Is that how you see my baby, Alice? As something little and unimportant? Is that how all of you see me? Well, let me tell you, this baby, Oliver's baby, my baby, means more to me than anything else, and that includes your friendship!'

'Maggie, calm down,' Stella intervened. 'This isn't doing you or the baby any good. Look, let's get the bill. Then we can all go home and sleep on things.'

'Yes!' Alice agreed with obvious relief. 'You did say that you didn't want to be late anyway, didn't you, Stella?'

Outside the restaurant they exchanged their customary hugs and kisses, but Maggie could sense awkwardness and constraint in place of their usual closeness. And it was all her fault. At least, that was obviously what the other three thought!

'You know, I can't help thinking that Nicki might have a point,' Stella commented as Alice drove out of the car park. 'I mean, Maggie has never been maternal. And if she is doing this because of Oliver...'

'She might never have said that she wanted children, Stella, but she was always terrific with ours. The twins in particular adored her. They thought she was so much fun.'

'Fun, yes. Maggie has always been that,' Stella agreed. Suddenly wanting to make amends to Alice for her earlier refusal to reassure and support her, she added reminiscently, 'Remember our pop group—that was Maggie's idea. A ground breaking all-girl band, even if we never made it beyond a couple of gigs at the local youth club. That was when you met Stuart, wasn't it?'

'Don't remind me.' Alice groaned. 'Those outfits...and that make-up! The music lessons our parents paid for, delighted by our desire to learn an old-fashioned accomplishment!'

'I know. My poor father's face when he walked into the garage and found us practising with our electric guitars.'

As they both started to laugh Stella's austere expression softened. 'Those were good times...' she had to acknowledge.

'Mmm. We thought we were so wild and cool, and in reality compared with today's youngsters, we were very naïve.'

'We thought you were sophisticated when you and Stuart started going steady! How does he feel about you doing this Open University course? I know he spends a lot of time away…'

'I haven't told him about it yet,' Alice confessed, starting to relax. This was better, more the kind of reaction she had expected, and Stella could always be relied on for her calm, practical advice. 'You know how he's always been, Stella,' she said tentatively. 'He's a wonderful man, kind, generous, loving…'

'But?' Stella invited, recognising her cue. And her role?

Were things perhaps not as good in Alice's marriage as they all assumed, Stella speculated inwardly. Certainly Stuart never made any secret of the fact that he had a high sex drive, and she had sometimes wondered if Alice ever tired of keeping up with a man who was so sexually demanding. Initially in a relationship no doubt having that kind of intensity focused on you was exciting and ego-boosting, but after thirty years of marriage?

'But… But nothing.' Alice shook her head.

It wasn't fair to criticise Stuart behind his back, even to her closest friends. After all, what if she did sometimes find him over-controlling? And then patronising her because she was so dependent on him… Compared to the appalling life Nicki had had to suffer with Carl, though, she had nothing whatsoever to complain about.

'Do you know,' she told Stella, changing the subject, 'I think that's the first time Maggie has ever mentioned the way Carl abused Nicki.'

'Well, it's a subject none of us likes to talk about, isn't it? I mean, we were there when they met, and when they got married, and none of us had any inkling of what he was really like. We saw Nicki every week, and yet none of us knew what he was doing to her, and we should have known.'

'She felt too ashamed to tell us. Her self-esteem was so low she had begun to believe Carl when he told her that she was the one who made him hit her. It was Maggie who found out in the end, and who made her leave Carl, helped her.'

They were outside Stella's house. Alice stopped the car.

'What do you think we should do about Maggie and Nicki?' she asked Stella hesitantly.

Stella's reply was prompt and unequivocal.

'Nothing! Except keep our fingers crossed and hope things sort themselves out.'

'Do you honestly think that they will?'

As she opened the door of the car Stella turned to look at Alice. 'I don't know,' she admitted, pulling the collar of her coat up around her neck against the chill of the sharp wind. Spring might only be several weeks away, but that didn't alter the fact that right now they were still in winter.

Being optimistic too soon and with too little cause was never a good idea, even if someone like Maggie could never be brought to accept that fact!

4

'Is Hughie back yet?' Stella asked Richard, slipping off her coat and going to fill the kettle.

'I heard him come in a few minutes ago. He went straight upstairs,' Richard told her. 'Pleasant evening?'

'No!'

Putting down his paper, Richard looked at his wife. She had been a slightly bolshy, outspoken junior probation officer when he had first met her—they had both belonged to the same ramblers group—and he had courted her steadily for two years before asking her to marry him. His widowed mother had initially been slightly hostile towards her, but that hostility had melted when Stella had produced Hughie.

'So what happened?' he asked curiously.

Handing him the cup of tea she had just made him, Stella sighed. 'Maggie announced that she's pregnant!'

'At her age!' Richard looked appalled. Much as he loved Hughie he had never been a 'hands on' type of father, Stella reflected ruefully. Night-time feeds and nappy changing had all been left to her. Not that she had minded. If she was honest, the love she had felt for her son as a baby had been far more intense and passionate than the calm, relaxed emotion she felt for

Richard. Which did not mean, of course, that she didn't love him. She did.

'I certainly wouldn't want to be in that position,' Richard told her.

'Well, we aren't likely to be, are we?' Stella replied wryly.

She knew it was unfair of her to remind him of the growing infrequency of their sex life. He was after all fifty-seven, they had been married for twenty-seven years, and sex had never been high on their list of shared priorities anyway. And at her age...

But she and Maggie were the same age, she couldn't help inwardly reminding herself. And the idea of Maggie deciding she was too old to merit a good sex life was as preposterous as...as Maggie's pregnancy? And it wasn't just Maggie, was it? There was Alice with Stuart, and Nicki with Kit. No, none of her friends lived a life where sex was reduced to a rare occurrence, that sometimes actually bypassed even 'high days and holidays'. Only she was expected to be nonsexual and like it!

Her frown gave way to a smile as the door opened and Hughie came into the room.

She and Richard were both tall, but Hughie was over six feet three, his body well muscled from the rugby he played. To her, though, Stella acknowledged, there was still something that was almost little-boyish about his face at times.

'Mum, have you and Dad got a minute?' he asked.

He was nervous, Stella could see that. Automatically her stomach tightened. This was something Maggie was going to have to get used to, this never-ending, relentless awareness of the vulnerability of one's child, coupled with the frightening realisation of how little one could do to protect them and keep them totally safe.

'Of course. Do you want a cup of tea? I've just made some,' she offered.

'No. No... Look...there just isn't any easy way to tell you this... I know you're going to be... Julie is pregnant and the baby is mine.'

Somehow or other, Stella discovered that she was sitting down, whilst Richard in contrast was now standing up, his shock showing in his eyes as he stormed furiously, 'What were you saying about him being intelligent? My God! How the hell much intelligence does it take to use a bloody condom?'

'I did... It burst.'

Nicki could see the Adam's apple moving in Hughie's throat as he swallowed. He was still a boy, really. A baby. Her baby! A wave of fiercely protective maternalism struck her. He was looking at her, waiting for her to say something, his puppy dog eyes pleading with her...trusting her...

Trusting her, Stella recognised as she forced herself to bite back the words, Are you sure it's yours?

Richard, though, felt no such restraint, or tact, she realised as she heard her husband bursting out with the words that were hammering inside her own head.

Instantly Hughie went white, his hands clenching as he stared accusingly at his father.

'Of course I am sure. Julie was...I was her first,' he mumbled, brick-red. 'Not that it's any of your business.'

'Maybe not, but what is our business is that our son, our clever, clever son, has got his girlfriend pregnant while she is still at school and he is in his first year at university! I thought you told me it was virtually over between the two of you.'

Richard was shaking his head, as though he still couldn't comprehend what he was hearing.

'It was…it is.'

'It's over?' Stella knew she would never totally understand the world of the modern young, where a couple could fall in love, and commit to one another sexually only to tire of the relationship within months, if not weeks, and decide to go their separate ways. It had been so different in her own day. 'So…so what…?'

'Our relationship is over,' Hughie agreed. 'But that does not alter the fact that I am the father of Julie's baby. And naturally I want to do the right thing for them both,' he added proudly.

'Naturally,' Stella agreed, a small spiky shoot of hope beginning to emerge through the shocked chaos of her anxiety.

'Of course, Julie wants to have the baby.'

The spiky shoot withered.

'Of course,' Stella acknowledged hollowly. Well, they did, these modern girls, didn't they?

'I will have to help support it…financially, I mean.'

'Yes, you damn well will,' Richard told him savagely. 'And if you think for one minute that I am going to put my hand in my pocket to pay for your—'

'Richard!' Stella interrupted him warningly. 'Obviously, we're still feeling the shock at the moment, Hughie, but tomorrow I think your father and I should get in touch with Julie's parents to discuss things.'

'No…you can't. There isn't any point.'

'What? Why not?' Stella asked.

'Julie's father refuses to accept what's happened. He's thrown Julie out. He says he never wants to see her again.'

'What?'

Now Stella *was* shocked. She had seen enough of what could happen to girls under such circumstances during her probation service days to feel genuinely protective towards Julie, and outraged by her father's attitude.

'Well, where has she gone—where is she?'

'Here,' Hughie told them uncomfortably. 'Upstairs in my room. Ma…what else could I do?' he appealed to Stella. 'She is my responsibility. They both are, at least until the baby is born. I couldn't just leave her. I mean, it's not as if she's got any other family to go to!'

'All right, Hughie. I understand. You'd better go upstairs and bring her down.' Stella sighed.

As soon as the door had closed behind him Richard exploded. 'No way. No way are we going to have her here. Stella…'

'What else can we do?' Stella asked him logically. 'And anyway, I don't imagine it will be for very long. Her father will probably come round. And since Hughie is the baby's father, I feel—'

'I doubt it, from what I know of him. He and I were both in a local "Think Tank Group" a couple of years ago. Originally he's from somewhere in the North—a small, very strait-laced mining town. He's still got an enclosed community mentality, he's very narrow-minded—bigoted, I would say. He wasn't a very popular member of our team, definitely got a chip on his shoulder from somewhere.'

Stella frowned. 'I didn't know you knew Julie's father—you never said.'

Richard gave a brief shrug. 'The project ended and we went our separate ways. Not the sort of chap one would want to keep in contact with, really. All I'm saying is that I wouldn't think he'd be someone w

'Three months.'

Stella thought she must have misheard her.

'Three months,' she repeated. 'No… I don't think…'

'It's three months!' Julie insisted stubbornly, shaking her head and begging Hughie, 'You tell her.'

As she saw the confirmation in Hughie's eyes Stella frantically grappled with the enormity of what she was facing.

'Julie! Your parents… When did you tell them?' she asked uncertainly. Three months! Had Julie registered with a doctor? The hospital? Had she…?

'When Hughie came home. I couldn't tell them before. I was too frightened…and I didn't want to tell anyone until I knew it would be too late for anyone to make me do…anything.' Her voice was stubborn, her facial expression saying that she felt proud of her actions, like a small child who thought she had outwitted the adults around her. Stella's heart sank even further.

And it was certainly too late for anyone to make her do anything now, Stella acknowledged. Julie was seventeen, six months pregnant and still at school, and her father had thrown her out. Stella closed her eyes.

'What am I going to do? I can't go home! My dad…' Tears were brimming in the huge washed-out eyes.

'What you're going to do for the time being is stay here with us,' Stella told her as calmly as she could, firmly taking control of the situation. Over Julie's downbent head she saw the look of relief and hope that Hughie was giving her, and her own eyes threatened to mist.

'Thanks, Ma,' he told her gruffly, coming over to give her a hug. 'I told Julie you'd know what to do!'

Things would have to be sorted out with Julie's parents, of course, a way found for her to go back home, but there was no point in them discussing that right now. Julie looked exhausted, and, now that she knew just how far advanced her pregnancy was, Stella felt seriously concerned for her.

Their house was an old Victorian three-storey one with plenty of bedrooms, and a granny suite on the top floor where Richard's mother had lived whilst she had still been alive, so there was no problem in finding room for Julie. But the sooner she was back at home with her own family, the better, Stella resolved.

It was all very well for Hughie to face up to his re-sponsibilities and to accept that he had them, but Julie's parents had their responsibilities as well!

'Mmm…I've missed you.'

'I've only been gone for four hours,' Maggie tried to protest, but Oliver was too busy kissing her to let her speak properly.

'Four hours, fifteen minutes and several seconds,' Oliver corrected her as he cupped her face and smiled down into her eyes.

Irresistibly his glance was drawn to her mouth. Maggie had the most wonderful, the most sexy, the most kissable mouth he had ever seen. In fact, so far as he was concerned, Maggie had the most wonderful, the most sexy, the most kissable, the most lovable ev-erything any woman possibly could have.

'How was The Club?' he asked her teasingly as he drew her closer, one hand in the small of her back, the other resting on her still-flat stomach. 'I suppose they've all rushed home to knit baby clothes.'

To his bemusement and her own chagrin, Maggie immediately burst into tears.

'Baby hormones,' she excused her reaction to Oliver, but as she said the words she could hear inside her head Nicki's voice, taut with anger and contempt, insisting, 'You can't be pregnant!'

As he registered the brief look of betraying bleakness in her eyes, Oliver demanded gently, 'Tell me what's wrong.'

Maggie closed her eyes and took a deep, painful breath.

'You are far too perceptive,' she told him wryly.

'We made a pact, Maggie,' Oliver reminded her. 'No game playing, no hidden agendas, no hidden anything between us.' Lifting her hand to his lips and placing a kiss in her open palm, he added, 'We agreed that our love deserves better than that.'

Now more tears were threatening her composure but for a different reason this time, brought on by a different emotion. Pain and joy—strange how in their intensity both could call forth the same physical response.

'How could I ever forget us making that pact?' Maggie answered him, her eyes luminous with her love.

Self-protection had been a necessity following the breakup of her marriage and had become a way of life for her. Strong, feisty, successful career women in their forties were vulnerable in a way that women one or two decades younger were not. All the more so when, like Maggie, they broke one of society's taboos by falling in love with a younger man. Because of that, Maggie was very protectively careful of her emotional responses. It was rare for her to make such an open admission of her feelings. That alone was enough to alert Oliver to the fact that something—or somebody—had seriously hurt her.

'Tell me,' he insisted.

'It's Nicki,' Maggie admitted shakily. 'She hates the idea of me having this baby.'

'She what?' Oliver frowned. He knew how important Maggie's friends were to her; he had heard the full history of their relationship, their shared traumas, and the way they had always supported and protected one another. He knew too how excited Maggie had been about telling them the news, and he could see beneath the brittle bravery of her smile just how hurt and shocked she was.

'She says that I'm too old,' Maggie told him. 'She says that I'm depriving another younger woman of the chance to have a child. She says that I'm doing it to…to keep you—'

'To keep me!' Oliver interrupted her. 'Maggie, there is no way on this earth that you could ever or will ever get rid of me. You know that. You know how much you mean to me. How much I love you. You know what I think…what I believe.' He looked at her, holding her gaze with his own. 'You…us…our love, they are my destiny, Maggie. You are the woman I have longed for all my adult life. If one of us deserves to be accused of holding the other to our love via our baby, then that one is me.'

Maggie felt the tight lump of anguish inside her easing. This conviction that Oliver had, and spoke so naturally and easily to her about, that he had been destined to love her, which he made sound so down-to-earth, so much an irrefutable fact, was something she simply could not discuss with anyone else. Because she was afraid she, they, Oliver would be laughed at?

Her friends were mature women and mature women did not believe in fate. Or that love could transcend time, cross the generation barrier? Why?

Because she herself dared not allow herself to believe it, no matter what Oliver might say? Because she suspected that had any other man but Oliver spoken to her in such a vein she would have dismissed him as being some daydreaming crank?

'Nicki's main concern is that I'm not aware of the problems of being an older mother. She says she can't understand how I can claim to want a child now when I refused to have one with Dan.'

Now it was her turn to look into Oliver's eyes.

'Isn't it time you told her the truth about that?' he suggested gently.

Restlessly Maggie moved away from him.

'It isn't as straightforward as that. Nicki has always thought a lot of Dan. He was her friend before he and I started dating. She actually introduced us. I don't want to…'

'Destroy her illusions?' Oliver supplied.

He had a habit of lifting one eyebrow when he asked a question and Maggie found herself wondering if it was a mannerism his son or daughter would inherit. Just to think about the coming baby made her heart turn over and melt with love and yearning.

'Which do you least want to destroy, Maggie? Her illusions or your friendship? Which do you think she values the more? Which would be most important to you? Don't you think she might even feel a little insulted to know that you believed both her friendship and her ego to be so fragile? Or are you afraid that she will be offended that you have withheld the truth from her for so long?'

'It wasn't a deliberate decision,' Maggie defended herself. 'And it wasn't so much that I wanted to withhold the truth from my friends…'

'No, what you wanted to do—your prime concern,' Oliver emphasised, 'was to protect Dan.'

'It wasn't his fault that he was infertile,' Maggie protested. 'He was devastated when we learned that the problem lay with him…'

'So devastated that he went out and had an affair!' Oliver agreed dryly.

'Oliver, you aren't being fair! Try to put yourself in his position. He desperately wanted us to have children. He had always wanted to have a family, and when nothing happened, he was wonderfully supportive of me.'

'Until he found out that he was the one who couldn't give you a child and not the other way round.'

'I think he had the affair to…to test out what he had been told,' Maggie responded quietly. 'I think it was a form of denial, coupled with a feeling of shock and bereavement, of grieving…and that afterwards he simply couldn't bear to stay with me because of the destruction of the hopes we had both shared for so long and because…'

'Because you knew the truth,' Oliver inserted grimly.

'Because he was afraid that my love might become pity,' Maggie corrected him gently.

'How long is it since he left you, Maggie?' Oliver demanded.

Would it ever go away, this tiny, gritty piece of jealousy over the man who had shared so much of her life before him; who had had so much of her, with her, before him? He knew how much she had loved her husband and how much she had suffered when their marriage had broken up, but his anger against Dan went deeper than jealousy. Dan was, so far as Oliver was concerned, responsible not just for hurting Maggie, but for undermining her, for letting her take the blame for the failure of their marriage and, even more importantly, for their failure to have children.

Maggie watched Oliver warily. In her younger days she knew she would have been tempted to feel flattered by such evidence of jealousy, but Dan was an important part of her past and of herself, and not even to please Oliver could she deny what she and Dan had once shared. What they had once shared…but what about her ongoing protection of him?

That was merely a habit, and nothing more, Maggie immediately reassured herself. But nonetheless, Oliver had raised an issue that Maggie knew she ought to deal with.

No matter what she might have said in the heat of her distress earlier, the friendship she shared with the others meant far too much for her to see it damaged. Nicki's reaction to her news had hurt her, yes, but that did not mean that she no longer valued what they shared.

She could tell Nicki that, but somehow she did not feel able to tell her the truth about Dan. Why? To protect Nicki, or to protect her ex-husband?

'I'm sorry,' she heard Oliver apologising ruefully.

A little guiltily Maggie shook her head. Oliver had obviously mistaken her absorbed silence in her own thoughts for anger and punishment.

Immediately she went towards him, leaning her head on his chest and wrapping her arms as far around him as she could. He had done so much for her; given her so much. After Dan she had believed there would never be another man she could love, another man who would love her enough to heal the pain of her loss.

'You should tell Nicki,' Oliver was insisting.

'I think there's more to her reaction than just the fact that Dan and I never had children,' Maggie responded. 'I'm concerned about her, Oliver. She was so wrought up, so…so unlike her normal self.'

'Maybe so, but my concern is all for you and our baby,' Oliver informed her.

Their baby… The baby her best friend felt she had no right to have!

These years of their lives they were going through now were, Maggie knew, a very, very dangerous rite of passage; a rite of passage that in many ways had become the last female taboo.

Maggie felt strongly that it was the responsibility of her own generation—the generation that had so successfully pushed back so many boundaries, and gifted so many freedoms to the decades of women following in their footsteps—to take up this challenge as they had done so many others.

This treacherous passage across the turbulence of the deep, dangerous emotional waters of these years were in their way as traumatic and life-defining as, perhaps even more so than, those of being a teenager.

Certainly no one—as far as she knew—wrote witty diaries featuring the hormone-induced miseries of her age group. Women of a 'certain age', to use a phrase that Maggie detested, had, it seemed, to be divided into two very different groups: those who clung gamely or ridiculously to the wreckage of their youth (depending on which paper and magazines one read) or those who simply opted to disappear and become 'past it' secondary people, useful only for the support they gave to others.

But why should this be the case? Maggie questioned. Where was it written down that it had to be so?

Was it that women stripped of their youth but left with their power were such a strong force that they had to be mocked and reviled, taunted and made to feel that they were now second-class citizens? Maggie didn't know. What she did know was that she was there in the vanguard, holding her breath, cheering on her own generation, waiting to see if they could perform the same transformation on this age that they had performed on every other they had passed through.

Her peers, her co-baby boomers, bulge yearers, were an awesomely powerful force, a huge wave of humanity, conceived in hope and celebration, a generation born into peace and prosperity, given unique gifts by their parents and their memories of those who had sacrificed their lives and freedoms.

Truly, if one wanted to look at it in such a way, a very special 'Fairy Godmother' had stood silently, rejoicing and hoping, in the wings at their births.

They'd been sprung free of the destructive trap of war that had snared their parents and grandparents, and no limits had been set on what they could achieve or what they could be.

Their lives had been a whole new learning curve for humanity, and, yes, there had been mistakes, foolishness, vanity, but also there had been spectacular life-changing, life-enhancing steps forward, 'giant leaps' for mankind of many different types, and this, their move forward into something so reviled and feared by folklore, was surely in its own way one very giant leap.

Get it right and, not just her own sex, but men and women alike of future generations would only look back in fond amusement that there could ever have been a time when a woman's fiftieth birthday was something she suffered in fear and shame. Get it wrong and they would be consigning not just themselves, but heaven alone knew how many future generations to a life as medieval in its way as that of refusing to allow women to learn to read and write.

And, Maggie felt, it was men like Oliver who would share and rejoice in her sex's crossing of this Styx-like river of fear.

The change of life! It was a turbulent and on occasion even frightening time, no one could deny that, but the strength it took to grow through it was life-enhancing and life-giving. Maggie knew far more about herself and her needs, her realities now than she had ever done as a girl. The things she had taken for granted then were infinitely more precious to her now, and those precious things included her friends. And her memories.

That her fellow humans had given her this chance to have the child she had so much yearned for, and with the right man, was surely something that should be celebrated, a glorious, wonderful gift that she had made a vow to appreciate and treasure, to love and send out into the world knowing how generously and with how much love he or she had been given life.

'Let's go to bed,' Oliver was whispering sexily in her ear.

Maggie hid a small smile. How many times in the early days of their marriage had she and Dan exchanged those very words? Young lovers did make up in bed. And Oliver was young—at least compared to her. On the list of dos and don'ts they had been given by the clinic had been the information that sex was okay, so long as they were careful.

When she had learned about Dan's affair her sex drive had deserted her completely, and she had believed that it had gone for good, destroyed by her pain, until Oliver had shown her otherwise! With him she had discovered the zest and excitement she remembered from her youth; she had relearned the pleasure of being physically loved, of giving and sharing that love. And she had also learned that perhaps the strongest aphrodisiac in the world was to be loved and desired by someone who simply wanted to put her needs first.

Dan had been a sexy, skilful, passionate lover, but it was Oliver who had shown her what sensitivity could bring to desire.

'Mmm...' she agreed, her eyes glinting with tenderness and teasing as she added insouciantly, 'They did say at the clinic that I should make sure I got enough sleep.'

'Sleep. That wasn't...'

As she started to laugh Oliver grinned at her.

'Okay, but just you wait until later,' he mock threatened her as they went upstairs, their arms around one another.

The sight of Stuart's car parked outside the house as she stopped her own made Alice's stomach clench a little. She had known he was due to return home this evening, but she had not been sure when.

The others had thought it very glamorous when she had first met Stuart and she had learned that he was an airline pilot, and if she was honest so had she! He had stood out dramatically amongst the boys who formed part of their extended crowd of friends, tall, tanned from his stopovers abroad, blue-eyed, blond-haired and so good-looking that Alice had wondered why on earth he'd been singling her out.

'Because you are stunningly pretty, and good and

sweet, and he's fallen in love with you, stoopid,' Nicki teased her gently.

'Yeah, and he's seen how sexy you look in those hot pants.' Maggie laughed, ignoring Alice's pink-cheeked protests.

The outfits Maggie insisted they wore for their 'gigs', Alice suspected, got them far more attention than their music.

Stuart obviously thought so, because one of the first things he did was ask her not to wear them.

'There's only one man I want you to look sexy for and that's me!' he told her with the same dizzyingly masterful maturity with which he swept her off her feet.

Stuart no longer flew commercial flights. Instead he worked for the airline as an instructor, flying only as a relief pilot when necessary, which was what he had recently been doing.

'Don't you ever worry about him...I mean, mixing with all those air stewardesses?' She was asked that question so many times over the years that she had her response off pat. A smile, a gentle laugh and small shake of her head. But of course she worried. Especially in the early years of their marriage. Stuart was after all a highly sexed man. But he was also a man who showed in many different ways that he loved her.

This house, for instance, that he insisted on buying when they first knew that her second pregnancy was twins. She was horrified at the cost of it—a very large detached house, set in its own immense garden, with an adjacent paddock. She protested that they could not possibly afford it, but Stuart was equally insistent that he wanted them to have it.

When the twins arrived, Stuart changed his own expensive car for a much smaller model and bought her a top-of-the-range four-wheel drive so that she could transport the children in comfort and safety. Zoë's riding lessons and her pony and all the other extra-curricular activities the children wanted, Stuart paid for without complaint. The allowance he insisted on giving her was a generous one, and the presents he brought her back from his trips drew the envious admiration of her friends.

No, Stuart never neglected her either in bed or out of it, something for which, if the stories she heard from other women were to be believed, she ought to be extremely grateful. And of course she was.

But the house, the allowance, the car, all of them were things she sometimes felt she would gladly have bartered just for the opportunity to sit down with Stuart and talk to him, to have her opinions sought and valued, to feel that he regarded her as an equal partner in their relationship, and that she mattered to him not because she was his wife, but because she was herself!

He was in the kitchen when she walked in, still an extraordinarily handsome man, his thick once-blond hair silver-grey now, the reading glasses he still pretended he did not really need adding an extra touch of subtle sexuality to his features. He always had been and always would be the kind of man who drew women's glances, and, although he might deny it, Alice knew that there was that little touch of vanity in his make-up that meant that he needed their female recognition of his maleness.

As he saw her he shuffled the papers he had been reading and stood up.

'Have you been in long?' Alice asked.

'A couple of hours. When I realised it was your

night out with the others, I went down to the gym for an hour.'

Unlike her, Stuart was something of a gym fanatic, his body still lean and muscular. Alice had at one stage endeavoured to become more exercise conscious, but Stuart had laughed at her, refusing to take her seriously.

'I love you just the way you are,' he had told her fondly, spoiling his compliment slightly by adding, 'Every single bit of you!'

He looked tired, Alice recognised, but diplomatically she did not say so. She had learned early on in their relationship that Stuart hated to admit to any kind of vulnerability or weakness, no matter how small. She suspected that this had a lot to do with the fact that his father had been a high-achieving, very macho man, a Second World War fighter pilot, decorated for bravery and revered by his wife and Stuart's three older sisters. Stuart had been reared in a family where his maleness had elevated him to almost godlike status, but the price for this had been that he'd never been allowed to show himself as mortal.

Her own father had fought in the same war, but the experience had affected his nerves in some way, and Alice could remember her mother's constant anxiety that Alice did not make too much noise or do anything that might upset her father, around whom their small household had revolved every bit as much as Stuart's had revolved around his.

To some extent Alice knew that she and Stuart had repeated this pattern. Stuart's job had meant that when he had been at home there had been times when she had automatically kept the children away from him so that he could catch up on his sleep. Times when she had in a number of small ways protected Stuart from the children and the children from him!

So, rather than commenting on his tiredness, and mindful of the news she had to give him about her plans, she said instead, 'I'm glad you've got some leave days now—'

'I wish!' Stuart interrupted her grimly. 'I've got a series of meetings coming up in the city.'

He had his back to her as he was speaking and Alice suddenly had the feeling that for some reason he didn't want her to see his face. A tiny sharp spike of unease touched her, like the beginnings of an unwanted spot, as yet unseen, but still felt beneath the outer skin.

And yet there was no reason for her to feel like that. Stuart was frequently away on business after all. Perhaps it was because she had been building herself up to telling him about her OU plans, waiting for the right moment. Yes, that was probably what it was, she reassured herself.

'How long do you think you will be away?'

'For heaven's sake, Alice, I just don't know. As long as it takes, however long that is. What is this anyway? What's all the fuss about?'

His irritation made her clench her stomach muscles defensively.

'I wasn't making a fuss,' Alice protested. 'It's just that… Well, there was something I wanted to discuss with you.'

'If it's about that idiot you hired who claimed he was a gardener, then we don't need to discuss anything. Sack him.'

'Stuart, it isn't about the garden! It's—it's about me!'

Now that she had his attention, Alice felt her apprehension increasing.

'You?' He was frowning. 'What do you mean it's about you? Look, Alice, can't we leave this for another time? Right now the last thing I want or need is an in-depth discussion on anything!'

He was getting annoyed, Alice recognised silently, registering all the tell-tale signs.

Her heart sank, but she was not going to back down.

'No, we can't leave it, I'm afraid, Stuart. It's too important for that. I...I've enrolled for an Open University degree course.'

'What?'

He was, Alice noticed, staring at her blankly, as though he hadn't properly taken in what she had said.

'I thought you said it was something important,' he challenged her. 'For God's sake, Alice! Don't you ever listen to anything I say? I've just told you that I'm up to my eyes in it at work and you're prattling on about some blasted college course.'

Alice could feel her stomach muscles clenching, but not this time with tension. She very seldom got angry, it just wasn't in her nature, but right now...

'You don't mind, then?' she asked him quietly.

'Mind?' He gave a brief, almost contemptuous shrug. 'I don't really see the point, but it's your choice.'

'Yes,' Alice agreed even more quietly. 'It is.'

Changing the subject, she questioned, 'You said you could be away for a few days?'

'Yes.' Stuart had turned away from her and was re-shuffling his papers. His voice sounded muffled and strained.

'It's the way things are these days, Alice. It's some-thing to do with a new policy decision. Even you must surely be aware of the changes the aviation industry is undergoing? The pressures on it? I mean, you do read something in the papers, don't you, other than the women's pages? God knows we get enough of them, judging by the bill.'

Alice stared at his white-shirt-covered back, the words of rebuttal and anger log-jamming in her throat in their furious need to be heard, but protectively she held them back.

Stuart was normally a calm, logical man—his job meant that he had to be—but just occasionally he could explode into undeserved and lacerating verbal criticism that was as unprovoked as it was unfair. Backing him into a corner or demanding an apology only resulted in him retreating into an iron-hard sulk, from which she would patiently have to coax him and right now... Right now she simply did not feel like doing any such thing!

'You'll never guess what happened this evening,' she said calmly instead, going to fill the kettle. 'Maggie told us that she's pregnant. She gave us all a shock, especially Nicki.'

Alice tensed as Stuart came up behind her, wrapping his arms around her and nuzzling the side of her neck.

'You never change, do you, Alice?' he told her as he bit sensually into her skin, oblivious to her rigid tension. 'We could be invaded by green men from outer space and you would still be more concerned about your own little life.'

Alice could hear the familiar note of mockery in his voice. It seemed to her sometimes that Stuart had spent most of their married lives mocking her or putting her down in one way or another.

'Come on,' Stuart demanded. 'Let's go to bed. I've missed you.'

Just for a second Alice was tempted to refuse, to pull

away from him, but he was already taking hold of her hand and tugging her towards the hall door. To challenge him to dare to mock her again! But typically she stopped herself.

And, after all, what was the point in deliberately creating a difficult mood between them? Didn't it make more sense to give in, to keep him happy? Wasn't that what her mother had always taught her by example? As she had taught Zoë. That men were people who needed to be pandered to and coaxed, pampered and protected. That either they or their love or both simply weren't strong enough to bear reality…

'You prefer the twins, you always favour them!' How often had Zoë accused her of that? Had she 'favoured' them or had she in reality done them anything but a favour?

The others considered her to be a perfect mother, a role model, but what was a 'perfect' mother?

'Where did you eat?' Stuart was asking her.

'The new wine bar. The food's Italian,' Alice replied.

As Stuart kissed her he smiled. 'And you didn't have garlic! Good girl!'

Good girl! Alice could feel her jaw tensing and her body chilling. But Stuart was as oblivious to the signals her body was sending out as he was to the fact that he was patronising her, Alice recognised.

'No, leave the light on. Please,' Oliver demanded softly as Maggie swung her legs out of their bed and at the same time reached out to dim her bedside lamp.

It had been Dan who had encouraged her to sleep naked, but, despite the praise Oliver heaped on her body and their lovemaking, she was still self-consciously uncomfortable about him seeing her unclothed in a way she had not been with Dan. Because she was older than Oliver and her body was no longer that of a young girl?

'I'm only going to the bathroom,' she told him.

'Why is it that you always want to hide yourself from me, Maggie?' Oliver asked her quietly. 'I love looking at your body. I love looking at you.'

He watched as she veiled her expression from him, dropping her lashes. She had so many small endearing habits that entranced him. She called herself old, but she wasn't. Her body was slender but softly curved, her skin creamily pale—as a redhead, she had told him ruefully, she had never been able to sunbathe successfully. The natural curves of her body aroused him in a way that shrunk, dieted-down, or unnaturally enhanced supposedly 'perfect' female figures never could.

When they had first become lovers he had tried to persuade her to wear soft loose clothes—and no underwear. Although she had tried to hide it, he had seen from her expression that he had shocked her. A little grimly, he had reflected then that at least there was *something* that she had not experienced with her ex-husband. His request had not been motivated by anything demeaning or controlling, but simply by his overwhelming feelings of love for her. Just to watch her move, just to see her lift her hand and grab at her wild curls—a habit she had—and to see her body move naturally and sensually flooded him with appreciation and desire. And now knowing that her body was holding and nurturing their child added a dimension to those feelings, to his love, that ran so deep and so powerfully that it went way beyond anything he had ever imagined he might experience.

In the bathroom Maggie looked silently into the

mirror as Oliver's reflection joined her own. Standing behind her, he wrapped his arms around her, bending his head to breathe in the scent of her skin.

'I love you, Maggie,' he murmured to her as he turned her round and kissed her. A slow, gentle, gifting kiss that melted away her hesitation.

'I love you too,' she answered, and meant it. How could she not love him? She closed her eyes as he stroked her skin. His hands cupped her breasts, his mouth caressing her throat. Desire ran through her veins, hot, heavy, drugging. In the mirror she could see her breasts swelling and lifting, her nipples taut. This pregnancy would change her body for ever. In about eight months a baby would be suckling greedily on the nipples Oliver was now gently plucking. The thought made her tremble with awe and excitement.

Here, protected by Oliver's love and desire, she could ignore the outside world, but she knew that Nicki wouldn't be the only person to criticise her.

There had been an increasingly antagonistic reaction to pregnancies like hers in the press over recent months, a passionately attacked and defended debate on the moral implications of such situations.

The irony of what she was doing was not lost on Maggie. As a girl, her generation had made full use of the contraceptive pill to prevent and delay pregnancy, thus interfering with the cycle of nature. And now that same generation was interfering with nature once again, only this time...

She heard Oliver groan as he reached for her hand and placed it against his body.

His erection was hard, his penis bulging and full, the veins standing out against his skin—a young man's erection. The sight of it made her shiver with sensuality. Slowly she caressed him with her fingers, fiercely barricading her mind, her memory against the intrusion of another life and another man.

Without releasing him she knelt down and took him slowly and skilfully into her mouth, caressing the head of his penis with her lips as she savoured the taste and feel of him before sliding her tongue along its stiff length.

Above her Oliver groaned out loud, burying his hands in her hair without constraining her, allowing her the freedom to dictate their intimacy.

Still holding him, Maggie licked teasingly around the distended head of his erection, using her lips and tongue to deliberately make him shudder with need before she took him back in her mouth. Holding him in its wet warmth, she caressed him with increasing intensity, taking him deeper and deeper, relishing the feel and taste of his flesh in this the most intimate of lover's ways. As she had known he would, he withdrew from her before he came, finding her own wetness with gentle fingers before he eased himself carefully into her.

No matter how often they made love it always surprised her that she climaxed so quickly and easily with him. Somehow it was as though the deepest part of herself and her body refused to accept the shackles of inhibition imposed by a society that said that she ought to feel ashamed of the maturity of her body.

Oliver had gathered her up before he entered her, supporting her body, and now as he let her slide back down to the floor he paused for a moment before finally releasing her to kiss her mouth with deeply tender passion.

In the early days of their courtship when she had often refused to allow him to give her oral sex, he had demanded, 'Why won't you let me?'

Somehow she couldn't explain to him that for her generation such an act from a man to a woman had been a much rarer pleasure than it was for his generation; a gift given on special days, at heightened moments of desire, rather than an accepted part of a familiar lovemaking ritual.

'I love the taste of you, the feel of you, the desire of you,' Oliver had told her passionately. 'Please don't deny those pleasures to me, Maggie.'

Hand in hand they went back to their bed, Oliver insisting on tucking her carefully beneath the duvet before joining her.

'Forget about Nicki and the others,' he whispered to her as he kissed her goodnight.

Forget? Maggie wished that were possible!

'Stuart...'

In the darkness of their bedroom, Alice tried to reach for Stuart's hand, but he pulled away from her, turning over, his back to her.

'Leave it, will you, Alice?' he demanded brusquely. 'For God's sake, let's not have an in-depth inquest. So I lost a bloody erection! So what? It happens all the time. You making a drama out of it isn't going to alter anything.'

Her making a drama out of it? Alice suppressed her desire to point out to him that she hadn't particularly wanted to have sex in the first place and that he had been the one to suggest it.

But she could feel Stuart's tension, and instinctively she wanted to comfort him. To reassure him, to reach out and hold him; but just as instinctively she knew he would not want her to. She could feel how shocked and disbelieving he was.

On his own side of the bed, Stuart lay staring into

the darkness. Never once in all the years they had been married had he suffered an erection failure. Never. Ever.

His eyes burned as though they were filled with grit, his body gripped by tension and a sickening sense of powerlessness. He knew why it had happened, of course. Of course! How could he not? It didn't need a series of expensive counselling sessions with a shrink to tell him. The miracle was perhaps that it hadn't happened before!

From his childhood he could hear his father's voice exhorting him, 'Be a man, Stuart.'

Be a man! His father had been a man. A very special man. Stuart had known all the time he was growing up that he could never hope to rival him, that his father belonged to a rare and exclusive club whose doors would be for ever barred to him. His father was, after all, a hero and he had the medals to prove it; the medals, and the stories, the reminiscences and tales of comrades who had not possessed his own luck and who had perished.

Stuart could still vividly remember how different his father had been when he had got together with his ex-comrades. At home he had been a distant, commanding figure, constantly exhorting Stuart to live up to his maleness. He had died shortly after the twins had been born.

'A man needs sons, Stuart,' he had pronounced approvingly after their birth. Sons...another marker of a man's maleness.

It was all rubbish, of course, and his views would be ridiculed now—Stuart knew that. Men and women were equal now. Equal...

Stuart closed his eyes against the burning pain seizing him. Just for a second he longed to bury himself against Alice's sleepy warmth, to take comfort from her and be comforted by her, but how could he, when he knew...?

What was she going to say when she found out? Would she despise him? Reject him? Blame him for letting her down?

Could he blame her if she did? He had tried to prevent it happening, but all the time, from the first moment he had met Arlette Salcombe, he had known it was inevitable. That single look between them, that meeting of glances. He had known then. And now there was no way out and no way back!

5

'What do you mean, a man telephoned asking for me?' The anger in Laura's voice made Joey cower away from her.

'What man, Joey?' Laura demanded. 'What did he say?' She could feel the heat in her face. Her heart was hammering against her chest, driven by anger. Anger and not excitement, no way was she going to allow it to be excitement.

Her fingers curled into her palms, making tight fists. It had to be Ryan. It couldn't possibly be anyone else. He must have got the number from Human Resources. He had no right to ring her. No right to...

'What did he say? Did he tell you his name?' Her voice rose, sharpening with each word, frightening Joey even more. He had intuitively picked up on Laura's antagonism towards his mother and that increased his fear of her.

'Did he tell you his name?' Laura was shouting now, too wrapped up in her own fear to be aware of Joey's. Right now he was just an irritating child who, through either malice or stupidity, was refusing to give her the information she so desperately needed.

'Joey?' Laura exploded, grabbing hold of him and giving him an impatient little shake before she could stop herself. Almost immediately she released him, but it was too late. Just as she did so Nicki walked into the kitchen.

'Let go of him! Let go of him, Laura!'

Furiously Nicki rushed to protect her son, kneeling down to gather him up in her arms as Laura released him.

'How dare you? How dare you touch my child?' she blazed. 'Joey, it's all right, it's all right, you're safe now,' she comforted her son, rocking him in her arms as Laura looked on in a mixture of contempt and bitterness.

'That's right!' she threw at Nicki. 'You rush to protect your precious child—but you can't always be here to protect him, Nicki. After all, I haven't forgotten that there was no one to protect me from you!' Instinctively Laura tried to defend herself and her actions.

'What? I never did anything to hurt you!' Nicki denied immediately.

'You're lying,' Laura spat out, giving her a thin-lipped, acid smile. 'But then you would, wouldn't you? Anyway, for your information, I wasn't hurting Joey. And if I were you, instead of treating him like a baby, I'd spend a bit more time making sure he knows how to take a telephone message properly.'

'It wasn't my fault,' Joey protested from the comfort of Nicki's arms. 'The man didn't say any name. He just asked if you were here.'

Laura had been terrifying her son half to death simply because of a phone call? Nicki's mouth compressed.

'Whoever he is, Laura, if he wants to speak to you enough he will ring back.'

Laura's face burned even hotter as Nicki made no attempt to conceal the smugly superior tone of her voice. Immediately she reacted to it, saying fiercely,

'It's typical of you to think what you're obviously thinking, but you're wrong. I don't want him to ring back. In fact, I don't want to speak to him at all. To speak to him or to see him. You see, unlike you, I have no intention of becoming involved in an affair with a married man or having sex with him behind his wife's back.'

As she listened to Laura's outburst Nicki's face went white. Releasing Joey, she told him huskily, 'Joey, go up to your room and watch your videos for a while before it's time for school, will you, darling?'

Over Joey's blond head their glances fought, neither of them allowing herself to give way. As soon as the door had closed behind Joey Nicki demanded, 'What is it exactly that you're trying to say, Laura?'

Laura shot her a bitterly cynical glare, hating what was happening but powerless to stop it. The words, the pain, the anguish had been dammed up inside her for too long to be controlled, now that she had released them.

'What do you think I'm trying to say? You know perfectly well what I'm talking about. And don't bother trying to lie about it. I was there! I heard you. They'd sent me home from school because I wasn't feeling well. I tried to tell them that there wasn't any point because there wasn't anyone there to look after me.' She gave a mirthless smile. 'After all, my mother had only been taken into hospital a few days earlier. To give my father a rest, that's what they'd said when I went to see her. But it wasn't a rest he was getting, was it, Nicki? He wasn't resting on the bed in the guest room at all, was he? No. He was lying there whilst you—'

'Stop it.' Appalled and sick with shock, Nicki covered her ears, her shock increasing as Laura flew at her, tearing her hands from her ears as she screamed.

'No! You will listen, just as I had to listen to the pair of you! Have you any idea how disgusting it sounds hearing your own father sobbing with sickening lust whilst his whore relieves him? I heard every word. Every sound...every sound,' Laura stressed savagely.

Tears of rage were pouring down her face—a face that was contorted into an expression of fury and loathing, the strength of the emotion emanating from her such that Nicki could almost feel it heating the air between them.

In contrast she felt icy cold with shock. She could feel herself shivering as the nausea churned unpleasantly in her stomach. She tried to defend herself, to stop the flood of obscenity pouring from Laura's mouth, protesting, 'Laura, it wasn't like that! You don't understand...'

'No, I don't!' Laura agreed furiously. 'I don't understand how my father could have possibly wanted to take you to bed in my home, my mother's home, whilst she was dying in a hospital bed. I don't understand how he can ever have wanted to touch you, never mind do the things he did to you.

'You couldn't wait, could you, Nicki? You wanted to desecrate my home, my mother, so badly that you couldn't even wait for him to undress you. I heard you begging him, screaming to him to take you, to fill you. I heard him... My mother was dying and the pair of you were shagging each other like animals. You couldn't wait for her to die, could you, Nicki? You couldn't wait to take her place. You *didn't* wait, did you?'

'It wasn't like that,' Nicki protested, white-faced. 'Laura, please listen to me.'

'Listen to you?' She gave a mirthless laugh. 'That's what *he* wants me to do! My boss…the reason I have had to come here, the one place where I know I'll be able to resist the temptation to give in to him, because you're here, Nicki, and every time I look at you I remember what you did and how much I hated you then and still hate you now for it.

'A married man with a dying wife. Was it good for you, Nicki, knowing that she was dying? Did that add that extra bit of something to your enjoyment? Did you think of her when my father was—?'

Laura gasped in shock as Nicki slapped her face. The sound ricocheted through the kitchen as her head snapped back.

Her eyes glittering with contempt, Laura ran to the back door, pulling it open.

Unable to move, Nicki heard the sound of the BMW's engine firing. Despite the fact that she was still shivering, sweat was now pouring off her, soaking through the shirt she was wearing. She could feel it gathering beneath her breasts. Just as it had done that day so very long ago.

Closing her eyes, she slumped against the kitchen wall.

It had taken her nearly two months to find a suitable housekeeper for Kit, and of course during those two months she had been obliged to speak to him both by telephone and in person on several occasions for professional reasons. And she had tried to keep things strictly professional. They both had.

She had tried to reassure herself, to tell herself that she had imagined, exaggerated that shockingly unexpected surge of awareness of him. After the experience of her marriage, the last thing she had been looking for was another relationship. Kit had been a married man, with a very sick wife. She'd had her professional position to consider. She was just not the kind of woman who went in for affairs. Oh, yes, she had been able to provide herself with any number of reasons for refusing to acknowledge what had been happening to her.

Kit had kept his own emotional distance from her, and she had actually begun to believe that the danger had been successfuly averted when he had arrived at her office late one afternoon, just as she'd been about to leave.

He'd explained emotionally to her that his daughter Laura had become very rebellious, in reaction, he'd suspected, to her mother's illness, and he had come to Nicki to seek help and advice, not knowing who else he could turn to.

She had, Nicki remembered, felt both flattered and afraid. Kit had persuaded her to come up to the house and meet Laura. Reluctantly she had agreed.

Laura had been thirteen then, the worst possible time surely for a young girl to be losing her mother, Nicki could remember thinking. She could remember too how sympathetic she had felt towards Laura and how much she had wanted to help and comfort her. Not just for Kit's sake but for Laura's own. Her thick wheat-gold hair, so like her father's, had made Nicki ache with protective pain, but she had determinedly refused to allow herself to swamp Laura with her own feelings, instead striving to treat her in as adult a way as possible.

She had introduced herself to her in her professional capacity and had asked her gently, 'woman to woman', how she considered Mrs Fulton the housekeeper had been getting on.

It had been the right kind of approach, and after an initial and natural hesitation Laura had begun to confide in her, so much so, in fact, that she had taken to calling in on Nicki at work on her way home from school.

Nicki had been happy to see her and to help her, but she had still determinedly kept a distance between Kit and herself—as he had done between himself and her. And so, foolishly perhaps, she had congratulated herself on having overcome any inappropriate feelings she might have had for him, until the first Christmas she had known him.

He had asked her to go shopping with him to buy a suitable present for Laura, and she had agreed.

They had been standing in the teenage clothes shop in the city, paying for the outfit she had told him she knew Laura wanted, when it had happened. The salesgirl had smiled at them both and said innocently, 'Is it for your daughter?'

Nicki had looked at Kit and he had looked back at her. Her heart had started to hammer and her mouth had gone dry. She had known what he'd been feeling because she'd been feeling it herself. She remembered how she had pulled away from him and run blindly out of the shop, terrified of her own emotions. He had come after her, catching up with her in the street. It had been a cold, raw day with a sharp east wind that had whipped her hair across her face.

Kit had pushed it out of the way, she remembered, his fingers tender against her skin.

'I wish more than you can know that things were different, that I was free to be yours and that you were mine, Nicki, and that we…' he told her, and then before she could stop him he kissed her! And she kissed him back, hungrily, passionately, giving in helplessly to a need she had no right to feel.

She felt bitterly ashamed afterwards, wrenching herself out of his arms and standing there on the pavement trembling with shock and sick despair.

It would have been bad enough if he had merely been married, but the fact that his wife was so desperately ill of course made her feel even more shamed and distraught.

She told him she never wanted to see him again…could not afford to see him again, but he pleaded with her for Laura's sake not to walk out of their lives.

Reluctantly she gave in, on the strict understanding that what had happened between them was never repeated.

Kit gave her his word that it would not be, and after that they were both meticulous about never knowingly being alone together.

At the back of both their minds but never actually admitted was the knowledge that ultimately they would have their chance to be together. But Nicki was determined not to taint either their own future or Kit's memories by allowing either of them to give in to their feelings while Jennifer was still alive. And she fully intended to stick to that vow!

As winter gave way to spring that first year, and spring to summer, Jennifer's health waxed and waned with the seasons. Her heart condition, initially caused by a severe bout of childhood rheumatic fever, had worsened after Laura's birth and was now chronic and fatal. All the doctors could do was buy her time, brief respites, when she was well enough to return home for a pathetically few days.

Without wanting to, Nicki became drawn into their

family circle. Mrs Fulton could not always be there, and Jennifer did not like strangers around her. She was very ill at that stage, with Kit her carer rather than her lover. Sometimes Nicki felt almost as though Jennifer sensed how she herself felt about Kit. She once said to her during her last summer that she hoped that Kit would remarry and be happy and that she didn't want Laura to grow up without someone to mother her.

Nicki said nothing, but that weekend for the first time she admitted to Maggie just how she felt. Predictably, Maggie hugged her fiercely and cried with her. Afterwards, again typically, she announced that she had arranged for them both to go on holiday together, a luxurious continental spa where they could let their hair down and be spoilt.

It was only later that Nicki realised that at the time Maggie's own marriage was in trouble and that Dan was having an affair!

The next winter she reluctantly agreed to spend Christmas Day with Laura and Kit, for Laura's sake. Jennifer was back in hospital, her condition deteriorating. She and Kit, she remembered, behaved towards one another like two awkward strangers, so much so that at one point Laura asked her in private if she didn't like her father!

The strain began to take its toll on her. She lost weight, and grew irritable and snappy, under the burden of her feelings of guilt and longing, but still she and Kit stuck rigidly to their agreement.

That spring Jennifer rallied—for the last time, the doctors warned Kit, and when he told Nicki in weary exhaustion of their verdict, she sensed the relief he wasn't voicing. Instinctively she knew it was not for his own sake, and certainly not for hers, but purely in every sense for Jennifer, who had suffered so much and for so long, and for Laura too who had spent virtually all her life watching her mother die. But as though he felt he had to punish them both—him for his feelings and her for sensing them—he immediately become angry and almost hostile towards her.

Unbearably hurt that he should be pushing her away just when she most wanted to be there for him, she turned to Maggie, for comfort. 'He feels guilty,' Maggie told her, confirming her own feelings. 'Let him go through this in his own way, Nicki,' she advised her gently. 'I know how much you want to be there for him, but perhaps in his eyes this is something he has to do alone for Jennifer and for their shared past.'

Their shared love, Maggie meant, Nicki knew that, and suddenly she was afraid that somehow Jennifer's death might take Kit away from her.

She stayed away from the house and from him, even distancing herself a little from Laura, and she would have continued to do so if Mrs Fulton hadn't had to give up her job to nurse her own sick mother.

It was Kit's wish that Jennifer should be allowed to die peacefully at home in her own bed, as she always said she wanted to do, but a sudden crisis meant that she had to be taken into hospital.

Nicki heard the desperation in Kit's voice when he telephoned her to ask her if she could possibly help him. The hospital agreed that Jennifer could return home for her final few days once her breathing was back to normal, and Kit naturally wanted to stay at the hospital with her, but because of her emergency admission there were domestic chores to do at the house.

Initially Nicki intended to find him a temporary substitute for Mrs Fulton, but no one was available, and in the end she went up to the house herself, using the key Kit had given her to let herself in.

Even the air inside the house felt heavy with grief and pain, and Nicki was instinctively affected by it. She felt for Jennifer as a woman. The last time she had seen her, Jennifer had shocked her by telling her that she was tired of her fight and that she longed for it to be over.

'I need to be allowed to die, Nicki,' she had said quietly. 'And Kit and most of all Laura need to be allowed to live. This shadowy half world which is neither living nor dying, which all three of us are currently condemned to, is benefiting no one. It's time for it to end.'

Nicki was upstairs, just finishing remaking the bed in the guest room, which Kit had taken to using leaving the main bedroom free for Jennifer, when Kit returned home. He had come upstairs before she realised he was there, standing in the open doorway and simply looking at her.

'Jennifer?' she demanded anxiously.

'The crisis is over for now, but...' He paused and then said bleakly, 'She's coming home tomorrow. She's always said she wanted to die here in her own bed.'

The look in his eyes tore her apart. Unable to stop herself, she went to him, intending only to offer him human comfort. She lifted her hand to touch his face, she remembered, and her palm was wet with his tears.

'Nicki!' He said her name in an explosive sound of raw agony, and then he reached for her, pulling her into his arms and kissing her with such furious need that she was not able to deny him, sensing that he was being driven by something that went way beyond mere sexual desire, and that it involved somehow a far more complex need; a form of grieving and losing himself and his pain that made her heart ache for him and for Jennifer herself.

Quite when that furious need to expiate his pain had turned to desire for her, she didn't know. All she could remember was suddenly realising that something had changed; that they were kissing and touching as lovers.

'Kit, no!' she forced herself to protest at one point, even though her body was already screaming for his possession, but Kit overruled her, begging her thickly, 'Nicki, don't deny me. Not now...I need you so badly... Please, please, Nicki.' And her will-power evaporated, burned away by desire.

All the months of denying themselves as well as Kit's pain and anguish, his guilt and despair at Jennifer's long decline, were exorcised in what followed. It was desire, need, hunger stripped down to its most basic components; rawly sexual, intensely tender, deeply emotional, the kind of intimacy that touched the soul and burned away inhibitions and conventions.

Afterwards Nicki felt both euphoric and shocked— the guilt came later when her body finally recovered from its satiated satisfaction.

For almost a week Jennifer lingered on the edge of death, brought home by Kit as he had always promised her he would do, and when Nicki finally managed to find the courage to visit Kit was distant and cold towards her.

She sensed instinctively that he felt guilty about what had happened and that he blamed her for it, even though he had been the instigator of their passion. His behaviour towards her fuelled her own resentment at being seduced into an act of betrayal she had begun to hate herself for committing. She hated knowing that their first time together had happened in such a way, and she came close to hating Kit for making it happen like that.

That it was the one and only occasion on which they were lovers until they were officially able to declare themselves as a dating couple made no difference; Nicki felt that she would carry the guilt of what had happened with her for ever.

Had Kit been prepared to talk about it, had they been able to find a way of exonerating themselves and allowing themselves to make a human mistake, things might have been different, but Nicki knew that secretly, despite their love for one another, both of them still felt uncomfortable about what they had done.

Initially, when both he and Laura withdrew from her, she thought it a natural consequence of Jennifer's death and she respected their need to grieve together as father and daughter. It was the school holidays and Kit took Laura away. Days, weeks, months went by without any contact from him, whilst Nicki waited patiently.

'Just give him time, Nicki,' Maggie counselled her consolingly, and that was exactly what she did.

On the day of her birthday in October, she received a simple bouquet of creamy white roses with a note attached to them in Kit's handwriting.

'Thank you—for being you,' was all it said, and she spent the whole day torn between elation and despair, wondering where he was and when—*if*—she was going to see him.

He telephoned her that evening to say that he had intended to be home to surprise her and take her out for dinner, but that Laura was not well enough for them to make the trip back.

Perhaps that was when she should have realised, guessed what was to lie ahead, but she hadn't done. Why should she? She and Laura had always had such a good relationship, it had never even occurred to her that Laura would turn against her, begin to hate her...do everything within her considerable power to break up their relationship!

And now at last she knew why.

She felt sick remembering what Laura had said to her and even sicker remembering what she and Kit had done.

'Where are you going?'

Maggie smiled ruefully at Oliver as she picked her car keys up off her desk.

'To see Nicki.' When she saw his expression she shook her head. 'I can't just leave things, Oliver. She's my best friend. We've been through so much together. I have to...'

'Placate her?' Oliver suggested.

Maggie shook her head. 'No!' she denied firmly. 'But if my friendship is as important to her as hers is to me we must be able to find a way to compromise, surely?'

'And if you can't?'

'Don't say that,' she pleaded with him.

Nicki stared at the cold cup of tea on the table in front of her. She had no recollection of having made it. Joey had gone to school, having been picked up by another boy's mother.

Nicki had no idea where Laura was, and she cared even less, she told herself savagely. And as for Kit! A bitter little smile twisted her mouth. Kit, lucky, lucky Kit, was away on business. She stiffened as she heard someone knocking on her kitchen door. Whoever it was, she didn't want to see them. She did not want to see anyone. Could not bear to see anyone. But the handle was turning and the door was opening and she could hear Maggie's voice calling out, 'Nicki. It's only me, Maggie…'

Maggie had been rehearsing what she was going to say all the way to Nicki's, but her hesitantly prepared words, along with her wariness, disappeared the moment she saw Nicki's white, tear-blotched face.

'Nicki! What's happened? What's wrong?'

Helplessly Nicki closed her eyes. Of course! Of course, it would have to be Maggie who found her like this. Why was it that whenever there was a crisis in her life Maggie always seemed to be there to witness it?

Maggie had been there the day Carl had beaten her so badly that she could hardly crawl, never mind walk; she had been there when Nicki had made the gut-wrenching decision not to see Kit again; and she was here now!

Pointless to try to deny that anything was wrong. Maggie knew her too well. They went back too far. Instead she closed her eyes and said carefully, 'I don't want to talk about it.'

Across the table they looked at one another.

Pulling out a chair, Maggie sat down opposite her and told her wryly, 'Tell me something I don't already know, Nicki, you never want to talk about it. I've never known anyone as determined to button her stiff upper lip as you.'

'And I've never known anyone as persistently determined to push a person to their limits as you,' Nicki retorted. In her own voice she could hear the echoes of so many similar confrontations. It irritated her to be forced to acknowledge how easily they both slipped into their childhood roles with one another.

She could see herself now. Eight years old, on her own in a corner of the playground of the new school her parents' house move had resulted in her attending, trying to escape from the bullies tormenting her and to hold back her tears of fear and shame.

Of course it had been Maggie who had come over to her, surreptitiously offering her a handkerchief whilst she poured scorn on the feared bullies, denouncing them as 'stupid'.

A sense of *déjà vu* filled her as, out of the corner of her eye now, she watched while Maggie reached in her bag and, without a word, produced a small pack of tissues, pushing them across the table to her.

'Is it Laura?' she guessed. 'You mustn't let her upset you. Wretched girl. You let people bully you too easily, Nicki, and Laura has always been a troublemaker.'

'A troublemaker!' Nicki tipped back her head and blinked fiercely, trying to contain her tears. 'Is she? Or is it me who simply attracts trouble? Arguments? Discord?'

Fiercely she blew her nose.

'I thought I'd got the whole victim bit out of my system during the counselling I had after Carl, but just recently I'm beginning to wonder; to question whether I bring it on myself, whether it's something in me...'

Getting up, she started to pace the kitchen floor as Maggie looked on in concern.

'You are not responsible for other people's failings, Nicki. Laura is paranoid with jealousy of your relationship with her father; we all know that. In her eyes you've taken her mother's place and—'

'No!' Nicki interrupted Maggie sharply, turning round to face her. 'In Laura's eyes, what I am guilty of is not taking her mother's place but inciting her father to betray her mother and their marriage. I found that out this morning.' Looking away from Maggie, Nicki told her in a muffled voice, 'And the worst of it is that she's right. Oh, God, Maggie, if I could rerun my life and wipe out that day! However much Laura hates me for what happened, it can't be as much as I hate myself!'

'Nicki, what are you talking about?' Maggie asked in bewilderment.

Agitatedly Nicki shook her head and then crossed her arms defensively over her body. She looked, Maggie recognised, very much as she had done the day Maggie had walked upstairs into the main bedroom of the house Nicki had shared with Carl to find her friend crouching in the corner of the bedroom, rocking herself back and forth, blood trickling from her cut face.

Now there was no blood, but the look of dark despair in Nicki's eyes was very much the same.

Putting her own feelings on hold, Maggie went over to her, firmly guiding her back to the table and pushing her gently into her chair.

'Tell me what's happened, Nicki,' Maggie demanded, adding, 'and before you say anything, just let me tell you that I am not leaving here until you do.'

'It's a long story.'

Nicki tried to sound dismissive, but Maggie ignored her, insisting, 'I've got plenty of time.'

Plenty of time. Time had been their enemy then, her and Kit's, Nicki reflected grimly. Their enemy and Jennifer's too. Abruptly her face crumpled.

'You know that Kit and I...that I fell in love with him while Jennifer was still alive,' she reminded Maggie abruptly.

'Of course I do,' Maggie acknowledged. 'And I know too how determined you both were, but most especially you, Nicki, to keep your relationship to a platonic and totally non-sexual friendship. After all, we spent long enough having heart-to-hearts about it. I truly admired you for that decision. We could all see how much the strain of what was happening was affecting you. I have to admit that I don't think I could have done what you did.'

'You told me that I would be better off finding someone else—a man who was free to love me.'

'I liked Kit, we all did, but I just didn't want to see you wasting your life waiting for a man whose freedom—'

'Could only come at the price of his wife's death?' Nicki supplied for her, white-faced.

Immediately Maggie shook her head.

'That was not what I was going to say,' she denied firmly. 'What I was going to say was that you, being you, would sacrifice yourself and your own happiness for Kit and to his marriage.'

'Kit and I did agree that there couldn't be anything physical between us while Jennifer was still alive.' Nicki shivered. 'That sounds calculating now, as though I was waiting for her to die, but it wasn't like that… I didn't want to…to do something—anything—I would later regret, to intrude on her marriage or her right to Kit's love…'

'I know,' Maggie assured her softly. 'I thought you were a saint.'

'A saint!' Biting her lip, Nicki got up and started pacing the kitchen again. 'Oh, no! I was anything but. I did the most awful, appalling thing, Maggie. I was guilty of the most dreadful kind of betrayal, of Jennifer, of Kit and Laura, and our love, but most of all of myself. I don't think that Kit has ever forgiven me for it and I know that I have never and can never forgive myself. It's there with me every single day. Every time I look at Kit…every time I look at Joey. Most of the time I can deal with it, live with it, but sometimes… You have no idea what it's like living with that kind of guilt on your conscience. Sometimes I think I wish that Kit and I had never met…that our love is flawed, wrong…'

As she listened to Nicki Maggie was aware of a growing sense of disquiet. Nicki had gone through a very difficult time when she and Kit had first fallen in love, she knew that. She knew, too, that Nicki had suffered from depression following Joey's birth, but she had quickly recovered, and she and Kit had seemed very happy together in their marriage. But the Nicki she was listening to now, the Nicki who had been so vehemently opposed to her own pregnancy last night, was disturbingly full of negativity and anger. Why? What had happened? Had something gone wrong, and, if so, what? And why hadn't she as Nicki's friend been more aware of it? Because she had been too wrapped up in her own life, her own love? Now it was Maggie's turn to feel guilty.

'Nicki, you can't say that,' she protested. 'You and Kit were made for one another. You told me yourself that you both believed that you were fated to meet and to share your lives.'

'Yes,' Nicki agreed tightly. 'It's amazing just what you will do to find an excuse for your own behaviour, isn't it? I expect you've told yourself that having this baby is something that was meant to happen, rather than the result of your own manipulation,' she challenged Maggie sharply.

Just for a second, Maggie was tempted to retaliate

and remind Nicki unkindly that Kit had insisted they marry after they had had unprotected sex and he had feared that Nicki might be pregnant, and that the charge of manipulating fate might just as easily be made against them. But there was something so vulnerable and disturbing about the way Nicki was behaving that Maggie felt that to do so would be cruel and unfair.

'Nicki, I don't know what has happened between you and Laura, or what's been said,' she sidetracked gently instead.

'But you want to know, don't you? You want to hear every sordid little detail.'

As Nicki's voice rose so too did the colour in her face. Seriously alarmed, Maggie tried to calm her down, protesting, 'Nicki, I don't want—'

'You don't want to what?' Nicki challenged her angrily. 'You don't want to waste your time listening to me? You don't care about what I think or feel, or suffer? No, neither does Kit. He hates me for what happened... I know that, and that's why...'

Her voice had dropped now, almost as though she was looking inward and backward; as though she had in a way forgotten that Maggie was there. Now as Nicki rewrapped her arms around her body Maggie was suddenly sharply aware of how thin she was.

'I know that Kit blames me for what happened, that day! Perhaps Kit is right to blame me. Perhaps deep down inside I knew that he would come to me and that I was tempting him...tormenting him.'

As she turned her head to look at Maggie, Maggie could see the raw pain in her eyes and she ached to be able to offer her some comfort.

'Whatever it is, Nicki,' she began softly, 'whatever happened, however bad things seem right now—'

'Right now?' Nicki interrupted her. 'I'm not talking about something that happened "now", Maggie.' She closed her eyes and took a deep breath. 'I've never told you or anyone else about this. I've always felt too shocked…too ashamed. But I swear I never meant it to happen.' Nicki's voice was suspended as though the words she was trying to say were choking her.

'You never meant what to happen, Nicki?' Maggie encouraged her, but she suspected she already knew the answer.

'I never meant to…to incite Kit into breaking his vow, and…and have sex with me, there in Jennifer's house…her home, whilst she…!'

Compassionately Maggie watched her. Did Nicki really think that all of them had not guessed that it was inevitable for two people as much in love and as much in need of each other as Kit and Nicki had been to take physical comfort from each other and their love?

Maggie knew how much Nicki prided herself on her self-control and her moral strength, but, after the trauma of what she had gone through at the hands of her ex-husband, of course she had needed the comfort of Kit's love. And equally how could Kit, who they all knew had not been able to have a sexual relationship with Jennifer for the years of her illness, have been able to resist showing her that love?

'Nicki,' Maggie protested quietly, ' I know you hate admitting as much but you are only human, you know. So you and Kit were lovers…'

'It was only the once,' Nicki defended herself immediately. 'It wasn't planned…and…I know we shouldn't have done it,' she told Maggie in a low voice, which to Maggie's relief was beginning to sound more rational, more as though it belonged to the Nicki she knew.

'I hated myself afterwards,' Nicki told her fiercely. 'And I know that Kit blamed me for what happened. That he has never forgiven me for being the cause of his betrayal of Jennifer and their marriage vows.' She gave Maggie a thin, bitter little smile. 'So you see, Maggie, I am not so much of a saint after all!'

'Nicki!' Maggie protested. 'You are being far too hard on yourself. You can't possibly think that Kit doesn't love you. He adores you!'

'Does he?' Nicki looked tired. 'I seem to have a knack of choosing men who end up hurting me, don't I? Dan, who left me for you; Carl, who turned out to be a wife-beater; and now Kit, who…'

Compressing her mouth, Nicki turned away.

'When he learns that Laura was in the house that day and overheard us…'

'What?' Now Maggie was shocked.

Nicki's mouth twisted. 'Oh, yes. Apparently she'd been sent home from school sick, but we were too engrossed in what we were doing to be aware that she was there. She heard everything. Every single intimate, personal detail,' Nicki told Maggie, her voice cracking with pain and distress.

'Nicki, it wasn't your fault,' Maggie tried to comfort her.

'Not my fault.' Nicki laughed bitterly. 'Of course it was my fault. I was shagging her father and she heard me. I hate that word—it's so…so degrading, so demeaning somehow. We never used it, did we? It was a man's word, used to denote the kind of sex that belittled and dehumanised women. This modern generation of women do use it, though. Laura used it today when she was telling me how she had been forced to endure the agony of listening to us…listening to her father shagging me whilst her mother was dying. I keep trying to imagine how I would feel if Joey was put in that position, and how I would feel about the woman who was responsible for putting him there. I would hate her, Maggie. I would hate her because she would deserve to be hated.'

Nicki's voice was rising again. Maggie could understand how shocked and distressed she must feel, but the sense she was getting from Nicki, that what had happened was somehow very much a current and contentious issue between her and Kit, rather than something that lay in the past, worried her.

'Come and sit down,' Maggie insisted, firmly taking hold of Nicki's arm and guiding her back to her chair. 'I can understand how you must feel, but it's a long time ago.'

Nicki didn't seem to be listening to her. Shaking her head, she said in a sickly voice, 'She told me this morning. There was the most terrible row.' Nicki put her fingers to her lips as she tried to stop them from trembling. 'All these years and she's never said anything until now.' She started to laugh hysterically.

'All these years when Kit and I have been so careful about not doing anything whenever she was around. All these years when I've begged Jennifer in my prayers to forgive me, when I've done everything I can to atone for what I did; when I've told myself that just so long as no one else knows everything could be all right. That just so long as Kit and I pretended that it never happened, he might one day forgive me! And now this. I can't bear it, Maggie. I can't bear her knowing…and I can't bear knowing that she knows.'

Every word Nicki spoke was increasing Maggie's anxiety and foreboding for her. Of course it was only natural that she should be very upset and shocked, but this was more than that—much more!

'Nicki, you need to talk to Kit about this,' Maggie told her.

'Talk to Kit about this! I don't talk to Kit about anything any more,' Nicki cried in a goaded voice. 'I can't talk to Kit about anything. He doesn't want to talk to me any more.'

As Nicki looked at her Maggie knew she had not been quick enough to hide her shock.

'This is what happens, Maggie,' Nicki told her bitterly. 'Sooner or later, this is what happens. This is the reality of the world you will be bringing your baby into, a baby nature would never have allowed you to conceive.'

'Nicki, please,' Maggie begged. She was beginning to feel seriously worried about Nicki's emotional and mental state.

'Nicki please what?' Nicki demanded sharply, her abrupt change of mood startling Maggie, who had put to one side her original purpose in coming to see her when she had seen how distressed her friend was. There was no reasoning with Nicki whilst she was in her current mood, Maggie recognised unhappily, hurt both by Nicki's outburst and her attitude towards her.

'Nicki, please tell me I'm wonderful? Please tell me what I'm doing is right? I can't, Maggie...I can't. I think you'd better go,' Nicki told her tiredly. 'Joey will be home soon and I don't want him to see me like this.'

'Nicki!' Maggie protested. She didn't want to leave her friend whilst she was in such a disturbed and distressed state, but she sensed that if she stayed she might only add to her obvious agitation, and that they might between them say things that could destroy their friendship for ever!

'There isn't anything more for us to say, Maggie. And right now I just don't want you here. Everything's always worked out well for you, hasn't it? You've always come up smiling and smelling of roses—you don't even begin to know what life is like for people like me...people who always lose out no matter what they do or who they choose. I know you, Maggie, you came here today hoping to get me to say I was pleased for you, because you always need everyone to be pleased for you, don't you, Maggie? To be pleased for you and to approve of you. Well, I'm sorry, but I don't. And as for the poor baby you are so selfishly determined to have...'

Compressing her mouth, Nicki got up and went over to the back door, opening it.

Silently, not wanting to risk saying anything she might ultimately regret, Maggie left.

6

Marcus checked his watch a little anxiously. Ten minutes to go before surgery started. His first surgery here in the market town partnership he had just joined.

Hebe had been furious with him when he had first announced his plans. There had been cracks appearing in their relationship before then, ignored by him in his desire to make it work, but his decision had been the cause of the final, unbridgeable split between them.

After all the effort he had put into maintaining their relationship, it had shocked him to discover just how little he was actually missing it.

'A habit, that's all you and I are, Marcus,' Hebe told him matter-of-factly when she announced that it was over. 'We've been together too long and for both our sakes now it's time that we moved on. We've got very different goals in life. I realise that now.'

That comment was made scornfully, contemptuously almost, and Marcus knew why. Practising medicine had never been a part of Hebe's life plan.

'Marcus, you know my views. There is no way I would ever want to tie myself down to some deadly dull GP practice in the middle of nowhere,' she told him irritably. 'That is not what I sweated through med school to get the best grades I could for. Research is where the excitement lies, the challenges, the—'

'The money,' Marcus interrupted her wryly.

'Yes, the money too,' Hebe acknowledged briskly. 'You're a fool, Marcus,' she told him, and she meant it.

'And as for this thing you've got about babies!' she derided him scornfully. 'It's my sex who are supposed to give in to the urgings of their biological clocks!' she pointed out mockingly.

Her sex maybe, but never Hebe herself.

'A baby? Marcus, are you mad?' she demanded when he first told her how he felt.

'It would be a commitment between us, Hebe, something of ourselves that we give to each other to create a new life.'

'Marcus, you are a doctor. Human life, as you very well know, can virtually be created in a lab,' she reminded him once she had stopped laughing, adding 'I thought you were too intelligent to come out with such sentimental emotional nonsense. If and when I choose to have a baby, naturally I shall want to ensure that it has the best possible genes available. And that means…'

'That mine are not good enough,' Marcus suggested lightly.

She looked at him speculatively.

'You know your trouble, don't you?' she challenged him. 'You are far too emotional. I should have seen the warning signs when you insisted on diversifying into paediatrics. Just because your cousin lost a child through meningitis does not mean that you have to train as a kiddie doctor. In fact you could do far more to prevent meningitis through research.'

They argued incessantly over his decision to train as a paediatrician and in the end Marcus was forced to concede defeat and to give up trying to persuade her to see things his way.

They parted on reasonably amicable terms, their relationship too worn out to even merit any passionate fights.

He knew that she blamed what she had termed his 'over-emotional' response to the death of his cousin's six-year-old son for his decision. All Marcus knew was that he had suddenly recognised how very important it was to him to have children. How sterile and empty his life felt without them. He was thirty. He had begun to hate city life, and he knew that he wanted to move out of hospital work and into a GP practice, that he wanted the sense of community and belonging that he had seen had been such a source of comfort and strength to his cousin.

He also knew that these were the very things that Hebe disdained and despised the most; the things she considered to be the foolish cravings of her emotion-dependent inferiors. Even so, he had still tried to explain to her how he felt.

She had told him as though in retaliation that she had been offered a very prestigious job in America, which she had already formally accepted!

He had known then that they had reached the end.

It was typical of Hebe, of course, that where another woman might have protested passionately that his desire for children was more important to him than her, Hebe simply rationalised his feelings as an inconvenient biological glitch.

Unseeingly, Laura stared out across the river. She had gone from Nicki's kitchen to the church where her mother was buried, sitting staring at the headstone that bore her name until her body was stiff with cold.

The scene with Nicki had brought back too many memories—and aroused too many disturbing feelings.

She knew she would never, ever forgive Nicki for what she had done; to do so would be to betray her mother. But she ached inside for the sound of Ryan's voice.

She had been aware of him from the first time she had walked into his office for her initial interview. Although he was not particularly tall, there was a magnetism about him that was instantly compelling. As Irish as his name implied, he had the broad-shouldered physique of the rugby player he had once been, a thick shock of night-black hair and the bluest eyes she had ever seen, all crinkly when he smiled, his mouth curling. And the heat in those eyes when they had looked at her and told her that he found her desirable...

Laura shivered. She was a modern young woman who considered herself to be sexually aware and experienced, but that look from Ryan!

He had taken her out for lunch within a week of her starting to work for him, and within a month he had told her about his disastrous marriage and the fact that for family and religious reasons he could not find it in himself to bring it to a legal end. He had arranged things so that they had to work late together, and then had taken her out for supper. He had asked her to work weekends and then told her that they would be working from the flat in the city where he lived as a bachelor whilst his wife and children remained at home in Cork.

She had been so tempted then and it would all have been so easy. Ryan would have made it easy. He was that kind of man. She had known just by looking at him how it would be, and she had ached for the plea-sure she knew he would give her.

But she could not allow herself to be turned into an-other Nicki, the woman she had despised and hated for so long. She had told him, bluntly, that she would not sleep with him.

Ryan had laughed at her and told her that she was wrong, that their coming together was inevitable; that they were destined to be lovers and that he intended to make sure that they were!

So, cravenly perhaps, she had waited until he was away on business and then she had handed in her no-tice and left. She hadn't even worked her notice pe-riod, which would no doubt look wonderful on her CV, she acknowledged grimly.

She missed Ryan with an intensity she could hardly bear, a pain that ached continuously through her. She was terrified that he would find out where she was and somehow persuade her to go back with him, and she was terrified too that he wouldn't!

And if she was honest there was a part of her that wished that he would.

A fine, damp, misting rain had started to fall. Ignoring it, she remained staring at the river.

'Julie, are you sure you don't want to come with me? They are your parents, after all,' Stella said firmly.

Immediately Julie shook her head.

'Dad said he never wanted to see me again,' she told Stella mutinously. 'I hate him. He wanted to kill my baby.'

Stella sighed. Julie was so immature. So young. Little more than a baby herself in many ways.

Coaxing and bullying her this morning to eat some breakfast had reminded Stella of the battle she had

had with her son when he had been a little boy. Then, like all young children, he had needed the security of knowing that 'Mummy knew best'. Even though she was seventeen, right now Julie was behaving in very much the same way, needing the security of handing her problem and herself over to someone else to deal with. She was, though, Stella acknowledged, mature enough and maternal enough to be determined to protect her coming child.

Hughie was on his way back to university. Watching as they said their goodbyes it had struck Stella how noticeably he and Julie treated one another as peers and friends rather than lovers.

'In our day,' she had told Richard in exasperation, 'at that age, falling in love meant sharing a few inexperienced kisses and, if it was really serious, a bit of heavy petting. Now it has to be full sex virtually on a first date. They treat it so casually.'

She had stopped speaking when she'd realised that Richard hadn't really been listening to her. The silence between them, which normally felt so comfortable, irked her a little. It was as though, having expressed his disapproval, Richard had totally distanced himself from the situation.

Stella had never met Julie's parents and as she drove towards their house she wondered just how accurate Richard's description of Julie's father was. He wasn't normally prone to exaggeration—far from it! She had already telephoned them, initially to reassure them that Julie was safe, and secondly to arrange to see them.

The house was in a quiet, well-maintained cul-de-sac of modern detached homes. There were two new cars on the drive, a large saloon car and a smaller runabout.

As she got out of her own car Stella was ruefully aware of its age and shabbiness.

Neither she nor Richard had ever been materialistic; people and not possessions were what mattered to them.

As she headed for the front door she was conscious of how quiet the cul-de-sac was. Their own street with its mixture of flats, small terraced houses and much larger ones like their own was busy and vibrant with life, and a good deal less up-market, Stella acknowledged as she rang the doorbell.

The woman who answered it was an older version of Julie, but a Julie without the younger girl's spirit and determination, a woman somehow crushed and made small and tired by life, Stella recognised.

Julie had told Stella that her parents had met when they'd both worked in the same bank but then her mother had given up work when Julie had been born, and that she had spent the last five years taking care of both her own and her husband's ailing parents.

The room Julie's mother showed Stella into was immaculate; not a cushion was out of place on the plumped up seats of the two sofas facing one another across a highly polished coffee table.

Gingerly Stella sat down, refusing her offer of a cup of tea.

'How is Julie? We've been so worried about her. She's such a headstrong girl,' Julie's mother told Stella. 'I don't know what she's said to you, but her father didn't mean…'

Julie's father was standing in front of the window with his back to her, and Stella could see the nervous look.

'Oh, yes, I did,' he corrected his wife flatly. 'Julie's chosen her own bed and now she can damn well lie on it. If she'd had any shred of sense or responsibility, she'd have made sure she told us in time…'

Stella's heart sank as she heard the bitterness and the anger in his voice.

'And if you've come here to try to persuade us to change our mind,' he told Stella grimly, 'then let me tell you that you are wasting your breath! No way is Julie coming back here, not until… Does your bloody son have any idea what he's done?' he demanded furiously, his anger breaking through his self control. 'That girl was supposed to be going to university. She'd virtually been guaranteed a place, all she had to do was to get the A-level grades her teachers had predicted she would get, so what does she do? She allows your bloody son to damn well impregnate her and then she doesn't tell us until it's too fucking late for us to do anything about it!'

'Gerald…' Stella heard his wife protesting in a small bleat. 'Language.'

'She's a social worker—she's heard it all before. Social workers, bloody interfering… It's people like you…'

'I actually retired from the social services many years ago,' Stella told him firmly. 'And I do understand how you must feel. After all, this isn't just your problem or your responsibility—it's ours as well.'

'Bloody high-minded, aren't you? On the side of the tracks where I was born there's only one person gets the blame when something like this happens, and it's never the lad who causes it. My God, after all we've given Julie, all we've done for her. The education she's had…when she knows… My sister fell pregnant at seventeen and it ruined her life. No decent lad would look at her. I was eleven at the time. They were all talking about her, saying that she was…' He stopped abruptly. 'If Julie had only told us earlier something could have been done.'

'If by "something" you mean a termination, Julie didn't want—' Stella began but immediately the girl's father overruled her.

'Never mind what Julie thinks she doesn't want. I'm her father and I know what's best for her. I've seen what happens. She's had every advantage, everything she's wanted, and this is how she repays us. Well, she doesn't come back here. Not until it's all over and everything's been sorted out.'

'Sorted out?' Stella queried.

'Yes. Obviously, the baby will have to be adopted.'

'And in the meantime?' Stella pressed him. 'Julie is still at school, she should be here at home...'

'No—no way does she come back here. Your bloody son is the one who's got her into trouble, let him sort it all out. He's the brat's father, after all.'

One look at his face confirmed to Stella that he was not going to change his mind. Out of the corner of her eye she could see Julie's mother nervously biting her lip.

'Very well,' she said as calmly as she could. 'If Julie can't come back here then she is welcome to stay with us.' Turning towards Julie's mother she added, 'If you want to come and see her...'

'She doesn't. Like I said, Julie's made her bed and now she can damn well lie on it.'

He was in shock and furiously angry, Stella knew, and it was obvious that the stigma of his sister's pregnancy had left its mark on him, but that did not alter the fact that he was someone she suspected she would never be able to bring herself to like. Guiltily, she admitted that she was glad that she was never going to have to try to do so, since thankfully he was not going to be Hughie's father-in-law.

Julie's mother saw her out, and glanced nervously over her shoulder as she opened the door before whispering urgently to Stella, 'Give Julie my love, won't you? Tell her that…that I'm thinking about her.' Her face suddenly crumpled. 'I'm so worried about her. What's going to happen to her?'

'Nothing,' Stella assured her firmly. 'She's going to stay with us until the baby comes, and for as long as she feels she needs to afterwards. You're welcome to come and see her whenever you like,' she added briskly.

As she got into her car she acknowledged fatalistically that she was committed now. How could she not be? Julie was carrying her son's child.

Busily, she started making mental lists. Julie had already admitted that she had not seen a doctor or had any of the normal check-ups. Her school would have to be contacted, and the hospital—there must be some kind of local support group for girls in Julie's position—and then they would need to prepare for the baby. She had to drive past the surgery on the way home. She could call in and make an appointment for Julie, she decided practically.

Stiffly Laura got up from the bench. It was hard to believe spring would ever arrive. Everything looked so grey, the dull sky, the river reflecting its dullness with a faint, pewterish sheen, and still full from the heavy winter rains they had had. Perhaps if she were to search the hedgerows she might be able to find the tiniest beginnings of new life, but she simply didn't have the spirit to be bothered. Her body ached for sun and warmth, for light and laughter—a physical manifestation perhaps of her inner hunger for the warmth of love?

She was reading too many magazines, Laura decided wryly. She wasn't used to having so much time for reflection, or for introspection. Until she had begun to work for Ryan, her career had absorbed every moment of her time and her energy.

She had never intended the job she had taken with his firm to be permanent or final—it was simply another step on the steep career path she had plotted for herself. Her career goals were already set out in her mind—by the time she was thirty she intended to be heading her own financial services company. She had already made several potentially very profitable investments that would ultimately fund this venture, but the arm of the financial industry where she worked was extremely close-knit, not to say incestuous. Any hint of weakness on her part would sink her chances of success. An affair with Ryan would not be deemed a weakness, but the way she felt about it inside certainly would if it were ever to become public knowledge! It was a business that didn't allow for close personal friendships, merely close personal rivalries, but her relationship with Nicki had surely equipped her to handle any amount of those.

When she had initially decided to come home to take time out, it had been the situation with Ryan that had been at the forefront of her mind, but now... Weird how easy it was to step back into the shoes of her teenage self! Weird, and extremely ego-deflating, not to mention exhausting.

Laura knew herself to be reasonably intelligent. It didn't escape her that in many ways with Ryan she was repeating the situation that had existed between her stepmother, her father and herself. Two women, both fighting for the exclusive right to the love of one man! And this was the twenty-first century!

In the distance she heard a clock chiming the hour. Five o'clock. It couldn't be! But when she checked her watch she realised that it was. She hadn't eaten any lunch and now suddenly she was both cold and hungry, but she shrank from the idea of going back and facing Nicki.

Deep down inside, Laura was already regretting her outburst—her retrograde step back into her childhood. Seeing Nicki so protective of Joey had been what had originally caused it; knowing that her stepmother, her father and Joey formed an exclusive little world from which she was indeed excluded. It had brought it all back to her: the pain, the sense of shock and betrayal she had experienced when she had realised that Nicki was not after all her friend and confidante but her father's lover, that the two of them had a secret relationship from which she was excluded. She had been so afraid already of losing her mother—her dying had in its way been a form of betrayal in Laura's then immature eyes—that to have to face another and far more destructive betrayal had been too much for her to cope with. All the tentative feelings of admiration and shy affection she had felt for Nicki had been destroyed by her discovery that Nicki and her father were lovers. She had hated Nicki for that discovery then and a part of her still hated her for it now.

Huddling into her jacket, against the briskness of the winter wind, she started to walk towards the town.

Laura was halfway down the town's tree-lined main shopping street when she heard someone calling her name.

'Laura. I'd heard you were back!'

She stiffened as she recognised Zoë, but Zoë seemed impervious to the 'I want to be alone' signals Laura's body language was giving out as she pushed her hand into her hair in one of the theatrically dramatic gestures Laura remembered from their schooldays and exclaimed, 'I've just finished work and the kids are at Ma's. Are you in a rush or have you got time for a drink? There's a reasonably decent wine bar round the corner.'

Uncertainly Laura hesitated. Despite, or more probably because of, the subtle pressure on them to be friends, she and Zoë had kept a wary if not outright hostile distance from one another when they had both attended the same local school. However, if they had not been particular friends, they had never been enemies either, and right now anything, anyone offering her an excuse for not going back and facing Nicki was an ally she could not afford to ignore.

Even so…

'Do they serve food?' she asked Zoë.

Zoë's eyebrows rose. 'You eat? I've often wondered. You're so incredibly slim.'

'I've got a fast metabolism,' Laura told her dryly. A fast metabolism and currently the kind of emotional trauma that virtually guaranteed female weight loss. In the words of one of her more cynical friends, 'Unavailable man plus in love woman equals weight loss. It's the best diet going—and it's free, in terms of money that is!'

'Lucky you,' Zoë sighed enviously as she pushed open the door to the wine bar. 'Two babies have not done my waistline any good. What brings you back here?' she asked curiously when they had ordered their drinks and found a table.

'It's my home,' Laura began, but she couldn't quite bring herself to look Zoë in the eye.

'Man trouble?' Zoë guessed.

Suddenly and unexpectedly, Laura recognised that she wanted to talk to someone about how she was feeling.

'Man trouble,' she admitted reluctantly.

'Join the club,' Zoë told her. 'Why is it that things are so hard for us, Laura?' she asked querulously as she drank her wine. 'My mother doesn't approve of Ian, my husband.' She pulled a face. 'She thinks I got married too young. Of course, what she really means is that she is afraid that I might manage to steal her crown. You know, the one she wears that says, "I was the perfect tender virgin bride". Well, I may not have been a virgin, but I beat her to marriage by three months, and the same when I had George…'

Laura stared at her in bemusement. Although she had known Zoë virtually all her life and attended her wedding, it had never occurred to her before now that anything less than perfect mother-and-daughter love existed between her and Alice. It was surely only wicked, ungrateful, selfish stepdaughters who criticised their nurturers?

'Of course, it was different for Ma. It always is.' Zoë picked up her glass and emptied it. 'My father swept her off her feet, she was too sweet and naïve to resist him, whereas I was the one who "persuaded" Ian into marrying me! He calls it blackmail. But it was his choice.'

She laughed when she saw the way Laura was looking at her.

'He travels all over the country—all over the world, it seems now—on business; he's an investment banker with one of the big American banks. He drives every-

where at ninety miles an hour, regardless of speed
limits! He was right up to his points limit on his licence—one more automatic fine and he'd have lost it.
He went through a camera and got caught. When the
letter came he told me he wanted me to say that I was
driving. As if—he never let me anywhere near the
driving wheel of his precious Porsche. I said I would
but only if he married me. He was furious about it, but
he needed his driving licence more than he needed his
freedom!' She gave a small self-mocking shrug. 'Do
you know, you're the first person I've ever admitted
that to! Not that Ian has ever let me forget it.'

'I expect he wanted to marry you, but was doing the
macho thing of pretending he didn't,' Laura offered
comfortingly.

'Ma disapproves totally of him,' Zoë continued morosely. 'She doesn't say so, but I can tell! She skirts
round the subject of course, asks me if I think he's being "supportive"' enough. For supportive you can
read "loving"—although how on earth she can question whether or not anyone else loves me enough
when she damn well never has! No, I was just the unwanted daughter she had on her way to producing a
pair of perfect, wonderful sons! And that of course
made her the perfect, wonderful wife. Sometimes I
just hate her so much. And not just her. All of them!
Mothers. And I include stepmothers in this, too.

'It's like their whole bloody generation is part of
some special untouchable race! God! They've become
like a mythological cult somehow—legends in their
own lifetime, ceaselessly reinventing themselves to
suit themselves. You name it, whatever it is and
they've done it first—and don't they just rush to let
you know it,' Zoë complained belligerently. 'And our
mothers and their peers are the worst of the whole

bloody lot! Doing drugs, fucking pop stars, being thin, hippying it out in India and finding themselves whilst they conveniently lost the babies they dropped nine months after they first dropped their knickers—I mean, why did they bother taking the pill? And now they're all writing books about it, and still refusing to let us into the playground. They act like they rule the world. They're so damned selfish but they pretend they're so sanctimonious—that it was all done for us. Balls. All they've done for us is make our lives bloody hard. I mean, what is there left for us to be? To *do*, other than follow in their pioneering footsteps?

'They've done it all before us, haven't they? Moved the goalposts, broken the rules, redefined what it means to be a mother and a wife; the only thing they haven't taught us is how to get their attention and keep it, because they were always too busy doing something else.'

'Have you ever thought of taking up politics?' Laura asked her teasingly.

'I'm on the Board of Governors for the local junior school,' Zoë replied, not seeming to pick up on the wryness in Laura's question. 'Ian thought it was a good idea.' Impatiently, she signalled to the waiter and ordered them both another drink.

Once he had gone she told Laura bitterly, 'My mother makes this big thing about being a mother, but the truth is that once the twins were born I might as well not have existed. Emotionally she just abandoned me! She's never really loved me! No one has!'

Suddenly Laura found her eyes filling with tears.

'My mother went one better than that,' she told Zoë, emptying her own glass. 'She got sick and died!'

'And then Nicki came along and stole your daddy,' Zoë offered. 'Life's shit, isn't it?'

Owlishly they looked at one another, united in a shared wine-fuelled sea of remembered grievances and pain.

'This is definitely a bonding thingy, Laura,' Zoë pronounced. 'Do you believe in fate? Shall we have another drink? Mothers! You'd think they'd have had the decency to leave us something to achieve that they didn't manage, but, no, they had to go and do it all... Anyway, I'm bored with talking about them! They're old! Past it. We are the future! Let's talk about something more interesting. Tell me more about this man trouble you're having?' she demanded.

A large glass of wine on an empty stomach had made Laura unusually reckless.

'He's married,' she told Zoë defiantly, 'and I think I've fallen in love with him.'

'You're in love with a married man... Join the club, so am I,' Zoë said to her.

Laura goggled.

'The only difference is,' Zoë continued, picking up her glass and taking a deep swallow, 'that the married man I love is my husband. And, like I've already told you, he doesn't love me!'

Laura stared at her. For once Zoë was not being theatrical.

'Zoë, I'm sure you must be wrong!' Laura tried to comfort her. 'You've got two children and...'

She stopped speaking as Zoë burst out laughing.

'Oh my God, Laura, and I thought my mother was naïve! What does having children have to do with love? Nothing!' she told her savagely. 'And anyway I was the one who had the children, not Ian. Oh, yes, he "begat" them...but he did not "have" them. He does not "have" them, and yet he has the gall to criticise me because I don't spend twenty-four seven with them. I took a degree, Laura. I had dreams. I wanted to travel...to live...to love and be loved, and yet here I am stuck in the same town I grew up in. I hate it all so much sometimes. And I hate myself even more!'

As she heard the anguish in Zoë's voice Laura tried to focus on the menu she had picked up. She knew she needed something to eat, but the intoxication, not so much of the wine she had had to drink but the confidences she and Zoë were sharing, the unexpectedness of feeling that she had at long last found herself an ally, coming so close on the heels of having felt so alien and alone, was pushing to one side such practical considerations.

'Ian hates me drinking. In fact sometimes I think he just hates me full stop,' she heard Zoë saying. 'His mother was an alcoholic!' Her eyes widened. 'You are the first person I've told about that. He hates anyone knowing about it.'

Laura took a deep breath.

'I had the most awful row with Nicki this morning. I mean, it was like my teenage years revisited!' she found herself confessing in return.

Conspiratorially, they smiled tentatively at one another.

'Don't look now but there's a man over there at the bar who just can't take his eyes off you,' Zoë hissed to her.

'What...where?' Automatically Laura looked towards the bar, her heart pounding as, illogically, she searched for Ryan's face and found instead that she was staring into a pair of chilly, disapproving, steely grey male eyes.

'Do you know him?' Zoë demanded.

Laura shook her head, suddenly conscious of her wine-flushed face and windswept hair. 'He's probably wondering what we're doing in here at half-past five in the afternoon, drinking,' she told Zoë a little uncomfortably.

'Balls,' Zoë retorted. 'He fancies you, I can tell. This is good, Laura. You and I have a lot in common. After all, we're both fellow victims.' She made a face and laughed.

'We both know what it's like to suffer from the "one for all and all for one" cabalistic terrorism of those women. God, do you know, Stella once saw me hanging out in the street with some other girls, trying to be cool, you know how it is, and she actually came up to me and told me that she knew it was past my bedtime. I mean, it wasn't like having one mother, it was like I'd got four of them! Of course, Maggie was always okay.'

'Well, Maggie's always been in a class of her own,' Laura had to admit. 'After my mother died she gave me a huge diary box with a lock on it. She said it was for me to put special memories of my mother in.'

'Yeah, her own mother died when she was young, didn't she? And she was brought up by some eccentric old aunt,' Zoë replied carelessly. 'How long are you going to be in town for?' she added eagerly.

'I don't know. I haven't got a job at the moment so…'

'I don't suppose you'd fancy a bit of child-minding, would you?' Zoë asked ruefully. 'Ma has the kids for me three days a week so that I can work—it keeps me sane. It's not that I don't love them to bits, I do. But…' She paused. 'Ma has suddenly gone all difficult about having them—heaven knows why, you'd think she'd be thrilled to spend time with them; they are her grandchildren, after all. Now, if they were the twins' kids…' Zoë closed her eyes. 'Of course I know why she's doing it. She thinks that I can't manage without her help; that I'm dependent on her! Well, I'm not! And I'm going to prove it to her. I'm going to find a live-in nanny and then…'

'Live-in?' Laura queried. 'What exactly would you be expecting? I mean, I'm not trained or anything, but I do like children, and I've worked on a voluntary basis at a local school—nothing dramatic, just helping out with the special needs kids.'

Zoë stared at her.

'Are you serious? I mean, I know you had this fantastic high-powered city job, and I can't afford to pay you much—I don't earn much myself…but I don't work for the money. It's the company, the sense of being part of the mainstream of life; of doing something that my wonderful mother hasn't done before me.'

Yes, she was serious, Laura acknowledged mentally. Anything to enable her to keep some distance between herself and Ryan. Anything, other than going back and living with her father and Nicki.

'I'm serious,' she confirmed. 'How soon do you want me to start?'

'Tonight? Ian's away on business for a few days and Ma has already warned me that she can't have the kids tomorrow. Oh, and of course it will depend on how they take to you.'

'Of course,' Laura agreed promptly. Her head was spinning, she recognised, and her stomach was churning nervously. So nervously that she no longer felt able to eat anything even though common sense told her that she ought to do so.

'We'll give it a trial run for, say, three days,' Zoë told her, 'and then if it looks like it's going to work out we'll sort out something more permanent.'

Lifting her glass, Zoë proposed solemnly, 'A toast, Laura, to us and to daughter power. It's time we united and showed the older generation that we are every bit as good as them.'

'Daughter power,' Laura echoed, muzzily.

As she put her glass down she realised that the man seated at the bar was still watching her—and she was pretty sure that the look in his eyes was not one of admiration!

'Oh, God, is that the time?' Zoë was exclaiming. 'I should have picked the kids up from Ma half an hour ago. Look, here's my address,' she told Laura, reaching into her bag and scribbling it down on a piece of paper torn from her diary, and then removing a small handbag spray of breath freshener.

'Just a precaution,' she told Laura when she had finished using it. 'It's ridiculous, I know, but some people, mentioning no names, think that enjoying a glass of wine turns a person into an alcoholic.' She pulled a face. 'I mean, if I was I'd be trying to hide it, wouldn't I? Stashing bottles all over the place. I mean, if I did have a drink problem, I'd know about it, wouldn't I? And I know that I haven't! You'd never think that Ma's generation were so heavily into the drug scene, would you? Not of course that Ma was ever likely to have indulged. Squeaky clean wasn't in it. I can't wait to tell her that you will be looking after the kids.'

'So when do you want me to start?' Laura asked her again.

'Whenever you like.' Zoë shrugged, pulling on her jacket. 'The sooner the better. Come round tonight if you can.'

Briefly closing her eyes Laura saw a mental picture of her mother's grave. Tears pricked the backs of her eyes. She was neither religious nor prone to otherworldly type thoughts, but right now... Right now if she was the kind of person who believed in the power

of love and prayer, she would be thanking her mother
for the escape route that had just been handed to her—
not just from Nicki but from Ryan as well. There was
no way he could track her down at Zoë's!

'Give me an hour,' she told Zoë determinedly,
reaching for her own coat.

On the way out, even though she had promised herself she would not do so, she glanced at the man at the
bar, grudgingly acknowledging that he was quite
good-looking if you liked the type; taller than Ryan
and not as heavily built. Younger, too, closer to thirty
than Ryan's forty. His hair was as dark as Ryan's, but
straight. Unable to stop herself she looked at his
hands. Hands were her thing; Ryan's were musician's
hands, long-fingered and supple, a magician's fingers.
Capable of all kinds of sleight of hand and deceit? This
man's were squarer, stronger, his nails immaculately
clean but not manicured. For a second Laura hesitated, not knowing what she was really waiting for.
Some kind of acknowledgement from him? Of what?
Zoë was already opening the wine bar door, and
quickly Laura went to join her.

Finishing his drink, Marcus paid his bill. The wine
bar had seemed like a good idea until the two women
had walked in. One of them had provoked a physical
reaction in him that had caught him off guard and an-
gered him. He had moved to the town to give himself
a period of reflection and not to make his life even
more complicated than it already was.

He knew if Hebe was with him she would be telling
him robustly that a decent sex session was what he
needed. Most men, he knew, would jump at the
chance to prove her right. Was he an idealistic idiot for
wanting more? Wasn't it women who were supposed

to find sex unfulfilling without an emotional commitment?

Maybe once, but with the breaking down of the social barriers that had imposed strict differences between the sexes had also come a breaking down of the rigid stereotypes that had accompanied them, allowing people's individual natures and not just their gender to dictate how they felt and behaved.

'How did you get on with Nicki?' Oliver asked.

Putting down the estate agents' details she had been studying, Maggie gave a small sigh.

'She was very upset when I got there. She'd had a row with Laura. Oliver...' She paused, her frown deepening. 'I'm worried about her. Not because of what she said about us and the baby, it's more than that...'

'She doesn't like having Laura there,' Oliver responded. 'You said so yourself.'

'Yes, I know, but... I don't know what it is. I can't put my finger on anything logical or concrete, but there's something there...something wrong. For one thing...' She hesitated. There was a strong code of loyalty between the four of them, which in its way transcended even her closeness with Oliver.

'What?' Oliver pressed her, coming over and wrapping his arms around her, holding her tenderly.

'It's hard to put into words,' Maggie told him slowly. 'But... Well, her reactions to everything, not just the baby, are so unlike her. She's always been so rational, so...so orderly in her thinking and her behaviour, even as a girl, but now— If you knew her as I do, you'd understand. Her behaviour, everything, even the way she moves and talks are different, out of character…just not Nicki. It's as though…' She stopped and shook her head. 'It's almost as though somehow she's become another person.'

'You mean you think she's got some kind of psychological problem?' Oliver questioned.

'I don't know,' said Maggie uncertainly.

'It sounds to me as though she needs professional help,' Oliver pronounced forthrightly.

'I don't think…' Maggie began and then stopped. 'It could just be me. Perhaps if I talked to the others they might…'

'Why not talk to Kit?' Oliver suggested. 'He is her husband, after all.'

'Yes,' Maggie agreed, but Oliver could hear the hesitation in her voice.

'What's wrong?' he asked her.

'Nothing. It's just that… Well, there's a sort of unwritten agreement between us all that husbands and partners are off limits, private territory, and to talk to Kit behind Nicki's back is something I just wouldn't feel comfortable doing. Nicki is my friend, Kit is her husband.'

'But you've known Kit for years. You like him, I've heard you say so,' Oliver exclaimed in disbelief.

'Yes, I know. But he is still Nicki's husband,' she insisted. 'I'll talk to the others,' she added reluctantly. 'If they haven't noticed anything then maybe it's just me…' Her voice tailed away.

'Anything of interest come from the estate agents?' Oliver asked, tactfully changing the subject.

'Not really. I have got some good news though. We've got the Egerton contract, and I've told them that you are going to be overseeing everything, because my pregnancy would mean that I couldn't be involved in the whole project.'

They had already agreed that if Maggie did conceive, Oliver should take over the lion's share of running the business, and Maggie had been grooming him for this purpose.

He had a good deal more artistic flair than her, she recognised, and she suspected that ultimately he would become the driving force of the business. A rueful smile curled her mouth.

'What's that look for?' Oliver demanded.

Maggie laughed, admitting, 'I was just thinking that at one time there was no way I would ever have allowed anyone else to take charge of my work because it was my "baby", but now that I'm having the real thing—Oliver!' she protested as he picked her up. 'We have to be careful,' she reminded him anxiously. 'Especially for these first three months.'

Although she had refused to let her see it, Nicki's brutal comments had left her feeling uneasy and anxious.

'The consultant said that everything was fine,' Oliver soothed her.

'I know,' Maggie agreed. 'I suppose I'm just being over-careful; over-protective.' It bemused her a little just how strongly protective she did feel towards the new life she was carrying; how fiercely and instinctively determined not to let anyone or anything harm it, even to the extent of resenting Nicki for thinking, never mind saying, what she had, just in case the baby might know and feel afraid.

Did she feel like this because it was an instinctive and automatic reaction, the reaction she would have felt had she become pregnant naturally, or were her feelings stronger and fiercer because she felt such a sense of gratitude and responsibility towards the woman who had made her pregnancy possible, such a sense of guardianship over her child?

It was at times like this that Maggie longed for someone to talk to; someone who knew and understood because they themselves had been through what she was experiencing now.

Somehow, instead of bonding her to her closest friends, her pregnancy was alienating her, setting her apart. Every day the weight of the responsibility she was carrying seemed a little heavier; every day she felt a little bit more anxious and afraid that she might not be strong enough, that somehow she might let down Oliver's child; that he or she might grow to hate and resent her because she was not really his or her mother, in the same way that Laura so obviously hated and resented Nicki.

She had never, Maggie recognised, felt more in need of the support of her friends.

7

Nicki was upstairs in the empty bedroom she used as an office, in the middle of trying to work on her VAT return, when she recognised from the noisy exhaust of their small car that Kit had arrived home. He was pointedly refusing to drive the BMW, which ridiculously actually made her feel hurt and rejected.

Now, though, the row they had had about the BMW had been pushed to the back of her mind by Laura's outburst.

Nicki's head throbbed with pain, the figures dancing indecipherably in front of her. She could feel the increasingly familiar sense of panic and sickness beginning to fill her. What was the point of her trying to make sense of them? What was the point of anything?

'Nicki?' Kit queried as he pushed open the office door. 'I saw that the light was on but I thought you must be out because the BMW wasn't there.'

'Laura has taken it,' Nicki told him shortly.

'Where has she gone?' Kit asked.

Nicki compressed her mouth. 'I have no idea. She's your daughter, Kit. Not mine.'

'What is this thing you've suddenly got, Nicki?' Kit demanded angrily. 'Why is everything suddenly divided into yours or mine?'

'Because that's the way things are,' Nicki told him flatly. Her head was pounding even more badly and she felt slightly sick. Stubbornly she refused to give in to the pain, again bending her head over the figures blurring her eyes.

Helplessly Kit watched her. There were so many things he felt they needed to discuss but recently she had been so irrational, so unlike her normal self, that he had become wary of saying anything to her.

'You're home late.' Challengingly Nicki lifted her gaze from the VAT figures and looked at him.

'Yes,' Kit agreed. 'I had a long meeting this afternoon with one of our main customers.'

Nicki could feel her stomach muscles clenching. They had agreed prior to Joey's birth that she would scale down her agency in order to give her more time to spend at home with their baby, but the downturn in Kit's business had made this impossible. At first she had not minded, telling herself that she was after all working for all of them, but now, when Kit's daughter was virtually living off her, driving her car, accusing her of…

'Don't tell me.' She sighed sourly. 'He isn't renewing his contract.'

'On the contrary,' Kit corrected her curtly. 'He is actually increasing it. And he isn't the only one. It looks as though finally business may be on the upturn.'

Once such an announcement would have had Nicki flinging herself into his arms, her face alight with love and pride. Once…

'I thought that perhaps we might go out and celebrate. Have dinner somewhere…' Kit suggested tentatively, offering an olive branch but not sure that it would be accepted.

'Now? Tonight?' Nicki gave him a bitter look, confirming his fears. 'We have a son, remember? But of course, unlike your precious daughter, you never really wanted our son, my son.'

'Nicki, that's not true,' Kit protested.

'I don't believe you,' Nicki told him flatly. 'Maggie came round today,' she added. 'I wonder how she would feel if Oliver told her that he'd changed his mind; that he wants her to get rid of his baby…to destroy it, kill it…'

Her voice had started to rise as her emotions threatened to get out of control, her eyes two dark burning pits of fury in her white face as she pushed back her chair and stood up, confronting him.

'Nicki, stop it,' Kit demanded. 'I never said anything like that.'

'Not in so many words, maybe, but you made it plain that you—'

'I simply questioned whether or not we should be having a second child. You said yourself that you hadn't believed that you were still fertile.' Kit cut her off. 'Joey is nine years old now, and to start again with a baby at our age, never mind the financial aspects of having another child… Yes, I was shocked when you told me that you suspected you were pregnant, but I never wanted…'

'You never wanted what? You never wanted me to miscarry? You weren't relieved when I did? Don't lie to me, Kit. I saw your face. And don't touch me either,' Nicki told him savagely as he took a step towards her, reaching out for her.

'Nicki, please don't be like this.' Kit groaned. 'I can understand how it must make you feel, knowing that Maggie is having a baby, when it's only a matter of weeks—'

'Sixteen weeks,' Nicki told him in a low voice. 'Six-

teen weeks and three days, that's how long I would
have been pregnant now, if... Not that you care.'

As her voice became suspended Kit tried again to
take hold of her, to comfort her, but immediately she
pushed him away.

'Nicki, Nicki. Of course I care.'

'No, you don't. You were relieved. Glad! And for all
I know you probably wish the same thing had happened to Joey. That way you'd only have your precious daughter—Jennifer's daughter...'

Helplessly Kit watched her. He had been shocked
when she had told him that she thought she was pregnant, but to accuse him as she was now doing!

'Your daughter is back,' Nicki informed him tightly
as the BMW's headlights swept the room. 'Why don't
you take *her* out to dinner to celebrate with you? After
all, no doubt she will benefit far more than either Joey
or I will. Who knows, you might even be able to buy
your own car for her to borrow.'

After he had turned on his heel and left her, Nicki
leaned her head against the cool wall of the bedroom
and put her hand over her mouth to stifle the sound of
grief racking her.

She wasn't crying. No, this sound she was trying to
stifle in the same way she had tried to stifle her grief
was the raw, savage sound of an animal in pain, the
howl of a mother deprived of her young. It made no
difference that she had conceived by accident, that she
hadn't had any plans to have a second child, not at her
age. She hadn't even had a chance—unlike Maggie—
to tell anyone other than Kit, to boast about her im-
pending motherhood. She had barely begun to accept
that she was actually pregnant when she had lost her
baby—the pain was still fiercely elemental.

When she had realised that she might be starting to

miscarry she had fought like a tigress to hold onto her baby—fought and lost. And now here was Maggie, who was incapable of conceiving a child of her own, who had refused to conceive Dan's child, smugly bragging about the baby she was carrying. Nicki actually felt as though she hated Maggie, as though somehow Maggie's pregnancy had been the cause of her loss.

Nicki could feel the pain filling her head, the confusion, the panic, the sick hopelessness. Sometimes she felt that she just did not want to go on living any more. What was the point? But what would happen to Joey if, like Jennifer, she were to die…if anything were to happen to her? Who would look after him? Love and protect him? Maggie was his godmother, but Maggie was going to have her own child. In her mind's eye Nicki could see Joey, alone, unloved, and it would all be her fault. There was so much danger out there in the world, so much pain, and there was only her here to love and protect him. Since losing her baby, she truly felt as though she could not bear to go on. She had even fantasised about how she might bring her life and her misery to an end. How she could block out for ever her pain—the pain that only she knew. After all Kit didn't care, did he? Not for her. Not for Joey and certainly not for the poor helpless little life she had lost. But she couldn't leave Joey behind to suffer, could she…? Which meant…

'Sorry I'm late, Ma,' Zoë apologised carelessly as Alice opened the door to her. As she smelled the alcohol on her daughter's breath Alice's heart sank. She had never been much of a drinker herself and she found it hard to understand this new modern culture that encouraged women to drink as heavily as their male peers.

When she had tried to express her concern about Zoë to Stuart he had merely shrugged tiredly, telling her, 'It's perfectly normal for a woman to drink more than your single glass of dinner wine on special occasions.'

Maybe it was, but where did one draw the line between drinking that was normal and drinking that was potentially something far more dangerous and destructive?

When Zoë bent down to pick up George he wriggled in her arms, pulling a face as she tried to kiss him, wrinkling his nose in distaste.

Irritably Zoë put him down. 'For God's sake! All I've done is have one drink. Why the hell does everyone have to react as though that's a major crime? Anyway, for your information,' she told Alice angrily, 'it wasn't my idea to call at the wine bar. I bumped into Laura, and she suggested it,' she fibbed.

'Laura?' Alice questioned, frowning. 'You mean Nicki's stepdaughter?'

'That's right. It sounds as though Nicki is giving her a really hard time. Of course she's always been jealous of the fact that Kit was married to Jennifer and had Laura with her.'

'Zoë, that's not fair,' Alice protested.

'Oh, come on, Ma.' Zoë sighed, rolling her eyes. 'Mind you, I suppose I might have known you'd rush to defend her. Your precious little circle of girl friends.' She grimaced. 'The most important people in your life.'

'Zoë, that's not true,' Alice told her sharply. Just how much had Zoë had to drink? she wondered worriedly. Certainly more than the one glass of wine she had claimed to have had.

Alice was convinced that it was Ian's influence, Ian's lifestyle that encouraged her daughter to drink as much as she did.

'No, of course it's not,' Zoë agreed cynically. 'And that's why you found it more important to go out to dinner with them than to be with your grandsons. Well, you needn't worry about having to look after them any more, Ma. Laura is going to come and work for me as a live-in child-minder.'

'What?'

Zoë couldn't help feeling pleased as she saw the look of shock on her mother's face.

'Come on, you two,' Zoë told her sons. 'Time to go home.'

'Zoë,' Alice protested.

'Sorry, Ma. I have to go. Laura will be coming round soon. Just for a trial at first, but I'm sure it's going to work out perfectly. She's exactly what the boys need. Someone young and energetic to play with them who understands today's culture. Someone who doesn't act like the world's about to come to an end because their mother enjoys a glass of wine!' she informed Alice smugly.

As she finished tucking the boys in bed Zoë couldn't resist giving them both an extra cuddle. She knew Alice believed that Ian had rushed her into marriage and motherhood, but the truth was that she had been the one to plead with him that they should get married, and to overrule him when he had suggested that they should wait a few years before starting their family.

'You're very young, Zoë, and if you tie yourself down with children now…'

'I want to be tied down,' Zoë argued, meaning that she wanted to make sure that she had him tied down, to make sure that he would never leave her, that he would be hers for ever. She knew that Ian, for all his faults, all his egotistical selfishness, would find it hard to desert his children. His own father had walked out on his mother, unable to cope with her behaviour, and Ian had never forgiven him for that.

'We have to get married. I love you too much not to,' she declared passionately when Ian protested that it was too soon.

'How do you know it's love?' He laughed at her.

'I just do,' she replied, warning him, 'You'll regret it if you don't marry me, Ian.'

'If you're trying to threaten me—' he began angrily, but she refused to give in, taunting him with deliberate sexuality.

'You'll do what? Punish me? Spank me? Tie me to my bed and torture me? Mmm…yes, please,' she breathed with an exaggerated sigh of pleasure.

She knew, of course, about his previous track record, the girls he had dated and then broken up with, and Zoë was determined to make sure that that did not happen to her.

She had wanted Ian the moment she'd set eyes on him; wanted him, desired him, hungered for him with an intensity that she had sensed had made him wary.

'My mother married young. It's in my genes,' she told him, adding provocatively, 'My father was the sexiest man around, just like you. It would be impossible for me not to love you, Ian. I'm pre-programmed to, and there's nothing you can do about it! Everything

my mother did I'll do, only better! I intend to be everything that she is and more…'

'You make it sound as though you're in some kind
of competition with her,' Ian mocked her.

'Isn't every daughter in competition with her
mother?' Zoë countered. For a while she thought she
might lose him and that her intensity—something she
did not get from Alice—had scared him off!

Even so, she suspected she would never have been
able to persuade him to marry her if it hadn't been for
the sudden spate of marriages amongst his contemporaries, suggesting that he could be in danger of being marooned high and dry in some now totally un-
cool, lonely bachelor backwater—that and the threat
of his unwanted speeding ticket! She knew how vital
it was to his continued business success that he was
able to drive—his Porsche was his favourite 'boy toy'
and there was no way he would ever relinquish it and
accept being driven by anyone else.

Even so, she didn't really expect him to agree. When
he did, she went public with the news of their engage-
ment immediately.

'Don't ever forget that you forced me into this marriage, Zoë,' he told her on the day of their wedding.
'Because I certainly won't!'

She didn't take him seriously—not then!

She looked at her mother, so secure in her father's
love, and decided that the best way to keep Ian was to
emulate her. To emulate her and to outdo her. After
all, it was a familiar mind-set for her, comfortable and
comforting!

So, like her mother, she ran a perfect home, and was
always on hand to entertain Ian's business associates
when he needed her to be. Like her mother, too, although, admittedly, with her mother's help, she was

virtually single-handedly raising their children, but unlike her mother Zoë suspected, she had a deep, hungry craving for her husband, her mate, both emotionally and physically, that never seemed to be appeased.

It kept her awake at night, gnawing hungrily at her as she lay in bed wondering where he was and who he was with, aching physically for him and yet knowing that even if he was with her, she would still feel hungry and in need, still be consumed by the nagging fear that he did not really love her as much as she loved him, that someone else could come and take his love away from her, usurp her, just as her brothers had taken her mother's love away from her.

That was why, unlike her mother, she sometimes liked a drink. It made her feel better, more relaxed, more…more the person she really wanted to be. More laid-back and less needy.

The phone rang as she closed the door to the boys' bedroom. The house she had persuaded Ian to buy was in a prestigious setting, larger than her parents'. She was currently trying to convince Ian that it would be a good idea to add an indoor swimming pool. She worked out at an exclusive local country club, but it would be fun to see her mother's face when she told her that they were going to have their own pool.

Hurrying into the bedroom downstairs, she picked up the receiver, her heart missing a beat as she recognised the number of Ian's mobile.

'I was just putting the boys to bed,' she told him, adding in a husky whisper, 'I wish you were here to do the same to me… Mmm…I miss you, Ian.' She closed her eyes and breathed deeply. 'If I was with you now, do you know what I'd be doing…?'

'Zoë. Cut it out,' Ian demanded, his curt voice slicing across her carefully rehearsed words. 'I haven't got much time. I'm meeting a client for dinner. And what do you mean you're just putting the boys to bed? Isn't it a bit late?'

'I was at Ma's,' Zoë told him immediately. 'She was in a bit of a flap, I suppose it must be her age. I think that having the boys is getting a bit much for her. She gives in to them far too much. When I think of how strict she was with me…'

'*She* gives in to them! Come off it, Zoë! She isn't the one who sits them in front of the television because she can't be bothered to spend time with them!'

Zoë could feel her tension increasing as she tightened her grip on the telephone cable. It was always like this. All she wanted to do was to talk to Ian about them, but whenever she tried to do so he insisted on talking about other things, other people. It reminded her of how she had felt as a child, wanting her father to notice her and pay attention to her, for her to be the first he fussed with and kissed when he came home, and not her mother.

'Oh, by the way, I saw your father today,' she heard Ian telling her. 'I took Philip Rowle to lunch at the Blueprint Café, and your father was lunching there at the same time.'

'Ma said that he'd got a meeting in the city,' Zoë told him uninterestedly.

'A meeting? This looked as though it was something much more intimate than that! In fact he was so engrossed in whatever he was talking about to the woman he was lunching with that he never even noticed me,' Ian told her derisively.

'Dad was lunching with a woman? How old was she? What did she look like? Who was she?'

'Thirty-something. Stunningly attractive, and I

don't know,' Ian replied laconically. 'Look, I must go, otherwise I'm going to be late. Kiss the boys for me…'

'Never mind them. Who's going to kiss me for you?' Zoë demanded. She loved the boys, of course she did, but sometimes she couldn't help wishing that it were just her and Ian, that she were the only person he wanted and needed. 'Ian…' she whispered. 'I wish I was there with you…'

'I've got to go.'

He had hung up before she could say any more. Reluctantly she replaced her own receiver.

She had still been a student when she had first met him. He had come to the university to address the students' union, a graduate who was now a high profile and very successful businessman, but it hadn't been his business skills that had interested Zoë. She had logged the designer suit, of course, and the confidently masculine air that had gone with it, but it had been what she had instinctively known had lain beneath the suit that had interested her.

Zoë had discovered sex at an age that she knew would have shocked her mother, just as she suspected that her enjoyment of it would have also shocked her, but Zoë did not share that shock. Instead she felt proud of her sexual expertise and the intensity of her sexual appetite.

After the first excitement of discovering how pleasurable sex could be, she had been choosy about her lovers, and protective of her own sexual health. It had been lust and not love that had driven her until she'd met Ian.

It was part of her family folklore, the story of how her father had fallen head over heels in love with her mother at first sight, told and retold by Stuart himself as well as Alice's friends, sending out a subtle message to Zoë's immature beliefs. In order to validate herself as a woman, to be as much of a woman as her mother, she too had needed to receive that gift of a mature, sexy, powerful man's instant adoration and adulation, and the moment she'd set eyes on Ian she had decided that he was that man.

During her own school days, her mother had been one of the leading lights of her school's prestigious debating club, and predictably Zoë had been determined to outdo her. She had become a member of her university's most prominent club—not a debating club, however, but a notorious all-girl drinking club who had given themselves the name 'Allez Katz'. It had been considered the height of cool by its members to challenge one another to perform outrageous public displays, their execution normally fuelled by copious amounts of courage-giving and inhibition-weakening alcohol. But Zoë hadn't needed the taunting dares of her peers to encourage her to make a play for Ian.

At first all she had known was that she had to have him, that he was exactly the kind of man she'd needed to take home and flaunt in front of her mother: rich, sexy, and with a sexual reputation even more dangerous and far more publicly known than that of her airline pilot father! Ian had been the perfect man to flaunt in front of her mother.

Then, she had assumed that she would become bored with him as quickly as she had done with the other men she had desired.

How could she have been so blind—and so wrong?

It had been easy enough to find out where Ian had been staying, and to get herself into his room so that she'd been waiting there when he'd returned to it, lying naked on his bed, her eyes huge and dark with self-given passion.

He hadn't seemed fazed at all to find her there, but neither had he seemed remotely excited by the fact that she'd been lying naked on the bed, her fingers stroking the wet warmth of her sex with lazy insouciance whilst she'd watched him.

Chillingly it had struck her that he might be gay, but somehow she had known that he was not, which had left her with the shocking and unpalatable discovery that he had simply not been interested in her; that she'd actually not been exciting or arousing him. It had been a situation she had never been in before.

'I don't know who you are or how you got in here, but you've got five minutes to get yourself out again before I call Security,' he told her curtly, before walking past her and into the bathroom, firmly closing the door behind him.

Zoë had left her own clothes in the bathroom but that was not why she got up off the bed and pushed open the bathroom door, her face red with disbelief.

He was just finishing urinating when she walked in, and she could see that either he was semi-aroused or he was considerably larger than any other man she had known, and that was enough to give her confidence the boost it needed.

Ignoring her, he turned to the basin and proceeded to wash both his hands and his penis.

Their eyes met in the mirror.

'You've got two minutes left,' he told her flatly.

Zoë discovered that she was holding her breath. 'Otherwise what?' she challenged him.

'Otherwise I call Security,' he responded.

She knew that he wouldn't, not when she could see with her own eyes…but as she moved towards him he reached for a towel and dried his hands and his body, and then zipped up his trousers.

'Time's up,' he told her laconically, without looking at her as he reached for the telephone receiver.

She was so sure that he was bluffing that she had to pull her top and jeans on without her underwear when she heard the doorbell to the suite ring.

Her face burned with humiliation as she saw the look the security man was giving her, but somehow she managed to keep her head held high as she left.

She didn't sleep that night for plotting just how she was going to get her revenge—and her man, because now she wanted him even more. And she didn't sleep the next night either, or the one after that, but she still wasn't prepared for it when, a week later, just as she was leaving her digs a Porsche drew up alongside her and Ian leaned across from the driver's seat and told her through the open window, 'Get in.'

She had no idea what she had expected, but it certainly wasn't that he would drive her at breakneck speed to a country park on the outskirts of the town, where he pulled up in the deserted car park and reached for her almost before he had switched off the engine.

He kissed her so hard that he bruised her lips. In return she bit his mouth in a frantic orgy of need and hunger. She was tugging his shirt out of his trousers before he pushed up her top and bared her breasts.

They came together, took one another with a ferocity that left Zoë, elated and exhausted, convinced that she had finally met the man who was her sexual match, her mate…convinced that she was finally in love.

'Satisfied now that you've got your own way and had what you wanted?' he taunted her, before admitting, 'I've been wanting that all week.'

'So have I,' Zoë responded, adding provocatively, 'And now that I've had it, I want it again…'

She licked her fingertip and ran it over his lips, followed by her tongue, and then she licked her finger again and ran it round the head of his penis.

She could still remember the exact way he had groaned and shuddered, just as she could still remember the scent and feel of him…the heat…everything. He was imprinted on her for ever.

After that she pursued him shamelessly, ringing him up, turning up at his office, perching on his desk and threatening to strip off and do it there, if he didn't take her out.

'My God, but you're reckless,' he said to her. 'Reckless and dangerous… Too dangerous for me.'

Then she thought that he was praising her and not warning her. The realisation that he considered his sexuality was something he thought should be controlled as strongly as she felt that hers was something that should be enjoyed came later…at the same time as she realised that it was not passionate longing and hunger she could see in his eyes when she came on to him openly in public, but, rather, disapproval and wariness.

Automatically she reached for a drink. To blur the sharpness of that look… And that was when Ian told her about his mother and how much he disliked women drinking.

She cried and told him how much she loved him; how he was the only man she could ever love. She told him about her family and her upbringing and her mother—her mother who never drank more than the occasional glass of wine and whom she could match and outdo in any way she chose.

'All I want is to be your wife and the mother of your

children, Ian,' she declared passionately, and she meant it!

'You're too young,' he told her firmly. 'And I'm not looking for a wife!'

'No, I'm not,' she denied, adding provocatively, 'I could even be pregnant now... I want to be.'

'I thought you were on the pill?' he challenged her, plainly not pleased.

'I am,' she agreed. 'But accidents can happen. And anyway...' she tossed her head and gave him a long, hungry look '...I wouldn't mind if I did get pregnant. In fact...'

'You mustn't,' Ian insisted tersely.

She told her friends that they were in love and about to get engaged, in an attempt to force his hand, and when Ian found out he was furiously angry with her. She thought then she was going to lose him and that she had overreached herself, but now he was hers. She had his name. She had his children... But she didn't have his love, did she?

And neither did she have the close support group of her own special coterie of friends. She knew people, of course, masses of them, but there was a deeply secretive part of Zoë's nature, a prickly defensiveness that refused to allow her to let her guard down with others. Everyone thought she was so lucky in having Alice as her mother. But Laura seemed to understand.

Of course, it went without saying, her mother would be mortified that Laura, Nicki's loathed stepdaughter, was going to be taking care of her grandchildren!

She could hear the doorbell ringing. Laura had arrived. Smiling triumphantly, Zoë went to let her in.

'I went to see Julie's parents today.'
Stella waited as Richard lowered his paper.

'And?'

'Well, it isn't looking too good. You were right about her father! He has flatly refused to have her back home until after the baby. I felt very sorry for her mother. She's such a cowed little thing. He's obviously a bit of a bully. He was ranting on about his own sister getting pregnant as a girl and it ruined her life and how he didn't want Julie's life to be ruined in the same way. He's furious with her because she concealed her pregnancy from him until it was too late for a termination.'

'Well, I can see his point. At best, even if you take the baby and the emotional angst its birth will cause, not just immediately but for the future as well, out of the equation, she is still going to put herself behind with her schoolwork by at least a year.'

'I called at the school with her, earlier. They're going to arrange for her to have special lessons—there are classes for young pregnant girls she can attend, and then, after the baby, the situation can be reassessed. She still seems determined to go to university, which is a good thing.' Stella shook her head in exasperation.

'You know, she amazes me, she's still so very young in many ways. On the way back from the school I had some shopping to do, and so we agreed to meet up in the shopping centre. When I got there she was staring into this shop window, and at first I thought—well, it had a display of baby paraphernalia, but no, what she was all excited about was the computer next to it. Apparently someone had told her that it might not be safe to use her mobile too much because of the baby and she was worried that she wouldn't be able to keep in touch with her friends.' Stella pulled a face. 'You know what these modern girls are like. They can't go more than five minutes without speaking to one another. And at least I suppose she'd thought about the baby...'

'So you bought her the computer,' Richard guessed dryly.

'Well, when she's gone we can use it ourselves. You know we've been talking about getting a second one. With all my committee work it would be useful. She can email her friends now, and play her music, as well as making use of it for educational purposes. She's upstairs in her room using it now.'

'*Her* room?' Richard enquired.

'Rich, what else can we do?' Stella asked him matter-of-factly. 'This baby is after all as much our responsibility—'

Angrily Richard folded his newspaper.

'No, it is not *our* responsibility.' He checked her. 'It is our son's responsibility—a responsibility which so far as I can see he is as happy to hand over to you as you are to let him. He's not a boy any more, Stella. He's a man and it's time he started behaving like one. And before you say anything, being a man takes more than fathering a child. In my day—'

'Rich, I know what you're saying, but—heavens, is that the time?' Stella exclaimed in relief. 'I've got to go, otherwise I'm going to be late. We're going to see if there's any way we can possibly raise some more money for the Shelter. It's appalling to realise how many people are homeless. I just wish...'

Stella stopped. Richard had already reopened his paper and his only response to what she had said was one of his customary grunts. There had been a time when she had complained to him that they no longer seemed to talk to one another.

'We've been married for twenty-odd years, Stella,'

he had answered. 'We don't need to talk to one another any more.'

She had understood what he had been saying and it was true that they knew one another so well that she knew how he thought and felt. But sometimes...

In her bag she had a list of all the arrangements that would have to be made for Julie's health care and her schooling. In the morning she was taking her to their local surgery for a check-up and then there would be hospital appointments, pre-birth classes, plus all the practical aspects of dealing with the baby's arrival and adoption.

The doorbell rang just as she walked into the hall. Answering it, she found a trio of giggling girls on the doorstep. Before she could say anything Julie came hurrying downstairs.

'They're my friends; it's okay if I take them up to my room, isn't it?' she asked Stella.

'Of course,' Stella agreed, wincing a little as she saw the neat little bare stomachs exposed by their cropped tops and low-slung jeans—and not just because it was cool outside! Their flatness, like their giggles, emphasised just how young Julie was.

Although she was fiercely determined to have her baby, so far as Stella could see she had not actually thought beyond that birth. The baby would be adopted, she had told Stella confidently, and she would get her A levels and go to university, her life back to normal.

'Sorry I'm a bit late,' Stella apologised to the other members of their fund-raising group as she hurried into the basement room of their chair's home.

'Don't worry about it,' Paul Howard reassured her as they exchanged hugs. They had worked in the same social services department together, which was how they had originally met, and it was Paul who had recruited Stella to their group, knowing what an asset she would be.

'Come and let me introduce you to someone I want you to meet, Stella,' he instructed. 'A new recruit. He's just moved into the area. You'll like him. As you do, he believes that good administration is a vitally important core base for any organisation. Todd!' he called out, reaching out to tap the shoulder of a man standing with his back to them, talking to their treasurer.

Only mildly curious, Stella waited, absently wondering why it was that some middle-aged men could still get away with wearing jeans and look terrific in them whilst others could not. This man certainly fell into the former group. His jeans revealed an enviably taut male rear view, a soft cotton checked shirt tucked into their waist, well-groomed thick dark hair liberally streaked with grey, worn at just the right length, brushing his collar.

Richard looked terrible in jeans. He had begun to develop a slight stoop, which he had defensively told her was due to the demands of their large garden, and whilst, unlike many of his contemporaries, he had not developed a paunch, no woman looking at him would ever feel drawn to give him a second look. Unlike the man who was now turning round and smiling at Paul.

'Todd, I'd like you to meet Stella,' Paul was saying. 'Like you, she's an administration junkie. It's thanks to her that our subscriptions and our paperwork are so well organised.'

Stella made a face.

'It sounds incredibly boring, I know.'

'Not at all.' The newcomer smiled. 'In my view orderliness is an under-appreciated virtue. My sons ridicule me because I never end up with odd socks, but that doesn't stop them raiding my sock drawer because they can't find a matching pair of their own. Whenever I go over to the States to see them I always know I'm going to come back minus a good few pairs.'

'They're studying over there?' Stella guessed, assuming from his appearance that he must be in his early fifties, but to her embarrassment he shook his head and told her easily, 'No. Actually they moved there with my ex-wife and her new partner. It's all right,' he added when he saw Stella's mortified expression. 'We've been divorced for nearly ten years now. Things were tricky at first and my elder son in particular was very, very angry with me and refused to have anything to do with me. So much so, in fact, that when he and his wife married, I was banned from attending the wedding, and my grandson was three years old before I got to see him. Now, that was hard.'

'Yes, it must have been,' Stella acknowledged.

Paul had moved away after introducing them, and somehow it seemed that they had become isolated from everyone else. Todd had discreetly but deliberately moved them so this could be the case, she realised on a sudden spurt of excited disbelief as she recognised belatedly that Todd was actually flirting with her.

For a moment she was tempted to show him that she was just not the kind of woman with whom men flirted, to take refuge from her own unwanted insecurity and react in the way she knew her friends would have expected her to, with a stern look and a cool, dismissive comment, but then a sudden surge of rebellion seized her. Why should she always be the one who was pushed into the background, the sensible one? Why shouldn't she flirt back with Todd?

Recklessly she smiled at him and watched him smile warmly at her in return, a sense of giddy exhilaration dizzying her.

Perhaps it was because he spent time in America that Todd was standing so much closer to her than his British counterpart would have done, his gaze fixing warmly on hers and holding it.

And then, unbelievably, he did something to her that she could never, ever remember any man doing, not even Richard. He reached out and tucked a stray strand of her hair neatly behind her ear, his fingers resting lightly, caressingly, she recognised in delighted bemusement, against her skin for just a second too long as he told her softly, 'Now I can see your eyes properly. What colour are they exactly? Blue…grey…'

'Er, yes. They're blue…'

Stella discovered that she could hardly breathe.

'Do you have children?' he asked her.

Children? Bemused, Stella had to think for a second before responding. 'Yes, one son, Hughie, he's at university at the moment…and his girlfriend's living with us. She's having his baby—an accident.'

Stella was aghast. What on earth had possessed her to tell him that? Julie's pregnancy wasn't going to be kept a secret, of course. But…but she prided herself on her businesslike attitude to her committee work, Stella acknowledged, and, whilst she was quite happy to exchange pleasantries with her fellow committee workers, intimate confidences were something she kept for her close friends.

'They happen,' he responded dryly. 'As I should know! My wife and I became parents whilst we were still at university ourselves—very accidentally. In those days—we are talking the very early sixties—it was the done thing, the decent thing to get married and so we did. We both tried to make the best of it, especially my ex-wife, but…'

The early sixties; that meant he must be older than she had thought—closer to sixty than fifty. Stella shot him a surreptitiously assessing look. He certainly didn't look it! Somehow she doubted too that he would be a candidate for Viagra or that he would spend his evenings in front of the television too tired or bored to make conversation, she decided boldly as her heart bounded around inside her chest.

'Have you just the one grandchild?' she asked him forcing herself to behave more appropriately, whilst inwardly her thoughts flung themselves giddily into avenues that led to a wild and totally unfamiliar surge of hectic excitement that she recognised with shock could just possibly be lust. Possibly? Didn't she mean probably?

'No, I've got three, two boys and a girl. It's amazing the way you feel about them; there's a tug, a gut-deep feeling; a bond that I have to admit is totally different from what I felt for my sons. To say that I'm besotted with my grandchildren is probably a gross understatement. When I'm away from them I email them virtually every day, and I'm working on getting Lainey, my daughter-in-law, to let them spend some time over here with me during school recess next summer. They've become, if not the biggest, then certainly the best part of my life, and yet to be honest I'm not particularly child-orientated. I wasn't a good father—for one thing I was too busy building my own career and my own ego.

'My ex used to say it was contemptible the way I competed with the boys when they were kids, but of course I refused to admit that she was right. With grandchildren it's different. Those three kids… Just you wait!' he warned Stella with a smile.

'Oh, it's not going to be like that for us,' Stella felt obliged to tell him. 'Julie, the baby's mother, has already decided that she wants to have the baby adopted.'

The look of pity she could see in his eyes shocked her, as did his quiet but sincere, 'I am so sorry to hear that. It must be very painful for you.'

'No, not at all,' Stella denied. 'I don't think of the baby as being a grandchild, and I don't intend to do so.'

When Paul suddenly reappeared, she didn't know whether she was relieved or disappointed to see Todd borne away to be introduced to someone else.

8

——◆——

The surgery was busy when Maggie arrived. She had been told that the appointment would be with a Dr Carter. His name wasn't familiar to her, but then she very rarely needed to visit the surgery.

The receptionist looked surprised when Maggie told her who her appointment was with. 'Are you sure?' she began, frowning. 'It's just that today is his day for seeing the new mothers to be...'

Maggie could feel her face growing hot. The other patients in the queue who were within earshot were looking at her with interest.

'Yes. I do know that,' she told the receptionist.

Maggie could see her pursing her lips as she found her name and ticked it off the appointments list. She also felt as though her disapproving look were burning a hole in her back as she started to walk away from the desk.

'Excuse me,' she called sharply after Maggie. 'The consulting room for pregnant mothers is downstairs, next to the nurses' room, and it has its own waiting area.'

Her face burning even more hotly than before, Maggie headed for the stairs.

As well as the normal antenatal classes and hospital visits, Maggie had several appointments during the course of her pregnancy at the fertility clinic so that they could monitor her progress, and this morning just before she had left Oliver had produced an article he had been reading advocating yoga classes for pregnant women. 'We could go together,' he suggested winningly. 'It would be good for you, very relaxing.'

'Antenatal classes, hospital visits, yoga classes, it's beginning to sound as though being pregnant is a full-time job. I still have the business to run, remember, and a new home to find...'

'Oh, talking of new homes,' Oliver interrupted her, 'I forgot to tell you, the estate agents rang yesterday. They're sending us details of somewhere that's just come on the market, although by the sound of it it's not going to be suitable.'

'Why not?' Maggie asked him.

'Well, for one thing it's huge, and for another it seems that it's going to need a hell of a lot of work doing on it.'

'Where is it?' Maggie asked him curiously. 'Did they say?'

'Draycotte,' Oliver responded, mentioning a small village a few miles away. 'Originally it was the local manor house, so it's called...'

'Draycotte Manor,' Maggie supplied softly for him.

'You know it?' Oliver asked her.

'Yes,' Maggie agreed. 'My grandmother lived in Draycotte and I used to play in the manor's gardens as a little girl. It was very run down at the time and the house was empty.'

Maggie prayed that Oliver wouldn't notice how flushed her face had become and ask her why. She had fallen in love with the old house as a girl, and in the early days of their relationship she had taken Dan to see it. 'One day, when I'm rich, I'm going to buy it for you,' he had told her. 'For us, Maggie, and for our children.'

'Well, we need to find somewhere soon,' Maggie reminded Oliver, quickly pushing Draycotte Manor and Dan out of her thoughts. Oliver was right, it was far too big and would need far too much work doing on it.

'Are you sure you don't want me to come with you to see the doctor?' Oliver asked her.

Maggie shook her head. 'You've got to see Ralph Frame—remember? He still can't make up his mind about which desk he wants. You'll enjoy yourself,' Maggie added, when he grimaced. 'His secretary has the longest legs and the shortest skirts I've ever seen.'

'So what? They'll be completely wasted on me,' Oliver responded, grinning at her. 'I'm a sucker for women of five feet two in maternity skirts. In fact,' he continued softly, taking hold of Maggie's hand and pulling her determinedly towards him so that he could feather his whispered words against her lips, 'there is only one woman, only one pair of legs that do it for me and you know it.

'Marry me, Maggie.' He said it abruptly, his hand tightening on hers. Reluctantly Maggie shook her head.

'Oliver. We've already been through this,' she told him.

'I know, you don't want to marry me because you think I'm after your money.' He was joking but she saw the pain in his eyes.

Shaking her head, Maggie corrected him. 'I don't want to marry you because I don't want to tie you down. To tie you to me, Oliver...'

He threw back his head and closed his eyes, his voice raw as he demanded, 'God, Maggie, we're having a child, how much more tied to you than that can I possibly be? What is it, Maggie? Why won't you marry me? Is it because of Dan? Because you still—'

'No.' Maggie stopped him immediately. 'No, it doesn't have anything to do with Dan.'

'Your friends, then, you're afraid that they won't approve?'

Fiercely, Maggie shook her head.

'Then why?' Oliver appealed thickly. 'God knows, you know how much I love you…'

Yes, she knew that. He loved her now! But how would he feel in five years' time…in ten? She had been far more self-indulgent, far more selfish than she had any right to be already in having his child; to marry him as well could only compound that selfishness. And besides… When she and Dan had married they had exchanged vows that should have lasted a lifetime, but they hadn't. Who was to say what would happen between her and Oliver, whom he might meet? A younger woman…*the* woman. How could she deny him the freedom to be with her? How could she claim to love him and not let him have that freedom?

The waiting room was beginning to fill up and Maggie was tensely conscious of how much older than the other pregnant women she was. Some of them arrived in twos and threes, their pregnancies well advanced, co-travellers down a uniquely bonding road.

She could still remember how envious and how excluded she had felt during her friends' pregnancies, how very much the odd one out.

She was still the odd one out, she recognised.

The surgery had begun. She overheard the two thirty-somethings seated next to her saying how good the new doctor was.

'He's a fully qualified paediatrician, which I suppose is why he's in charge of this clinic. He certainly knows his stuff. I saw old Dr Harris with my first. He didn't have a clue. Mind you, the midwife was almost as bad. I thought she was going to have a fit when I told her that I wanted to have a Caesar.'

'Mmm. My mother was horrified when she discovered that I was planning to have Tom delivered by Caesarian section. She was one of the natural childbirth and no pain-killers generation—it took her twelve hours to deliver me and after twenty years of hearing a blow-by-blow account of it, there was no way I was going to go through that. Talk about inflicting guilt!'

Absently Maggie listened to them, glancing over as the waiting-room door opened.

As Stella pushed open the door the first person she saw was Maggie and immediately her heart sank a little. As yet she had not had the opportunity to tell anyone about what had happened. She could see the way Maggie's eyes lit up as soon as she saw her, her expression changing to one of confusion as Stella stepped back and ushered Julie into the room ahead of her.

Before they could sit down Julie's name was called. Giving Maggie a brief smile, Stella hurried her to the door.

Marcus frowned a little as he saw Julie. The irony of him being given the task of monitoring the pregnant mothers had not escaped him. The evidence of their fecundity increased his own longing for a child. That had not surprised him at all, but what had was the number of mothers-to-be who had told him ruefully that it had been their partners who had initially wanted a child.

'It's this new man thing,' one thirty-something had told him wryly. 'Personally I'd just as soon not have bothered, but I got so tired of Eddie gazing longingly at other people's sprogs that I had to give in.'

'So you're not entirely happy about your pregnancy?' Marcus had asked her.

His patient had laughed.

'I'm delighted,' she had informed him. 'Now! But if you'd told me twelve months ago that I'd be spending every spare minute reading baby-raising books and loving every second of it, I would never have believed you.'

'So, Julie,' he began gently as he studied the pale-faced teenager sitting in front of him, once he had finished examining her behind a curtained screen whilst Stella waited anxiously. 'You say that you are just over six months pregnant. Have you given any thought to what you want to happen afterwards, when your baby has been born?'

'She's going to have the baby adopted and go back to school,' Stella supplied impatiently for him. With barely three months to go before the baby was due, surely it was more important to sort out all the practical arrangements for its birth, rather than discuss the one decision that had already been made.

'Is that what you want, Julie?' Marcus asked, giving Stella a brief look. 'This is your baby, you know,' he stressed, in a way that made Stella's face burn with indignation. 'And any decision regarding his or her future must be yours. We have a counsellor here at the surgery if you would like to talk to someone, and of course social services will—'

'Julie has already made her decision, and she has made it by herself,' Stella insisted.

Marcus gave her a steady look. Stella struck him as a formidably organised woman, but before he could say anything Julie burst out, 'I do want the baby to be adopted… I couldn't have…have killed it like my father would have wanted me to, but I…I don't want it…'

As she spoke tears filled her eyes, and Stella felt her own anger melt away.

'I'd like you to see the nurse before you leave,' Marcus told her. 'She will arrange for you to talk to the midwife, and sort out antenatal classes. You will be able to discuss with her any preferences you might have as to the way you give birth.'

'Everyone says that it's really going to hurt.' Her voice wobbled.

'Well the word "labour" certainly implies that it will be hard work,' Marcus agreed carefully, looking at Stella properly for the first time as he continued. 'I don't…'

'Giving birth varies from woman to woman, Julie,' Stella offered promptly, coming to his rescue. 'I was lucky with Hughie, although I have to say he was reluctant to get himself into the right position and we did think for a time that he was going to be a breech delivery.'

Giving Marcus a rueful smile, she added, 'My midwife lost patience with him after she had turned him round twice—she said then he would probably be a stubborn child and she was right. You mustn't worry,' she told Julie calmly. 'I'm sure—'

'I want my mother to be there,' Julie told her shakily.

Over her downbent head Stella exchanged looks with Marcus.

Whilst Julie was seeing the nurse, Stella went to sit down next to Maggie.

'Julie is pregnant with Hughie's baby,' she explained in a low voice. 'I haven't had a chance to say anything yet. We only found out ourselves a matter of days ago. Her father has virtually thrown her out and so she's going to be living with us until after the baby's born.'

'A grandchild...' Maggie smiled. 'Oh, Stella...'

'No!' Stella denied sharply. Why was it people automatically assumed that she was not just ready but eager to claim her relationship with this baby who in reality meant nothing to her?

'Julie is going to have the baby adopted,' she told Maggie. 'It's the most sensible thing to do and it's what she wants to do,' she added firmly.

'She and I both seem out of place here.' Maggie sighed. 'She because she's too young and me because I'm too old. At least, according to Nicki.' She paused and frowned. Perhaps now wasn't the moment but, the more she had thought about Nicki's behaviour, the more concerned she had become for her friend.

'Stella,' she began tentatively. 'Have you noticed anything different about Nicki lately? Only—'

'I know she upset you, Maggie. But I wouldn't take it too much to heart,' Stella interrupted. 'To be honest you gave us all a shock, and...'

She stopped as Maggie's name was called. Getting up, Maggie recognised that it was perhaps just as well that their conversation had been brought to an end. It was obvious to her that Stella felt she was overreacting to Nicki. Was she?

'Mrs Rockford.' Marcus smiled as Maggie walked into his room and closed the door behind her. 'You are in the early stages of pregnancy, I understand?'

'Yes.' Maggie smiled hesitantly. 'I know you must think that at my age…' She stopped whilst Marcus watched her.

He had checked her medical history before his surgery and knew that she had gone through a multitude of tests before it had been discovered that the failure to conceive with her husband had been because of a problem with his sperm.

'You are fifty-two and, so far as I can see, in extremely good health,' he told her calmly. 'Moreoever, since you have conceived by egg donor, your baby will already have been screened for any potential…problems. The fact is that you statistically have every chance of producing an extremely healthy baby.'

His smile and his words immediately put Maggie at her ease.

'I know everyone doesn't approve of a woman of my age doing what I am doing.'

'Why shouldn't you? Men do it all the time,' was Marcus' calm response. 'Although we are now just beginning to recognise that the ability to produce sperm does not guarantee the birth of a healthy child, and that a man's sperm becomes less healthy as he grows older.'

'A…a friend of mine has warned me that until I am over my third month I could miscarry the baby,' Maggie said worriedly. Nicki's warning had been on her mind ever since her friend had issued it.

'That is true, of course, but the majority of spontaneous abortions before three months are caused either because nature has decided that the foetus is not viable for one reason or another, or because of the mother not being able to maintain the pregnancy. That is hardly likely to happen in your case, because the egg has already been screened before it was fertilised and implanted, and your own health has been thoroughly checked out. Of course, if you were to behave in a way that might prejudice your pregnancy, such as taking up a physically rigorous sport, for instance, then, yes, there would be a risk, but I really don't think you need to worry,' he reassured Maggie gently. 'According to your medical notes you are perfectly healthy, and so, too, I am sure, will your baby be.'

Her baby! *Her* baby...

As she left the surgery Maggie realised that for the first time when someone had referred to the baby as being hers she had not felt an immediate need to correct them. Her baby... Hers and Oliver's. Theirs!

Maggie hummed as she let herself in through the front door and picked up the post that had arrived in her absence. She felt energetic and excited, full of joy and love.

She would go and see Nicki again; perhaps she had overreacted, been over-imaginative. She was pregnant, after all, and her hormones would be all over the place.

A wide, almost girlish grin curled her mouth. Pregnant... There was so much she needed to do. They hadn't looked at nursery equipment as yet, or baby clothes. Nursery equipment, baby clothes...first they had to find a house, she reminded herself humorously. Hopefully, the estate agents might have sent them details of something worth looking at. She felt so much better since she had seen the doctor, so much more like her normal optimistic self, so much more positive and focused. She felt, Maggie recognised with delight, that she really and truly now was pregnant; that she was going to be a mother. And she intended to be the best, the most loving, the most grateful mother there could be.

Dizzy with relief and happiness, she went into the kitchen and made herself a cup of tea before sitting down to open her letters. She was not expecting Oliver back until later in the day. She had some work of her own to do, though, and…

Tea slopped dangerously from the mug she was holding as she stared in disbelief at the letter she had just opened and read.

Shock, nausea, fear—all of them surged through her, locking her stomach muscles, making her hands shake.

'No…' she whispered in horrified rejection, her immediate instinct to crush the letter into a tight ball, to rip it into shreds so that she never had to see it again, but she knew that every word it contained was already imprinted inside her head, and so instead she put it down on the table and read it slowly again.

Maggie
I had to write to you! I would have preferred to talk to you but I knew you wouldn't listen. You aren't a listener, are you, Maggie? You're too selfish for that. You've always been selfish, I know that. I know everything there is to know about you, Maggie. I know you inside out. I know all about you and Dan!
How can you live with yourself? How can you bear to face yourself every day knowing what you have done? The baby you are carrying belongs to someone else. You have stolen it and deserve to be punished. You will be punished for it, Maggie! It will grow up hating you because you have stolen it from its rightful mother.
When I saw you the other day I knew that you

shouldn't be having a baby. Perhaps you shouldn't be allowed to go on living! What do you think, Maggie? You know that I'm right, don't you? Think about it. Think about what you've done!

Maggie was barely aware of the door opening and Oliver walking in until she saw him standing in front of her.

'Oliver,' she whispered blankly. 'What are you doing here?'

'I had to come home to find out how you went on at the doctor's,' he began. 'I… Maggie, what is it? What's wrong?' he demanded as he saw her face, dread sharpening his voice as he asked hoarsely, 'The baby…?'

Numbly Maggie shook her head.

'No. The baby's fine… It's this,' she told him, tears filling her eyes as she showed him the letter.

Like her, he had to read it twice, and when he had he put it back on the table and told her quietly, 'This will have to go to the police.'

'No!' Maggie denied immediately.

'Maggie, it's a poison pen letter,' Oliver told her. 'The…the person who sent it is sick and needs help.'

'Oliver, I don't want to involve the police. I…'

'Why not?'

Maggie shook her head.

'We both know who this letter has come from, Maggie. You said yourself that Nicki—'

'No!' Maggie protested despairingly. 'No… She would never do anything like this. Never… She's my friend, she's… Oh, Oliver, she can't have done it. Please, please promise me you won't go to the police. Please promise me you won't do anything,' she begged him huskily. 'Let's just forget it. Let's just forget that it ever happened. Please!'

'Forget it?' Oliver was appalled. 'Maggie, we can't! For Nicki to have sent you this letter she must be seriously unbalanced, and perhaps even dangerous.'

'We don't know that it was Nicki!' Maggie protested immediately, but she could tell from Oliver's face that her panic had given her away.

'Who else could it possibly be?' he demanded. 'Who else could possibly know so much?'

'She's my friend,' Maggie protested. She was almost in tears—tears of shock. Tears of pain, tears of grief and anger and disbelief that this could be happening.

'Is she?' Oliver's expression had hardened. 'You said yourself that her reaction to your news had upset you,' he reminded her. When she remained stubbornly silent, he added in exasperation, 'Maggie, I don't understand you. I know what you've put yourself through in order to have this baby, and I know just how much it means to you, and yet here you are behaving as though suddenly Nicki is the most important person in your life…protecting her at the potential expense of our child! Deliberately blinding yourself to what she's doing!'

'Oliver that's unfair…unjust,' Maggie objected fiercely. 'Nicki would never, ever deliberately hurt a child.'

'Really. But she doesn't mind hurting you, does she, Maggie? And you are *carrying* a child…our child. Surely she must realise the effect receiving a letter like that could have? And if she doesn't, then it's damned well time that she was made to realise, via the law if necessary. And if you won't report this letter—'

'Oliver, if you take that letter to the police—'

Maggie stopped, white-faced, as they confronted one another.

For the first time in their relationship an argument had produced a mutually hostile silence.

Oliver ached to reach out to her, to hold her, but he ached too with hurt that she should put Nicki before him and their baby.

Maggie was also distraught. Why couldn't Oliver understand how she felt, how reluctant she was to accept that Nicki could have done something so terrible? And, more importantly, why. To Maggie her friends were her family, the closeness they all shared the foundation of the life she had built for herself in the aftermath of her divorce. To think of Nicki sending her that letter was to think the unthinkable, and that was what she had wanted Oliver to say to her.

She ached for the strong comfort of his arms, the warmth of his protective body, his protective love, but she couldn't let him go to the police!

Maggie ached all over, inside and out. She went to the bedroom and, curling into a small protective ball in the middle of the bed, she squeezed her eyes tightly shut against her tears.

Oliver found her there, small and vulnerable in their big bed, and he couldn't help himself as he pulled her into his arms.

Tears choked Maggie's voice.

'I'm sorry I let you think that Nicki is more important to me than you or the baby,' she told him sadly. 'She isn't. But she is my friend, Oliver, and I can't...'

'Maggie, Maggie. Please don't cry,' Oliver begged her as he held her tighter in his arms. 'The last thing I want to do is to upset you. It's just that I feel so damned angry and so damned helpless.'

As she looked at him, unable to stop himself, he

kissed her. Maggie gave a small emotional shiver, and wrapped her arms closely round him.

'I'm still not happy about what Nicki's done,' Oliver told Maggie softly. 'But...'

'But you agree that I should be the one to deal with the situation and that you won't go to the police,' Maggie insisted.

'I agree,' he sighed, 'but you'll never convince me that she didn't send it or that she should be allowed to get away with it. She's your friend, Maggie, and now that you've explained to me how you feel I have to respect those feelings, but I don't think I will ever be able to accept what she's done.'

Then they kissed again, relieved that they had cleared the air between them.

9

Zoë groaned as she woke up. Her head was pounding nauseatingly and her heart thumped with nervous, guilty anxiety.

The bottle of wine she had brought upstairs with her last night—now empty—was on the bedside table, next to a cold cup of tea.

As she struggled to sit up Zoë looked at the alarm clock. Eleven o'clock! It couldn't be!

The boys! Frantically she pushed back the bedclothes, gritting her teeth against the wave of pain and sickness that gripped her. And then she remembered about Laura. The relief and guilt that filled her made her feel even worse than her alcohol-induced nausea. Her body was beginning to shake whilst her heart pounded furiously. The tips of her fingers and her toes felt slightly numb as her blood-sugar level plummeted. She could remember suggesting to Laura last night that they had a drink, and she could remember Laura shaking her head and refusing. She could even remember the first glass of wine she had poured, but after that…

Getting out of bed, she made her way to her bathroom.

'More! Do some more,' William demanded imperiously, tugging on Laura's sleeve. Obligingly she reached for a fresh sheet of paper. Who would have thought that the simple paper shapes she had learned to make as a child would prove so absorbing to today's generation?

Laura had always liked children. At one stage, as a young girl, she had even considered working with them, but that had been before her mother had died.

Even so, when she had arrived at Zoë's the previous evening she had been wondering if she was doing the right thing.

This morning, unsure of what the boys' routine was, she had gone into Zoë's bedroom to ask her, only to discover that Zoë was deep in an obviously alcoholic sleep.

Laura had got the boys up and dressed, and made both them and herself some breakfast, waiting an hour before taking Zoë a cup of tea, but to her dismay Zoë had still been deeply asleep.

Laura frowned as she recalled her new employer's reaction the previous evening when Laura had refused the glass of wine she had offered.

'God, I hope you aren't going to be boring, Laura. I get enough of that from my husband and my mother,' Zoë had complained. 'There's nothing wrong in enjoying a glass of wine, you know. In fact, it's very good for you!'

A glass of wine might well be, Laura reflected now, but a bottle was surely a different matter.

They were in the middle of a counting game, much to the excited enthusiasm of the boys, when Zoë walked into the kitchen, grimacing and closing her eyes as she exclaimed sharply, 'For God's sake, you two, stop that noise!'

'I'm sorry,' she apologised when she saw Laura's

expression. 'It's just that I've got the most dreadful headache. I think that bottle must have been corked...'

'Mummy, look what Laura's done,' William demanded, reaching excitedly for the paper aeroplane Laura had made.

'What on earth is it?' she asked, wincing when William showed her by launching the plane towards her.

'Oh, very good!' she told Laura, sniffing disparagingly. 'Although it's hardly rocket science, is it? Hell, I'm sorry,' she apologised contritely and almost immediately. 'I can be such a bitch at times. I don't know what gets into me... Yes, I do,' she corrected herself ruefully. 'It's my way of rebelling against having a perfect mother. Perfect so far as everyone else is concerned, that is. I'm glad you're here, Laura,' she continued. 'You and I have a lot in common. We're both victims of the Fabulous Foursome. Thanks for sorting the kids out, by the way. I was in a real panic when I woke up and realised what time it was.'

'I wasn't sure what their routine was,' Laura told her warily. She wasn't sure she was ready for the instant intimacy that Zoë seemed to want to share with her. In the cold light of day, agreeing to come and work for her looked as though it could be an impulsive decision she was going to regret making. But then, she reminded herself, she had not had much option, had she?

Her face burned as she remembered her row with Nicki.

Kneeling beside her mother's grave the previous day, she had whispered to her, 'At least I've told her now. At least I've done something...' Her tears had flowed as she'd relived the pain and anger she had felt listening to her father betraying her dying mother with Nicki, wanting to remind her father of where his loyalties should lie, wanting to protect her mother too, and hating herself for not being strong enough to do so almost as much as she had hated Nicki for what she'd been doing.

And yet telling Nicki what she had heard, throwing in her face the evidence of her guilt and deceit, had not given her the satisfaction she had anticipated.

'You should have seen Ma's face when I told her that you were going to be looking after the boys,' Zoë gloated.

Laura gave her a startled look.

'Your mother knows that I'm here?'

'Oh, yes,' Zoë confirmed carelessly. 'She thought she was indispensable and that I couldn't manage without her. Well, now she knows she was wrong.'

Laura frowned. All she had told her father was that she had got herself a temporary live-in job.

'Really, I should have done something like this ages ago,' Zoë was saying. 'I mean, with Ian away such a lot it makes sense for me to have someone living in. There's a small studio flat over the garage. It's empty at the moment but it wouldn't take much to get it furnished for you, and that way you would have your own privacy…'

And, far more importantly, she would have Ian to herself when he was at home, Zoë decided. Fortunately Laura wasn't Ian's type, she was too thin, and serious-looking. And as for her clothes! They were sensible enough for wearing around small children but they were hardly sexy, Zoë decided smugly.

'You were going to tell me about the children's routine,' Laura prompted.

'What? Oh, yes. Well, Ian insists that they have

good table manners, and of course I only allow them
to have natural organic foods.'

Silently Laura raised an eyebrow. The fridge and
cupboards when she had opened them this morning
had been full of TV meals and pre-packaged foods.
Not that she objected to what Zoë was saying. She believed in eating healthily herself. Nicki had always
been very particular about the food they all ate, and
indeed she still was.

Irritably Laura reminded herself that Nicki was
supposed to be her enemy, and that therefore, surely,
her cooking was to be despised, even if she did make
the best risotto that Laura had ever tasted!

'They both go to playschool, and then there's their
gym class. I'll give you a list. Oh, God, my head,' Zoë
complained.

'How about a cup of tea and a couple of aspirin?'
Laura suggested.

'The tea, yes, but the aspirin, no,' Zoë replied with a
shudder. 'I doubt my stomach could take them.'

Laura had just finished pouring the tea when
George ran in, announcing excitedly, 'Grandma's
here.'

'Oh, God, no,' Zoë moaned. 'She's come to check up
on you,' she warned Laura. 'Bet you...'

Alice hesitated as George opened the kitchen door
and flung his arms round her. She had been unde-
cided about whether or not she should call, but in the
end, for the sake of the boys, she felt that she had to.

'Hello, Ma,' Zoë greeted her laconically. 'No prizes
for guessing why you're here. Laura, come and be in-
spected by my mother.'

Laura knew that her own face was burning but it
surprised her to see that Alice's was as well.

'Laura made us aeroplanes,' George told Alice. 'Look!'

Alice started to smile as she saw what he was showing her. 'Heavens, it's years since I've seen one of those. I used to make them for the twins.'

'Don't remind me,' Laura heard Zoë muttering.

'Can you make those things that you write words on?' Alice asked Laura reminiscently. 'I remember we made them at school and Nicki—'

'I think so.' Laura laughed.

Really, when she was not being defensive Laura was an obviously confident and attractive young woman, Alice decided. She certainly seemed to have gained the boys' confidence. A little warily, Alice studied Zoë. Her face looked pale and puffy and there was a look in her eyes that warned Alice that she was in one of her most difficult moods.

'I didn't realise you were used to working with children, Laura,' Alice commented gently.

'Ma, I thought you said that Dad had gone to the city for a meeting,' Zoë overrode her rudely.

'Yes, he has,' Alice agreed.

'Well, he wasn't in a meeting when Ian saw him sharing a very intimate lunch with some woman yesterday! According to Ian they were so engrossed in one another that Dad never even saw him.'

Zoë knew that she was embroidering Ian's comments, but it gave her a savage sense of pleasure to see the look in her mother's eyes and to know that she had caught her off guard. It was time that Alice acknowledged that their roles were now reversed and that it was she, Zoë, who had the most power. Ian earned far more than her father, her home was much bigger than her mother's, her circle of friends far, far wider, and as for her sex life, well, she doubted that her mother had ever given her father the kind of satisfaction that she gave Ian. Her mother probably wasn't even properly orgasmic. She wasn't the type!

'I think I'll just take the boys out into the garden whilst it's dry,' Laura suggested diplomatically. Did Zoë regularly drink as much as she had done last night, Laura wondered uneasily, and if she did did Alice know about it?

Alice waited until the door had closed behind Laura and her grandsons before asking Zoë with quiet dignity, 'What exactly are you trying to imply, Zoë?'

'I'm not trying to imply anything,' Zoë denied virtuously. 'I'm just telling you what Ian told me—that he saw Dad having lunch with another woman. You said he told you he had a meeting. I thought that you'd want to know—I certainly would in your shoes! Of course, I can understand how difficult it would be for you if there was someone else. After all, you're totally dependent on Dad financially, aren't you?'

Was this really her daughter, her child, speaking to her like this, deliberately trying to frighten and hurt her? Alice closed her eyes. Her immediate, instinctive reaction was to ask Zoë why she was behaving like this, but she already knew the answer from years of experience. Zoë was behaving like this because this was the way she liked behaving. Because she was Zoë!

'A meeting covers a variety of situations, Zoë,' she responded as calmly as she could. 'Ian—'

'Ian would never be unfaithful to me,' Zoë interrupted her furiously. Her face had gone even whiter, and her voice rose sharply in panic and denial. 'Never!'

Zoë shook her head melodramatically, and as Alice watched she felt a familiar sense of helpless irritation and despair wash over her. Zoë was a first-class architect of confrontational situations, of arguments that always led to the same place—that place being the pain her mother had condemned her to as a child, or so she claimed!

There was no guilt like a mother's guilt, Alice reflected wearily, no sense of failure more aloe-flavoured and haunting than that of a woman who had failed her child.

'Well, for your information—' Zoë continued, stopping abruptly as pain splintered through her head and her stomach heaved.

As she rushed to the cloakroom to be sick Alice followed her, her irritation forgotten in her maternal anxiety. In the enclosed space of the cloakroom Alice could smell the alcohol fumes mixed with the vomit.

Zoë's drinking was something outside her experience, and beyond her comprehension. Heavy drinking as a socially acceptable pastime for young women and one they could openly boast about, describing themselves as 'well bladdered' and 'totally pissed', was an aspect of the modern 'ladette' culture that Alice knew she would never be able to accept with equanimity.

'Zoë!' she protested, unable to stop herself.

'What?' Zoë demanded, flushing the lavatory and splashing her face with cold running water.

'Your drinking,' Alice began uncomfortably.

'What about it?' Zoë asked angrily, heading back towards the kitchen, leaving Alice to follow her. 'Everyone does it, Ma. The days are gone when a woman was only allowed to sip genteelly on a bloody Babycham. Don't you ever read the papers, or watch television? Modern women drink and why the hell shouldn't we? Anyway, haven't you got things you should be doing? Comparing washing powders with all the other has-been miseries, that sort of thing? It's different for us, Ma, we're a different generation, a new generation and we do things our own way. And if that means enjoying a drink and living life, then I'm all for it. Have you any idea just how boring you are, Ma? Personally, I wouldn't blame Dad if he did find someone else. I mean, who stays with the same partner for as long as you and Dad have any more?'

Even as she spoke Zoë could feel her own panic growing. If her father could be unfaithful to her mother…leave her mother…then just how vulnerable did that make her? Her mother had no right to allow such a thing to happen. It couldn't happen, nothing could happen that might threaten her own fragile security. Her parents' marriage was her own benchmark of what security and love was, and she had convinced herself that if she could just mirror her mother's life then her own would be safely secure, *she* would be safely secure. But she still couldn't stop herself from deliberately goading Alice.

'Poor Dad,' she claimed. 'He must be bored out of his mind.'

Alice could feel the anger rolling down over her and with it a desire to retaliate. But Zoë was her daughter, her creation, hers and Stuart's!

Where had they gone wrong? How had they produced a daughter so cynical and self-centred, so implacably determined to put herself first and do whatever she wanted, so devoid of any sense of responsibility towards others, and so devoid too of any responsibility towards herself? Alice had read somewhere that the current late teenagers and early twenty-somethings had been so cosseted by their parents and the system, so protected, so often and unceasingly indoctrinated with the belief that they and their self-esteem were the most important things on earth, that they were completely incapable of understanding, never mind accepting, a situation in which this was not the case.

Which, if it was true, of course meant that the blame lay with their parents, mothers like her.

And she did feel to blame, Alice acknowledged. She felt to blame and, if she was honest, she also felt cheated and angry, cheated of the daughter she would have loved to have had, and angry because Zoë was the way she was.

'Oh, by the way, Ma,' Zoë suddenly announced, 'there's no need for you to keep coming round so often. Not now that Laura's here to look after the boys.'

Alice could feel the pain of her daughter's comment scorching her face.

'I'm very pleased to hear that, Zoë,' she managed to respond calmly, her pride coming to her rescue as she added, 'You see, I'm going to be starting an Open University course in September, and so in future I shan't have as much time to spare.'

Alice thought that her daughter's shocked expression should perhaps have given her more pleasure.

'You're doing what?' Zoë demanded. 'You've got to be joking. You doing an OU course! What on earth for? I mean, what *is* the point? It isn't as though you need a degree, is it, or as though you'll be using it for anything? Oh, I get it,' she derided Alice mockingly. 'It's the empty-nest syndrome thingy, isn't it? Dear Agony Aunt,' she mimicked savagely. 'What shall I do now that all my children are grown up? I suppose Maggie or one of the others have put you up to this, haven't they?'

'Actually, Zoë, it was my own idea,' Alice told her sharply, adding emphatically, 'Contrary to what you seem to think, I am perfectly capable of making my own decisions.'

Laura and the boys were still playing in the garden when Alice left. Both her grandsons came running up to her to hug and kiss her. The fresh air had brought welcome colour to the two small faces, which she often felt were too pale, but George the elder, caught at her heart as he asked her in an anxious voice, 'Is Mummy all right now, Grandma?'

'She's fine,' she reassured him. Over his head her eyes met Laura's and she could see the discomfort in the younger woman's eyes before she looked away.

According to Nicki, Laura was a possessive monster, a potential marriage wrecker, a daughter who hated the thought of anyone else having any kind of emotional relationship with her father. But the boys had obviously taken to her, and Alice knew what would happen if she tried to question Zoë's decision!

As Alice drove away the new mobile that Laura had acquired rang. Immediately she tensed as she saw the number flashing up on her screen and recognised it immediately.

She was reluctant to answer the call, but she knew that sooner or later she would have to respond to it.

Taking a deep breath, making sure that she could see the boys, who were enjoying the unfamiliar freedom of being allowed to exercise their imaginations and play out in the garden, she said firmly, 'Hi, Dad.'

'Laura! Thank goodness! What's going on? Where are you? Are you okay? Why didn't you—?' he began immediately.

'Dad…Dad… Everything's fine,' Laura interrupted him. 'I'm at Zoë's. Alice and Stuart's daughter,' she added. 'I bumped into her in town yesterday and, well, to cut a long story short, she's offered me a live-in job helping out with her sons, and I've taken it!

'Yes, I know that with my qualifications working as a child-minder isn't...but to be honest, right now anything that gets me a roof over my head that isn't also over Nicki's has got to be good news. Look, I'm going to have to go,' she told him. If she stayed on the line he might start asking her about the row she had had with Nicki, and it just wasn't something she wanted to discuss, just as she didn't want to analyse why even mentioning it brought her an unwanted sense of defensiveness. After all, she wasn't the one at fault, was she?

10

After leaving Zoë, Alice went into town. She was committed now. There was no going back, and an uncharacteristic sense of bravado was driving her and energising her. Buoyed up by it, she had decided to buy herself a computer to use during her OU degree course. She had a vague idea of how they worked—thanks to the twins, who had taught her how to receive and send email messages before their departure—but she was reluctant to use the one they and Stuart shared and so had decided to invest in her own.

She knew that either Stuart or indeed Maggie, Nicki or Stella would have been only too pleased to give her their advice as to what she should buy, and in the case of her three friends no doubt help her to learn how to use it properly, but she had made up her mind that it was something she was going to do on her own. She was just coming out of the shop, having listened very carefully to the advice of the young salesman, and opted for the equipment he had recommended, when she saw Stella emerging from the nursery outfitting store on the opposite side of the road.

'Looking for something for Maggie?' Alice asked her with a smile. She was feeling so pleased and excited about her purchase, her reluctance to use anything technical being a joke amongst them all, that she immediately wanted to tell Stella all about it.

'You'll never guess what I've just done!' she began, but, instead of urging her to explain, Stella looked as though she had barely heard her, her frown deepening.

It had caught her off guard to see Maggie in the doctor's surgery when she had gone there with Julie, Stella acknowledged, too engrossed in her own thoughts to pay much attention to what Alice was saying.

Unlike Maggie, who was always so impulsive, Stella preferred to assimilate and chew over things before discussing them. She would have much preferred to tell her friends what had happened at a time of her own choosing, but now of course Maggie already knew.

'Alice, have you made any plans for lunch?' she demanded abruptly. 'Only there's something I want to tell you.'

'Lunch would be lovely,' Alice agreed immediately. She had planned to get home and start clearing out the boxroom that she intended to turn into her study, ready for the delivery of her computer, but automatically she put her own plans on hold, sensing Stella's anxiety.

Ten minutes later, as they faced one another over their warming bowls of home-made soup to keep out the chill of the day, Stella explained tersely, 'We've just found out that Hughie's ex-girlfriend, Julie, is pregnant. That was what Hughie had come home to tell us.'

'Oh, Stella, what a dreadful shock for you,' Alice commiserated sympathetically, knowing instinctively how difficult and upsetting Stella would find such a situation. She was a stickler for order, and for being in control of her life. 'What…what will happen?' Alice hesitated delicately.

'Well, it's too late for… That is, Julie has already made the decision that she intends to have the baby, and sensibly she's also decided that it will be adopted. She and Hughie had already decided that their relationship was over when she found out she was pregnant. She didn't tell him until he came home at Christmas! Apparently she was afraid that pressure would be put on her to have her pregnancy terminated, which she didn't want. Since the baby was conceived during the summer holidays, when they actually told us she was already six months pregnant—she's one of these ultra-slim modern girls and, of course, she's been wearing those huge baggy clothes, so that no one, not even her own mother, guessed.

'Hughie was in such a state of shock that he went back to university in the New Year without telling us—but he recognised that the pair of them couldn't go on keeping it a secret for ever, and that, quite apart from anything else, Julie ought to be receiving proper medical attention and that proper plans needed to be made. He persuaded her to tell her parents, and came home himself to support her and tell us.'

'Well, that's very responsible of him, Stella,' Alice commented tactfully, correctly recognising in Stella's voice her determination to protect and defend her son from any criticism.

'Oh, yes. Well, he is the baby's father, even if he had no idea that…and Julie has made it clear that she has no regrets about them breaking up.'

As she listened to her Alice was trying to imagine how she would feel if one of her sons were in Hughie's position, if she were in Stella's position! The thought of a child, any child, having to be separated from its mother tore at her tender heart, but when that child was also her own grandchild… She said nothing of her feelings to Stella though, partially out of tact and consideration for her and partially because she knew that Stella would deride her for her sentimentality.

'Well, at least you know now,' she began. 'And Julie's parents will—'

'That's the problem,' Stella interrupted, guessing what she was going to say. 'Julie's parents, or rather Julie's father, has refused to do anything. In fact her father has virtually thrown her out!'

'What?' Now Alice couldn't conceal her feelings. 'Oh, the poor girl! Stella, she's barely seventeen…'

'Yes. I know. But according to Rich, who knows him vaguely, her father has very old-fashioned views, and a bit of a chip on his shoulder—something to do with his own upbringing. Anyway, naturally, I've said that Julie must stay with us at least until after the baby's born. We've got the room after all, and, well, I just couldn't not offer to help!'

'Oh, Stella,' Alice repeated. 'Heavens, you must be run off your feet. When is the baby actually due?'

'So far as can be worked out, in a little under three months.'

'Three months!'

'Yes. I know. Fortunately, according to the doctor, both Julie and the baby are healthy. And at least Julie is being sensible enough to give the baby up for adoption, once it's born,' Stella repeated, checking when she saw Alice's expression before Alice could conceal it from her.

'I can see that that would be the most practical thing to do,' Alice agreed carefully.

Stella's mouth compressed. She knew Alice well enough to know she wasn't deliberately trying to have a dig at her, but it still grated to hear both her instinctive use of the word 'practical' and the note of uncertainty in her voice.

'Well, getting all emotional and giving in to sentiment isn't going to help anyone,' she countered more sharply than she had intended. 'Julie is still at school after all, and Hughie is only just in his first year at university. They aren't even a couple any more. And Julie's such a child herself still. I mean, they think they're so grown up, so streetwise, these girls, but in reality... I don't think she has a thought in her head about the baby—not really. Oh, I know she's been determined to make sure that her father can't pressure her into having a termination, but apart from that...' Again she sensed that Alice was hesitant about saying anything.

A little exasperatedly, she exclaimed, 'I suppose I sound dreadfully unsympathetic, but to be honest I'm still in shock!'

'How has Richard taken the news?' Alice asked her.

'Well, you know Richard.' Stella gave a small shrug. 'Other than tearing a strip off Hughie, he hasn't said much at all. I think he's hoping that if he doesn't acknowledge that it's happening, then somehow it won't. He's no more prepared to be a grandfather than Julie is a mother,' she told Alice waspishly. 'I tried to persuade her to come shopping with me today. I know she intends to have the baby adopted, but there are still some things she's going to need.'

'I think that Zoë might still have Will's baby things,' Alice told her. 'I could ask her if she wouldn't mind Julie borrowing them, if you like?'

'Would you?' Stella gave her a relieved look. 'I don't even know where to start—I mean, it's twenty years since I—' She paused and shook her head. 'Do you think that Maggie really knows what she's letting herself in for? She was attending the same antenatal clinic as Julie.'

'Did she say anything about Nicki?' Alice asked her eagerly. 'Have they made things up?'

'Well, she did say that she'd been to see her, but...' Stella frowned. 'I really don't feel I want to get drawn into taking sides, but I was a bit taken aback when Maggie started to hint to me that she felt that Nicki might be having some kind of problem. I mean, it's the oldest defence in the world, isn't it, that kind of emotional manipulation—laying the blame on the other person's shoulders by claiming they have a problem?'

Alice frowned as she heard the underlying criticism in Stella's voice.

'I don't think that Maggie would ever do anything like that. She's never been devious or manipulative.'

Stella raised her eyebrows.

'Hasn't she, Alice? Think back and take off those rose-coloured glasses. When did Maggie ever give up on anything until she'd got us all to do and think exactly what she wanted? The rock band! The weekend in Paris she coaxed you to get Stuart to get us all cheap flights for? That time she encouraged you to dye your hair? The puppy she almost foisted off on Rich and me...to name but a few instances.'

'Oh, yes, but those were all done for a purpose, because she thought it was for the best...a good idea...'

'Mmm, because she thought... You've always put her up on a bit of a pedestal, Alice! If you ask me, she's come up with this suggestion that Nicki "might be having a problem" because it's an excellent get-out for her!'

Alice looked at her uneasily. 'You sound almost as though you agree with what Nicki said.'

'Well, I wouldn't have put it so…dramatically, per-haps, but yes, I do think she has a valid point, if only from a practical point of view. Let's face it, Alice, Maggie has gone through life doing exactly what she wants to do, when she wants to do it. I mean… remember that villa holiday she had you organising, the one we all went on just before it came out about Dan's affair? It was Maggie's idea, but you were the one who ended up doing all the organising.'

'I enjoyed doing it,' Alice protested. Stella's com-ments were making her feel anxious and upset. Their friendship had always been strongly based on their support of one another and yet suddenly it seemed as though what they were actually doing was undermin-ing one another!

'So, like Nicki, you don't approve of what she's do-ing either?' Alice guessed.

'It isn't a matter of approval,' Stella corrected her. 'It's just this habit that Maggie has of pigeon-holing us all. You, the sweet stay-at-home one, with the perfect husband and the perfect marriage, me the sensible, practical, unsexy one, and now Nicki the neurotic one! Right now I think it's probably very convenient for Maggie to draw attention away from her own behav-iour by suggesting that Nicki is reacting against her pregnancy to offset the pressure of other problems in her life! I know that Nicki has Laura living with her—'

'Not any more,' Alice interrupted her.

'What? She's gone back to the city?'

'Not exactly.' Alice took a deep breath. 'As it hap-pens…' She paused, and then continued, 'Zoë has asked Laura to move in with her and look after her boys.'

'What?' Stella yelped. 'Well, we all know what

Zoë's like, but I would have thought she'd have had more sense than to do something like that!'

Alice flushed a little.

'As a matter of fact, Laura is very good with them,' she told her stiffly. 'I called round there this morning.'

Stella realised that she had been tactless.

'Alice, I'm sorry,' she began. 'I didn't mean...'

'It's all right,' Alice reassured her with a smile. 'I was a bit taken aback myself initially, but, truthfully, Laura was really good with the boys. And I won't be able to look after them as much myself once I start on my Open University course. I know I won't be starting it officially until September, but I've got a list of back reading I want to make a start on and, and this morning...'

'Oh, yes, I'd forgotten about that,' Stella acknowledged carelessly. 'So you've told Stuart and Zoë, then?'

'Well, yes, but I haven't been able to discuss it in any great detail with Stuart yet. He's in the middle of a busy time at work. He's away at the moment, in fact, in the city.' Alice paused, her body suddenly tense. There was no logical reason for her to suddenly start feeling anxious and on edge, just because Zoë had said that Ian had seen Stuart having lunch with a woman!

'And as for Zoë,' she told Stella, pushing away her unwanted introspective thoughts, 'she was furious with me the other night when I couldn't have the boys because I was having dinner with all of you.'

'And this is her way of retaliating? Paying Laura to look after them instead?' Stella guessed shrewdly.

Privately Stella was wondering why on earth Zoë needed to have help looking after her children—her 'job' handing out details in the local estate agents' a couple of days a week could hardly be called challenging, and it wasn't even as though she needed the money! Stella didn't want to hurt Alice by mentioning the gossip she had heard about Zoë's behaviour and heavy drinking. After all, they all knew what a difficult child she had been and how hard Alice had always striven to both appease and protect her.

'You mustn't let her bully you, Alice,' Stella reproved her sternly. 'You've done more than enough for her already. You are the boys' grandmother, not their mother, and you of all people deserve to have some "me" time. You've already told us just how much this degree course means to you.'

'It's not so much the course itself,' Alice sighed honestly. 'It's what it represents for me—it's doing something to prove that I'm an intelligent, thinking, viable person and not just Stuart's wife and the children's mother. Am I being unrealistic and selfish, Stella?' she appealed to her friend.

'Certainly not,' Stella told her robustly.

'I do hope that Maggie and Nicki patch things up before our next get-together.' Alice sighed. 'I felt dreadful when Maggie made that comment about wanting our support; as though we'd let her down.'

'You know your trouble, Alice? You're far too tender-hearted,' Stella told her forthrightly.

Later, when they had said their goodbyes, Stella reflected privately that, whilst no one could ever accuse Alice of selfishness, so far as Stella could see she was certainly being unrealistic if she expected either her husband or her family to give up willingly the total dedication to their needs and their egos that Alice had always lavished on them.

She loved Hughie and she loved him with a deep, fierce, protective, maternal love that was the strongest and most intense emotion she had ever experienced, but she had never allowed him to rule her life.

She loved Richard too, of course, but that love… A little uncomfortably Stella acknowledged inwardly that she did not want to either quantify or analyse the degree to which the word 'love' applied to her feelings for her husband!

Apprehensively Nicki placed her hands to her aching temples. Her heart felt as though it were being jerked on a piece of elastic, and then thrown against her chest wall. Her mouth had gone dry and the fear that was filling her was almost a physical presence in the room with her.

It was nearly two o'clock and she had no idea just where the morning had gone!

She had known fear before; as a child at school, a misfit, afraid of the taunts of the other children, and then later as a young wife, lying in bed waiting for Carl to come in, terrified that when he did she might somehow have said or done something that would cause him to lash out at her, sometimes beating her so badly that she had been left unconscious.

Then there had been the fear of other people discovering the truth about her marriage; about her weakness and her inability to have a normal marriage, the kind of marriage where a husband did not physically attack his wife because she was so useless. But thanks to Maggie she had learned how to overcome that fear and to leave it and her marriage behind her.

But that had not been an end of her fears. She had feared loving Kit and then she had feared losing him. She had feared the power that Laura had over him and she had feared the effect of his first wife's death on him. She had feared their breakup and then afterwards she had feared their reconciliation. She had feared hearing him say that he had felt trapped into marrying her because of their making love without using protection.

But her biggest fear of all was for Joey. Joey, her most precious, wonderful child; so much loved, so very, very deserving of being loved and yet surely so much damned by the fact that she was his mother; so much at risk from the vagaries and cruelties of the same vengeful fate that had taken that new life from her, destroyed her baby in her womb.

Just lately she had barely been able to sleep at night for worrying about Joey, afraid to close her eyes in case some dreadful fate befell him due to her negligence, her inability to protect him. Sometimes she felt as though she were just waiting powerlessly for Joey to be hurt—to be destroyed in an act of vengeance whose real target was her! But how could that be fair? She was the one who should be punished, not Joey. No, Joey had done nothing except be born!

Why was she being persecuted like this? Was it because she had already proved herself to be an unfit mother by not being able to protect her new baby? Her heart felt as though someone had flung it hard—too hard—to the floor. The resulting bounce made her feel giddy, breathless, sick.

'Nicki?'

It took her several seconds to register Kit's voice and by that time he had walked into the kitchen, frowning as he looked from the messy kitchen table with its clutter of unwashed mugs to her own congealing breakfast toast, to her uncombed hair and shiny nose.

She couldn't remember him saying that he intended

to come home early and his unexpected arrival made her tense defensively.

'Nicki, are you all right?' Kit demanded.

'I've been busy—working,' she lied defensively. 'One of us has to!'

The air between them smouldered acridly with hostility as she looked belligerently at him. She already knew exactly the sour expression she would see on his face, the downturn of his mouth—the same mouth she had once thought so generous and sexy and exciting; the same mouth she had once loved to touch and kiss, and be touched and kissed by.

'I tried to ring you but you didn't answer,' Kit told her, ignoring her dig. 'So I came home instead to tell you… I thought you'd want to know that I've spoken to Laura. Apparently she's got herself a job working for Alice's daughter, looking after her children, and she's going to be staying there as well.'

Very deliberately Nicki got up and walked away from him.

'Nicki!' she heard him protesting.

'You came home just to tell me that? Why? Laura is *your* daughter,' she told him coldly. 'Not mine. I don't care what she does, Kit, or where she is, just so long as it isn't here! She was trying to hurt Joey,' she reminded him passionately, and as she spoke all the protective fury she had felt on seeing her son cowering away from her stepdaughter came back to her. She had cowered away from Carl, her ex-husband, in just the same way! What was it about her that drew these violent, dangerous people into her life? Was it, as she was beginning to fear, because there was something intrinsically bad about her? Something so bad that she had to be punished, that she deserved to be hurt? Wrapping her arms tightly around her body, she started to rock rhythmically to and fro. She might be bad but Joey wasn't! He didn't deserve...

'Nicki, look.' Kit frowned when she refused to respond or answer him, persisting doggedly, 'The other night we were both overwrought. Things were said...' Her behaviour bewildered him. Nicki had never been a sulker or a manipulator, her choice of weapons was more cerebral than emotional—sound, sustained, calm argument, not emotional pressure.

'I don't care what you say, Kit. I am not having Laura back here—ever. It's Joey you should be thinking about and not her! She wants to destroy our marriage!' Suddenly Nicki was virtually screaming at him. 'And if she could, she would destroy Joey as well!'

Kit took a step back from her, shocked by the fury he could see and hear in her face and voice.

'Nicki, you know that isn't true!' he protested.

'Do I?' Nicki challenged him bitterly.

Helplessly, Kit watched as she got up and left the kitchen, slamming the door angrily behind her, in a warning that he was not to follow her. He could hardly recognise the woman he had fallen so passionately in love with in the person that Nicki had become.

Maybe, with hindsight, it was true that he hadn't been as supportive about her losing the baby as he could have been, but he had still been in shock from the news that she'd been pregnant at all!

Alice opened the door to the boxroom and took a deep breath. It had been later than she had planned when she had got back home. She walked over to the old-fashioned desk that had originally been her father's, and began to open its drawers.

Half an hour later, kneeling on the floor surrounded

by their contents, she wondered ruefully if she might not have made life simpler for herself if she had bought a brand-new modern workstation. If she had, she wouldn't now be faced with wondering what on earth she was going to do with all the memorabilia she had removed from the desk drawers. As she started to stand up she noticed that a couple of photographs had become dislodged from one of the several albums she had removed from the two deepest drawers. Automatically she bent to pick them up.

They were holiday snaps, the first one of her and Stuart, taken a year after they had married. Stuart looked impossibly tanned and sexy and sure of himself, posing in his seventies-style swimwear, whilst she stood at his side, looking pink and gazing up adoringly at him, wearing a towelling bikini, which she remembered she had felt very self-conscious about wearing because of the brevity of the briefs.

She had bought it from a small boutique, feeling flustered and excited, after Stuart had announced that he had booked them a surprise last-minute trip to the Seychelles to celebrate their anniversary—in those days a holiday destination so exotic and exclusive that hardly anyone she knew had known where it was, never mind been there!

For their honeymoon he had taken her to Venice. She had thought herself the most fortunate, the most loved of women then.

In Venice on their honeymoon he had made love to her in a bedroom in what had originally been a Renaissance prince's palace, to the sound of the water lapping against the walls. Afterwards they had sat on their balcony and he had wrapped her in his arms whilst they'd watched the reflection of the huge full moon on the lagoon.

They had spent hours exploring the city on foot and by water, and hours too making love. There was something about the very air of Venice that breathed sensuality. When she had said as much once to Stella, she remembered that her friend had laughed and said that, so far as she was concerned, Venice's air breathed bad drains!

They had had such plans then, she and Stuart. She had loved the excitement and the intimacy of travelling with him. In that first year of their marriage they had visited over a dozen European cities, each visit a tiny glowing jewel of happiness to be stored away in her private memories.

The holiday in the Seychelles had been especially special, the island the nearest place to paradise she could possibly have imagined. Zoë had been conceived there, and it had also been there that Stuart had persuaded her to go skinny-dipping with him. In fact, she had always suspected that Zoë had been conceived whilst they had been skinny-dipping, although Stuart had always claimed it was impossible for her to know that.

He had been so thrilled when she had told him that she thought she was pregnant, and so jealous when Zoë had been born. She could still remember how pulled between them she had felt. Zoë had seemed to have the knack of waking up screaming the moment Stuart had touched her, and Stuart for his part had always seemed to want her attention the most when Zoë had been at her most demanding and difficult. She had often wondered if he would have behaved in the same way had Zoë been a boy, and had felt dreadfully guilty for that thought. As the only one of the four of them to have had a baby at that stage, she had half expected that the other three would grow as irritated by the maternal demands on her time as Stuart, but instead they had proved wonderfully supportive.

It had been Stella who had decided, when she had not been able to get a babysitter so she could come and join them for a meal, that they would come to her and they would bring the meal with them. It had been Nicki who had booked her into a local beauty salon for a 'full works' treatment, as a special birthday surprise, and Maggie who had come and spent the day with Zoë to make sure that she could enjoy it.

There had been pressures on them then that could have fragmented their friendship but that had only strengthened it, so why now, after all these years, did it suddenly seem as though they were pulling against one another?

Tucking the photograph back inside the album, she picked up the other one.

Coincidentally it had been taken on the group holiday they had all shared and which Stella had referred to earlier. As Stella had said, it had been Maggie who had suggested that they all go away together, but Alice had been the one who had organised everything. She remembered how much she had enjoyed doing so. Making lists, keeping files...organising!

'You should do this on a professional basis,' Maggie had teased her admiringly.

'Alice run a business? Never!' Stuart had laughed. She had laughed too, but secretly she had been hurt by his comment.

Was Oliver right? Was she wrong to want to shield Nicki, to protect her and to give her the benefit of the doubt? This wasn't a situation she could deal with on her own, Maggie recognised, putting down the contract she had been trying to read.

They might have talked everything through and
made up their quarrel, but that didn't alter the fact
that the letter was still there, its malevolence lying
heavily on her heart, seeping slowly out to poison her
trust and her happiness. She needed to talk about
what had happened, and how she felt, she recognised.
She needed the help, the support, the comfort of sharing her fears with her closest friends. The friends who,
unlike Oliver, knew Nicki every bit as well as she did
herself. And who, also unlike Oliver, would be able to
give her opinions that were unbiased and non-
judgemental.

Of the four of them, Stella was the most practical,
the most analytical. On the point of dialling Stella's
number, Maggie hesitated. She had felt the ambiguity
of Stella's attitude when she had initially told them
her news, and Stella now had problems of her own.
Alice would understand, though, and like her she
would want to do what was best for Nicki as well. Unlike Oliver she would understand how and why
Maggie felt so protective towards her, so reluctant to
acknowledge the truth of Oliver's insistence that the
letter could really not have come from anyone else!

Quickly she dialled Alice's number.

Alice had just finished finding the photograph albums a new home when the phone rang.

'Maggie!' She began to smile and then stopped, asking anxiously instead, 'Is everything all right...the
baby...?'

'The baby's fine,' Maggie assured her, swallowing
hard as she fought back the impulse to say, But I'm
not!

She had been worrying for hours about what she
should do, not just for her own sake but for Nicki's as

well, and now she was desperate to unburden herself to someone she knew would understand.

'Alice… I… There's something I wanted to talk to you about. I…I wondered if I could come round. I need your advice… I'm worried, Alice, about Nicki,' Maggie burst out. She couldn't tell Alice about the letter over the phone!

On the other end of the line, Alice felt her heart drop.

'Maggie, I do understand how…how upset you must have been by Nicki's reaction to your news,' Alice responded awkwardly, 'but…well, it was a shock for all of us, and… Well, baby hormones do make one…what I mean is, I shouldn't take Nicki's comments too much to heart if I were you. I mean, she is under a lot of pressure what with Laura, and Kit's business not doing very well. She probably spoke in the heat of the moment, and you know sometimes things are said that are best overlooked. We've all been friends for such a long time… I don't think any of us would want…' Uncomfortably her voice trailed away.

'I understand what you're trying to say, Alice,' Maggie told her. She was unable to stop herself adding bleakly, 'I wonder if you can understand, though, how it feels to know that my baby is the cause of… I wanted him or her to have your love, Alice, not to be rejected by you all before even being born!' Maggie burst out emotionally. Closing her eyes in despair, she acknowledged that now she had probably totally confirmed Alice's awkwardly expressed belief that she was suffering from an overdose of emotionalism.

'Maggie, of course we'll all love your baby,' Alice soothed her. 'It's just that… Please don't take this the wrong way, will you, but, well, life's not entirely easy for the rest of us right now. Of course, that doesn't mean that we aren't happy for you, of course we are,' Alice told her hastily.

'But what's happening to me isn't that important?' Maggie supplied for her. 'Well, it was important enough for Nicki to—' Abruptly she stopped. All she had wanted to do was to discuss her fears with Alice, to get together with her and Stella and show them the letter she had been sent…to ask them to assure her that it could not possibly have come from Nicki.

'Of course we care, Maggie,' Alice told her gently. 'It's just that— Look, we'll be getting together as usual in three weeks' time. I'm sure by then that Nicki will have calmed down and come round.' She stopped speaking as a small warning sound indicated that she had another call coming through, and when she looked at her telephone screen she could see that her caller was Stuart ringing on his mobile.

'Maggie, I have to go,' she exclaimed urgently. 'Stuart's trying to get through and I do need to speak to him.'

Quickly she ended the call, but it was too late. Stuart had hung up, having left her a message.

Maggie looked bleakly at the phone. So much for confiding in her friends and getting their advice, she reflected a little bitterly.

Despite the centrally heated warmth of the room, Maggie gave a tiny little shiver. She knew that in general other people thought of her as someone who didn't allow things to get her down, someone who was continually pushing back the boundaries, someone who took risks, who was upbeat, optimistic, and self-confident. But they were other people, not her closest friends! They, she had always believed, knew different—better! They knew and understood her as no one else could. Her need of their support, their closeness—the bond between them went very, very deep for her. Their shared friendship was of primary importance to her and she valued it as such. That had always been a given for her, one of the strongest foundations on which their friendship was built. For them, with them, she had no need to pretend, or to be brave and resilient! To them she would always be able to turn. That was what she had believed, just as they in turn could always come to her.

Now shockingly, disturbingly, she was questioning whether the others shared those feelings. If she was perhaps alone. And that was a very frightening and alienating place to be, Maggie recognised soberly.

The poison pen letter was on the table in front of her. She looked at it as bleak despair filled her. Had she been wrong after all to insist to Oliver that he allow her the right to deal with the situation herself?

A little uncertainly Alice dialled the number of Stuart's mobile. She had played the message he had left for her—a terse announcement that he might be tied up in meetings in London for longer than he had originally anticipated, and that he did not as yet know which day he would be returning home. 'Don't ring back,' he had instructed her. 'I'm going straight into a meeting now, and I don't know when I'll be free. I'll ring you.'

That had been over two hours ago, and he still hadn't rung back. She had tried to ring him, but his mobile was switched off.

11

Dan grimaced as he swung the SUV off the road and into the narrow rutted lane that led to Draycotte Manor. He had only picked the vehicle up the previous evening and was still getting used to it. Another thing he was going to have to get used to, he reminded himself grimly, was to drop his acquired Americanisms and revert to his native English. The top-of-the-range Land Rover he had just acquired was a four-wheel drive, and not a Sports Utility Vehicle.

It was a surprisingly mild day. One of those days that teased you into believing that summer was really only just around the corner, even though common sense and experience should be telling you that it was no such thing!

He still wasn't sure just why he had decided to turn his back on the life he had made for himself in America. And as for his decision to view Draycotte Manor! Pure nostalgic self-indulgence.

Dan gave a small wry shrug. He was fifty-five and he had worked his ass off for the last ten years. In fact he had worked so damned hard that he had gained a reputation in New York and the Hamptons, where so many of his clients owned properties, for being a confirmed workaholic. And for what?

He hadn't even been in New York on nine eleven. But what decent-thinking human being could put their hand on their heart and say honestly that they hadn't been affected by the trauma of the event at some deep and profound level? Surely it was impossible to be human and not to feel the shock waves that had rocked the world?

He could see the house in front of him now—an ancient tangle of buildings, parts of which dated back as far as the fourteenth century.

The course of the financial ups and downs of those who had lived in it could be charted from the various additions, both in bricks and mortar and to the land.

It was far too large for his needs, and it would cost a fortune to turn it into anything like a comfortable modern home. The agents themselves had as good as admitted that! Financially it would make more sense to knock it down and start again, although since it was listed that would be impossible.

The land was in an even worse state than the house, thanks to the combination of bad management and lack of investment, plus a disastrous venture by a previous owner who had attempted to turn part of it into a pheasant shoot and had had the full force of a very wrathful and powerful local anti-bloodsports group turned against him for his pains. As a result, so Dan had been told, the local area was awash with semi-tame escaped pheasants, plus a band of marauding peacocks, which had apparently been bought in an ill-fated attempt to open the house to the public.

His architectural training told him that taking on the house would be like pouring money into a bottomless pit, and if a client had come to him saying that he wanted to buy it Dan would have strenuously tried to persuade him not to do so.

It was just nostalgia that had brought him here, he told himself as he stopped his Land Rover beside the half-collapsing outbuildings. There was no way he could ever be tempted to buy it. Not even if it had come without the listing and wrapped up with a twenty-four-carat planning agreement to knock it down and rebuild it as an investment!

Although he didn't lack the money. He had sold the architectural practice and consultancy he had set up in New York for a sum that put him very comfortably into the millionaire class.

He had the money—and he certainly did need the challenge! And the sense of continuity, of passing a small part of himself into the future, in a way that a man who had fathered children took for granted, Dan told himself grimly as he automatically redirected his thoughts.

He had sold up and stopped work, he reminded himself firmly. He already owned a property in France and another in Florida. If he really felt he had to have a home in Britain, then he should be looking at a modern, purpose-built, low-maintenance apartment, and not this haphazard collection of other men's broken dreams and hopes!

'Hi there!'

'Todd!' The art of flirtation had never been one of Stella's accomplishments but this was the first time she had found herself so intensely and immediately regretting its lack, she acknowledged as she tried to control her foolish, flustered reaction to the unexpected sight of him.

'I was just on my way to have a coffee.' He mentioned the name of a well-known chain of American coffee bars that had just opened in the high street. 'Can I persuade you to join me?'

He was wearing sunglasses against the bright glare

of the unexpected sudden burst of mild weather, and he removed them as he spoke to her so that, heart-stoppingly, she was suddenly looking right into his eyes. The sensation was so intimate that it fused her to the spot.

'Persuade' was the wrong verb, Stella admitted, shakily aware of just how fiercely electrical the charge thrilling down her spine was, of her whole body's high-octane physical response. She grappled for a disgracefully short few seconds with her conscience, before quickly accepting his invitation, and experiencing the totally unfamiliar sensation of wishing she were wearing something more exciting than jeans and an old suede jacket over a plain white shirt.

It didn't seem to matter that that coffee bar would normally be her last choice of somewhere to have coffee, or that her coffee shop of choice was normally the small café run by two elderly sisters, whose clientele was several decades removed from the young mothers and bleary-eyed teenagers who were the predominant customers of this new concession.

It was sheer bliss to have Todd walk on the outside of the pavement as he escorted her protectively towards the coffee bar, opening the door for her, and—had she imagined it?—actually pausing as she went through it to look down into her eyes and give her a smile that reduced the universe to the small circle of intimacy that suddenly seemed to be enclosing them in a very private and very dangerous little bubble.

'This is a real piece of good luck,' he told her. 'I was going to get in touch with Paul to ask him to let me have your phone number.'

'You...you were?'

She was stuttering with a self-consciousness that even a girl as young as Julie would have probably derided with lip-curling contempt, Stella admitted to herself. Hopefully she could blame the sudden colour burning her face on the heat of the coffee bar. The heat burning her body was a different matter!

Stella's admiration for Todd grew as he not only managed to find an empty table, but also, miraculously, persuaded the blank-eyed teenager who had turned her back on them when they'd walked in to abandon her conversation with her friends and to remove the used plates from the table and wipe it down for them.

'What will you have?' Todd asked her. 'Or do I have to guess? They say that you're either a tea or a coffee person! I've never been a tea drinker—unlike my ex-wife,' he added disparagingly.

Mentally consigning her secret longing for a cup of strong, hot tea into oblivion, Stella smiled and lied enthusiastically that coffee was quite definitely her choice of drink, wondering at the same time just what on earth had come over her!

The smile he gave her was toe-curlingly sexy, she acknowledged as she watched him walk towards the counter. It was a very novel sensation, being treated with all those little man-to-woman courtesies that she had deemed ridiculously unimportant and even laughably out of date and old-fashioned as a young woman, but which now suddenly were a blissful pleasure that made her feel wonderfully feminine and cherished. A pleasure that the role into which Maggie and the others had thrust her had denied her, she reminded herself.

Todd was still standing at the counter. As she'd noticed before, he was lean enough to look good in the jeans he was wearing and mature enough to have had the good sense to team them with a good quality soft checked shirt instead of trying to emulate a younger generation.

Idly she wondered about his private life. Somehow he did not strike her as the sort of man who would spend his evenings falling asleep in front of the television, as Richard did.

No, there was something openly vigorous about Todd; something vibrant and…exciting. Exciting. A tiny thrill of forbidden speculation was stirring her senses; an awareness that she was very conscious of the breadth of his shoulders, the narrowness of his waist and the muscular definition of his backside, and that the awareness had a sexual undertow to it that she should not be allowing it to have.

'These kids make me feel so old,' Todd complained with a rueful shake of his head as he came to sit down and handed her her coffee. 'Mind you, I suppose in their eyes I am! My grandchildren will soon be their age, after all.'

Stella sipped her coffee. It was aromatic, but slightly bitter, and the huge mug contained far too much for her.

'Have you made any firm plans for them to come over to see you yet?' she asked him, guessing how much he wanted to talk about them.

'Unfortunately, no. It's still under negotiation! However, I am hoping that it won't be too long before I have them here. But before I do, I am going to have to find somewhere else to live. The flat I'm currently renting is fine for me, but it only has one bedroom. I've just been to the estate agents', but, to be honest, I would appreciate a little more help than they were able to give me. I don't suppose that you…' He paused and waited, whilst Stella's heart thudded furiously. He was asking her to help him. He wanted her to...her mind automatically baulked at what she was thinking. She was letting her imagination run away with her, because of her flustered reaction to the unexpected sight of him, she told herself severely. Men did not proposition women like her, not even discreetly, cloaking their intentions in outwardly legitimate requests!

And if by some remote chance Todd was actually coming on to her, then of course she was going to refuse to...

'I'd be pleased to do whatever I can to help,' she told him a little breathlessly, 'but I must warn you that I'm no expert so far as property is concerned!'

'I was thinking more of other things, like whether or not an area might be a good one for kids, what the facilities are, and what the drawbacks could be. That kind of thing. Where local knowledge makes a difference,' Todd told her smoothly.

He was looking right into her eyes, focusing on her with the kind of intensity surely more appropriate for lovers. She reached for her drink and discovered that her hand was trembling. Quickly she snatched it away, but Todd stopped her, taking hold of it.

'What's wrong?' he asked her softly. 'Frightened of getting burned?'

This could not be happening...not to her.

'The cup is hot.' She heard herself half stammering and half whispering, as though she were a mere teenage girl and not a mature woman!

Todd was smiling at her. And he was still holding onto her hand!

'You really are an incredibly sexy woman,' he told

her outrageously, and surely untruthfully. 'But I expect you already know that. Your husband is a very lucky man.'

Stella goggled at him.

No one—*no one*—had ever, ever, described her as 'incredibly sexy' and just for a second she wished that the others had been here to hear it! To hear her, practical, sensible Stella, being described by a man like Todd as 'incredibly sexy'! And then reality broke into her little daydream, and she snatched her hand back from Todd, giving him a reproving look.

'Well, today has definitely been my lucky day. And not just because I'll be getting the benefit of your advice, but because I'll be enjoying the pleasure of your company as well! How can I get in touch with you?'

Dizzily Stella gave him her address and mobile number.

All she was doing was arranging to help him, she told herself later. After all, helping him to find somewhere to live was hardly indulging in anything clandestine or lover-like, was it?

Was it?

Maggie stared unseeingly out of the kitchen window. She had barely slept, waking over and over again during the night from horrifying dreams, her face wet with tears, which Oliver had wiped away as he'd comforted her.

Oliver had begged her to go to the office with him this morning.

'Don't be silly,' she scolded him, adding gently, 'Nothing's going to happen, Oliver. I won't let it. Not to me and most of all not to our baby. But, please, you have to trust me and let me do what I believe is right. We agreed that you would,' she reminded him firmly.

'I don't like leaving you here on your own,' he protested, but they both knew that he couldn't cancel his morning's appointments at such short notice, and, besides, Maggie did not want him to. This was something she had to come to terms with on her own, for all their sakes.

But the morning had dragged. She felt sapped of her normal energy, nervous and on edge, starting at every sound, uncomfortable with the solitude of her own thoughts, but unable to dismiss them. She ought to go and see Nicki, but she knew that she would not— could not—do so. She felt too fragile, too bruised…too afraid? But neither could she allow Oliver to do what he had wanted to do and hand the letter to the police. She was, she admitted, still desperately trying to cling to a tiny thread of hope that there would be an explanation, that Nicki would get in touch with her, and that somehow things could be put right!

At lunchtime she had pushed away her meal barely touched, and now… She had folded the letter up and put it to one side, refusing to keep on re-reading it, but its words were burned into her memory.

How could Nicki have done it? And why? They had always been so close, shared so much!

The Nicki she knew and loved might disapprove of what she, Maggie, had done, but she would never, ever do something so calculatedly cruel and damaging. Not Nicki, who had suffered so much herself!

But a tiny niggling worm of doubt refused to go away as she remembered the way Nicki had reacted to her news, her vehemence, her fury, the sheer un-Nickiness of her response.

It still hurt, too, that Alice had not made any attempt to get in touch with her after her phone call to her yesterday, and that neither she nor Stella had somehow telepathically recognised her need and responded to it, even though she told herself sternly that she was being unreasonable and irrational.

There was, after all, nothing to stop her telephoning them. No, nothing at all, other than a painful feeling of alienation, and, surely ridiculously, of being an outsider!

Suddenly she couldn't stay in the house any longer, with her tormented thoughts going round and round in circles. She had to go out, breathe fresh air…escape!

Maggie had told herself that she was simply driving around aimlessly, but as soon as she saw the turning for Draycotte Manor she knew that somewhere deep down inside herself she had meant to come here. To this special place where she had come so many times before, seeking solitude and peace; seeking to renew herself and reaffirm all those things in life that were so important to her.

Once this had been her and Dan's special place: their wish-fulfilment house, the place they had laughingly told themselves would one day be theirs if by some miracle they became millionaires!

She had come here to cry over Dan and to grieve for the love she had lost, the emptiness of life without him; to mourn his loss in the places they had made their own.

And after Dan had gone and she had been left with the empty shell of her life, so cracked and damaged that it had literally taken her years to painfully collect all the pieces and painstakingly patch them together, she had still come here. To remember and to listen to her own thoughts, to be grateful for all that she had had and all that was still to come.

The last time she had come here had been the day after she'd finally acknowledged Oliver's love. She had come to say a final goodbye to the house, a final thank-you for all that it had given her. To tell it that, now she had Oliver, she no longer needed to lean on the emotional security of the dreams and the hopes it had kept, in secret and in safety, for her!

Engrossed in her own thoughts, parking her own car in front of the main house, Maggie didn't notice the four-wheel drive vehicle tucked neatly almost out of sight round the side of the ramshackle stable block.

Oliver frowned as he stared at his office wall. He had hated leaving Maggie this morning, knowing how upset she had been during the night. They might have made up their original quarrel, but he still felt sharply, painfully aware that at some very deep level she didn't totally trust him to be able to protect her and keep her safe, when she still thought that the full responsibility of looking after herself rested on her own shoulders. When she doubted his judgement!

Had he been Dan, would she have behaved in the same way, or would she have allowed him to decide what should be done? Would she have felt she could rely on him to protect her and their child?

Oliver's frown deepened. He had recognised very early on in their relationship that a part of him was always going to be jealous of Maggie's ex-husband, just as a part of her was always going to love him, even if Maggie herself insisted that this was not so.

Sometimes he felt as though he knew her better than

she did herself. And the truth was, no matter how much Maggie herself might try to deny it, there was a part of her that she tried to keep hidden that was so intrinsically generous and loving that it was impossible for her not to gift that love to those she cared about.

Nicki was a case in point. Oliver was sure that Maggie must be as aware as he was himself that that letter could logically only have come from Nicki, and yet Maggie had still stood by her friend and defended her. He must not upset Nicki.

Upset Nicki! What about Maggie? Didn't she deserve not to be upset? How could they be so absorbed in their own lives, and so selfishly oblivious to Maggie's longing to be a mother?

Maggie had never told them the truth about her marriage to Dan as she had him, Oliver reminded himself.

'Oliver?'

He looked up as Kath, their office administrator, knocked briefly on his half-open door and walked in.

'There's someone outside asking to see Maggie. She hasn't got an appointment. She said she was hoping she could have a chat about a proposition she wants to put to her.'

'I'll have a word with her,' Oliver told her. 'Where is she now?'

'She's in the outer office going through one of Maggie's albums.'

Oliver smiled. Maggie had kept photograph albums of all projects, and there were copies in their reception area for visitors to look at.

At Oliver's own instigation, a more modern visual treatment incorporating small details from a variety of projects had been turned into a series of stunningly arty wall displays, and Maggie had enthused excitedly over what he had done.

As he walked into the reception area the woman was standing with her back to him studying one of his displays.

'These are good,' she said as she turned to smile at him. 'Your work?'

'Yes,' Oliver confirmed. 'I'm Oliver Sanders, by the way, and you are…?'

'Yes, I thought you must be.' She beamed. 'I've learned such a lot about Maggie that I feel I know her already. She began the business after her marriage broke down, didn't she? I really admire her for that. And you're the arty one. You look as though you would be. I've been told that I'm rather arty myself.' Her smile faltered. 'Unfortunately, though, I haven't been able to develop that side of my nature as much as I would have liked. Necessity has meant that I've had to take on a rather more mundane type of work. We aren't all as lucky as Maggie. And she has been lucky, hasn't she? She says as much herself, I know. Even more lucky, now that she has met you!'

Although she was still smiling, her voice had developed a slightly sharp undertone, and Oliver wondered when she was going to get to the point of her visit. He might have promised Maggie that he wouldn't do anything about that letter, but he was far from convinced that he ought to have given in to her. The police should be informed. What if there were more? What if…?

'Of course, I know that Maggie's services don't come cheaply. They wouldn't, would they? And my little venture will probably be much smaller than she's used to. Rather beneath her notice, I suppose, really.'

The woman gave a sigh. 'It must be wonderful to be as successful as Maggie is. To be able to afford to have anything you want. To buy anything you want.'

Oliver focused on her. The woman really was a little bit odd. Not that she looked it particularly. She was too nervy for his taste, moving edgily around the reception area, picking things up and putting them down again, her eyebrows drawn together in a dissatisfied frown that matched the tone of her voice.

'It's a pity that Maggie isn't here,' she was adding. 'It was her I wanted to see, really. Where is she?'

'She's actually out seeing a client, I'm afraid,' Oliver told her, untruthfully. He had met her type before, and experience told him that she was all too likely to demand that Maggie come into the office to see her if she knew that she was at home.

'If you'd like to leave your name and address, I can get her to get in touch with you,' he offered.

'Yes, I suppose I should do that,' she agreed, her voice suddenly vague. 'Only, you see, I was hoping that I could see her today. I thought that she would be here.'

Oliver had had enough.

'Well, I'm sorry, but she isn't,' he told her shortly.

He knew that Maggie was the one who had started the business and that she was the one who people tended to associate with it. Normally it didn't bother him in the least when people insisted that it was her they wanted to deal with, but for some reason this woman was really getting under his skin.

Because he was still worrying about that letter?

Perhaps if he just went round to see Nicki himself…
He had, after all, only agreed not to contact the police, and in his view Nicki needed to be made aware of the

criminality of what she was doing—instead of being shielded by Maggie out of loyalty, and potentially to her own detriment. So far as he was concerned, Maggie needed to be protected, whether she was prepared to acknowledge as much herself or not!

The woman was leaving, much to Oliver's relief.

The office door opened and Kath walked in.

'I've got to go out,' Oliver told her, coming to a decision. 'I'm not sure how long I'm going to be. If Maggie rings, tell her… Tell her… Tell her I love her!' he told Kath gruffly.

12

Although she had the selling agent's details on the car seat next to her, Maggie didn't make any attempt to read them—she didn't need to, and anyway she hadn't come here to look round the house.

This wasn't somewhere she would want to live with Oliver and their baby. No, for them she wanted something like Alice's home, a sturdy 1930s architecturally designed house with a large garden and some land—there were several of them in the area.

No, she hadn't come here to Draycotte Manor to view it as a potential buy. So why had she come?

Swinging her legs out of the car, she stood up and took a deep lungful of air.

Somehow the air here at Draycotte always tasted different. The house was built on a small and indiscernible hill, which raised it slightly higher than the surrounding land. It also had clear views to the distant hills, and three fields away an ancient river meandered lazily through its equally ancient water meadows. Perhaps it was these things that gave its air its unique taste!

Of old, soft-focused dreams and tender, cherished hopes? Of a wistfulness and the now gentle ghost of a pain once so sharp that she had hardly been able to bear it?

But that had been then…this was now.

As she headed for the small summer house in the garden, which had always been one of her favourite spots, the sun glinted on the warm richness of her hair, the breeze tousling her curls. She lifted her hand automatically to push them away, and that was when Dan saw her, rounding the corner of the stables he had been inspecting. He came to an abrupt halt, whilst his heart hammered against his ribs as though he were still a hormone-driven schoolboy, and his mouth went dry with eagerness and apprehension.

Maggie! Even though she was standing half turned away from him, he knew immediately it was her. The different hairstyle, the unfamiliar clothes, even the fact that his wedding ring no longer showed a soft gold band on her finger made no difference. He would have known her in a hundred other women, a thousand.

He closed his eyes in a reluctant salute to his own senses and waited for the world to stop rocking beneath his feet.

He waited for her to turn round and look at him, to sense him. To come running towards him, her curls flying, her arms outstretched, her eyes alight with love and happiness.

He could see the arch of her eyebrow, the hollow of her eye socket, those ridiculously long lashes she had always had, the rounded curve of her cheekbone and the tender line of her jaw. There was something about her that would always and for ever give her that certain special youthfulness. Even in old age she would still possess it, and she was far from close to old age now.

To Dan, familiar with the nipped and tucked faces and bodies of New York women who fought time with the same aggressive, single-minded determination with which they fought everything else, including any other woman foolhardy enough to try to take their man, Maggie's face had a genuine youthfulness about it that caught at his heart.

This was their place, the place where they had laughed, lived and loved. And the place where they had cried. He could almost feel those emotions surrounding him now.

Maggie! Her name filled his heart. Flooded it.

Maggie stopped in mid-step, suddenly unsure about whether she actually wanted to be here. The sun was still shining, the air was still warm, but somehow she felt as though the weight of her past sadness were actually chilling the air.

She had brought Nicki here once, when she had been trying to persuade her that she was strong enough to leave Carl. She had told her that this was a special place, a place that would give her courage and make her feel empowered, but Nicki had shaken her head and laughed, denying that she could feel the essence of the place in the same way that Maggie did.

Nicki! Instinctively Maggie placed her hand protectively against her still-flat stomach.

The sun had gone behind a cloud, the wind abruptly developing a sharp bite. Shivering a little, Maggie told herself that she was stupid for having come here.

She had a relaxation and yoga class for pregnant women to attend, she reminded herself.

And Nicki?

She would talk to her, she promised herself, but not today. Not yet.

Dan held his breath as Maggie turned round. All she had to do to see him was to look towards the stables. All he had to do to talk to her was to call her name.

Some places, some things were best not revisited, Maggie acknowledged as she got back into her car and started the engine.

Bleakly Dan watched her as she drove away.

He shouldn't have come here, and he didn't really know why he had!

Nicki stared at the clock on the wall. Was it really nearly three o'clock?

A little uncertainly, she looked at her desk. What had she done all day? Where had the time gone?

It was almost time for her to pick Joey up from school, but first she had to go into town to post a parcel. Her heart was still beating heavily and somehow out of rhythm, so that each heavy thud increased her sense of nausea and disorientation.

Upstairs she splashed cold water on her face and then stared at her reflection in the bathroom mirror. Frighteningly, there was nothing there that she felt she could recognise; no sign of the woman whom Kit had claimed that he loved! Nicki could feel her anxiety levels cranking up and tightening.

Her tee shirt looked slightly grubby and she studied it critically, somehow distanced from and unconnected to the angry feeling of contempt her refusal to change it was causing her. In fact, oddly, there was almost a feeling of grim satisfaction in her own scruffiness, her own lowering of her strictly adhered-to standards. What did it matter if she didn't change it? Who cared how she looked? Who even noticed? Certainly not Kit. No, he was far too busy thinking about his precious Laura!

* * *

Oliver turned into the road that led to Kit and Nicki's house. All the way over from the office he had been rehearsing what he would say; how he could best deal with the situation and let Nicki know how dangerous what she had done was! How could she call herself Maggie's friend and send a letter like that? Why had she done it? He would be perfectly justified in going to the police, and he intended to tell Nicki as much, and Kit too, if he was there. Nicki needed to be made to understand that, unlike Maggie, he was not prepared to protect and shield her. No, the person his protection was for was Maggie herself, and of course their unborn child.

Oliver was the first to admit that he owed it to Maggie to recognise not just the strength of the bond the four women shared, but also her right to make her own decisions. But he had decisions that needed to be made as well, objectives, agendas; and right at the top of them was Maggie. If she could not protect herself, then he was damn well going to make sure that he did.

He had no idea what spite, what malice, what sheer cruelty was motivating Nicki, and right now he didn't care! Not about her, not about her problems, not about the friendship she was so obviously trading on. All he cared about was Maggie, and he intended to let Nicki know that if she so much as dared to give Maggie even a look that suggested that she was not overjoyed for her, then he, Oliver, would know about it and he would have no compunction whatsoever in taking both her letter and his own suspicions to the police! Which was, after all, what he ought to be doing right now anyway!

And yet…and yet… Abruptly Oliver brought his car to a halt several houses away from Kit and Nicki's.

Maggie had asked him for a promise and he had

given it to her. What was a relationship worth if it was not based on trust, on the belief that the other person would keep their word once given? Maggie trusted him. She trusted him to keep his promise to her, not to do anything about the letter or his suspicions.

Yes. She trusted him. She trusted him to protect her and their unborn child, he argued passionately with himself. And he would be ignoring that trust if he did not speak with Nicki!

But if he went behind her back…

It would be for her own good…to protect her….

To protect her from the pain of receiving another vile letter, but how could he protect her from the pain of knowing that she could not trust him?

Sombrely Oliver put the car in reverse.

He had almost turned round when his mobile rang. Completing the manoeuvre, he switched off the car engine and answered the call.

'Oliver, where are you?'

Just the sound of Maggie's voice was enough to lift his heart.

'In the car. Why?'

'I was wondering if you could get home early?' Maggie responded.

'Why, what is it? Is something wrong?' Immediately he felt concerned—anxious, cursing his own folly in not going ahead and seeing Nicki.

On the other end of the line Maggie forced herself to smile. She had spent enough time worrying and agonising. She owed it to Oliver and to the baby to concentrate her time, her energy, her love on them. After all, she reflected a little bitterly, no one else seemed to want them, or her—certainly not the friends who suddenly seemed so frighteningly remote and distant.

This afternoon at Draycotte Manor, she had felt as

though she had undergone a small death, and she had left with a sense of loss and of loneliness. But driving away she had reminded herself firmly that she had a new life to nurture, and that she had Oliver's love to help her do so. She knew that a part of her would always mourn the friendship she felt she had lost, without knowing how or why she had lost it.

Taking a deep breath, she told Oliver, 'No, everything is fine. More than fine. In fact, it's so fine that I think that tonight we should celebrate! After we've gone and got totally blissed out on nursery shopping. Do you realise that we are running out of time to get this baby, our baby supplied with a new home?' Maggie paused and then, determined to be upbeat, continued brightly, 'I've been thinking. What we could really do with is a house something like Alice and Stuart's. What do you think?'

'It's a great house,' Oliver confirmed, too relieved to hear the happiness and excitement in her voice to care where they lived, so long as it made her happy.

'That's good,' Maggie laughed. 'Because I've jumped the gun a bit and been in touch with a relocation agent, asking them to search one out for us. When do you think you can get home? I'm dying to shop. And not just shop,' she whispered teasingly, a husky meaningfulness deepening her voice.

'I'm on my way,' Oliver assured her fervently.

'So what did you think of Draycotte Manor?' the young man in the estate agents' office asked Dan eagerly. 'I would have sent someone to view it with you, but, as I explained, unfortunately we're unexpectedly short-staffed today.'

'It doesn't matter,' Dan assured him truthfully. 'And anyway...' He paused. Of course he wasn't interested in buying the manor. That wasn't why he had gone to see it. Anyone even thinking of taking it on would have to be half crazy and have a bottomless wallet to finance their craziness.

'It's in one hell of a condition,' he heard himself saying.

'The executors of the late owners' estate are prepared to negotiate,' the estate agent told him swiftly. 'In fact, if you like I could arrange for you to meet with them today...'

'Hey.' Dan stopped him. 'I'm not really...'

'Look, why don't you sleep on it?' the other man was pressing him. 'I mean, the land itself could be a really good investment buy, with planning permission...'

'Anything that was worth building on was sold years ago,' Dan told him dryly. 'What's left is basically water meadows—great if you want to raise watercress, but not much use for anything else.'

The estate agent gave a small shrug, obviously losing interest as he recognised that Dan wasn't a serious potential buyer. And yet, to his own bemusement, instead of requesting that he be provided with details of properties more suitable for his requirements, Dan heard himself saying, 'I can't see that I'd be prepared to make anything like the kind of offer you've indicated, but I suppose it can't do any harm to meet with the executors.'

The agent looked pleased.

'Let me set up a meeting,' he told Dan. 'We'll have your address on file, I know, but if you could just give it to me again...'

The post office had been busier than Nicki had expected and it would take her several minutes to walk through the town to where she had parked her car. The small, carefully chosen private school Joey attended was several miles outside the town. It had a first-class reputation and acted as a feeder for the area's most prestigious fee-paying senior school. Kit had baulked a little at first when Nicki had insisted on private education for Joey.

'Laura went to state schools,' he had reminded her, 'and she got an excellent degree.'

'That was some time ago,' Nicki had pointed out impatiently. 'Things are different now, Kit. For one thing, the school that Laura attended has closed down; all the area's secondary school age pupils now attend the same comprehensive. I want the best for Joey,' she had insisted fiercely. 'And I intend to see that he gets it.'

She was halfway down the main street when she saw Dan walking towards her, and for a second the shocking sense of *déjà vu* that overwhelmed her rocked her to a standstill.

'Dan!' As she breathed his name she felt a fierce gust of intense happiness and excitement flood over her, and suddenly she was twenty again, and deep in the throes of her first sexual and emotional fantasy love.

'Nicki!' Dan's face creased into a warm smile as he saw her. He had dated her a couple of times before he had met Maggie, more as a friend than a potential lover. He had enjoyed her company and her friendship, and he was delighted to see her now.

'You're back,' Nicki whispered. She was trembling, dizzy...unable to stop looking at him.

All those years ago she had considered him to be the sexiest, most dangerous man she knew, and there was still that unmistakable air of raw maleness about him now, she recognised, even though his once dark hair was now tinged attractively with grey. Tinged with grey, but still thick, she acknowledged.

Kit was tall, but Dan was that little bit taller, that little bit broader, giving off a certain male something that said subtly that his body would be heavily muscled, powerfully male, that he was still very much a man in the prime of his life. No wonder the two young thirty-something women who had just walked past had paused to give him a quick once-over, Nicki decided jealously.

'I certainly am,' Dan agreed warmly. 'Something happened after New York—I don't know what. I just know that suddenly making money or rather making more money no longer seemed as important as it had done. I felt I wanted to come home. So here I am, looking for somewhere to live and something to do. Here, take my card so you know where to get hold of me.

'Nothing seems to have changed. Looking round here today, it's hard to believe I've been away for over ten years. Especially when I look at you, Nicki,' he told her with another smile.

He had meant the words as a semi-teasing compliment, but to his consternation Nicki's eyes suddenly filled with tears, her face becoming pinched and pale.

'Nicki!' He felt both concerned and embarrassed, unsure of what to do or say, unsure of what was happening.

'You're wrong, Dan,' Nicki told him passionately. 'Things have changed. Everything has changed!'

There was a look in her eyes that disturbed him, an inward-looking darkness that his instincts told him wasn't good.

'I...I have to go,' Nicki told him. 'I was just on my way to pick up my son, Joey.'

'Your son?'

'Yes. He was born not long after you left.'

Dan felt as though she was waiting for him to make some comment, to compliment her perhaps, and tell her that motherhood suited her, but the words stuck in his throat because the truth was that it didn't, or rather something didn't. She looked pale and strained, haunted somehow.

'How is everyone else?' he asked her instead. 'The others...Maggie?' He said her name quickly, afraid to let the taste of it lie too long on his tongue, glad to have shaped and ejected it before he gave too much away.

'Maggie?' Nicki could almost taste her own bitterness and resentment. 'She's fine,' she told him in a brittle voice. 'In fact, she's more than fine. She's blooming, as they say.'

'Blooming?' Dan focused sharply on her.

'Yes,' Nicki told him flatly. 'Maggie is pregnant! Not so much a miracle of nature as a miracle of modern science!' she added bitterly, darkly. 'Maggie has a younger lover, and she is desperate to give him a child. I must go, Dan.' She broke off as she heard the church clock chiming. 'I mustn't be late to collect Joey.'

The panic that thought caused swamped her bitterness about Maggie. Her heart jerked painfully against the string on which it was being jerked by her inner tormentor, the unseen enemy that had somehow taken up residence inside her.

Silently Dan let her go. Maggie was pregnant. Maggie had a younger lover. Maggie...

Laura frowned as she drove past Joey's school and saw her young half-brother standing outside.

Laura planned to use some of her savings to buy a car, but in the meantime Zoë had had Laura's name added to her own car insurance, or rather her husband Ian's PA had, and Laura had insisted on taking a solo drive in the car to make sure that she was familiar with its controls and felt confident driving it before she agreed to take the children as passengers. Now she was on her way back to the house, having called at the supermarket to pick up some shopping for Zoë.

She might only have been working for Zoë for a couple of days, and she might have taken the job on impulse rather than because she actually needed it, but already Laura could see that it was not going to be a sinecure.

Her friends in London would no doubt be amused if they could see her. Laura, the high-flyer whose goal was to run her own business, working as a glorified au pair! But it was still preferable to her other options, which were either living with Nicki or going back to London and risking giving in to Ryan.

Ryan! Just thinking about him turned her belly liquid and made her ache so much that she was grinding her teeth together.

It appalled her that, despite the fact that they had barely touched, never mind actually had sex, she could want him as intensely as she did. And she did want him! God, but she wanted him...wanted him...wanted the strong, hot feel of him inside her, the sharp, savage, sexual bite of his teeth against her skin, the rough male touch of his hands against her body, the hot, urgent feel of him inside her, filling her, stretching her, making her...

Laura groaned, glad that the car was an automatic as her body reacted fiercely to the sexuality of her thoughts. As she checked her rear-view mirror she realised that Joey was still standing on the footpath.

Laura frowned. Nicki was ferociously protective of

her son, and if, as Laura suspected, it was her own father who was responsible for picking him up and who
had not made it in time, Nicki would make her dis-
pleasure very apparent.

Laura felt almost as protective of her father as Nicki
did of her son, especially since she had returned home
and seen the way that Nicki was treating him. More as
though he were an office junior she felt able to harry
and bully than her husband, the man she was supposed to love. The man she had claimed she loved so
much that she had crawled into his bed, in the house
he shared with her own mother and…

Laura grimaced as she brought the car to an abrupt
halt and then reversed it a little too fast. Joey was not
her responsibility, she reminded herself as she
switched off the engine and got out.

The relief in his eyes as he saw her gave her a tiny
little ache. He was extraordinarily like her father to
look at, and almost too sweet-natured, in that way that
young boys had before life and their peers hardened
them. For a moment Laura had a ridiculous urge to
gather him up in her arms, this child brother who was,
after all, related to her by blood, flesh of her own father's flesh.

He looked far too vulnerable standing there on his
own, potential prey to heaven alone knew what kind
of lunatics and perverts who might be around.

'Laura.' She could hear the tiny betraying crack of
relief in his voice as he started to hurry towards her.
'That's not our car,' he told her.

'No,' Laura agreed.

Nicki saw the car—a strange car—as she drove up,
parking hers awkwardly and getting out, frantic with
anxiety as she saw the woman bending towards her
precious son, and not realising that it was Laura until

her stepdaughter suddenly straightened up and reached out as though...

'Don't you dare touch him!' Nicki screamed as she flung herself between her son and her stepdaughter. 'Don't you dare, *dare* touch my son!'

Laura recoiled with shock as she heard the high-pitched hysteria in Nicki's voice and saw the vitriol in her eyes. She hadn't heard Nicki arrive and had been trying to reassure Joey, who was obviously distressed, and Nicki's furious outburst had caught her off guard.

Joey had started to shiver, as though he, too, was shocked by his mother's behaviour, but Nicki predictably seemed to think that it was Laura who had upset him, dragging him even closer to her side as she hissed at Laura, 'Keep away from Joey, Laura. Just leave him alone.'

And then she was hurrying him away, without giving Laura the opportunity to point out that Nicki was the one who had left him alone and frightened outside his school.

Nicki was behaving like a madwoman. A madwoman, a drunk or an adulterer—what a choice! Was there something she didn't know about herself? Some baggage she was carrying with her from a previous karma perhaps? Laura wondered self-mockingly.

She certainly wasn't doing very well in the relationship stakes right now!

13

'Did you enjoy your yoga class, Julie?' Stella asked brightly as she watched Julie pushing her early supper disinterestedly around her plate. Every instinct Stella possessed urged her to insist that Julie should be eating properly, if not for herself then for the baby she carried. She really was far, far too thin, and seemed to prefer snacking on chocolate bars and picking at the trays of fast food that Stella was continually finding congealing in her kitchen than eating a proper meal.

Blank-eyed, Julie played with the piece of chicken that Stella had cooked and chargrilled especially for her because she had said it was what she wanted. Stella's muscles bunched as she watched whilst Julie focused all her concentration on slowly and methodically scraping off the blackened outer layer of the meat before cutting it up into minute pieces, and then cutting it up again.

'It's not fair!' she suddenly burst out, pushing the plate away, ignoring Stella's tension. 'I hate being like this. Having this horrid baby. All my friends are going out enjoying themselves, going out clubbing, having a good time. I never wanted this to happen. It isn't my fault. It's Hughie's!'

To Stella's dismay, she pushed her uneaten food away and stood up. 'I hate being like this. And I hate being here...' Sobbing noisily, she headed for the kitchen door.

Automatically Stella made to follow her, but to her surprise Richard shook his head.

'Let her go,' he told her. 'Poor kid, it's a natural re-action.'

'But you heard what she said about Hughie,' Stella fumed. 'Blaming him...'

'What do you expect?' Richard asked her. 'After all, he *is* to blame, isn't he? And in her eyes—'

'Oh, yes, you would say that,' Stella exploded. 'That's typical of you, Richard. You're always so ready to criticise Hughie, instead of praise him.'

'I'm not criticising him, Stella, I'm simply stating facts. Hughie is the baby's father. We all know that. And as for not praising him—well, if you want my opinion, you do enough of that for both of us. You always have done.'

Whilst Stella stared at him, Richard opened his pa-per and started to read it. About to challenge him, Stella frowned as her mobile rang, and saw that the caller had withheld their number.

She answered a little tersely, and was shocked to hear Todd's voice asking softly, 'It's Todd, Stella. Can you talk?'

Maggie gave a small sigh of relief as she sank down into a chair in the bar of the restaurant. A shopping trip on top of her yoga class had perhaps not been a good idea, she acknowledged as she surreptitiously removed one of her shoes and massaged her aching foot.

It had been Oliver's idea that they should eat out in-stead of going straight home. She had so much to look forward to, Maggie reflected. And so much to regret?

As Oliver headed back to their table with their drinks, the door to the restaurant opened and Marcus walked in. Recognising him, Maggie slipped her shoe back on and smiled warmly at him.

Marcus hesitated before going over in response to Maggie's friendly smile, acknowledging that not to do so would be bad manners. Quickly introducing the two men, Maggie was pleased when Oliver immediately asked Marcus if he would care for a drink.

'Well, I don't want to intrude.' Marcus hesitated.

The truth was that, absorbing though his work was, socially he still felt something of an outsider. The other partners in the practice were all older than he was, and married with families and well-established lives. At thirty he considered himself a little too old for the local wine bar scene, but after a full week of eating on his own he had been desperate for some company, even if it was only at second hand.

The restaurant had been well recommended by his partners and so he had decided on impulse to eat there. It hadn't occurred to him that he might meet one of his patients, but, as though she knew what he was thinking, Maggie was making it discreetly plain that her conversation was going to be strictly social. Marcus started to relax a little.

He had already known from the extremely comprehensive records the private clinic had provided that Maggie's partner was younger than she was, so meeting Oliver didn't disconcert him in any way, even though his obvious love for Maggie intrigued him a little. He did not consider that he had any prejudices against an older woman-younger man relationship, but there was no doubt that it was one that statistically seemed doomed to be short-lived.

* * *

'Yes!' Alice gave a small crow of pleasure as she finally managed to get the computer to do what she wanted it to do.

The only problem was there was no one with her to share her pleasure in her small triumph.

She looked at the phone. Maggie would understand, although no doubt she would laugh at her. Grinning to herself, she dialled Maggie's number.

The sound of the answering machine deflated her excitement. The house suddenly felt empty and lonely.

Stuart was due home tonight. He had been evasive and short with her when she had finally managed to speak with him, telling her which train he would be catching, then ending the call quickly, as though he'd been reluctant to talk to her.

Maggie knew what it was like to have an unfaithful husband; to go through the trauma of her partner having an affair.

At the time Alice had believed that she had understood what Maggie had been going through, but did one ever truly understand someone else's situation unless one had experienced it personally?

Her small triumph with the computer had gone, leaving her feeling not merely deflated but actively on edge. What if Stuart was having an affair? What if...? Bleakly she stared at the computer screen.

Instinctively Stella moved out of earshot before speaking to Todd, closing the door between herself and Richard as she walked into the hall. How easy it was to adopt the ways of self-protection and camouflage, of intrigue and deceit!

'Todd...' she began shakily. Just the act of saying his

name gave her a sharply illicit thrill of pleasure! Illicit? Her grip on her mobile tightened.

'Can you meet me? Tonight? I've got to see you, Stella… Please…'

His voice was urgent, its unspoken message of desire dizzying her.

'Tonight? I…I…'

'Eight o'clock? In town?'

'I… Yes,' Stella heard herself agreeing weakly.

Her hand was shaking so much when she cancelled the call she could barely press the button. Her face felt hot. Inside she was shaking so badly she was surprised that she could still stand.

'Stella?'

Richard had opened the door and was looking at her.

'I…I almost forgot,' she began, but to her relief, before she was forced to lie, Julie came downstairs.

It was not as though she was doing anything wrong in agreeing to meet Todd, she reassured herself. He was simply a friend, that was all. A friend? When he made her feel… She and Richard had never had an intensely passionate relationship, but until recently, Stella had never particularly minded that, preferring it to be smooth and calm.

So when had she begun to suspect that smooth calmness was merely a self-deluding garment to hide the paucity of their relationship, to cloak its dullness and boredom? Since she had met Todd?

Uncomfortably she pushed the thought away.

'I've got some good news for you, Julie,' she announced, trying to make herself concentrate on something else. 'I bumped into a friend of mine today whilst I was out, and she was saying that she was sure that her daughter had finished with her baby stuff and that she wouldn't mind passing it on to you.'

'No!'

The vehemence with which Julie made her denial flummoxed Stella.

'Julie!' she protested, aghast.

'No,' Julie repeated angrily. 'No, no, no! No way is my baby having grotty second-hand stuff! I want a running stroller like you see the pop stars with and…and a sheepskin baby carrier, they're cool.'

'Julie, we're talking about a baby you've already decided to give up for adoption, not a fashion accessory,' Stella reminded her tartly.

Thank goodness she had had a son and not a daughter.

'Oh, that's typical,' Julie exploded. 'You…my dad…you're just the same, you think you know everything. Well, you don't!'

Stella winced as Julie stormed out of the room, slamming the door so hard behind her that it rattled in its frame.

'Did you hear that?' she asked Richard in exasperation. 'You'd think that she would be grateful! A stroller like a pop star. Whatever next!'

'She's a child, Stella, and she's frightened,' Richard told her quietly. 'Surely you can see that?'

Stella frowned. It was unlike Richard to comment on any kind of emotional situation, never mind question her understanding of it! But he'd done it several times now.

'I can certainly see that she's behaving like a spoiled brat!' she responded tartly. 'You'd think that she'd realise just how lucky she is!'

'Lucky? To be pregnant at seventeen? Oh, come on, Stella! How many times do you suppose she's asked herself what her stubborn bravado is going to cost her? She's a bright kid. Do you honestly want me to believe that in her shoes you wouldn't be having moments when you panicked, when you questioned whether or not you'd made the right decision? And, poor kid, no matter whether you're for or against termination no doubt there must be times when she probably wishes she had gone for that option! I've got to go out,' Richard told her. 'There's a meeting of the bowls club finance committee.'

She and Hughie had both laughed when Richard had taken to playing the odd game of bowls with the elderly residents of the local care home with which he had become involved in the course of his work. But, Richard being Richard, he had remained stoically unconcerned by their teasing mockery, and had announced that he enjoyed the game and the company of his co-players.

That had been a couple of years ago, and now he not only played regularly but was also a member of the committee that ran the local bowling green.

Richard was going out, which meant that there was no need for her to lie to him…which meant that she was free to go out and meet Todd!

The nearer his train got to his home, the more uncomfortable and ill at ease Stuart felt. He was dreading having to talk to Alice, to explain to her the life they had shared for so long was now over. It was pointless trying to convince himself that she would understand. How could she? He barely understood himself. All he knew was that there could be no going back!

It wasn't that he hadn't tried! He had! He had fought to stop this from happening, but in the end…

A woman sitting on the opposite side of the aisle gave him a subtle but thorough visual inspection, noting the handsome tanned face and the white evenly spaced teeth, the hair, silvering in a way that made it and him look very distinguished; the expensive dark suit, and the handmade shirt and complementing tie. A sexy man, a rich man. She gave a discreet glance at his left hand and expelled a faint sigh of regret as she saw his ring. A married man. But experience had taught her that they were often the best!

The train started to slow down. His station was next. Stuart looked bleakly out of the window at the postcard-pretty countryside. The house would have to be sold. The buffet-car sandwich he had eaten earlier lay queasily on his stomach. The temptation to simply stay on the train and not get off, not go back, was so strong that for a moment he almost gave in to it.

Stuart's train was pulling into the station. Alice felt her stomach muscles lock.

In the early years of their marriage she had sometimes frightened herself by wondering what she would do if he ever fell out of love with her and in love with someone else, but during this last decade she had ceased to do so. Sex had gone from being exciting to becoming mundane, and from that to something which, if she was honest, had become almost a chore. She wasn't highly sexed; for her, sex was only truly enjoyable as an expression of her emotional love. If someone had asked her six months ago how she thought she would feel if Stuart's sexual appetite were to diminish, her honest reply would have been that she would feel rather relieved. But now that it was happening, now that he was turning away from her in bed, her prime feeling was not one of relief, but of anxiety and vulnerability.

Her life was a busy one, filled with a hundred and one small activities. Stuart had often been away for days at a time, and she had somehow not felt worried or threatened, but this time…

Was it because of what Zoë had said to her? Or had it been Stella's unthinking remark about her role within their quartet as the happily married one that had jarred like something touching an exposed nerve? Alice didn't know; all she did know was that it had shocked her to discover just how strongly she felt, how powerfully intense the jealousy stirring inside her was, the possessive fury at the thought of another woman usurping her role in Stuart's emotions.

The train had stopped disgorging its passengers. It had been a wet day, but now the sky was clearing, lemon-yellow towards the horizon, the final sharp rays of the sun dazzling the eyes, so that it took her several seconds to actually see Stuart.

He was walking slowly, his head bent, everything about his body language crying out aloud his reluctance to be where he was. And to be with her?

'And this is Laura. I told you about her, Ian. She's going to help me with the kids.'

Laura found herself holding her breath as she was subjected to Zoë's husband's boldly sexually predatory gaze.

He had to be the most aggressively and openly sexual man she had ever met. His sexuality surrounded him like a forcefield, and she had to take a step back to prevent herself from breathing in the physical heat he seemed to generate.

She saw his mouth twist in a taunting, knowing

smile as she did so, watched as he gave her a slanting look that raked her insolently from top to toe, lingering pointedly on her breasts and the apex of her thighs.

Quite undoubtedly he was sexual dynamite, a walking, talking powerhouse of male testosterone and machismo who obviously looked on every woman who crossed his path as potential bed fodder, but, oddly, she herself did not feel in any way attracted to him.

Zoë was watching him with a betraying mixture of sick, hungry longing and wary anxiety, and Laura could see his nostrils twitch fastidiously as he obviously caught the smell of alcohol on her breath.

'So Laura, you're going to take care of the kids, are you?' he demanded, turning away from Zoë to concentrate exclusively on Laura. 'Know much about them, kids, do you?' he challenged, launching the question at her like a guided missile.

'Some,' Laura returned coolly. 'After all, I was once one myself, and a pretty obnoxious one at that. Although I have to say that George and William are both absolute honeys.'

She had used their names deliberately, and she saw that he knew it from the slight change in his expression.

'Really? You surprise me! If it was left up to my darling wife—'

'That's not fair,' Zoë interrupted him furiously. 'I do my best, and, for your information, if you and my mother didn't undermine me all the time—'

'Undermine you?' Ian laughed sardonically. 'You do that to yourself, Zoë. Where are they, anyway, the kids?' he demanded of Laura.

'Upstairs in bed,' she responded. 'Zoë wasn't sure what time you would get home and, although it's old-fashioned, I believe that children should have an established bedtime.'

'So that you girls can have all the more time to do your own thing, eh? How many bottles have you got through this time, Zoë, or did you stop counting?'

Laura could almost taste the savagery and hostility emanating from him as Zoë took a step back.

'I only drink because you leave me here on my own so much,' she told him, accusingly. 'You know that. If you took me away on your business trips…'

'You've got two kids, remember?'

Laura had had enough. She might not hold a particularly strong brief for Zoë, but there was no way she was going to stand here and be forced to be a passive onlooker to Ian's cynical cruelty towards his wife.

'I'd better go up and check on the boys,' she announced, and without waiting for any response she left the kitchen.

She could still hear the raised voices coming from downstairs when she opened the door to the bedroom the two boys shared.

'Dad's back.' George was sitting upright in bed, his body tense. His younger sibling, William, slept. 'He's not going to make Mum cry, is he?' George was asking her, his dark eyes too old and knowing in his anxious little face.

Laura ached for him. She knew all too well herself what it meant to be a child lying awake at night dreading hearing the sound of a parent's grief, only in her case it hadn't been because her parents were quarrelling that her mother had cried, but because she had known that she was dying.

Sitting down on the bed, she pushed the floppy dark hair back off his forehead.

'Grown-ups do cry sometimes,' she told him.

The look he gave her said that he knew when he
was being fobbed off. Anxiety still shadowed his face,
and for some reason it reminded her of Joey's anxiety
when she had seen him outside his school.

Nicki's reaction had been totally uncalled for, totally over the top! She had had no intention whatsoever of hurting Joey.

Laura started to frown. One of the things she had always reluctantly admired about Nicki, as well as resented, had been her cool demeanour and her calm
control. Nothing had ever seemed to faze Nicki. No
amount of teenage insults, sulks or arguments, no
amount of banged doors, or furious outbursts. Nothing! Until now.

George had gone back to sleep and she could no
longer hear the raised voices from downstairs. Zoë
had insisted on delaying supper until Ian returned,
and Laura's stomach was beginning to rumble pro-
testingly. Quietly leaving the bedroom, she went back
downstairs. The kitchen door was open but as she
stepped inside she froze as she saw the scene in front
of her.

Zoë was on the kitchen table, her head thrown back,
the whole of her upper body arched in sexual urgency,
her top pulled up to expose her naked breasts, her
flesh revealing the imprint of Ian's fingers, her face
suffused with an unmistakable flush of arousal.

Her skirt was up around her hips, her bare thighs
pale against the darkness of Ian's suit as he stood between them, her knees gripping him as she moaned in
frantic sexual hunger.

Totally unable to move, Laura was distantly aware
of the thrusting movement of Ian's hips, hypnotic and
mesmerising. Zoë was moaning a string of commands

to him, obscenities punctuated with guttural cries and the harshness of her breathing.

'I want to come…make me come, Ian,' Laura heard her sobbing frantically.

'You stupid bitch, you're too drunk.'

The flat tone of disinterest and detachment in which the harsh words were delivered shocked Laura out of her paralysis. Hastily backing out of the kitchen, she hurried back upstairs to her own room, her face burning. Not with embarrassment over what she had witnessed, but with anger. Anger against Ian for the way he was treating Zoë. Anger against Zoë herself for letting him do so, and for so patently enjoying the way in which he was demeaning her.

Just as she would be demeaning herself if she ever gave in to Ryan?

'Stella!'

Automatically Stella took a step back as Todd came towards her, glancing quickly over her shoulder.

'I'm so glad you could make it,' he told her. 'Look, it's far too cold to stand here. Why don't we go back to my place?'

Stella hesitated, her mouth suddenly very dry and her heart racing. She felt as giddy as though she had been caught in an oxygen-laden slipstream of terrific force, and was euphorically high on the resultant adrenalin rush.

Back to his place! Already she could mentally envisage its shadowed intimacy and privacy. Her thoughts scattered in a dozen different directions, shot through with a dozen different emotions.

'Todd, I don't think…' She could hear her own aching disappointment, protesting volubly against her decision, so clearly that she was surprised that Todd could not hear it as well.

But he was already apologising, explaining. 'I'm sorry. I wasn't thinking straight. I'm so damned wound up at the moment... What about that place over there?'

Stella turned her head uncertainly towards the wine bar. There wasn't really any reason why she shouldn't have a drink in public with Todd, was there? They were on the same committee, after all, and if she hadn't actually told Richard yet about Todd's request that she help him to find a flat, it was only because she simply hadn't had time, not because she wanted or needed to be secretive about it.

'Yes, all right,' she accepted.

The wine bar was busy, but Todd found them a small table tucked discreetly into the shadows.

'I just can't believe what my ex has done,' he announced angrily as soon as they had been served their drinks. 'You know I told you that my daughter-in-law had okayed a visit here by my grandchildren? Well, now it seems she's having second thoughts, thanks to my ex who has told her that she doesn't think it's a good idea. I can't believe she's done that! I mean, why? To get at me? Okay, so I wasn't the best husband in the world, but I've paid for that. She saw to it that I did. You wouldn't believe what those lawyers of hers managed to get out of me!'

Stella listened to him in silence. He had brought her here because he wanted to talk about his family...his ex-wife!

Her disappointment felt like a cold, heavy weight pressing down on her body. Chagrined, she continued to listen. And then, just when she had tusselled with her conscience and decided that it was far better, far wiser, far safer for her to think of him merely as a friend, he reached across the table and took hold of her hand, breaking off his diatribe against his ex to tell her huskily, 'Stella, the way I feel right now, it's probably just as well you were sensible enough to refuse to go back to my place. I need you so badly! No, don't look at me like that. We aren't a couple of immature kids, who need to play games with one another, to tease and test each other. I knew the moment I saw you how I felt, and I know it was the same for you, otherwise you wouldn't be here. We're old enough not to have to waste precious time going through the motions of a pointless move and countermove game of hide and seek. I want you in my bed so badly right now. I need you so badly right now. I need you to lose myself in…to…'

Frantically Stella snatched her hand away.

'Todd, I'm married,' she protested shakily.

Taking her hand back, he lifted it to his lips. 'So?' he challenged her softly.

'I've got to go,' Stella insisted. 'My…Rich will be home soon. I've got to go, Todd.'

'Okay… If you insist. But next time…'

14

'I can't believe it's nearly two months since we last got together and that we're into April already. Things have been pretty hectic for all of us lately, though, so it's not surprising.' Alice sighed as she slipped off her coat and handed it to the hovering waiter before sitting down.

'Aren't the other two here yet?' she asked Stella, looking round the restaurant.

'Well, Nicki isn't coming,' Stella replied. 'When I rang her she said she couldn't make it because she was looking after Joey. Maggie's coming, though.'

'I saw Nicki in town the other day,' Alice broke in. 'She was on the other side of the street, but by the time I had managed to cross she'd disappeared. I think she's a bit miffed with me at the moment because of Laura working for Zoë.'

'Oh, heavens, Alice, don't you start looking for problems where they don't exist. Things are bad enough with Maggie still on her high horse.'

'She and Nicki haven't made things up yet, then?' Alice asked, firmly refusing to allow herself to take umbrage at Stella's outspokenness.

'Well, I told you what Maggie said to me when I bumped into her at the surgery, and… Oh, Maggie's here.'

'Hello, you two.' Maggie greeted them both warmly before exchanging hugs.

Maggie had always been the most tactile of all of them, Alice reflected, returning her hug. She had recently begun to realise just how sterile life could be without the loving intimacy of physical contact with another human being. She and Stuart might be sharing the same bed, but it was beginning to feel as though there were an unscalable wall between them!

Stella would probably laugh at her if she told her how miserable and insecure Stuart's unfamiliar lack of desire for her was making her. Maggie would probably laugh too, but for a very different reason. Stella had never made any secret of the fact that she considered herself fortunate in having a relationship with Richard that was based more on friendship than sex, and as for Maggie…well, deep in the throes of love and passion as she was at the moment, the very thought of not having sex would no doubt fill her with amused pity! Anyway, she didn't really want to even think about the change in Stuart, never mind talk about it.

'Maggie, you look blooming.' Alice smiled instead. 'How many weeks are you now? It must be twelve…'

'Nearly,' Maggie agreed, smiling at the waiter who was holding out her chair for her. She had made herself a promise before coming out that she was not going to accidentally dominate the evening's conversation with baby talk. 'How are you progressing with the OU course?'

'Well, it doesn't begin officially until September, of course, and at the moment I'm still struggling to get to grips with my computer. I decided that it made sense to learn how to use one, but so far…'

'Heavens, Alice, you should have said. I would gladly come and sit with you to help you. Oliver's taken over the bulk of the work in the business so I'll be free to concentrate on the baby, so I've got plenty of time on my hands. Which reminds me, we're going to have to look round for a proper assistant for Oliver. You don't think that Zoë would be interested, do you? I mean, I know she's got that job at the estate agents', but with her degree…'

Alice hesitated. What Maggie was suggesting would be an ideal job for Zoë, challenging, with plenty of incentives and room to develop a strong career role for herself that would still allow her to spend quality time with her children, but what about Zoë's drinking? How would she, Alice, feel if in a few months' time Maggie were to turn round and announce that Zoë was going to be asked to leave?

'I'm not sure, Maggie… You know what Zoë can be like,' she added lamely.

'It was only a thought,' Maggie told her briskly.

'Perhaps Nicki might know of someone?' Stella suggested.

'Perhaps,' Maggie agreed, her gaze suddenly intent on the cutlery. 'It was just that I couldn't help thinking, Alice, that if Zoë has inherited your organisational qualities she'd be ideal. Come to think of it, you would be ideal.' She laughed. 'But of course I know you wouldn't be interested, and I doubt that Stuart would want you to work anyway, would he? I know you're doing your OU course, but he's always been the kind of husband who wants you close at hand, we all know that.'

She was, Alice suddenly discovered, reducing her bread roll to uneatable crumbs!

'And so Julie's baby is due in a matter of weeks?' Maggie asked Stella.

They had finished their main course and were waiting for their coffees to be served

'We're not exactly sure when,' Stella said. 'Julie is a bit vague as to when she actually conceived.' She looked surreptitiously at her mobile as she bent down towards her handbag on the pretext of looking for a tissue. Todd was texting her most days—often several times a day—and she looked forward to his messages with the avid, intense hunger of an addict awaiting her fix, which in reality was what she probably was, she acknowledged as the screen proved disappointingly blank.

'Have you seen anything of Nicki?' Stella asked Maggie as she straightened up.

Maggie's stomach muscles cramped. Since the receipt of the poison pen letter she had heard nothing from Nicki, and, if she were honest, she wasn't sure what she would do if she did. Logically she ought to have tackled her about the situation by now, but the reality was that she had no idea how to deal with the subject. It was a minefield of potentially lethal hidden dangers, from which their friendship could not hope to survive. She lacked the single-mindedness to give their relationship the *coup de grâce* that it probably now deserved, Maggie recognised. There was still somewhere deep inside her a feeling that she owed Nicki, and that somehow she had let her down. But these were not feelings that she could put into easily voiced words, especially not to Stella, whose unexpressed disapproval she could still sense.

And neither, if she was honest, did she want to put herself in the position of being told a second time that she was overreacting.

'Not really,' she replied as casually as she could.

Coffee had arrived for the other two, along with the tea she had ordered. No risk of her baby not having perfect health was too small for her to ignore, no sacrifice for its well being too big to make... So long as that sacrifice wasn't Nicki?

Marcus looked up from his newspaper as he saw the girl walking into the wine bar. She was vaguely familiar, but it wasn't until Laura returned his tentative smile with a freezingly cool look that he recognised her as one of the pair of women he had seen drinking in the wine bar a few weeks previously.

Well, tonight at least she was sober, he acknowledged. Sober and alone! Like him.

Laura could feel her face threatening to burn as she refused to return Marcus' smile.

She had known that it wasn't a good idea to come here on her own, but she had desperately needed to put some space between herself and Zoë. The truth was that it was now more her growing sense of responsibility towards the boys that was keeping her working for Zoë. Zoë on her own she could just about tolerate, but Zoë when Ian was around!

She decided that she would tell her own friends to shoot her before they allowed her to degenerate into the state that Zoë got into around her husband. It both sickened and infuriated Laura to see the way that Zoë debased herself in front of him. That wasn't love, not in Laura's opinion, it was more a form of self-denigration...more like self-hatred!

It had definitely not been a good idea to come in here on her own, she decided, when she had had to fend off the hopeful advances of another couple of single men who had seen her and made a beeline for her. She had lost her appetite anyway.

As she stood up Marcus didn't know whether to feel intrigued or infuriated by her.

She was obviously out to attract as much male attention as she could, walking in by herself, sitting down, and then getting up again and walking out without ordering anything, all the time wearing that look of hauteur like a tragedy queen. Well, he certainly wasn't going to allow himself to react to it! Not that she was likely to notice, not with those two other guys at the bar salivating openly over her!

Stella checked and glanced warily over her shoulder before going into the building that housed Todd's rented flat.

He had telephoned her just after lunch, inviting her out to dinner. Of course, she had had to refuse, but he had come back to her saying that if she wouldn't or couldn't have dinner openly with him, then would she meet him at his flat?

Initially she had refused. Initially...

She shook back her hair as she waited for him to answer the door. It was newly cut and styled—a mere coincidence, since she had already made up her mind that she was ready for a change, and as for the new, more fashionably styled jeans she was wearing...well, she had had to buy a new pair because of the unexpected amount of weight she had lost over the last few weeks. All that running up and down those stairs after Julie, no doubt, and nothing whatsoever to do with the fact that she felt as interested in food as a lovestruck teenager! The jeans bought on impulse in the kind of shop she would normally never have dreamed of spending money in—chain-store clothes were far more hardwearing than ridiculously overpriced designer items—along with a white tee shirt that had done astonishing, almost miraculous things for her shape. Luckily a sudden warm spell had allowed her to wear it without the necessity of either a cardigan or her standby navy blazer!

The door opened, and her heart bounced against her chest wall as though it had been slammed by a centre court champion.

Like her, Todd was wearing jeans and a tee shirt, but unlike her his hair was damp and his feet were bare.

The significance of those two small facts burned a path through her attempts to remind herself that she was (a) fifty-one and (b) married, like a light set to a trail of gunpowder. Inside her shoes, her toes curled in helpless reaction, newly painted toenails and all.

Without a word Todd moved sideways, one hand on top of the door so that she had to walk beneath his arm to enter the flat. For the first time in her life, Stella experienced the sharply excited, sensual reaction of her own body to the scent of freshly showered male flesh. She went hot and then hotter and for a delirious, unbelievable second she was actually tempted to stand there and bury her face greedily against his body so that she could fully absorb the reality of him. The sexual rush scorching her both thrilled and appalled her.

Without breaking eye contact with her, Todd closed the door and then leaned back against it, taking hold of her hand and drawing her to him.

'I've been thinking about this moment from the second I set eyes on you,' he told her softly. 'This moment and all those other moments we are going to spend exploring and enjoying one another, sexy Stella. I hope that you are as hungry for me as I am for you. Are you, Stella? Do you want me?' he whispered huskily to her as he kissed her mouth lightly, and then looked at her, as though searching her expression for something, before smiling slightly and kissing her again and then again, each time a little more deeply.

Somewhere at the back of her mind Stella recognised that she was in the hands, quite literally, of a very practised lover, but she refused to acknowledge just what that might mean.

Skilfully Todd moved their bodies so that, without her knowing how he had done it, suddenly she was the one with her back against the door, his body holding her there, leaning into her so that she was immediately and intimately aware of his arousal. Even as a young couple, she and Richard had never behaved like this. They had kissed, touched, yes…but never with such open sexual intimacy, such…such dizzyingly intense desire.

Todd's hand was on her breast. Stella quivered. Once a long time ago, a very long time ago, Richard had told her that she had perfectly shaped breasts…

Richard. Thinking about him was like having a bucket of cold water thrown over her, dousing the flames that Todd had so expertly been fanning.

Suddenly she felt guilty and ashamed. If she were to become involved with Todd then she wanted it to be openly and honestly as a free woman.

'No!'

She could see from Todd's expression that he didn't want to believe her.

'No,' she repeated firmly. 'I need time.' Time to distance herself from Richard; to leave their marriage. A marriage, she decided, that had become an easy habit for both of them; something she allowed to exist simply because they had nothing they wanted to put in its place. Until now…until Todd.

He wasn't pleased, Stella could see that, but he didn't make any attempt to stop her from leaving.

She had parked her car several streets away in the town's main car park, just in case, and she had just reached it and unlocked the driver's door when she realised that Maggie was walking across the car park towards her.

'Stella,' she heard her exclaiming warmly. 'I've just been to the twenty-four-hour store. I've got the most desperate craving for pickled onions of all things…'

Maggie's voice tailed away as she looked at Stella, and saw the tell-tale soft bruising swelling her mouth. Her pregnancy hormones had enhanced her sense of smell to such an acute state that she could actually smell the male cologne scenting Stella's clothes.

Immediately and unassailably, Maggie knew that whoever was responsible for that scent and whoever had been kissing Stella hard enough to leave that tell-tale sign of his passion on her mouth, it wasn't Richard.

For a moment the two women looked at one another in silence, and it was Stella who looked away first.

'I'd better go,' Maggie told her quietly. 'Take care, Stella,' she added gently.

Stella's face was burning as she got into her own car, but she couldn't bring herself to make any response.

Thoughtfully Maggie watched her drive away. There were some truths one kept to oneself discreetly, some one gossiped about with enjoyment, and some that one simply put carefully in a very, very safe place labelled 'forget'. What she had just unexpectedly witnessed quite definitely belonged to the latter category.

'So where are we celebrating?' Oliver asked Maggie teasingly.

'Celebrating?' Mock innocently, she affected not to know what he meant, but he refused to give in.

Laughing, he told her, 'You know as well as I do that it's twelve weeks and one day today since you conceived. I've seen them crossed off the calendar.'

Twelve weeks and one day. Maggie gave a small sigh of happiness as she snuggled into his arms.

'We've done nothing but celebrate ever since we knew,' she reminded him.

'So?' Oliver gave her back a gentle little rub of loving affection. 'Is there a rule that says we have to limit our happiness or how many times we celebrate it?'

'No…' Maggie allowed.

She had firmly tucked all the shock and unhappiness of Nicki's behaviour to a safe, dusty little corner of her mind. She couldn't understand how she could have done such a thing, but she certainly didn't want to persecute her!

'I've got a date for my scan,' she told Oliver. 'And it looks like they're going to deliver the baby midway through October, possibly on the fifteenth as I shall be just a couple of days short of the full forty weeks then, and they don't want to have me go into labour naturally, just in case there are complications. I wish they would let me give birth naturally though, Oliver.'

This had been a small bone of contention between them and between Maggie and her consultant, but the latter had remained adamant. In view of Maggie's age and the fact that this was her first child, he was not prepared to take any risks. 'And I'm not just thinking of you, Maggie,' he had told her. 'A long, slow birth could have serious repercussions for the baby, and I know that that's something neither of us would want.'

'Have you any plans for today?' Oliver asked her as he finished his breakfast.

'Not really,' Maggie replied. 'I'm going to ring the estate agents and chivvy them along a bit. If we don't find somewhere soon we're going to end up knocking on doors and begging someone to sell us their house.' She laughed. 'And I've got some shopping I want to do later.'

'More pickled onions?' Oliver guessed.

'No!' Maggie denied.

She was upstairs in the bathroom when she heard the car driving up, and by the time she got back down again it had gone.

The letter was there, though. Lying face down in the hall, the envelope looking innocuous enough, but somehow she just knew.

Typewritten and bearing just her name, it gave nothing away, but Maggie's hands still trembled as she opened it.

'Twelve weeks, Maggie. I didn't think you'd make it this far! You have surprised me! Don't get too confident though, will you? I haven't changed my mind,' it read.

That was all. But it was enough...more than enough.

Maggie tore it into shreds, her hands trembling, and then she buried it as far down as she could in the trash where it belonged.

Now Nicki had gone too far! But, liberatingly, instead of frightening her, the letter had driven her through fear and into the cleansing freedom of anger.

And she *was* angry. So very, very angry! So tempted to go straight round to Nicki and tell her what she thought of her, to punish her by warning her that Oliver wanted to report what she had done to the police. She could feel her heart jumping, frighteningly heavily. Quickly she put her hand on her body. If she was frightened then how must her poor baby feel?

'It's all right,' she soothed softly. 'Everything's all right... It's just your silly mummy getting angry.'

Angry. At least anger was cleansing, unlike her previous emotions. Only sick, inadequate people wrote poison pen letters. She ought to feel sorry for Nicki instead of angry with her, she told herself as she began to calm down. Instead of confronting her, the best way to deal with the situation was to ignore it. Wasn't it?

She didn't really want to get drawn into confrontations or arguments, Maggie recognised. She didn't want to expose her baby to the rank bitterness she felt sure would flood from a meeting with Nicki, like pus from a wound.

She wasn't going to allow anything to dent the strength, the love she intended to pour into making her baby. Fiercely, she brushed away her tears. Nicki had made her choice, and now Maggie was going to make hers! If Nicki felt that giving vent to her anger at what Maggie had done was more important than her friendship, then so be it. She certainly felt that surrounding her growing baby with love and good vibes was way more important than trying to rescue a relationship already brutally sabotaged.

But she still wasn't going to tell Oliver about the new letter!

Stella put down her article with a small sigh of exasperation. She was surprised that the incessant beat of the music that had drowned out every sound in the house since Julie had put it on over an hour ago had not brought the ceiling down!

She was a patient person, or so she had always thought, but she had had enough. Standing up, she opened the sitting-room door and headed for the stairs.

Outside the door to the flat, she took a deep breath and then knocked firmly.

No reply. She waited, and counted to ten, and then ten again, and knocked a second time. The third time she only counted to ten once, before grasping the handle and turning it.

The music, deafening enough downstairs, was at a painful, ear-hurting crescendo inside the small flat. There was no sign of Julie in the sitting room. Exasperatedly, Stella turned the music off and then frowned as in the blissful silence she heard a tiny, moaned whimper.

'Julie!'

She found her in the bathroom, doubled up on the floor, clutching her stomach, her face streaked with tears and her eyes full of pain and fear.

'Julie! What is it? Is it the baby?' Stella asked her as calmly as she could.

Officially Julie still had at least a week to go, and it could of course be merely a false alarm, but as Stella watched her her whole body contorted and tensed with the unmistakable rigour of a full contraction.

'Come on, Julie,' Stella instructed her. 'Let's get you to the hospital.'

'No,' Julie moaned. 'No... I can't... Please don't make me. It hurts... It hurts...'

Somehow, by a mixture of coaxing, pleading, praising and downright bullying, Stella managed to get her safely downstairs and into the car. Once she was there, Stella felt as stressed and exhausted as Julie looked.

'I want my mum,' Julie sobbed as Stella got in the car beside her and turned on the engine.

'I'll ring her just as soon as we get to the hospital,' Stella promised her soothingly.

She wanted to ring ahead to warn them that she was

bringing Julie in, but she dared not take her attention off the road to use her mobile, and she knew she couldn't ask Julie to make the call herself.

In the end, as luck would have it, as she pulled up outside the main entrance a porter happened to be passing with a wheelchair and she was able to persuade him to help Julie into it and take her inside whilst she parked the car.

By the time she had returned to the maternity wing, Julie was already on the labour ward. Going back outside to use her mobile, Stella rang the number Julie's mother had given her, but to her dismay there was no response. She left a message, and then tried Julie's parents' home number which she had got from Hughie 'just in case'. She was fully prepared to risk Julie's father's fury, but only the answering machine cut in.

Hughie, predictably, had his mobile switched off, and Richard hadn't even bothered to take his out with him. Whilst she was making her calls, a number flashed up on her screen that she immediately recognised as Todd's, but for once she felt no answering response of feverish sexual excitement, instead mentally brushing the realisation that he was trying to reach her away as she concentrated on what right now were more important matters.

'Julie?' she asked the nurse on duty anxiously as she hurried back onto the ward.

'She's doing fine,' the nurse told her. 'She's asking for you,' she added with a smile. 'So if you'd like to come and gown up?'

Julie was asking for her? Stella suspected that the nurse had mistaken her for Julie's mother, but since she was the only person who was here she felt duty bound to give Julie whatever support she could.

It was strange how little really did change, Stella reflected ten minutes later, standing beside Julie, holding her hand, feeling her sharp little nails dig into her flesh as she stroked the damp hair off her forehead and spoke encouragingly to her.

Giving birth was as fundamental to human civilisation now as it had always been, as awesome, as mystical, as downright blood, sweat and tears, Stella acknowledged as she praised Julie for her hard work, and told her what a clever, strong girl she was being.

'It hurts. It hurts!' Julie screamed. 'I hate it, I hate you and I hate this bloody baby.'

Over her body, Stella and the midwife exchanged wry smiles.

'I told mine to stay where he was,' the midwife told Stella. 'I hated him more than I had believed I could hate anyone or anything, other than his father, until the moment he was born and I held him for the first time. Then… Yes. Come on, Julie. No! Don't push! Not yet… Just take a breath. That's a good girl… Take another…yes. I know it hurts but you're being wonderfully, wonderfully brave.'

As births went it was relatively quick, but as Julie gave an animal howl and the final push to bring her child into the world Stella felt as exhausted herself as though she had run a marathon—two marathons. And yet at the same time she felt more elated, more euphoric, than she could ever remember feeling before.

'Yes. Julie, that's it… Oh, yes. You've got a gorgeous, gorgeous, perfect baby boy,' the midwife was crooning happily as she placed the baby on Julie's sweat-slick trembling body.

Just for a moment, before Julie enclosed him protectively in her arms, Stella caught a glimpse of him and felt her heart turn over inside her chest.

She had thought with Todd she had experienced the most important emotional and physical love of her life, but now immediately she knew she had been wrong. This was what had been missing from her life; this feeling flooding and totally absorbing her, imbuing and endowing her, redefining the whole meaning and purpose of her life, Stella recognised emotionally as she looked at her grandson for the first time. What she felt could not be analysed or rationalised, it simply was. In the act of being born, her grandson had transported her from one set of needs and values and loyalties to another, and the feelings she had had for Todd quite simply ceased to exist.

The baby was the image of Hughie. A perfect replica of how he had looked when he had been born.

Love flooded over her and her eyes filled with tears. This tiny scrap of humanity was her son's son. Her grandchild…a part of her…a tiny human link in an eternal chain. Stella ached to reach out for him, to pick him up and hold him to her own body. She could actually feel the echo of a retraction of her own womb, the tensing of her breasts.

The midwife was tidying Julie up, and shooing Stella gently but firmly out of the room.

'Time to let them get to know one another now, and Julie needs to sleep.'

As she walked out into the corridor on unsteady legs Stella felt as though she were floating on a cloud of pure gold joy. As though she had experienced something so wondrous, so life-changing that she could never be the same person again. She reached for her mobile. She had to tell Richard, and the girls, her friends. Todd had tried to ring her again. Without a second's compunction she deleted the call without bothering to return it.

What twenty-four hours ago had seemed essential, exciting and necessary now seemed tawdry and pathetic—her behaviour with Todd that of another woman, with whom she no longer had anything in common!

15

---◆---

'Stuart, what is it? What's wrong?'

'Nothing's wrong, Alice.'

'Yes, there is,' Alice persisted. 'Ever since you came back from that last trip to London you've been... different.'

She had already anxiously mentioned to him that Ian had seen him having lunch with a woman, but Stuart had simply shrugged and said that she had been a colleague. And Alice had told herself that she had no concrete reason to doubt him. But...

'And last night...' she began carefully.

'For God's sake! So I couldn't get it up,' Stuart exploded, raking angry fingers through his hair. 'What the hell does that prove? I don't know why you're complaining, anyway. After all, it isn't as though you've exactly been gagging for it, begging me for it, these last few years, is it?'

Alice knew that her shock was showing in her face. It was so unlike him to speak like this.

'Stuart!' she protested.

'"Stuart,"' he mimicked back, adding irritably, 'You know what your trouble is, Alice?'

'No, actually, I don't,' Alice answered him, suddenly as angry in her own way as he was in his. 'But I can see that you're eager to tell me. So why don't you,

Stuart? Why don't you go ahead and tell me what my trouble is?'

She heard him curse under his breath as he raked his hair again, pacing the floor of the kitchen impatiently, like a man caught in a trap, she recognised, suddenly sharply aware of how very tense and on edge he was.

'Sometimes I think you've spent so much damn time fussing around over the kids, running around after them, especially Zoë, that you can't see what's happening under your nose,' he told her.

Alice felt her heart lurch unsteadily from one side of her chest to the other as a sickening wave of anxiety washed coldly over her.

'Well, perhaps you'd better tell me what is happening under it then,' she suggested quietly.

'Alice, I just don't want this right now.'

'And you think that I do?' Alice challenged him.

'Look, ever since they were born you've made the kids your priority, but they're adults now, and it's high time they were fully independent. I can't go on financing them for ever!'

'Financing them?' Alice felt confused. She had been dreading Stuart telling her that their marriage was over and that he had found someone else, but instead he seemed more interested in complaining about the children. Was this some roundabout way of broaching the subject of a potential divorce with her?

With every day that had passed since his return she had sensed him distancing himself a little more from her, just as with every day that had passed she herself had grown more panic-stricken and filled with pain at the thought of him leaving. She was even missing having sex with him, so much so that the previous night, after he had turned his back on her and gone to sleep, she had been left lying wide awake on her own side of the bed, literally, physically aching for him! She could remember once reading in a magazine that there was no sex quite like breakup sex, with its explosive mix of anger, pain, and desperation.

'God knows, I've worked my balls off to support them all over the years, to make sure they've never gone without anything. And look at them now! Not one out of the three of them has ever so much as earned a penny towards their own keep. Zoë went straight from university into marriage and plays at working—God knows why, given what Ian earns! And as for the boys, swanning off around the world—at my expense! When I think of what their school fees were alone!'

There was a strained, almost desperate note in his voice that made Alice frown. Stuart had never quibbled about how much money was spent on their children—in fact, she had often thought that he actually felt proud of how expensive their lifestyle was. He wasn't the kind of man who boasted about material assets as such, but Alice had always been aware that he enjoyed the subtle superiority of others knowing that his family were so well provided for.

Whenever she had tried to suggest that their children already had enough, it had always been Stuart who had insisted that they should be allowed the additional private classes, the riding lessons, the school trips, and, in fact, the twins' expensive and supervised gap year, claiming that he wanted to know that they would be safe, instead of allowing them to do their own self-funded thing.

'Alice, I've been thinking.'

He sounded awkward, and uncomfortable, Alice recognised uneasily, his voice lacking the sureness and positivity that was such a familiar part of it and of him.

'This house…it's far too big for the two of us. Why don't we put it on the market? Move to something smaller, easier to manage. Looking after it is a full-time job and if you're going to be studying…'

'Sell the house?' Alice stared at him.

'It makes sense,' Stuart told her. 'I haven't said anything yet, but there's a chance that I might have to…to be based closer to the airport for a while. A new venture. Can't tell you much about it, all quite hush-hush at the moment, but the bottom line is that they're going to need me to be there more or less on call for quite some time.'

'You're saying that you want us to move closer to Heathrow?' Alice questioned him.

He had always been the one who had insisted that there was no way he wanted to live close to the airport, and that he was quite happy to commute to and from his work so that his family could enjoy the benefit of living in a quiet country town.

'No!'

The alarm she could hear in his voice and see in his eyes startled her.

'No…' he repeated in a quieter voice. 'Not move… not both of us. No, I was thinking more of selling this place and buying something smaller here, and then perhaps I could rent somewhere, just a bedsit type of place…'

Alice was too shocked to know what to say. In the space of one brief conversation her world was threatening to turn from the safe, secure place she knew into somewhere alien and potentially very unsafe indeed.

Was Zoë right? Could Stuart be involved with

someone else? Shamingly, Alice knew that she did not have the courage right now to ask him.

'Yes, he's a month old now, and exactly like Hughie was at his age. No, Julie, don't jiggle him up and down like that after you've fed him, you'll make him sick. Oh, dear. You'd better give him to me,' Stella told her firmly, taking charge of the baby who had fulfilled her warning by posseting some of his milk on Julie's top.

She exchanged an 'I told you so' look with Alice, who had called round at Stella's invitation, in lieu of their normal monthly meal out, to see the baby and have a cup of coffee.

'Oh, Alice, no, I can't possibly, not this month,' Stella had exclaimed when Alice had rung her about their regular get-together. 'I can't possibly leave Jack for a whole evening yet!'

Alice, remembering how they had all managed to stick to their routine when they had had their own babies, had tactfully not reminded Stella of this, but she did say gently, 'Maggie should be having a scan soon, I imagine, so we should be having some baby pics to look at. She came over the other day to sit with me and help me get to grips with the technological monster lurking on my desk. She's looking really well, but she seemed a bit quieter than usual. She won't admit it but I think she's still very upset about what happened with Nicki.'

'Well, you know my views on that subject,' Stella informed her firmly. 'They're both intelligent adult women and it's up to them to sort it out between them.'

'Well, yes, but Nicki does seem to have withdrawn from us all, Stella.'

'She's probably just very busy. You mustn't dwell

on things so much, Alice. It only builds them up into something they don't have to be.'

Was that what she was doing with Stuart? Alice prayed that it might be!

Ignoring the sullen look that Julie was giving her, Stella beamed indulgently at her grandson. Out of the corner of her eye Alice saw Julie fidgeting and looking bored.

'I think I'll take Jack round to Mum's,' she announced. 'Dad will be at work.'

'Oh, but…' Alice could see that Stella was looking put out, but Julie had already picked up her son and started to walk out of the room.

'Honestly, Alice, Julie just doesn't have a clue about looking after a baby,' Stella told her the moment the door had closed. 'And she's become so obstinate and difficult. I mean, when I suggested Jack as a name she totally refused to entertain the idea, until her mother said that it had been her grandfather's second name.

'And as for Julie's mother! Well, I sometimes feel that she might as well have moved in here, she's here so often!'

'Has her father come round yet?' Alice asked.

'Well, he's been round once to see Julie and Jack, but that's all. According to her mother, he's still very upset about everything. Hughie's been home to see Jack. I got out all his old baby photographs. You wouldn't believe just how alike they are. Although I do think that at Jack's age, Hughie was quite a bit heavier. Julie just couldn't take to breast-feeding. Well, she isn't the most patient of girls. I did try to persuade her to keep on trying, and I told her how important it was for Jack's sake, but she totally refused to listen to me. He really is the most wonderful baby, though, Alice. Sometimes I can't believe that he's actually here.'

Stella paused, unable to find the words to express just how she felt about the wonder of the new life that was so much a part of her. He was the first thing she thought of when she opened her eyes in the morning and the last person she wanted to see before she went to bed at night, tiptoeing up to his room to kiss his baby cheek before going back downstairs to her and Richard's bedroom.

'As I've already said to Richard, you'd think that Julie would be more appreciative of my help, but all Rich says is that Jack is her child!' Stella told Alice, looking affronted. 'I had to point out to him that Julie is still a child herself, and that as such it's up to us to guide her and advise her.'

Although she wasn't ready to confide totally in anyone else as yet, Stella had her own plans for Jack's future.

'Heavens, is that the time?' Alice exclaimed, getting up. 'I must go, Stella. It was lovely meeting Jack…'

Stella was the last person she would have imagined becoming such a doting grandmother, but there was no mistaking the intensity of her friend's feelings for her grandson! Alice could see problems ahead for Stella, when the time came for Jack to be adopted, and she had felt totally unable to mention this subject in Stella's presence.

After Alice had gone, Stella glanced at her watch. It was time for Jack's feed. She hoped that Julie would remember and bring him home on time…perhaps she ought to ring her and remind her?

Before she could do so, the phone rang. Quickly Stella answered it only to discover that her caller was Todd.

'I was hoping you'd have been in touch with me before now,' he began without preamble. 'You did say you would ring.'

'Oh, yes. I'm sorry, Todd, but I've just been so busy with Jack.'

'Well, how are you fixed tonight? We could—'

'No, Todd. I really can't.' Stella gave a distracted second look at her watch. Poor little Jack would be starving.

'Stella,' Todd was demanding urgently. 'You and I…'

Stella frowned in irritation. She wanted to end the call so that she could ring Julie. 'I'm sorry, Todd,' she told him. 'But I really don't think… I'd have liked to help you to find a new flat, but I'm afraid that just isn't going to be possible any more. Julie needs me to help her with Jack and—'

'It's okay, Stella. I think I've got the message.' His voice was terse but Stella barely registered his anger, or the fact that he ended the call without saying another word to her.

Making sure that Jack did not miss his feed was far more important to her than soothing Todd's bruised ego! Whatever foolishness had caused her to believe that he was someone she wanted in her life was over, and she was thankfully now restored to her old sensible self.

'You're late again, Zoë. That's the second time this week.'

'Oh, for God's sake, Andrew, don't be boring,' Zoë protested irritably, scowling as she switched on her computer and broke one of her nails. 'I mean, it's not as if we even open for another half an hour.'

'That isn't the point,' Andrew responded huffily. He was the agency's branch manager and the only reason he had taken Zoë on in the first place was because of her husband's contacts. They were the oldest agency in the town—a relatively small family-owned concern with only a handful of offices—and needed all the help they could get to compete with the big nationals. But so far, instead of increasing their business as he had hoped, Zoë's presence appeared to be having the opposite effect.

There was that house she had gone to measure up, only to inform one of her friends later in the wine bar, in a voice loud enough to be overheard by a neighbour of the potential vendors, that the house was crap and the decor total shit, and that she personally wouldn't live there if she was paid.

And then there had been the afternoons when she had mysteriously never reappeared in the office after lunch, and the even more annoying ones when she had—decidedly the worse for drink.

Andrew had already been forced to give her a verbal warning—twice, but the last time she had totally unnerved him by interrupting him in mid-sentence to ask him conversationally if he actually preferred shagging dogs. Her reference to his current girlfriend, the plain, dumpy daughter of a local property developer, had thrown him so completely that he had totally lost his thread.

'We've got clients complaining, Zoë,' he told her in a hectoring voice. 'You were supposed to send details of flats out to Todd Fairbrother. He telephoned three days ago to complain that he hasn't received them.'

'He wants an apartment with three double bedrooms with walk-in "closets" and their own bathrooms, plus a computer room, access to a gym, and a rumpus room, whatever that is. He's crazy,' Zoë told him unrepentantly.

Andrew glowered at her.

'You'll have to do without a lunch hour today to make up for the time you haven't worked,' he told her crossly. 'I've got a meeting at twelve with a potential client and the executors of Draycotte Manor.'

Zoë gave him an insincere smile. Did he honestly think she was going to stay here in this boring office when she could be in the wine bar? No way!

Ian was away again and she was bored. Laura had become as obsessed by the boys and their routine as her mother had been, and had flatly refused to join her for a drink after work.

'Zoë, I can't,' she had protested. 'What about the boys?'

'What about them?' Zoë had yawned.

'I can't just leave them...'

'Give Ma a ring. She'll be ready to come to heel by now. I'll bet she's just itching to check them over and make sure you haven't been abusing them in some dreadful way.'

'You pay me to look after them,' Laura had reminded her. 'It's my job.'

'God, Laura,' Zoë had protested. 'Have you any idea how boring you sound? No wonder you don't have a man!'

Idly Zoë went on line and checked her horoscope, and then just to be on the safe side she checked Ian's, scowling when she read that it was a good day for connecting with other people.

Ian. Just thinking about him made her body ache for him. He wasn't due home for another three days. How did he feel going without a shag for days on end? Or did he not go without! Jealousy, white-hot and feral, clawed at her insides, a living, tearing tormentor, mocking her. Viciously she punched her keyboard and then realised she had just wiped the details of a new sale she was supposed to be listing.

Oh, hell! Well, she would just have to make them up!

'Where are we going?'

Laura knew the boys pretty well now. It was always George who asked the questions, looked anxious and constantly checked everything she said and did, until he felt totally secure that he understood. William was much more laid-back than his older brother.

'To the doctor's,' Laura answered patiently as she drove them there in the car she'd recently bought out of her savings. It was much more convenient not having to share Zoë's car. 'Remember, we talked about it yesterday. You have to go and be weighed and measured, because the doctor needs to know how much you are both growing.'

It wasn't completely true. George had apparently had breathing difficulties in the early weeks of his life and was supposed to attend the local surgery for regular check-ups, but Laura had only discovered this when Ian had asked Zoë if George had kept his appointment.

Sulkily Zoë had admitted that he had not and blamed her mother for this oversight, and it had been left to Laura to ring the surgery and apologise and make a fresh appointment.

It had crossed her mind that George might be inclined to be slightly asthmatic. He certainly seemed to wheeze slightly and have trouble breathing properly whenever he became anxious, but Zoë had dismissed her concern with an airy, 'Oh, for God's sake stop fussing over him, Laura. There's nothing wrong with him.'

* * *

Marcus had had a bad week. One of his patients had gone into labour too early following a car accident, and had lost her baby. She and her husband were both devastated—the baby had been a much-longed-for sister for their eight-year-old son, and Marcus had felt totally helpless in the face of both parents' shocked grief. The mother had lost so much blood they had thought they were going to lose her as well at one stage. And Marcus had stayed at the hospital with the husband until they knew she was safe.

Today was his morning for repeat visits. He frowned as he looked at his list. George Chambers.

So far he had missed three appointments, and the mother had apparently been told that there was a degree of concern that her child could potentially be asthmatic.

George was his first patient. A little grimly, he flicked his intercom.

When she heard George's name called, Laura calmly detached William from the toys he was playing with and guided both boys out of the waiting room.

Marcus' eyes widened and then narrowed a little as his door opened and Laura walked in. He recognised her immediately from the wine bar. Unable to stop himself, he said coolly, 'Ah, good, I'm pleased to see that you were able to make it.'

Laura gave him a level look.

'Yes, I'm sorry about the missed appointment. I did explain.'

It irritated Marcus that she should be so calm and so unapologetic. Ignoring her, he turned to George and started to check him over.

'Has he been having much difficulty breathing recently?' he asked Laura, without looking at her. 'Only there seems to be a degree of inflammation in his lungs...'

'He does sometimes get slightly breathless when he is anxious,' Laura confirmed.

'I'd like to refer him to the asthma clinic,' Marcus announced when he had finished examining George, giving the boy a reassuring smile as he saw the worried look in his eyes. 'I see from our records that he didn't keep the appointment before last either. You were away skiing at the time, I believe.'

'Actually—' Laura began, but Marcus refused to allow her to finish.

'Mrs Chambers.' He addressed her sternly, steepling his fingertips together as he looked at her over them. 'Childhood asthma is on the increase. Normally I have anxious mothers demanding that I send their offspring to the asthma clinic to be checked out if they so much as even threaten to wheeze, but you for some reason seem to think...' Realising that he was going too far, Marcus stopped. But that lost baby had been so very much wanted, and here was this woman who seemed to have such a cavalier attitude to her child's health!

'I don't have your records here or your husband's. Is there a history of asthma in either of your families?'

Laura smiled unkindly at him.

'Actually,' she began again, 'I am not George's mother. I am merely his temporary nanny.'

Not his mother. Marcus felt acutely discomfited.

'Oh, I see. I'm sorry. I naturally assumed...'

William, growing tired of the proceedings, tugged on Laura's tee shirt. Obligingly and correctly interpreting his wishes, she picked him up and settled him on her knee, where he promptly leaned into her and closed his eyes.

Zoë had insisted on keeping both boys up far later than their normal bedtime the previous night, and Laura was not surprised that William was tired.

Distractedly Marcus noted the way the younger of the two boys snuggled into Laura's body, quite plainly feeling at home with her.

Now that he was not judging her with prejudice, Marcus was suddenly aware of how naturally and instinctively she nurtured both boys. A small pang spiralled through his body.

'Laura, what's asthma?' George asked her unhappily half an hour later as she drove home.

'Nothing for you to worry about,' she comforted him, but she could see that he was not totally reassured.

'Was that the post?' Maggie asked Oliver with a smile.

As casually as he could, Oliver nodded.

'Anything interesting?'

'Not so far as I can see,' he replied, glancing quickly through the envelopes in his hand. The postman had been later than usual this morning. Normally he managed to pick up the letters and go quickly through them whilst Maggie was still upstairs. He remained convinced that they should have reported the poison pen letter to the police, but Maggie was so visibly happy and excited that he couldn't bear to do or say anything that might upset her.

'I saw Stella in town yesterday with her new grandson,' Maggie told him. 'Did I tell you?'

'Nope, only half a dozen times,' he replied with a grin. 'Let me see. He's gorgeous and looks just like Hughie did at his age, and…'

'All right,' Maggie laughed. 'So I did tell you. Oh, Oliver, I can't wait for our baby to be born. I just wish...'

As he saw the look she was giving him he shook his head firmly, knowing what she was going to say.

'No, Maggie,' he told her. 'You know what the specialist said. He doesn't want to risk either of you in a natural birth.'

'I know,' Maggie acknowledged with a small sigh. 'And of course our baby's safety is the most important thing, but I can't help wishing that I could give birth as nature intended, Oliver. I want to feel that my body has delivered our baby into life, and not the surgeon's knife.'

Tenderly Oliver put down the post and took her in his arms. He knew immediately what she was thinking and how she was inwardly comparing their child's conception to his birth and condemning herself because they were both 'manufactured' events. How could he not, when she had spoken about this so many times to him?

'I know that I couldn't have conceived myself, but to at least have given birth,' she had protested. 'To at least have done that...'

'You will be delivering our baby into life, Maggie,' he told her emotionally as he wrapped her hand in his own and held it against his face, before turning to place a kiss in her palm.

'You know,' he told her thickly, 'sometimes I can't believe that all this is actually happening, and that you are a part of my life—the most wonderful, precious part of my life, Maggie, now and for always. And yet at the same time another part of me knows that this was always meant to happen, that loving you is my destiny, and the most important thing I will ever do.

Whatever happens in the future, I want you to know that. I want you to know that even without this—' gently, he patted her stomach '—you have given me the happiest days of my life. And yet you are only mine by default, really. I know that…if Dan hadn't been such a fool…'

'Oliver!' Maggie protested, shaken by what he was saying and immediately wanting to reassure him.

'No. Let me say it, because it's true. If Dan hadn't been such a fool, there would never have been any opportunity for me to play a role in your life.'

'Oliver, I love you,' Maggie whispered in a choked voice.

'Yes, I know you do,' he agreed softly. 'Oh, Maggie, please don't cry.' He rubbed his thumb along the line of tears glistening on her face. 'I want you to promise me that, if anything should ever happen to me, you'll remember that more than anything else I want your happiness.'

Happen to him? Maggie stared at him.

'Oliver…' she protested.

'I know…' he agreed ruefully. 'It's just that sometimes I have to tell you how precious you are to me. How very, very special, and how very, very much I love you. Pity we still haven't had details of anything suitable from the estate agents' yet,' he continued so mundanely that Maggie had to laugh.

They'd looked at over half a dozen properties now, but none of them had come anywhere close to being what they were looking for.

Maggie had a mid-morning meeting with an old client, who was now considering downsizing and wanted to talk to her about designing an office for him in his home, and Oliver was due to visit a new small joinery business they were thinking of using, having seen samples of their work.

As they kissed outside the front door Oliver waited to watch Maggie walk towards her own car. Her pregnancy was showing now and it suited her, he reflected tenderly.

Sensing that he was watching her, Maggie turned round before unlocking her car. She raised her finger tips to her lips and blew him a kiss. She had laughed the previous weekend when he had insisted on taking her to the city to buy her far too many ridiculously expensive, specially designed mix and match maternity outfits, but there was no doubt that she felt good in them. Based on plain black and white stretch pieces enlivened by additions in a bold black and white large abstract pattern, the French maternity range had a style that far surpassed anything else she had seen.

Tight tops, bare midriffs might be the preferred look of younger mothers to be, but it certainly wasn't for her. In contrast the slim-fitting elegant black stretch skirt with its matching scoop-neck, short-sleeved top, embellished with the 'bikini top' style patterned piece that pulled down over the top, made not just a positive statement about her pride in her pregnancy but also made her feel that she looked good as well.

Oliver couldn't have done anything more to show her how much he loved her or how thrilled he was about this baby, Maggie acknowledged as she started her car, reaching for her sunglasses to shield her eyes from the May sunshine. They had been told that they could soon expect to feel the baby's first movements, and Maggie had promised herself that she would not allow herself to feel them until Oliver was there with her to share that special moment. 'So no kicking until your daddy is with us,' she warned her bump with a tender smile that illuminated the whole of her face as she put her car in gear.

Oliver thought that she didn't know why he encouraged her to take her time coming downstairs every morning, but she was well aware of his surreptitious scrutiny of the mail. Neither of them had mentioned the letter she had received after she had made him promise not to do anything about it, but Maggie knew that Oliver hadn't forgotten about it, any more than she had herself—or the arrival of the second one. But right now she was feeling so filled with happiness, so at one with the world, so totally confident and happy in her pregnancy that nothing and no one could hurt her. She could actually feel the tenderness of her love spilling from her heart to embrace everything and everyone around her. She had, Maggie acknowledged, quite simply never known a joy like it. It was unique, wonderful, a special, special gift to be shared with those she loved!

Nicki was reading the paper when she heard the front doorbell ring. Kit had complained earlier in the week that he thought it unnecessary that they should have every single one of the national newspapers delivered every day. Nicki had simply refused to listen. She needed those papers. And the magazines she had taken to buying surreptitiously every time she went into town.

She hesitated before opening the door, but then she reminded herself that it was all right, because Joey was safely at school.

The man standing on her doorstep was a stranger to her. Tall, and dark-haired, he was wearing an obviously expensive business suit and an equally expensive tan, his cool blue gaze making her aware of the fact that she had neither combed her hair nor put on her make-up.

'Hi there. I'm sorry to be bothering you,' he told Nicki with a smile. 'But am I right in thinking that Laura is living here?'

He was looking for Laura? Immediately Nicki tensed. His accent was Irish but educated, and he had the kind of commanding air that successful men the world over carried about their persons.

'I know that this is her father's address,' Nicki heard him persisting. 'She used to work for me and...'

Laura had worked for him! He must be the 'married boss' she was trying to avoid.

Something about the way he was looking at her was making her feel uncomfortable. She lifted her hand to her hair, instinctively trying to smooth it, vaguely aware as she did so of an odd sense of confusion and even revulsion as she looked down at her creased clothes. A fierce spiral of shock and fear shot through her. What was happening to her? Why wasn't she properly dressed, her hair clean and gleaming, her appearance pristine, her nails polished?

'Is Laura here?'

Blankly she stared at her persistent caller.

'No. No, she isn't,' she told him dizzily, and then stepped back quickly, closing the door, and leaving him standing on the doorstep.

Ryan lifted his hand to ring the doorbell again and then thought better of it. He had an aunt, over in Dublin, who was known for her eccentricity and her piety, and the woman he had just been speaking to reminded him of her a little.

When Laura had walked out on him, he had never expected that he would have to come after her. No. He had assumed that she would be the one to come back to him. The fact that she had not done so had piqued his interest, and a coincidental meeting out of the city had given him the opportunity to seek her out.

Women simply did not walk out on Ryan. And he never walked out on them. He simply, subtly, but oh, so unmistakably let them know that their time with him was over and that for their own sakes they needed to move on. And, of course, he had the excuse of a jealous Catholic wife, and the brace of children he had with her, who could never be put on one side. 'You do understand how it is, don't you, my darling?' was a line he had always found did the trick.

And when they did leave him, Ryan always had the pleasure of knowing that they would remember him with longing for the rest of their lives. For, whatever else he might not be, Ryan was a wonderful lover; he made sure of that…made sure that every woman he seduced and then bedded with such care and expertise enjoyed the kind of sexual pleasure that meant that no other man could ever supplant him in their memory. All over the world there were women for whom he would always be the supreme shag!

Not that Ryan would ever use so crude or indeed, even worse, so unlyrical a word to describe the act he had perfected, indeed elevated into an art form! No, what Ryan did was enable women to fulfil their destiny, to experience the full, rich extent of their sexuality; what he did was give them the most wonderful and the most precious gift of their lives, and what they gave him in return was a guaranteed, unassailable place in their hearts and their memories.

Ryan's first success had been with the young novice at the convent where his sister had been a pupil. He had pursued and persuaded her, and then when the time had come he had parted from her with pleas for her forgiveness and regrets that he had fallen so far as to attempt to steal her away from her calling.

He still glimpsed her occasionally, whenever he collected his own daughter from the convent.

Yes, she had been the first, and there had been many, many others since.

And Laura should have been one of them. Mother of God, Laura was still going to be one of them, he had promised himself, already imagining the rapt delight with which she would fall into his arms when he turned up at her home.

Getting into his car, he turned in the direction of the small country town he had just driven through. Maybe Laura had a job there now...

Maggie's meeting hadn't taken as long as she had expected. It was a lovely sunny day and she decided on impulse to go into town. And then, without knowing why, she discovered instead that she was driving down the familiar road that led to Nicki's. She didn't need to do this, she told herself. There was no law that said that she had to try to understand, and even less of one that said she should try to find a way to put things right. Why should she? Nicki had made her position plain enough. And she, Maggie, owed her nothing. Nothing at all.

But she owed the life she was carrying inside her everything she could give. One day her child might ask her to explain the meaning of loyalty and friendship and when that day came she wanted to be able to tell it just what those things meant. She could even show

Nicki her precious scan pictures of the baby, she decided wryly—if Nicki would allow her to do so!

Nicki breathed heavily down her nose as she heard someone knocking on her back door. Again! She had just finished cutting out everything she needed from the day's papers. It was extraordinary—and frightening—to realise just how much there was to be cut out and carefully pasted into the record book she was keeping. Every day children were snatched, stolen, disappeared. She felt a sharp thrill of fear and triumph as she studied the neatly cut pieces of newsprint scattered on the table. All of them proof of just how right she was to be concerned about Joey's safety.

She frowned as she re-read one piece, about a child snatched on the way home from school. She wasn't convinced that it was safe for Joey to be going to school. He could, after all, be taught here at home with her, where he would be totally safe.

Another piece caught her eye. A horrific story of a jealous stepsibling murdering a younger child. A cold shudder gripped her.

Would Joey ever be safe? Laura hated him, just as she hated her.

On the other side of the door, Maggie hesitated, and then, reminding herself sternly of all the years when she and Nicki had been the closest of friends, she gripped the handle and pushed.

Nicki was seated at the kitchen table, surrounded by discarded newspapers, but it was not these that caused Maggie to come to a full stop and stare in consternation at her, unable to keep the shock from her eyes.

Still gripping her scissors, Nicki frowned at Maggie. Maggie felt her stomach muscles tense as she studied her friend. What on earth had happened to her? She looked…she looked…Maggie swallowed and bit her lip, all the more shocked by Nicki's neglected, untidy, downright unkempt appearance because she knew just how fastidious her friend had always been. Even when she had been suffering unbelievable physical cruelty at the hands of her first husband, Nicki had still presented an immaculate appearance to the world.

'Nicki?' Maggie began unsteadily.

'What do you want?' Nicki asked her sharply.

'I…I was passing and I thought I'd call and see you. Talk to you.'

Nicki was frowning. 'I can't talk to you. I'm too busy.'

Silently Maggie looked at the mess of newspaper on the floor and all over the table, the pieces cut out.

'Nicki,' she began hesitantly and very gently. But before she could continue Nicki stood up, waving the scissors she was holding in the air, and demanding angrily, 'I want you to go, Maggie. Now…and I don't want you to come back here ever again. You know that you shouldn't be having that baby, don't you?' she hissed. 'Something will happen to it, Maggie. Something very, very bad…'

Maggie felt sick and shocked. Tears stung her eyes as she turned blindly towards the still-open kitchen door.

She could hardly recognise the friend who had meant so much to her in the woman she had just seen. Shakily she got back in her car and restarted the engine.

And then as she drove away she felt it—the tiniest of movements, a flutter, nothing more, as though the baby itself wanted to defy and deny Nicki's horrible words.

Now her tears were caused by relief and joy, Maggie recognised as she shook her head and whispered emotionally, 'I told you, you've got to wait. This will have to be our special secret now... You do realise that, I hope?' she challenged her bump mock severely.

16

'Maggie!'

Maggie stopped in mid-step as she heard Alice's voice.

'You look wonderful,' Alice told her fondly. 'Very glam. I remember when I was pregnant having to wear huge baggy tops and the ugliest pair of maternity dungarees ever made.'

'And you looked like a madonna in them,' Maggie told her, adding with a sigh, 'But then of course you were young.' A small shadow crossed her face. 'I just called round to see Nicki. Alice, I'm really worried about her. Not...not because of the way she feels about me...about this,' she added, patting her stomach gently. 'She just didn't seem like the Nicki we know. In fact...' She stopped. Life was complicated enough already without her adding to those complications by confiding in Alice about the poison pen letters.

'Maggie, there's something I wanted to talk to you about,' Alice was saying, looking so uncomfortable and embarrassed that Maggie immediately guessed.

'Don't tell me—the computer is acting up and you want me to—?'

'No. No, it isn't that. Actually, I was wondering if you'd found a house as yet,' Alice told her awkwardly. 'Only, you see, Stuart wants to put ours up for sale and you did say that you thought a house like ours would be ideal and so...' As her voice trailed away Maggie stared at her.

'But you love that house, and so does Stuart. I can remember the day he bought it for you. How excited and thrilled he was, you both were...'

'I know, but he says that it's too big for us now. And I suppose he's right. And besides...'

Stuart had consistently ignored her tentative overtures in bed recently—the mere fact that she had had to make them in the first place was unusual enough to add further fuel to her suspicions, without the bombshell he had dropped about wanting to sell the house, and needing to spend so much time working and living away from home.

She had to face it. Stuart was a prime candidate for a middle-aged extra-marital affair, if magazines and newspapers were anything to go by.

It had shocked her to recognise how primitively possessive and anguished she had felt at the thought of another woman having sex with him. How jealous and desperate not to lose him. He was her husband, her partner...hers! Her own sex drive might never have been particularly high—her nurturing talents lay in other directions. But she had often suspected that Stuart enjoyed the challenge of coaxing and arousing her; that he was that rather old-fashioned kind of man who believed that a woman was of more value to him for being that little bit unobtainable, and instinctively she had refused to change her own personality to meet the sexual fashion requirements of the times. But now, suddenly, she was discovering that she was nowhere near as sanguine as she had always assumed she would be at the thought of Stuart, her husband, her mate, sharing the most intimate essence of himself with another woman.

Normally, the first people she would have turned to with her fears would have been her friends, but suddenly it seemed as though there were barriers between them all, differences. She no longer felt able to reveal her feelings of insecurity and misery, which would have allowed her to expose them to some much-needed fresh air and common sense. Instead, she kept them enclosed inside herself, in a way that was only serving to hothouse and force her fears into a very dangerous and terrifying threat.

Now, having witnessed Maggie's shock at her disclosure that Stuart wanted to sell their home, she felt even more threatened.

'Stuart's got some new responsibilities at work,' she explained brittly. 'And he feels that he needs to be closer to the airport, so he thinks we should buy something smaller here and then he can rent somewhere to live during the week.'

She was almost holding her breath as she waited for Maggie to see through the façade of acceptance she had erected and to demand to know more; to give her the opportunity to express her feelings in full. But instead Maggie simply nodded and shrugged her shoulders almost dismissively as she acknowledged, 'Well, I can see his point.'

Unaware of what Alice was secretly feeling, Maggie was tusselling with her conscience. Although she might teasingly have said to Alice that she wanted a house like hers, she knew that she would never, could never move into the house that had been Alice's home. She would always feel as though she were a guest there, a voyeur, almost a trespasser. For her, the house would always be Alice's, and she knew that she would feel as though she were stealing something from her friend if she were to move into it.

Trying not to feel hurt by her friend's inability to sense her anxiety and guess at what lay behind it, Alice squared her shoulders and determinedly changed the subject.

'Talking of houses,' she commented brightly, 'you know of course that Zoë works at Sheridans, the estate agents'?'

Maggie nodded.

Alice gave her a slightly awkward look. Here again was a case in point where she would have welcomed the forum of their group friendship in which to air this particular piece of news! She felt torn between distressing Maggie by revealing it, in case she had not already heard it from someone else, and keeping it from her, with the result that she would ultimately feel betrayed and let down when she *did* find out because Alice had not passed the news on to her.

This was a situation where Nicki's calm good sense was called for, and where Alice felt very much in need of the back-up and support of the others, not just for herself but for Maggie as well.

'Well, I don't know whether or not you've heard yet, Maggie, but apparently Dan is back.'

'Dan?' Maggie instinctively placed her hand to her body, her shock registered in her eyes and her voice. 'No,' she admitted faintly. 'No, I hadn't heard.'

'Well, I only know because Zoë told me that he's interested in buying Draycotte Manor.'

To Alice's consternation, if anything Maggie looked even more shocked.

'Oh, Maggie, I'm sorry,' she apologised awkwardly. 'I didn't mean to upset you.'

'You haven't,' Maggie told her immediately, forcing

her lips into a smile as she shook her head and tried to gather her scattered thoughts. 'I…I just didn't realise. But then, there's no reason why I should have done. Dan and I are history, after all—and very much so. I just didn't imagine that he would ever want to come back here. I thought he was settled in New York…'

'Look, I was on my way to the library to get some books for my course and then I've got to pick the boys up from Laura because she's got a dental appointment, but why don't we go and have a cup of coffee?'

'Alice, I'm fine,' Maggie insisted.

Dan was back. Her heart was jumping unevenly inside her chest, and she could feel her face starting to burn.

It struck her that her reactions were not exactly dissimilar to those she had experienced when she had first known him.

'Who is *that*?' she had demanded breathlessly of Nicki, the day Nicki had introduced them.

'Oh, just someone I know…a friend,' Nicki had responded airily. And she had believed her. Because she had wanted to believe her! Because she had known already that she was going to fall in love with him, and because she couldn't bear to think that Nicki herself might be closer to him than she was saying.

Dan… Although she had never admitted as much to the others, knowing that they believed her to be wild and adventurous, Dan had been her first lover. Her first love!

And she had loved him with such passion. Such intensity, such completeness.

It had torn her apart when he had been unfaithful to her. It had felt as though someone were ripping her heart out of her body and that she simply could not continue to live. And yet at the same time she had been so close to him emotionally that she had understood the male need that had driven him into someone else's arms, someone else's body!

She had pleaded with him not to leave her, to give their love a second chance, and he had told her that he could not. That he could not bear to be with her knowing that it was because of him that they could not have children. That it was tearing him apart, to know that she knew…that she was protecting him…

'You make me feel so much less of a man, Maggie.'

'Not in my eyes, you aren't,' she had told him stubbornly.

'Maybe not in yours,' he had replied. 'But I am in my own! And I can't live with the burden of that any more.'

With the burden of her, he had meant, though, and Maggie had known then that she had to allow him to go.

And now he was back.

She placed her hands on her body. On her stomach, where Oliver's child was growing inside her.

'Have you seen much of Stella, and her new grandson?' she asked Alice quietly, and Alice recognised that the subject of Dan was not one Maggie wished to pursue.

Instinctively, Laura touched her new filling with the tip of her tongue. Her jaw felt a little bit tender, and her lip was tingling a little, but thankfully the anaesthetic was wearing off.

She had never been very keen on going to the dentist. Her friends had always laughed at her for making a fuss, and even her father had not really understood her aversion to the drill.

In fact, the only person who had ever seemed to

realise how she felt had been Nicki. Laura frowned as she remembered being taken to the dentist's once by Nicki when her mother had been in hospital having treatment.

'Do you think that Mum gets frightened?' she asked Nicki as they waited in the reception area. She didn't realise then that Nicki wanted her father, and was still treating her as a friend.

'I think we all get frightened about certain things, Laura,' Nicki told her. 'But your mother is a very special person, and a very brave person.'

'I want to be brave,' Laura said. 'But then I hear the drill.'

Nicki looked at her watch, Laura remembered, and then got up and said something to the receptionist. 'I won't be very long,' she told Laura, and then she disappeared. When she came back she was carrying a small package, which she handed to Laura.

'Open it,' she had told her.

Uncertainly, Laura did so. Inside was a small personal stereo system complete with a tape of her then favourite group.

'You can listen to it whilst the dentist is using the drill,' Nicki said simply.

There were times when Laura desperately wished that she had simply not returned home that day, that she had never been forced to confront the reality of Nicki's relationship with her father. Perhaps, then, when they had married...

But she could never forget the way in which Nicki had betrayed her mother. Or the way that Nicki had deceived her. She had believed in her! Trusted her! Felt that she had known her, but the woman she had believed she knew would never have behaved in such a way.

Starkly Laura stared into a shop window without really seeing its display.

'So there you are, my darling girl. Tell me now, and the truth if you please, have you not missed me at all?'

'Ryan!' Her eyes widening, Laura swung round and watched dizzily as the familiar lazy, triumphant smile curled his mouth.

'The very same,' he acknowledged in that rough, soft, deliciously accented English that tugged so dangerously at her heartstrings.

'I was in the area, and I thought… Ah, no,' he told her, shaking his head. 'I can tell that you have me for a liar… The truth is that I was missing you so much that I persuaded the dragon in Human Resources to give me your address and… Have you any idea just what you're doing to me right now? Isn't it a mercy that we're standing here in the street in full view of the townspeople? Otherwise, I might just—'

'Stop it, Ryan!' Laura told him sharply.

'Stop what?' he demanded mock innocently. 'Stop wanting you? Stop aching for you so bad that I can't think for the longing for you? Oh, no, my darling girl, I can't do that. I wish I could, but you are just too—'

'Ryan…' Laura warned.

'Come back to me,' Ryan pleaded with her. 'Come back with me now, Laura. Let me show you how much I've missed you. How good it can be between us…'

His voice was a seductive whisper that tugged dangerously on her senses.

'You know you want me,' Ryan was murmuring. 'And I sure as hell want you.'

Laura closed her eyes. He was married. He had children, and although it wasn't love they were talking about sharing but sex, if she gave in to him, to herself she would be exactly the same as Nicki.

'Ryan, it's no good,' she began.

'Laura, please. All I want is just to talk to you. Just to talk, I promise. Have lunch with me. Please...'

Lunch! Laura looked away from him.

The boys were with Alice for the rest of the day, and it was her night off.

'Yes, all right,' she agreed reluctantly. Despite her trip to the dentist, she was feeling hungry. Perhaps over a shared meal she would be able to make it clear to him that what he wanted—her—was quite definitely not on the menu!

'Good girl!' Ryan told her in delight, taking hold of her as he added, 'My car's this way.'

His car! Laura frowned, but Ryan was already tugging her arm firmly into his own and hurrying her down the street.

'Nicki, what's going on?' Kit demanded in exasperation as he walked into the kitchen. He had arrived home to discover two men measuring up the gateway, and when he had asked what they were doing they had explained that they were measuring up for special electronic security gates.

'What do you mean?' Nicki asked him.

'I mean, what are those men doing measuring for security gates?' Kit told her sharply.

Nicki looked away from him.

'I need to make sure that Joey is safe.'

Kit frowned as he looked at her. The kitchen floor was covered in pieces of newspaper, and Nicki was wearing the same clothes she had been wearing the previous day and the day before that.

'Joey *is* safe, Nicki,' he told her. 'In fact he's so damn

safe that the poor kid is in danger of being suffocated. He's a boy, Nicki, and he needs to be allowed some freedom. Can't you see what you're doing to him?'

'I'm protecting him,' Nicki shouted at him. 'I have to protect him.'

'Protect him? From what?' Kit demanded irritably. 'For God's sake, Nicki…'

'From Laura,' she told him fiercely. 'Laura wants to hurt him.'

Kit stared at her.

'Don't be ridiculous. Laura wants to do no such thing. Look, I know you've got this thing about her, Nicki, but to accuse her of wanting to hurt Joey! That's crazy!'

Nicki felt her stomach starting to churn. It was just as she had begun to suspect. Joey was in as much danger from his father as he was from his half-sister. Kit thought that he could overrule her, deceive her, that she was too stupid to realise how he felt, but she wasn't. She would never let either of them hurt Joey. Never…

She took a deep breath.

'Kit, I want you to leave,' she told him. 'I don't want you living here any more.'

'What?' Kit could hardly believe his ears. 'What are you saying? I'm your husband, Nicki…'

'No, you aren't,' she denied. 'You're Laura's father and that's all that matters to you. She's the only person who matters to you. Not me. Not Joey.' She gave a small shudder. 'I know that you never really wanted him… I suppose you wish that he'd died…like…'

'Nicki!' Appalled and shocked, Kit made to go to her, but immediately she backed away from him, her eyes filling with rage.

'No. Don't touch me…don't come near me! I can't

bear it if you do. You've got to leave, Kit. I just don't want you here any more.'

Kit shook his head wearily. He simply couldn't make any real sense of what she was saying. He hardly recognised her as the woman he loved any more. Nothing and no one other than Joey seemed to matter to her, and certainly not him. If, recently, Joey had become much more her child than his, then that was because she had made things that way. He had felt increasingly that he had become someone that she had initially tolerated and now resented.

He knew how hard it must have been for her when his business had gone through such a bad time, and she had had to be the one to support them all, and he knew too how upset she had been about the baby she had lost. He had handled that badly, not realised at the time…been too caught up in his own feelings of fear, inadequacy and the panic of worrying that he simply couldn't finance another child! He had sensed for a while that she had begun to despise him, to feel contempt for him because of the failure of his business, and he couldn't blame her for that. But he still felt that she was overreacting, especially now that financially things were getting better for him.

'Nicki,' he pleaded gently. 'Let's sit down and talk about this…'

'I don't want to talk about it, I just want you to leave,' Nicki insisted.

Helplessly, Kit looked at her.

'This is my house,' she told him. 'I'm the one who pays the mortgage.'

His face started to burn. Technically, what she had said was true. His mouth compressed. He hated the arguments that resulted from these dark moods she seemed to be suffering from so often recently. It was impossible to talk to her, to reason with her, and, he recognised bleakly, a part of him was tired of trying to do so.

'Very well, then. If that's how you feel,' he agreed quietly. Perhaps she did need some breathing space. Perhaps they both did. Things hadn't exactly been easy for them lately, he acknowledged, what with the financial pressure they had been under and then losing the baby, and, of course, Laura coming back home.

Tensely, Nicki watched him. It was all there in the newspaper cuttings she was collecting. Fathers who murdered their children because they hated them. Joey would never be safe whilst Kit lived with them. At first she had thought it was only Laura she had to protect him from, but now she realised her mistake, thanks to what she had read. She had done her best to make sure that Joey was protected. The new security system would help, but not if his father was locked inside it with them. No.

'I'll have to find somewhere to live,' Kit began. 'So—'

'You can stay in a hotel until you do,' Nicki told him quickly. 'You must leave now, Kit. You must.'

White-faced, he looked at her. She was looking at him as if she hated him. He felt as though he simply didn't understand her any more. As though she had become a complete stranger to him. Everything he tried to do to make things better between them only seemed to make things worse. And it all seemed to date back to when she had lost the baby. To when he had refused to acknowledge her feelings...to when he had let her down, he admitted guiltily.

Even though her declaration had shocked him, shamingly, a part of him felt relief at the thought of not having to come home wondering about what kind of mood she would be in; worrying about doing or saying something that would send her either into a furious outburst of temper or a withdrawn unbreakable silence.

Time out—wasn't that the new buzzword for dealing with volatile personal situations?

Zoë was scowling when Kit walked into the estate agents'. Andrew had refused to allow her to go for any lunch, staying in the office himself so that she could not sneak out behind his back, claiming that she had to make up her 'lost time'.

She wasn't hungry, but her body was suffering the effects of being deprived of alcohol, and Zoë gave Kit a churlish look as he explained what he was looking for.

'A flat?' she demanded suspiciously. What did Kit want a flat for? To buy for Laura? Was Laura thinking of leaving her?

The thought of being cooped up at home with her children panicked Zoë. She needed Laura. She needed her to be her friend, to support her, side with her and like her. And the thought that Laura might not need to be any of those things to her both frightened her and made her feel resentful. People were always taking advantage of her, and using her. She had thought that in Laura she had found someone different, someone who understood, someone who would be on her side. The paranoid, illogical thoughts of the alcoholic jumbled together inside her throbbing head.

Conscious of Andrew watching her from his own desk, she provided Kit with the details he was asking for.

Nicki knew that she had at least two hours before she needed to pick Joey up from school, but, nevertheless, she glanced anxiously and nervously at her watch before getting out of her car and walking to the front door of the house that Dan was renting.

He had given her his card the last time they had met and she had kept it in her purse ever since.

'Nicki.' Dan gave her a bemused look as he opened the door to her.

'I was just driving past and I thought I'd call and say hello,' Nicki fibbed.

'How nice. Come on in,' Dan invited her warmly, holding the door open for her. 'I'm afraid it isn't very comfortable, I rented it ready furnished. It was either that or live in a hotel. Can I offer you a drink? Tea, coffee?'

'Tea, please.'

She had made a special effort for this visit. Washing her hair and putting on her once-familiar uniform of immaculate business suit and a crisp white shirt. Putting on the clothes had felt oddly alien, as though she were stepping into another woman's persona.

'Have you found anywhere permanent to live yet?' Nicki asked Dan conversationally as he handed her the cup of tea.

'Only sort of.' He gave her a wry look. 'I've decided to buy Draycotte Manor, although it will be a long time before it is properly habitable.'

Nicki almost dropped her cup.

'The old house that you and Maggie used to be so besotted with?' she demanded angrily. 'But it's virtually falling down. I could never understand what you saw in it, but I suppose it was Maggie who persuaded you to want it. She was always like that. Wanting anything and everything she couldn't have. In fact she still is,' she told him bitterly.

Dan was frowning now, but Nicki was unaware of either his silence or his cool watchfulness.

'Take this baby she's insisted on having. She has no right to be having it. No right at all. And I told her so! After all, if she'd really wanted to have children, she could have had yours when she was married to you instead of—'

'No, Nicki, she could not have had mine,' Dan interrupted her quietly.

Nicki stared at him.

'What do you mean?' she asked him. 'Of course she could have had your children! She was your wife! You married her! You loved her!'

Dan winced a little as he heard the long dammed-up bitterness infecting her voice. He had always known that Nicki had hoped for more from their youthful relationship than mere friendship and that he had been guilty of deceiving Maggie when he had insisted that Nicki would not mind them dating. But he had seen for himself how much she now loved Kit, and he had always suspected that part of the reason Nicki had decided she loved him in the first place was because he had loved Maggie. Close friends they might have been, but Nicki had always had a competitive edge to her, a determination. Unlike Maggie, who had never or could never, ever resent the happiness of another person.

'Yes. I did,' he agreed calmly. 'And in fact, if I'm honest, Nicki, I still do.'

'No!' Nicki denied fiercely. 'You don't love her. You can't! You left her because you wanted children and she refused to have them. She was too selfish. Her career was too important to her.'

Dan's frown deepened as he listened to her.

'No, Nicki. That isn't true. The reason that Maggie

and I didn't have children was because I could not give her them. I am infertile. To put it in the vernacular, my equipment only fires blanks!' he elucidated bluntly.

'No! I don't believe you!' Nicki protested. 'You're only saying that to protect Maggie.'

To her chagrin, Dan threw back his head and laughed cynically.

'Me, protect her? My God, you don't know how much I wish that I could claim that I had. No, Nicki. She was the one who sheltered and protected me, the one who hid my weakness from the world. She was the one who sacrificed herself to save my pride. And how did I repay her? I destroyed our love by indulging in a stupid, meaningless, sordid sexual affair because I wouldn't, couldn't... Because I simply wasn't man enough to accept that the doctors were right and that the reason we could not have children was because of me.

'You see, even with the evidence written down on my medical report, I still refused to believe it. I still insisted that I was not the one at fault. It was Maggie who could not conceive, I told myself. I could have a child...with the right woman...

'But there was only one right woman for me, and I—' He stopped abruptly.

'Maggie gave up her chance to be a mother because of her loyalty to me,' he told Nicki sternly. 'And she protected me from anyone else knowing the truth by pretending that she didn't really want children—and, weak, selfish fool that I was, I let her. I didn't care about her pain. Only my own. God, when I think... If she has chosen to become pregnant now, then she had every right to do so, and I for one—'

'It isn't really her baby,' Nicki reminded him

sharply. 'It's Oliver's baby by another woman. All Maggie is doing—'

'All?' Dan stopped her incredulously. 'My God, Nicki, I thought you were supposed to be her best friend and yet here you are... Nicki?' he demanded as she suddenly banged down her cup and headed for the door, but it was too late. Dan cursed as he watched her get into her car.

Just having to think about Maggie being pregnant with her new partner's baby made him ache with remorse and longing. He closed his eyes. Now was he finally going to acknowledge just why he had come back?

Only today he had finally committed himself to buying. It was too late for him to change his mind. Contracts had been exchanged and he had paid over a substantial amount of money.

Wearily Kit looked round the apartment he had just agreed to rent. It was in a small purpose-built block and had a relatively low rental because the owner only wanted to let it out for a few months. Another advantage was that it was fully furnished and he could move into it virtually straight away once the legal formalities had been sorted out.

He had booked himself into the local country-club-cum-hotel for tonight—a part of him was still half expecting Nicki to ring and say that she had changed her mind.

How could this have happened to them? Their love had seemed so strong, so right. Nicki had been a tower of strength to him both during Jennifer's illness and after her death. The problems they had experienced had—or so he had thought—only brought them closer. Joey's conception, whilst unplanned, had given

him a chance to see fatherhood from a very different
angle. With Laura he had had to be both mother and
father, as well as the husband of an extremely sick
wife; with Joey, his role had simply been that of being
his father, and he had relished that.

Because of Jennifer's illness their sex life had been
virtually non-existent after Laura's birth, whereas
with Nicki...

Outwardly prim and even perhaps a little strait-
laced, in the privacy they shared as a couple she had
always been amazingly responsive and sensual. It was
completely true to say that he had only discovered the
extent and depth of his own sensuality through his relationship with Nicki.

Andrew glanced surreptitiously at his watch as he
waited for Kit to finish looking round the apartment.
He had had to leave Zoë in the office on her own, but
he had warned her that she was not to leave it unat-
tended. If she ignored his instructions then... His
mouth compressed. Hannah, his girlfriend, had told
him that he was a fool for not sacking her, and her father had agreed.

The wine bar was busy and Zoë had had to sit on a
stool at the bar.

'I'll have another vodka,' she told the barman. 'A
double.'

Andrew wasn't going to tell her what to do, she told
herself defiantly. He had had no right to stop her having her lunch hour.

She picked up her drink, and then frowned as she
realised that Andrew's girlfriend, Hannah, and her
property developer father were seated at one of the ta-
bles having something to eat.

Deliberately she stared at them until Hannah

turned her head and saw her. An uncomfortable flush stained the other woman's face and she leaned across the table and said something to her father, who turned round to look disapprovingly at Zoë.

Picking up her drink, she got down off her stool and made her way towards their table.

'Well, if it isn't Andrew's girlfriend and her daddy.' She smiled. 'Has he fucked you yet?' she asked Hannah conversationally, enjoying the gasp of shocked outrage the other woman gave as bright red colour ran up under her skin, and her father made an angry sound and started to stand up.

'Now look here,' he began, but Zoë was enjoying herself too much to listen, driven on by her own alcohol-fuelled, dangerous exhilaration.

'If he hasn't, I wouldn't bother if I were you,' she continued with a kind smile. 'I mean! He'll probably tell you that it's this big…' She made an insultingly small measurement with her thumb and forefinger, much to the sniggering delight of the youthful male occupants of the next table. 'It isn't. It's this big!' she told her triumphantly, halving the distance. 'You won't feel a thing…'

Andrew frowned as he looked round the empty office. Closing the door, he made for the wine bar, and then came to an abrupt halt as he opened the door and saw Zoë standing beside the table where Hannah and her father were seated.

'You're drunk!' he heard Hannah gasping as he reached them.

'Oh, really?' Zoë laughed. 'So I am. But at least tomorrow I'll be sober, whereas you will still be an ugly lard-arse.'

'Zoë!'

As the sound of Andrew's furiously angry voice penetrated her dizzy euphoria Zoë turned round, swaying slightly on her feet.

'Andrew. I was just telling Hannah about your little problem…'

'Hannah, Mr Webster. I'm really sorry about this,' Andrew apologised, red-faced with fury and embarrassment. 'And as for you! You're sacked!' he told Zoë.

'What? You can't do that!' Zoë protested, suddenly sobering up.

'I told you not to leave the office. You've already been warned about your behaviour, Zoë.'

'I was just having my lunch hour,' Zoë protested. 'You can't sack me for that.'

'You're sacked,' Andrew reiterated savagely. 'And, what's more, you're banned from ever, ever setting foot in the office again.'

'What, just for saying that you're a little prick?' Zoë demanded, but he was ignoring her, turning instead to comfort Hannah.

'Mmm. That was a wonderful meal,' Laura enthused blissfully.

'I'm glad you enjoyed it.' Ryan smiled back at her, reaching across the table to take hold of her hand in his own before she could stop him as he told her softly, 'There's no end to the number of wonderful things you and I could do together, Laura.'

Laura was not naïve. She had known when she had accepted his invitation to have lunch with him what he'd intended it would lead to, and she had been prepared to be propositioned by him. But what she was not prepared for was her own dangerous, reckless longing to agree.

Something, and she didn't wholly understand herself just what, had made her realise these last few weeks just how much her body was missing the physical pleasure of having really good sex. She did not consider herself to be a particularly highly sexed woman—far from it. There had been men, relationships, but rather fewer than those of her peers.

And, although she could never find him personally attractive, the sheer animal sexuality of Ian had made her achingly aware of the emptiness of her own bed.

She had even caught herself fantasising about the children's admittedly extremely fanciable doctor, she acknowledged ruefully, despite having turned down an invitation from him for dinner!

And now here was Ryan offering her the perfect opportunity to indulge her body in a bout of totally emotion-free physical sex.

But Ryan was married!

Maybe so, but she wasn't planning to break up his marriage, was she? Or to take him away from his family. All she wanted from him was sex, and somehow, her inhibitions loosened by the consumption of an excellent wine, in direct ratio to the heightening of her physical hunger, her loathing for Nicki's behaviour with her father no longer seemed to have the power to deter her in the way that it had. What harm in reality would it do to go along with what he was suggesting and indulge herself? They would, after all, only be sharing a physical relationship, which would not affect his marriage any more than any of his other flings had done. Why should she set herself up as a guardian of his fidelity to his wife? Why should she deny herself something she needed and wanted because of her own feelings about her stepmother?

'Why don't we have our coffee upstairs in my suite?' Ryan was suggesting softly.

Laura gave him an old-fashioned look. The hotel where he was staying was renowned for the luxury of its accommodation, and it was a favourite place for honeymooners and romantic trysters.

'No doubt it comes complete with candlelit Jacuzzi, and champagne,' she mocked him.

'I'm not sure about the candles. They would probably set the smoke detectors off.' He laughed. 'But there is certainly a Jacuzzi, and champagne, and a plethora of strategically placed mirrors.' Ryan gave her a smile that made her toes curl as desire ached through her.

It was her night off, and theoretically there was nothing to stop her from staying overnight with Ryan. Nothing!

After all, she was not Nicki, and Ryan's wife was not her mother!

Inwardly exultant, Ryan watched her. She was trying to appear cool and in control but Ryan knew women. She wanted him.

Summoning the waiter, he asked for the bill, and, without releasing his hold on Laura's hand or her gaze from his own, he signed when it came and then stood up, expertly drawing her to her feet with tender care.

'Coffee,' he murmured. 'Upstairs. In my suite.'

The suite floor had its own private lift, a huge plush affair in keeping with the whole ambiance of the hotel itself. The doors hadn't even closed properly before Ryan took her in his arms and began to kiss her with a fierce, silent passion that excited her far more than if he had said anything to her.

Somehow or other he had pushed her back against the side of the lift, the pressure of his thighs heavy and hot against her own body.

The shirt she was wearing was plain white cotton and not in the least bit sexy, or so Laura had believed, at least until Ryan had plucked firmly at her nipple through it, rubbing it between his thumb and forefinger until it was stiff and aching and then dextrously sliding her breast free of her bra cup beneath her shirt. Dragging his mouth from hers at the same time as he picked her up, he placed his mouth over her breast and sucked—hard—on her tight nipple.

The explosion of sensation that rocked her arched her back, tightening her whole body into a bow of sexual readiness, and brought a small mew of pleasure to her lips.

The lift rocked gently to a standstill. Ryan released her, smiling as she gazed at him with glazed, disbelieving eyes. As the doors opened and they stepped out of the lift Laura caught a glimpse of herself in their mirror. Quite clearly, through the damp patch of cotton clinging to her breast, she could see both the dark pink aureole of her nipple and its even darker thrusting peak.

17

The letter was waiting for Maggie when she got home. It had been pushed beneath the door and lay face down in the hallway, but immediately she knew what it was, her stomach churning nauseously as she stared at it, willing it to disappear.

When it didn't, she skirted carefully around it and headed for the kitchen. It had been a day of unexpected emotional intensity in several different ways, and she already felt as though her emotional batteries had been drained, leaving her with nothing with which to recharge her defences.

Oliver's words of love to her this morning had touched the most sensitive and protective part of her; Nicki's behaviour had left her feeling bruised and aching with sadness for the friendship she seemed to have lost; but it had been Alice's news about Dan's return that had had the most intense effect on her.

The past was the past and she had no desire whatsoever to revisit it, but she had loved Dan with a passion, a completeness, a mixture of emotions that had gone soul deep and could never be entirely rooted out of her.

When he had left her, she had prayed that he would find what he so badly wanted with someone else, so that at least in one way the pain she was going through would have some real meaning, some real worth.

The kettle had boiled, but Maggie ignored it, drawn compulsively back into the hall and the letter lying there.

As she bent to pick it up the baby gave a flurry of small kicks, as though it too wanted to escape from its dangerous menace.

Protectively Maggie placed her hand over the place where the small foot was making a tiny but very definite bulge in her flesh.

'It's all right,' she reassured. 'Everything is all right… We are all right…'

Instead of laughing at her when she talked to the baby, Oliver joined in. They had decided not to be told the sex of the child she was carrying, but Oliver was convinced that it was a boy, and he was already planning the excursions they would make together to watch his own favourite football team.

'He, if he is a he, might not like football,' Maggie had teased him straight-faced, bursting into laughter when she had seen his expression.

But she wasn't laughing now.

Her fingers trembled as she held the envelope, carefully turning it over.

A jumble of odd-sized letters cut from magazines and newsprint spelled out her name. 'Maggie—Baby Thief.'

Common sense warned her not to open it, to simply throw it away unread, but already she was walking into the kitchen with it, holding it in one hand whilst the other cradled her bump as though she were already protectively cradling Oliver's child in her arms.

* * *

Stella gave the empty kitchen an irritated look as she hurried in. She had a committee meeting this evening and she was already running late. Not that she was sure she would be able to go out yet. Jack had started to get very fussy about who gave him his feed, often refusing to take his bottle unless Stella herself was the one who gave it to him.

'Honestly, you can't blame him when you see the way that Julie shoves the teat in his mouth,' Stella had told Richard.

'Give the girl a chance, Stella,' Richard had responded, adding, 'It might make things a bit easier for her if you helped her occasionally instead of always being so ready to criticise her.'

If she was quick, she would probably have time to run upstairs and give Jack his bath before she went out, she decided, ignoring her rumbling stomach.

The door to the top-floor flat was open, and as she walked through it Stella could hear both Julie's voice and Richard's.

Frowning slightly, she pushed open the door into the small sitting room, which had originally been furnished for her late mother-in-law, her frown deepening at the unexpectedly domestic scene that greeted her.

Julie was leaning against the wall, holding a mug of coffee, whilst Richard sat in a chair, holding Jack. For some reason the fact that the baby was contentedly guzzling down the contents of his bottle whilst his grandfather and his mother chattered amicably over his head only added to Stella's irritation, especially since when she had previously tried to persuade Richard to take an interest in the baby by pointing out to him how much he looked like their own son, he had steadfastly refused to do so.

'Look, if you want to go out this evening, Julie,' she announced, 'I can look after Jack.'

'It's okay, I've already arranged to drop him off at Mum's,' Julie told her.

Before Stella could say anything, Richard reminded her frowningly, 'I thought you had a committee meeting tonight.'

'Yes, I do, but it isn't an important one and I could have cancelled it.' She flushed a little when she saw the look Richard was giving her, although he didn't say anything until a little later on after Julie had gone out and they were on their own in the kitchen.

'I know how much Jack means to you, Stella,' he began. 'But you've got to remember that he is Julie's child and she has her own plans for his future.'

'He may be Julie's child, but he's also Hughie's child and our grandson,' Stella pointed out quickly.

'Hughie might have fathered him,' Richard told her, 'but that doesn't make him his father. Hughie doesn't want to be his father. He doesn't want the responsibility of a child.'

'No, and neither does Julie. I know that,' Stella agreed, seeing an unexpected opportunity to tell Richard what she wanted them to do. 'Julie intends to have Jack adopted, but he's our grandchild, Richard. We are his family, his blood.' She took a deep breath. 'I want us to adopt him. It wouldn't be difficult,' she rushed on. 'I've checked with a few people I know who…who deal with this sort of thing, and the feeling is these days that it's preferable to place a child within its own family where possible…'

'Stella! No!'

The authoritative severity of Richard's denial shook her a little. She had been expecting him to protest, and even to argue a little—Richard instinctively objected in principle to anything that might interfere with his own hallowed routine. But the stern way in which he was regarding her was so out of character that for a moment she did not know how to react to it.

But then she quickly reminded herself of all the many occasions in the past when she had had to act for the greater good of everyone concerned and take charge, even if it had meant overruling Richard in the process.

'Look, it's the obvious thing to do,' she insisted. 'After all, a hundred years ago it was quite common for grandmothers to bring up their grandchildren alongside their own children. And look at Alice, she's virtually bringing up those two boys of Zoë's. It makes sense, Richard. Julie will be able to go back to school, and then on to university, and of course she'll be able to see Jack whenever she wants to. I mean obviously, at some stage, she's going to get married and no doubt want to start a proper family, but that's a long way in the future and—'

'And when she does we will be free to keep Jack. Is that what you're thinking?' Richard challenged her sharply.

Stella frowned, not comprehending the reason for his anger or its intensity.

'Well, why not?' she demanded. 'It makes sense, surely you can see that…'

'Does it? What if Julie should have plans of her own for Jack?'

'You mean having him adopted, but I've already explained to you. We can do that. Oh, honestly, Richard. Haven't you listened to anything I've been saying? That's your trouble, you know. You never really listen. Anyway, I don't care what you say! I've made up my mind. Jack is going to stay with us!'

'I have been listening, Stella,' Richard told her grimly. 'But you are not the person who has the right to make decisions about Jack's future. Julie—'

'Oh, Julie!' Stella interrupted him dismissively. 'She loves Jack, of course, but she's so young, Richard. She'll be only too pleased to have us take over the responsibility of caring for Jack from her. She's much more interested in going out with her friends than she is in being a mother, anyone can see that.'

Richard was still frowning, but Stella ignored both his frown and the grave look he was giving her. She knew she was right. And besides, the thought of anyone other than herself mothering Jack and bringing him up was unthinkable, unbearable!

'Where's Dad?' Joey demanded as he looked at the clock. 'He's normally home by now!'

'He's…he's had to go away on business,' Nicki lied. She would have to tell Joey that Kit wasn't coming back, of course, but not yet. One day, when he was older, he would understand why she had had to do the things she had done…why she had needed to protect him.

As he bent his head over his homework she studied him with aching, tormented love. Yes, he was safe now! But for how long? What if Kit tried to take him away from her?

Her heart started to beat frantically.

Her conversation with Dan had left her feeling confused and upset. She knew that he had been lying to her and that he had been trying to protect Maggie, because he still loved her.

But she didn't care about that. She was even glad about it. Reawakening her love for Dan, sharing herself with someone other than Joey, just wasn't something she wanted to do, she realised now. It was too complicated, too stressful. In order to keep Joey safe she needed to be free to dedicate herself totally to him. And besides, in the animal world male animals sometimes killed the young they had not fathered themselves. And at bottom human beings were still programmed by the same feral instincts for survival as animals. Maggie, Maggie, what was it about her that made her so special? Nicki wondered resentfully. Why should she be having this baby when her own...?

But at least she had Joey. For now. Until something, someone took him away from her.

But she could not let that happen. The thought of him being unhappy or in pain tore at her until her emotions were raw with agony.

This world was just not a fit place for her precious son to live in. It was not a safe place for him to live in!

'Mum, when I've finished my homework can I go out and play?' Joey asked her pleadingly.

'No! No, Joey. You have to stay in. It isn't safe out there,' she told him frantically. 'You must stay inside, in here with me.'

Laura moaned, her face contorting, her hands reaching up above her head to grip the bed head as, with every powerful, deliberately slow, tormenting thrust of his flesh within her own, Ryan drove her further and further up the bed.

It was sex as she had never known it and never even thought previously of wanting, stripped bare of emotion and perfected into a physical art form that left her shocked by how much she wanted it, begging for more as Ryan had slowly and sensually aroused every one of her senses. Long, long before he had finally entered her she had forgotten why she had ever thought it necessary to run away from both him and her own desire for him.

Her orgasm came quickly and intensely; so intensely that the only sound she could make was a guttural shocked exclamation of almost unbearable pleasure as it gripped and possessed her, contorted her from head to toe and convulsed her into spasms that stole her senses and her breath

She heard the phone ringing as she started to come down, Ryan cursing as he apologised ruefully to her.

'Holy Mother of God, I clean forgot to switch it off. It's my youngest, Liam. Probably wants to know why I haven't telephoned to read his bedtime story.'

Laura knew that he was trying to be humorous, but the last thing she felt like doing was laughing. Listening to him, too sexually exhausted to move, Laura was filled with a self-revulsion almost as intense as her orgasm had been.

She could hear Ryan talking to his son as he got up off the bed and headed for the privacy of the suite's sitting room, blowing her a kiss *en route.*

Like an automaton, she gathered up her clothes and headed for the bathroom, locking herself in while she did what she had to do and then showered and dressed. Her fingers felt numb, trembling over buttons and zips, but her mind wasn't numb. How could she have done what she had just done? How could she? And even now when her mind, her emotions were crawling with self-loathing, her body was still glorying, gloating in the physical aftermath of her self betrayal! Was this how Nicki had felt?

'Oh, it's you.' Narrowing her eyes drunkenly, Zoë stared at Laura. 'Decided not to stay in your new flat, have you?' she demanded in a disgruntled voice.

Laura frowned as she looked at her. Even without the evidence of the vodka bottle on the table and the almost empty glass, the overly careful way in which Zoë was trying to form her words would have given away the fact that she had been drinking.

'I suppose the boys are asleep, are they?' Laura asked her.

'S'pose so.' Zoë shrugged. 'I dunno, though. They're at Ma's. I rang her and asked her to keep them until the morning. So when are you going to leave, then, and move into your new flat?'

'What new flat? Zoë, I—'

'The flat your daddy was in our office renting for you today,' Zoë spat viciously at her. 'And if you think I don't know what you're up to you can think again. You're after Ian, aren't you? Well, there's no way—'

'Zoë.' Laura stopped her sharply. 'I am not "after" Ian, and as for this flat I think you must have made a mistake.'

'Isn't a mistake. Only mistake I made was in trusting you and thinking you were my friend,' Zoë told her morosely, her speech deteriorating into a thick slur.

Uneasily Laura watched her as she reached for the almost empty bottle and poured what was left of it into her glass.

'I don't think—' she began, but Zoë interrupted her immediately.

'Don't pay you to think,' she said nastily. 'Don't pay you to shag my husband either... You're all the same. Everyone's the same,' she hiccuped, tears of self-pity flooding her eyes.

Laura suspected she might have felt more compassion if she had not already witnessed more than half a dozen similar episodes, although this was the first time that Zoë had actually been verbally abusive to her.

Refusing to listen any longer to her, Laura went upstairs to her room and dialled the number of her father's mobile.

What Zoë had said about him renting a flat was nonsense, of course, but...

'Dad?' she exclaimed when Kit answered. 'Look, I know this sounds crazy, but you haven't been in the estate agents' where Zoë works today, have you? You have?'

On the other end of the line, Kit sighed. He should perhaps have expected this.

'Look, I can't go into everything now, Laura. But, well, Nicki and I have both agreed to give our relationship a bit of breathing space. And I called at the estate agents' to check out some flat details.'

'Where are you now?' Laura demanded anxiously.

'I've booked myself into the country club for a couple of nights.'

'I'm coming over,' Laura told him firmly.

When she went back downstairs she could see Zoë slumped across the kitchen table, talking to herself, and oblivious to her departure.

Stella had been a few minutes late arriving for the committee meeting. She had seen Todd out of the corner of her eye and had been relieved when he had not made any move to come over to her. Whenever she thought about her ridiculous behaviour with regard to him now—which was as infrequently as she could— she was filled with a sense of scornful disbelief, tinged with alarm. How could she ever have imagined that she wanted him? She could hardly bear to think of what might have happened, of what she could have missed if she had allowed herself to become involved in a fully fledged affair with him. She might have lost Jack! The very thought made her blood run cold.

It had been a busy meeting with a full agenda, without any opportunity to socialise. She had seen Todd just before she had left, though. He had been deep in what had obviously been a very intense and intimate discussion with one of the other female members of the committee, his head bent towards her, his free arm resting against the wall in a way that enclosed them both in their own private space. He had looked up as Stella had walked past, and then deliberately looked through her, totally blanking her. She knew that his action was designed to hurt and humiliate her, but what she had actually felt was a definite sense of relief. It was impossible to believe that she had actually contemplated leaving Richard for him. The stable, long-standing marriage she and Richard shared was the very best kind of home background for Jack.

She looked at her watch. Another ten minutes or so and she would be home. Jack would be in bed asleep, of course, but she could still go up and see him…

'I'll just go up and see Jack,' Stella announced, pausing in the kitchen just long enough to remove her jacket.

'He isn't here,' Richard told her.

'What? Where is he? Has something happened? I knew I shouldn't have gone out—'

'Stella, calm down. Jack's fine. Julie rang half an hour ago, to say that she's decided to stay over at her parents' tonight. Her mother is on her own.'

'Stay over? Oh, right. Well, I'd better drive over there and bring Jack back…'

She was already reaching for her jacket, but Richard

stopped her, an expression of pity mingled with exasperation in his eyes.

'No. Stella, you can't do that.'

'Of course I can,' she protested. 'I must. This is his home. His things are here, his cot and—'

'Jack's home is with Julie. You must understand and accept that, Stella, otherwise...' He stopped and shook his head.

There was a look in his eyes she didn't understand, didn't want to understand, a part of her recognised as she said quickly, 'Well, I suppose we can't stop her from staying with her mother, but really she should have said something instead of just acting on impulse. I'll have to have a talk with her when she gets back. It isn't good for Jack to have his routine disrupted like this. I've been thinking, Richard, we really need to get him a decent pram. That silly three-wheeler thing that Julie insisted on buying is all very well, but I'm hardly likely to go running with him, am I? No, I know it's a bit extravagant, but I think we should get him a proper old-fashioned pram, and of course something more modern we can use in the car.'

'Stella, I really don't think it's a good idea to be making these kind of plans.'

'Oh, Richard,' Stella sighed. 'That's so typical of you. Honestly, if I left things to you nothing would ever get done, and Jack would be walking before we got a pram.' Shaking her head, Stella went to fill the kettle. She would need to have a word with Nicki and find out what she thought of the private school she sent Joey to. Where a child's education was concerned, it was never too early to start making plans, especially with the competition for places at all the better schools. When Hughie had been growing up they had not been able to think in terms of private education, but now it was different.

'Dad. What's going on? Are you all right?' Laura demanded anxiously as she hugged her father and then stepped back to study his face.

'I'm fine,' he reassured her. 'I'm worried about Nicki though, Laura.'

Laura shot him an incredulous look. 'Why on earth should you worry about her when—?'

'Laura, I know how you feel about…about Nicki and my marriage to her, but in this instance…' He paused. 'This situation with Maggie being pregnant has affected her badly, and that's my fault.'

Laura looked blankly at him.

'I don't understand. What do you mean?'

'Nicki was pregnant,' he told her awkwardly. 'An accident… And I… Well, at the time I was struggling to keep my business afloat, and Nicki was working all hours God sends to pay the mortgage, and the bills, and I just didn't think… I didn't feel… I didn't know how on earth we could cope with another child. Having Joey hadn't exactly been planned, and to have to start again with another baby… In the heat of the moment I overreacted and panicked…said something that I realise with hindsight I should not have said, and that Nicki misconstrued.'

'Nicki was pregnant?' Laura repeated slowly. 'Dad…'

Kit could see the shock and the horror in her eyes.

'Dad, you didn't… Nicki couldn't…' As she fought for the words to say what she could scarcely bear to think Laura recognised instinctively that Nicki would never, ever have agreed to have her pregnancy terminated.

'No, no,' Kit assured her quickly, guessing what she was thinking. 'No, Laura, Nicki lost the baby… naturally…a few days after I had told her that I…I wasn't happy about her pregnancy.'

Laura swallowed, hard. Against her will she found herself imagining how she might have felt in Nicki's shoes, and recognising with a savage sense of shock that she was instinctively in sympathy with her step-mother. Of all the things she might have felt justified in accusing Nicki of over the years, not being a loving mother was not one of them. Nicki was as fiercely protective of Jocy as Laura had always secretly longed for her mother to be of her, as nourishing, loving and proud as Laura knew instinctively she would be with her own children. Laura tried to imagine how she would feel if her partner were to tell her that he wasn't 'happy' about a conception they had created together.

Laura loved her father, intensely so, but suddenly she was seeing him from the viewpoint of a woman looking at a man and recognising that he had failed to meet the high expectations she had had of him, the high criteria she had for the potential father of her children; a woman feeling saddened and disappointed by his weakness…his man-ness…and his inability to match her hopes.

'Because of that, Nicki seems to have got it into her head that I don't love Joey…that I didn't want him, and that…'

Shaking his head Kit burst out, 'I just can't seem to get through to her any more, Laura. She's changed so much, become someone I can scarcely recognise.'

'She must have been very upset when she lost the baby,' Laura suggested sombrely.

'Well, yes. Yes, she was,' Kit agreed. 'She actually said to me afterwards that she thought she was being punished for marrying me, and that she should never have changed her mind about ending things between us.'

'Ending things?' Laura queried, frowning.

Kit gave her a rueful look.

'Well, yes. After your·mother died, and it became obvious that you weren't happy about...about her, Nicki decided that for your sake it would be better if she and I split up. I felt so torn between my love and responsibility for you and my love for her! And I'd already put her through enough! After your mother died I—'

'I heard you and Nicki in the bedroom...having sex...before...whilst Mum was in hospital. They had sent me home from school, and I was in my room... I heard you,' Laura heard herself interrupting him to blurt out. 'I told Nicki about it.'

'Oh, Laura...' Kit's voice was muffled as he enfolded her in his arms. 'That was my fault too. Nicki had made me promise that nothing physical would happen between us whilst Jennifer was alive. She said that she couldn't live with herself if it did. But then that day...' He paused. 'She begged me to be strong for both of us, to remember my marriage vows, but I needed her so damned badly. Day after day in that hospital room, surrounded by the sounds and smells of disease and death. I needed to lose myself in her wholeness, her healthiness. She never wanted it to happen like that, and afterwards... I loved your mother very much, Laura, but her sickness meant that my love for her became that of a carer rather than a lover, a parent for a child if you like, whilst my love for Nicki was very much that of a man for a woman. She told me herself that she hated feeling that she was taking the love that should have been another woman's, and that she couldn't bear the thought of knowing she had enabled me to break my marriage vows. I thought I was going to lose her then!'

Laura couldn't say anything. She was trying to come to terms with what he had just told her; the revelation that it was not Nicki who had seduced her father away from her mother, callously claiming him as her lover in her mother's home, but her father who had been overwhelmed by his own need.

As she had been by hers earlier this evening?

A child knew nothing of the fierce, compulsive savagery of sexual hunger and need, but she was not a child any longer.

'Perhaps it was wrong of me to love Nicki whilst your mother was still alive, but I don't believe she would have condemned me for it, or have wanted me to burden myself and Nicki with the guilt I did burden us both with after her death,' Kit continued sombrely.

'In fact, I didn't realise until I almost lost her just how much I did love Nicki, and even then she almost refused to change her mind.'

'Because of me…' Laura guessed.

'Partially,' Kit acknowledged. 'She felt that it would be unhealthy for you, growing up with a wicked stepmother as a role model, even if you had created her yourself. She wanted to give you so much, Laura. She had an unhappy childhood herself, and then, with the physical abuse she had endured from her first husband, she felt very strongly that it was important that you grow up with the strongest, most positive feelings about yourself she could help you to have. She often used to talk about it before…whilst Jennifer was still alive. She even put herself through a course of therapy because she wanted to make sure she didn't pass on to you any negative feelings about what it means to be a woman. She suffered quite badly from depression during her first marriage, and then after Joey was born there was some concern. Of course, being Nicki, she refused point-blank to let anyone but me know about it, not even Maggie and the others, and fortunately she recovered very quickly from that.

'Despite what you think, she was always concerned about ensuring that your mother remained a part of your life. Having lost her own mother before she grew up, and never being allowed to talk about her out of a misguided belief that it would be too upsetting for her, she wanted things to be different for you. She wanted to help you to keep your mother alive in your own thoughts and memories, and to ensure that you would always feel able to talk about her and remember her. She wanted you to feel that you could always be open with her, always talk about Jennifer and make her a continuing part of your life.'

As he spoke images, memories were springing into vivid life inside Laura's head: events, conversations, things which, in the light of what her father was saying, she could see she had wilfully and destructively sabotaged in order to hang onto her vengeful desire to hurt and reject Nicki. And all because deep down inside, secretly, where she had locked the knowledge away so that no one, not even herself, could view the shame of it, a part of her had actually wanted during her mother's lifetime for Nicki to be her mother, to have a mother who was not confined to her bed, always sick, always tired, always to be treated with care.

She could still remember the innocent comment of a school friend, which had turned her secret longing into coruscating, destructive guilt. 'I bet you wish that Nicki was really your mother, don't you?' was all she had said. An innocent, naïve comment, not meant to hurt or maim, but which had done both of those and so very much more.

Yes, she had wished that Nicki were her mother. Had wished it, longed for it, and even prayed for it sometimes.

Laura felt the hot, cleansing salt burn of the tears stinging her eyes. She was, she recognised, crying for the child she had been, for the love she and Nicki could have shared, for the mother who had been too ill to be a mother, and perhaps most of all for the woman who would have been so many things for her if only she had allowed her to be.

'I don't know where or why it's all gone so wrong,' Kit was saying wearily. 'This obsession Nicki's got at the moment about Joey! He's my son as well as hers but from the way she behaves, you'd never think so.'

'Dad, why don't you go back and see her, talk to her?' Laura suggested, determinedly putting aside her own thoughts and feelings.

Kit shook his head. 'It's too soon. We're both feeling too raw. We both need time.'

'But you love her and she loves you,' Laura told him urgently.

'I thought we did,' Kit agreed bitterly. 'But according to Nicki, I don't know what love really is. If that's true, why the hell does she think I've been flogging myself half to death to get the business back on its feet? It isn't because I enjoy it! Given the choice I'd sell it off tomorrow and buy a little place somewhere in Italy, like I used to talk about, spend my time growing olives.'

'Have you told Nicki that?' Laura asked him curiously. 'That you want to move with her to Italy?'

Kit shook his head.

'How the hell can I? She's worked flat out to keep

things going whilst my business has been in trouble. It's only right that I repay her.'

'Maybe you could repay her far more effectively by being happy,' Laura suggested. 'Okay, so you can't move to Italy while Joey still needs to be at school, but there's nothing to stop the pair of you buying yourselves a small property, if that's what you both want, and spending time there together.'

'Maybe,' Kit acknowledged. 'We'll see!'

Laura's mobile rang as she was on her way back to Zoë's.

'Can we talk?' she heard Ryan asking her as she answered the call.

'We can,' she told him as she stopped the car at the side of the road, 'but I don't think there's any point.'

In the end, the decision she had known she would have to make from the moment she had accepted Ryan's invitation to lunch was much easier than she had envisaged.

'I enjoyed this afternoon with you, Ryan,' she told him honestly, smiling as he tried to speak but refusing to let him do so until she had finished what she wanted to say. 'Probably I shall never experience such intensely carnal and satisfying sex ever again. But the truth is that I can't live with the guilt of what having sex with you really means, whereas I can, if I have to, live without the sex.'

'No, you can't,' Ryan told her flatly.

'I can, Ryan,' Laura insisted. 'And, just to make sure that I do, if you try to persuade me to change my mind, then I shall get in touch with your wife and tell her that we are having an affair.'

Through the silence, she could almost hear the pressure of his thoughts.

'You don't mean that,' he said at last, but she could hear the note of angry unease splintering his certainty.

'I do, but in any event we both know that you wouldn't want to risk putting me to the test, don't we? After all, Ryan, you can always find a willing body to fill your bed and satisfy your ego. But I could never find a working and permanent salve for my conscience.'

She waited for him to argue with her, but she had not fully appreciated either the size or the vulnerability of his ego, because after a few seconds of silence he simply ended the call and hung up.

It was probably relatively easy to contemplate a famine with a full stomach, Laura reflected ruefully. The time to judge how well she was coping with her decision would be six months from now, lying awake at night with her whole body aching for the pleasure that she could now only enjoy in her memory.

18

Zoë frowned as she concentrated on the road in front of her. She had woken up with only one thing on her mind, and that was telling that little prick Andrew that there was no way he was going to sack her!

A car pulled out of a side street in front of her and she swerved round it, gesticulating at its elderly driver and sounding the horn of her car.

Her head still ached from the mixture of wine and vodka she had consumed the previous day. She turned onto the dual carriageway that formed the town's ring road, recklessly ignoring the warning signs for the police speed camera, pressed her foot down hard on the accelerator and laughed as she felt the car surge forward, oblivious to the fact that, up ahead of her, a lorry was pulling out to overtake a slower-moving vehicle...

Alice was making a list of the books she was going to need when the telephone rang. Anything to stop herself from having to think about what might lie behind Stuart's uncharacteristic behaviour. Before leaving for work this morning, he had informed her that he could be late back, his voice terse.

The temptation to say equally tersely, 'Again?' had been so strong she still wasn't sure how she had been able to resist it. But then, fear could be an extremely strong motivating force, as she was beginning to discover. And what if he did not come back? What if he simply rang her to say he was never coming back? Her hand shook as she reached for the telephone receiver, and perhaps because of the intensity of her inward dialogue it took her several valuable seconds to comprehend what she was being told. She lost several more in the panic and despair that followed that comprehension, but eventually she was able to understand that the hospital was ringing her to tell her that Zoë had been brought into their accident and emergency department following a road traffic accident, and that she had requested that the hospital inform her mother of what had happened rather than her husband.

'What—? Is she…? Can I see her?' she demanded shakily, the most terrible images flooding through her head.

'Fortunately, she isn't seriously injured,' she was told. 'But we will be treating her for shock and various scrapes and bruises.'

'Can I see her?' Alice repeated, her voice choking with tears.

There was a small pause, and Alice took immediate advantage of it.

'I'm coming to the hospital now!' she announced, and then hung up, rushing into the kitchen to collect her car keys.

What if the hospital had been lying to her? What if Zoë were far more seriously injured than they had indicated? Alice had never understood why she had wanted such a powerful high-performance car. Unable to see properly through her blurred windscreen, she switched on the washer and the wipers, and then realised that the blurring was caused by the tears filling her eyes and not dirt on the windscreen.

Zoë! Oh, please God, let her be all right, she prayed as she drove towards the hospital. Zoë, her precious first-born child, so much wanted, and yet so very, very difficult. As a child she had been constantly falling over, into and out of things and hurting herself, much more so than the boys. There had been regular emergency drives to their local hospital, but fortunately the damage had never been as dire as Alice had always feared.

And then there had been that time when they had thought she'd had appendicitis and she'd had to stay in hospital for several days. Alice had stayed there with her, until Stuart had insisted that she come home to catch up on her sleep. Zoë had screamed and tried to follow her. Alice had felt terrible, only getting as far as the car park before turning round and going back. When she had reached the ward, she had been greeted by the sight of a serene, laughing Zoë happily watching a television programme. A car accident, though!

Alice shuddered. The hospital was up ahead of her. She turned into the car park, mercifully not full at this time of day, and got out of her car.

Sombrely, Nicki stared down at the sleeping form of her son, her most precious and beloved child.

Last night, pacing the floor of her bedroom, unable to sleep, tormented by her fears for him, she had suddenly realised what she had to do, the only thing she could now do to protect him from ever being harmed. Once she had come to her decision, a wonderful sense of calm and purpose had descended on her, a healing sense of rightness and peace.

She had been very careful to crush up the sleeping tablets she had given to Joey into a powder so fine that he wouldn't be able to taste them, mixing them with his favourite juice. There were things she'd had to do—important things, and she hadn't wanted him to wake up and be afraid whilst she'd been out doing them.

Her hand had shaken a little when she had woken him to give him the drink she had made. Sleepily obedient, he had swallowed the contents of the glass she had held to his mouth.

Afterwards, she had lain down with him until she'd been sure he'd been safely asleep, then she had got up and driven her car to the large out-of-town hypermarket that stayed open twenty-four hours a day.

The girl on the till had been yawning and bored, uninterested in her purchases. She had panicked a little, worrying that she wasn't going to be able to find any garden hose, but then she had spotted some tucked away at the back of a shelf. She had filled the car with petrol before coming home, unsure of how much she would need, that same sense of beatific calm and purpose filling her with a powerful euphoria.

Her final action had been to go down to the special place in the garden where she had made her own secret shrine to the baby she had lost, a special place where she went every day to think and to mourn.

And then she had watched dawn pale the sky, filled with a soaring sense of relief and release that this would be the last dawn she would have to see, the last day she would have to face in fear for her precious son.

And now she was gently kissing Joey as he slept, smiling as she saw how peaceful he looked.

Soon now it would be time. A feeling of purposeful elation filled her.

'Mmm. Do I really have to go into the office?'

As he breathed a relaxed sigh of pleasure against

her skin, tickling her slightly, Maggie laughed tenderly and pushed Oliver away.

Maggie had been woken early by the baby's gentle kicking, and she had shaken Oliver out of his own sleep so that he could feel its movement.

He had insisted on getting out of bed to make her tea and toast, and then she had teased him into making love to her. Now replete and content, she turned her head to look at him. A small pang of remorse scorched her heart. Oliver looked so young: his hair ruffled, his jaw slightly stubbly, the clear morning light highlighting the smooth suppleness of the bare flesh of his torso.

Her own skin could no longer bear such a remorseless and unforgiving light.

'Mmm… No, I really don't think I will go to work today,' Oliver continued, nuzzling her skin a bit more determinedly.

Making a soft sound of pleasure, Maggie asked him, 'Have I ever told you how much I love you and how lucky I think I am to have found you?'

Oliver lifted his head to look at her.

Words of love from her were so rare—not because they meant nothing to her but, he knew, because she felt they meant so much and should never be used carelessly. He could feel his emotions reacting to her declaration.

'No, Maggie,' he told her gruffly. 'I'm the one who's lucky.'

Smiling at him, she leaned over to kiss him. 'Are you sure you don't want to go to work?' she asked mock innocently, whispering the words against his mouth. 'Only, isn't it today that you are supposed to be seeing Amelia Ainsworth, the footballer's wife?'

Maggie laughed when she saw his expression. Amelia had initially sought out Maggie after she and her husband had moved into the area. As an ex-model turned photographer, she had wanted to consult Maggie about an office she wanted to commission for the new house, which both she and her husband could use, and which in addition could serve as a homework room for their two young children.

'Amelia Ainsworth,' Oliver breathed. 'How could I have forgotten about her? It's your fault.' He addressed Maggie's bump. 'If you hadn't distracted me...'

Still laughing, Maggie slid out of bed.

'You know, you are one very clever lady,' Oliver told her ruefully an hour later as he finished his breakfast. 'And if I didn't know better I might even suspect that you had an ulterior motive for not wanting me around today.'

Maggie pulled a face. 'As it so happens, I do have,' she told him. It was, after all, the truth, even if Oliver believed that she was merely teasing him. As he grabbed his jacket and leaned over to kiss her before hurrying towards the back door her face became slightly shadowed. She hated not being able to be totally honest and open with him about anything, but in this instance she knew he would not like what she was planning to do, and the last thing she wanted to do was to quarrel with him about it.

While in principle she believed very strongly that honesty and trust were essential ingredients for any meaningful relationship, right now she was experiencing a conflict of loyalties that was putting those beliefs under a pressure they could not withstand.

What she planned to do today was something she

had to do. She owed it both to herself and more importantly to a relationship that predated her love for Oliver by many, many years.

She had known ever since she had spoken to Alice when she had bumped into her in town that she was going to have to face this moment, and she recognised that it could not be put off any longer.

'I've come to see my daughter,' Alice explained anxiously to the nurse on duty. 'The hospital rang me. She…there was a car accident, and she, my daughter…'

'What is your daughter's name?' the nurse asked Alice calmly.

'It's Zoë…Zoë Palmer,' Alice told her, quickly correcting herself. 'No, I'm sorry, it's Zoë Chambers. She's married now, you see, and…'

The nurse was glancing down a list on the desk in front of her, and had begun to frown.

'Zoë Chambers. Oh, yes. I see. Well, you can see her, Mrs Palmer, is it? But only for a few minutes, because the doctor will be seeing her soon, to do a blood test.'

'A blood test,' Alice repeated. 'What's wrong with her? Whoever telephoned just said that she was shocked and bruised and…'

'It's this way.' The nurse was still ignoring Alice's questions as she walked down the ward, coming to a stop outside a private room at the end.

Through the open door Alice could see Zoë lying on the bed. Her eyes were closed, a bruise swelling her cheekbone, and some scratches on her face. The hand that was lying on top of the bedclothes was bandaged and Alice could see that there was dried blood matted in her hair.

Immediately she hurried to her side, exclaiming in distress. 'Zoë...'

'Ma...' Zoë opened her eyes so quickly that Alice realised that she could not have been asleep, as she had first thought.

'Ma. Thank God you're here. What on earth took you so long? I told them ages ago that I wanted to see you. Tell me you haven't rung anyone and told them about this! Ian—he mustn't know...'

As she spoke Zoë leaned forward, grabbing Alice's arm in such a tight grip that Alice could feel her nails piercing her skin—feel her nails and smell the unmistakable scent of alcohol on Zoë's breath.

Instinctively she recoiled, both from the physical evidence of Zoë's drinking and from the shocked thoughts pouring into her head.

It was only just gone nine o'clock in the morning! Zoë could not possibly have been drinking, could she?

'Ma, answer me! You haven't told Ian about this, have you?'

'No. No, I haven't,' Alice answered her, white-faced. She hated confrontation of any kind, but now she knew that she was going to have to confront Zoë with her shocked, horrified suspicion that her daughter had been driving her car under the influence of alcohol.

'Zoë,' she began. 'I...'

She stopped as she heard Zoë's indrawn breath and felt her flinch. Turning her head, Alice saw a uniformed policeman and a white-coated doctor standing in the doorway.

'What's he doing here? That prick in the uniform. I haven't done anything wrong,' Zoë was demanding in a furious high-pitched voice. 'I'm in hospital. Tell him, you stupid arsehole.' She swore at the doctor. 'Just because I like a drink, that doesn't mean that the accident was my fault. It was that fucking lorry driver, if he hadn't pulled out when he did... I don't have to say or do anything. You can't make me. Tell them, Ma, tell them that they can't make me...'

Unable to speak, Alice stared at the wild-eyed, almost hysterical young woman she could hear uttering pleas so childish and unstructured that they tore at her heart, intermingled with the kind of language that made Alice's face burn with shame. This was her daughter, this pitiful, disgusting creature in front of her, who was gabbling like a madwoman, screaming and crying, trying to pull herself free of Alice's hold and then lashing out at her with such ferocity that her nails clawed the side of Alice's face, sending blood showering down onto the bedcover.

'Calm down, Zoë, we just want to take a blood sample,' the doctor was saying coolly.

'Yes, so that you can say that I was pissed! Well, I wasn't, and you aren't pissing well taking anything from me. Nothing until I've seen a solicitor! Do you understand? I know my rights. You can't make me stay here. I want to go home. Ma, take me home... now!'

'Zoë...' Alice implored her helplessly.

'You aren't leaving this hospital until it's been medically proved that you aren't suffering any after-effects from the accident,' the doctor told Zoë firmly. 'You are damned lucky to be alive at all, do you know that? There was a young mother in the other car, and four children she was taking to school. You were driving so fast that you crossed the central barrier and smashed into her head-on.'

He stopped speaking to look briefly at Alice as she gave a shocked exclamation of distress.

'Oh, for Christ's sake, you're exaggerating,' Zoë protested. 'I barely clipped the damned woman's car, and if she hadn't been driving like a prat she could have quite easily avoided me.'

'Zoë!' Alice protested, shocked and appalled by her daughter's lack of remorse.

'Zoë what?' Zoë mimicked. 'God knows why I told them I wanted you here. You're useless. Worse than useless. And if you think that I'm going to—'

So abruptly that Alice had no inkling of what was happening, Zoë stopped speaking and slumped across the bed.

Instinctively she moved out of the way to allow the doctor better access to the bed and to Zoë. And as she did so, she heard the unmistakable sound of Zoë being violently sick.

'Please, tell me what happened,' she begged the policeman as the doctor rang for a nurse to come and assist him with Zoë, who was moaning and swearing in between bouts of sickness. 'What's going to happen to…to my daughter?'

He frowned before answering her.

'Well if, as we suspect, it is proved that she was over the legal alcohol limit, then she will be charged accordingly. She's lucky that she isn't facing a charge of manslaughter, never mind anything else,' he told Alice grimly. 'Both cars are complete write-offs, and how they all escaped unscathed, I have no idea. The lorry driver who witnessed it said it was a miracle. We're going to need to interview your daughter properly, of course, but I have to warn you that we have several witnesses who say that she was driving dangerously.'

Alice blenched as she listened to him.

This wasn't something she could handle on her

own, and if Zoë had refused to allow the hospital to contact Ian that meant that she would have to ring Stuart.

Zoë had stopped being sick now and Alice could hear her sobbing violently and claiming that none of it was her fault.

'It's all that wanker Andrew's fault.' She hiccuped. 'If he hadn't sacked me… Him and that fat ugly cow of a girlfriend of his are going to love this. And bloody Laura. She's just waiting to get her claws on Ian, pretending to be such a goody-goody, and whining all the time about me having a drink.'

Ashamed both for Zoë and for herself, Alice felt her face burn. 'Zoë, I'm going to go and ring your father,' she began, but immediately Zoë started to scream.

'No, no! You mustn't tell Daddy, you mustn't!'

'Zoë, I have to,' Alice insisted. 'From what the policeman has just told me you are going to need help, a solicitor. I don't…I can't…'

'Oh, that's typical of you,' Zoë yelled. 'Dear, sweet, helpless Mummy, who can't do a thing without a big strong man to help her, but it's all a lie really, isn't it, Ma? You just pretend to be like that to get them on your side!' Zoë collapsed on the bed in a heap, crying noisily.

Alice hesitated. How many times in the past had she protected Zoë from the consequences of her actions, lied for her, shielded her from other people's anger and other people's criticism? She couldn't do that this time. It was appallingly obvious to her that Zoë's current condition was not the result of one too many glasses of wine over dinner the night before, but more likely an entire night of heavy drinking. It was useless trying to hide the truth from herself any longer, Alice recognised bleakly. Zoë was not just someone who oc-

casionally had too much to drink—Zoë had a serious
drink problem.

Standing up, she repeated as calmly as she could,
'I'm going to ring your father, Zoë.'

She could hear Zoë's screams the full length of the
ward, and, of course, she could not use her mobile until she was physically outside the hospital, sitting in
her car. She went through her address book until she
reached Stuart's mobile number.

The first time she got the message that the number
was not recognisable, she thought somehow the
phone had misdialled, but by the third time she realised that for some reason Stuart's mobile must be out
of action. And she needed desperately to contact him.
The only way she could do that would be for her to
ring the airline, and ask his PA to pass a message on to
him for her.

When the switchboard answered her call, she asked
for Stuart by name. There was a long pause and then
she was told, 'I'm sorry, but I don't have any record of
anyone of that name working here. Are you sure you
have the right person?'

Alice felt like laughing hysterically and telling the
girl that she felt pretty sure she knew her husband's
name, but instead, too on edge to argue or to protest,
she asked instead to be put through to the PA Stuart
shared with three other senior pilots.

Nancy Lucas was very much a career spinster of the
traditional sort, who had always made it plain that she
did not have very much time for her pilots' wives
who, she considered, should not waste valuable working time by telephoning their husbands with petty domestic problems. Alice felt her stomach muscles
clenching a little as she came on the line.

'Nancy. It's Alice Palmer,' she introduced herself. 'I'm sorry to bother you but I do need to speak rather urgently to Stuart. The girl on the switchboard couldn't seem to be able to trace him and his mobile isn't working. I wonder if you could get a message to him from me?'

The silence that met her request was so long that Alice actually thought the other woman must have hung up, but then just as she was about to hang up herself in exasperation she heard her saying uncomfortably, 'Alice…Mrs Palmer. I'm so sorry… But Stuart… Mr Palmer doesn't actually work here any more. I…I think I'd better put you through to our human resources department,' she added hurriedly before Alice could say anything. 'Just hold on, will you?'

Stuart didn't work there any more. What on earth was she saying?

The cool-voiced young woman from Human Resources was matter-of-fact and there was no sign of any discomfort in her voice as she told Alice briskly, 'I'm sorry, I can't tell you anything.'

'But is it true that my husband doesn't work for the airline any longer?' Alice pressed her.

'That is true, yes,' she agreed evenly.

Alice took a deep breath.

'My—our daughter has been involved in a car accident this morning and I need to speak to him urgently. He must have left you with a contact number.'

'I'm sorry,' the girl repeated, quite plainly not sorry at all. 'I really can't help you, I'm afraid. Oh, by the way,' she continued crisply, 'if he does get in touch with you, you might remind him that he still hasn't handed his work-issued mobile to us. We have informed the network to invalidate his line, of course.'

Trembling, Alice switched off her mobile. Had

Stuart been sacked? Had Stuart been sacked and not said anything at all to her about it!

Fear and panic filled her. Without knowing she was doing so, she rocked to and fro in her seat, like a needy child.

She was on her own, confronting a situation she had no idea how to deal with, and with no way of getting in touch with Stuart.

She could of course ignore Zoë and ring Ian. She reached again for her mobile and then stopped.

Hadn't one of her complaints been that she was never allowed to be responsible, never treated as though she was capable of being responsible?

Getting out of the car, she took a deep breath and started to walk back towards the hospital.

Laura had dropped the boys off at their morning playgroup, and had three hours to fill before she needed to pick them up again.

Her conversation with her father, and Nicki, were very much on her mind. She had an impulsive urge to go and see her stepmother, to try to talk to her. She started to frown.

Before she started her car Maggie read the letter again.

The clumsy letters were no less stomach-churning for being so mismatched and stuck onto the paper at odd angles, much as a child might have done.

'You are going to die and so is your baby. You have no right to live. You are a thief and a murderess.'

She knew the words off by heart—the letter was printed indelibly inside her head. She knew that Oliver wouldn't want her to do what she was doing, but she had to.

Before she could change her mind she started her car.

She didn't care what the 'evidence' might say, and whilst she respected and understood how Oliver might feel, he did not, could not know of that inner voice, that inner person prompting, insisting that she made one last attempt to reach out to Nicki! It was as though the baby itself were urging her to do so, as though he or she were somehow offering Nicki a depth of love and compassion that Maggie knew she herself had been on the verge of withdrawing. That knowledge shamed her a little. She and Nicki went back so very many years, after all.

'It was just that I wanted to put you first,' she whispered to her baby. 'But if you want me to do it…'

A firm little kick answered her soft promise.

Maggie knew there were those who would say she was being over-emotional and reacting accordingly, that it was simply not possible for the life growing inside her to communicate with her in the way she somehow felt he or she was doing. Perhaps not, but that wasn't going to change Maggie's mind—or her decision!

Maggie had no wish to be confrontational with Nicki, to accuse, bully or threaten her in any way. But she knew she had to speak with her again.

It was as though a sense, a something, a someone deep down inside herself, were insisting to her that it wasn't merely an issue of their friendship being in jeopardy, but Nicki herself! That same inner urgency was pushing her to go and see Nicki, despite the fact that she had already decided that their friendship was over, ended by Nicki herself. There was a debt between them that, for whatever reason, Maggie had woken up this morning knowing she must honour, and with that knowing had also come a sense of freedom and strength, so strong that she felt able to overlook the cruelty of the letters she had been sent, in order to repay that debt. A debt of knowing, and of times past. A debt of love!

Draycotte Manor was his! He had signed the final legal documents that had transferred the house and the land into his ownership, and Dan still didn't know whether he was quite sane.

He frowned as he stepped out of his solicitor's office into the bright sunshine. It was on his conscience that he had perhaps been a little hard on Nicki when he had last spoken to her. It wouldn't hurt to drive over to her place and offer an apology, explain that he had spoken in the heat of the moment—and out of the intensity of his love for Maggie, he acknowledged as he unlocked his car.

Getting Joey into the car had proved harder than Nicki had expected and taken up precious time. She had been terrified that he might wake up, but to her relief he didn't.

Her mouth trembled as she automatically reached out to fasten the seat belt around him and then stopped. He wouldn't need it where he was going; neither of them were ever going to need any kind of restraints ever again.

The men working on the automatic gates had told her that they couldn't finish the job until the following week, but that didn't matter now.

Before getting in the car herself, she checked that everything was in order. The garage door was closed and locked, and the windows were closed. The house doors were locked too.

She took a deep breath, got into the car, and then switched on the engine.

It was difficult holding Joey in her arms with the steering wheel in the way but she managed to do it.

She wasn't sure how long it was going to take... Not long, she hoped. She could smell the fumes already... She closed her eyes and pressed her lips to Joey's forehead.

19

'I don't know what you're making such a fuss about,' Julie told Stella angrily. 'Why shouldn't I stay at my mother's if I want to?'

'All Jack's things are here,' Stella reminded her. 'His bottles, the steriliser...'

'Mum has bought one, and she says that the teats on his bottle aren't the right kind. She says that's why he's getting wind.'

Stella stared at her, shocked by the sullen, openly hostile edge to Julie's voice.

'You were supposed to take Jack to be weighed this morning,' she reminded Julie, rallying.

'Mum took him,' Julie told her. 'He's put on two pounds. Dad can't believe how well he's doing.'

'Your father has seen Jack?' Stella couldn't conceal either her chagrin or her disbelief.

'He came home early. Mum says she's got a photograph of Dad when he was a baby and that Jack is the spitting image of him.'

Stella stared at her.

'Jack looks like Hughie,' she reminded her curtly, but Julie was ignoring her, turning away from her, lifting Jack out of his pram and deliberately refusing to make eye contact with Stella.

'I've got to go out shopping,' Stella told Julie as affably as she could. 'Is there anything you need?'

Shaking her head, Julie walked away from her.

* * *

Maggie frowned as she approached the roundabout and saw that the exit she needed to take was closed and that diversion signs were posted offering a much longer way round.

She hesitated, gnawing at her bottom lip. She had an appointment with the hospital later, only a routine check-up but she didn't want to miss it. Perhaps she ought to put off going to see Nicki until later? The baby gave her a very firm kick. 'Okay,' she agreed ruefully. 'That's fine, if that's what you want.'

She checked her driving mirror as she swung her car back onto the roundabout and did a full circle to bring her back to the posted diversion.

The sight of Nicki's new semi-installed security gates made Maggie frown a little. They lived in a market town that had a very low incidence of crime, and where virtually everyone knew everyone else, and where the issue of privacy was one that came more frequently into people's conversation than that of security.

There was no sign of Nicki's car parked on the gravel in its normal spot, but still Maggie stopped her own car and switched off the engine, getting out.

Nicki was a keen gardener, and the small bed at the front of the house, flanking the front door, was always filled with deliciously scented plants, but today it was not their scent Maggie could smell as she walked across the gravel, but the far more ominous odour of car exhaust fumes.

From the very start of her pregnancy Maggie had developed a nauseous reaction to exhaust emissions, becoming extra sensitive to their smell, and she lifted her hand to her nose in a gesture of discomfort as she looked round.

And then she saw it, creeping with stealthy, deathly intent from beneath the closed garage door, a pall of odorous grey-coloured mist.

Her heart lurched and banged against her ribs, her body suddenly freezing cold, her legs refusing to carry her. Immediately, instantly, without knowing how or why, she knew. In the same heartbeat as she offered up a prayer for Nicki, she offered another of thanks that she had listened to that oh, so faint whisper of instinct. And then somehow she was moving, running clumsily towards the garage, shouting Nicki's name as she tried to open the locked door, banging frantically. When the door refused to open, she ran desperately to the house, trying all the doors, but not really surprised to discover that they were locked.

Frustrated again, she ran round the side of the garage, where she knew there was a side door and a window.

The door was locked, but through the window she could see Nicki's car, and in it… There was no time to call for help, no time to waste at all. Reaching for the first thing she could find—a piece of stone lying on the ground—Maggie picked it up and hurled it with all her might at the window.

The sound of it shattering made her sob with relief, but she knew she needed to get inside the garage. Blindly she tore at the broken glass, desperate to remove enough of it to allow her to climb inside, ignoring the cuts on her hands and the blood running from them. Somehow she would have to find a way to breathe through the noxious fumes; somehow she would have to find a way to manoeuvre her pregnant body safely through the broken aperture, somehow…

She was leaning into the window, half choking on

the fumes as she tried to lever herself upwards, when Laura drew up, bringing her car to a skidding halt as she saw the smoke.

'Maggie!' Laura protested in shock, running to her side and dragging her back from the window.

'Nicki's in there, in the car...' Maggie sobbed '...and Joey's with her. She's locked all the doors.'

'I've got my keys,' Laura told her. 'Get back from the smoke, Maggie.'

'I can't just leave her, I have to get to her!' She continued to struggle to get back to the window, and it took all of Laura's strength to drag her away.

'Ring the emergency services,' Laura instructed her as she ran for the door.

Her hand was trembling as she fitted her key into the garage door. It was Nicki who had provided her with her set of keys, her mouth tight with bitterness and dislike as she'd done so.

Laura coughed, choking on the powerful fumes as she pushed the door open. She could barely see Nicki's car for the exhaust.

She could hear Maggie on the phone, explaining to the emergency services what was happening.

Frantically she hurried into the garage, fighting against the choking, lung-burning taste of the fumes, her heart hammering with adrenalin and fear.

Through the smoke she could see the still figure of her stepmother inside the car, her eyes closed, her arms wrapped protectively around Joey who was lying against her.

The first thing Dan saw as he turned into the drive was the two cars, the second was Maggie, her face streaked with smoke, and tears, her clothes covered in bloodstains as she turned round without seeing him and ran into the open garage from which he could see fumes pouring.

Getting out of his car, he followed her, ignoring the shocked look on her face as Maggie saw him run round to the rear of the car and yank the pipe from the exhaust.

'Dan, the car's locked,' Maggie cried as he turned to face her. 'Nicki's inside it with Joey.'

'Have you rung the emergency services?' he demanded tersely.

Maggie nodded.

He could see now that there were two of them, Maggie and a younger woman, her face grimly set as she tugged futilely on the locked car door.

'Get back outside, both of you,' he instructed them, adding firmly, 'Maggie, you shouldn't be in here inhaling these fumes.'

'What are you going to do?' Laura demanded.

'Try and break the rear window,' he told her curtly.

'The rear window?' Laura protested.

Dan gave her a brief look. 'If I break the windscreen it could set off the air bags. Now get Maggie out of here.'

Instinctively obeying him, Laura went to Maggie's side and started to guide her outside. They both paused as they heard the sound of breaking glass, turning to look back. Maggie pulled against Laura's constraining grip, but Laura refused to let her go.

If, as she feared, it was already too late to save Nicki and Joey, then Maggie should not be the one to make that discovery.

To her relief Laura could hear the sound of sirens, heralding the arrival of the emergency vehicles.

Her mind in overdrive, she acknowledged that she

really ought to ring her father. Maggie was shudder-
ing silently at her side, the bulge of her belly and its
promise of new life as grotesque in its way as the bril-
liance and warmth of the sunshine, given what was lying behind them.

Tears burned Laura's eyes. Nicki, her stepmother,
whose love she had never acknowledged or accepted.
Joey, her half-brother, whom she had barely started to
get to know. Her life would be painfully diminished
without them.

Gravel spurted under the tyres of the ambulance as
it pulled into the drive. The fire engine was behind it,
and Laura could hear the authority and activity of the
men as they moved into action.

Someone, a uniformed police officer, had somehow
materialised at her side and was suggesting quietly
that she and Maggie should go inside.

Numbly Laura took hold of Maggie's arm and drew
her towards the house.

'It might be an idea to put the kettle on and make
some tea, love,' the police officer was suggesting
gently, whilst one of the ambulance crew was heading
for them, giving Maggie a professional look.

'It's okay, I'll take over here,' she told Laura.

'She got here first and I think she's inhaled a lot of
the fumes,' Laura told her in a staccato voice. 'She
broke a window, to try to get in...'

'It's all right,' Laura heard the nurse saying gently.
'You have a good cry...'

Cry? She was crying? Laura lifted her hand to her
face, surprised to discover that it was wet.

'Nicki, my stepmother, and my brother Joey...'

'The men are breaking into the car now,' the nurse
told her, 'but I don't...' The look in her eyes confirmed
Laura's own fears.

'Come on, let's get you upstairs,' she was urging Maggie.

'I can't,' Maggie protested. 'I've got to go, I should be at the hospital for my antenatal class...'

'They'll understand why you can't make it.' The nurse was soothing her. 'Let's get you cleaned up a bit and then I can check on junior although, from the looks of this—' she smiled as she reached out and touched the bump in Maggie's belly where a small bulge was protruding '—it looks like he or she is pretty much okay.'

How was it possible to laugh at such a time? Laura wondered. But she was laughing, sharing the moment of relief and joy with Maggie and the nurse as all three of them smiled down at the small kicking foot.

Once Joey must have done something similar, a small bump carefully protected inside his mother's womb. How could a woman take her own child's life when she had gone through so much to give him that life? Any woman, but most especially a woman like Nicki, who had always revered everything that lived, refusing to even allow Laura as a girl to so much as kill a fly?

Dan watched as the emergency services lifted the inert bodies of Nicki and her son from the car. The silence in the garage was as thick and heavy as the exhaust fumes had been.

'Mrs Palmer. Please sit down.'

Alice gave the doctor a slightly uncomfortable look as she sat down opposite him. She had made the appointment on impulse after leaving the hospital, having been told by the doctor there that Zoë would have to stay in overnight to ensure that she was not suffering from concussion.

They had told her at the surgery that the new doctor had a spare appointment that she could take if she wished. She had hesitated uncertainly, and then accepted the appointment, but now she was not so sure she had done the right thing.

The doctor at the hospital had been too busy to answer the questions she had wanted to ask, nor had she felt able to unburden herself to him and discuss her fears.

Marcus smiled at his patient and checked her notes. There was nothing on them to suggest why she might have come to see him. He could see, though, that she was very anxious and agitated.

'I wanted to talk to you about my daughter,' Alice burst out. 'There was an accident this morning. She's in hospital.'

Patiently Marcus waited, listening carefully to the jumbled sentences.

'The thing is, you see,' Alice told him, taking a deep breath, 'she... The hospital... She'd been drinking.'

Marcus frowned. If she had come here to ask him to intercede in some way on her daughter's behalf...

'I knew that she sometimes drank too much. I feel so guilty,' Alice confessed. 'If I had done something earlier... But I...I just tried to pretend that it wasn't happening. They said at the hospital that it was a miracle that no one was killed. The woman in the other car was taking four children to school.' Without knowing she had done so, Alice had started to cry, slow, seeping tears of anguish and shame that rolled gently down her face.

'The policeman said that they had been able to smell the drink on her breath at the scene of the accident. It wasn't even nine o'clock in the morning and she was drunk!'

In her voice Marcus could hear all the bewilderment, anguish and shame of a middle-class mother who had probably never drunk anything more than the occasional Christmas sherry and celebration champagne.

'She wouldn't let the authorities send for Ian, her husband, so they got in touch with me instead. I could see what they thought of her...and of me. She was sick whilst I was there, and...and abusive to the doctor and the policeman.' Biting her lip, Alice raised her head and looked imploringly at him. 'I don't know what to do...how to help her. There must be things, treatments...'

Marcus relaxed a little as Alice unwittingly revealed that the help she wanted for her daughter was medical and not legal. In Marcus' experience, it wasn't unheard of for a certain type of parent to attempt to browbeat a family doctor into protecting an adult child from the consequences of his or her addiction.

'Well, yes, there are,' he agreed. 'But first we have to find out to what extent your daughter has a problem, and the only way we can do that is for her to come and see us.'

'But she won't do that,' Alice told him in panic. 'She doesn't realise how serious things are. She...'

Marcus sighed. Alice was practically wringing her hands as she pleaded with him to supply her with hope, answers, something—*anything* that would enable her to help her child, he recognised, but of course he couldn't.

'I'm sorry,' he told her. 'But in order for your daughter to receive any kind of treatment she has first to decide herself that she needs it.'

'But she does need it,' Alice interrupted him anxiously. 'They said at the hospital…'

'She may need it, but until and unless she recognises that herself we cannot do anything for her,' Marcus told her firmly.

'For one thing it would be totally unethical for us to force anyone to have medical treatment they did not want, and for another it is clinically recognised that, unless a patient accepts the fact that they have an addiction problem—whatever that addiction might be— no treatment on this earth is going to work.'

Alice stared hopelessly at him.

'You mean that Zoë has to come to you herself and say that she is—' Alice stopped and swallowed emotionally '—that she has a drink problem, before you can do anything for her?'

'Yes,' Marcus had to confirm. 'I do understand how hard this must be for you,' he said gently. 'There is an organisation for people who…who have family members who are addicts. It provides a forum where you can talk in complete confidence about the…situation. It's called Al Anon,' he told her, 'and you should be able to find the address of your nearest group in your telephone book.'

'But Zoë needs help,' Alice told him piteously. 'She's married, a mother with two small children…'

Marcus sighed. He understood what Alice was trying to say.

'Perhaps if you sit down with her and talk with her? Explain that you are concerned about her. Tell her that you love her and that you want to support her, but make sure she understands that she has to face up to what she is doing to herself and to those who love her. Perhaps her husband…'

'Ian?' Alice gave him a brief look. 'She doesn't want him to know.'

'I'm sorry that I can't be more help,' Marcus told her, signalling discreetly that it was time for her to leave. 'However, if your daughter should want to come in and see us here... You may find that the hospital will suggest to her that she looks at her lifestyle and perhaps she'll acknowledge that she has a problem that needs to be addressed, but, at the end of the day, what she does or does not decide to do rests entirely with her.'

Without being aware of having done anything Alice discovered that she was outside in the street, staring blindly in front of her.

She could see the estate agents' where Zoë worked—had worked, she corrected herself numbly. Her throat felt dry and her head was aching. She had some headache tablets in her bag somewhere. Perhaps if she went and had a cup of tea... What time was it? It gave her a shock to look at her watch and discover that it was lunchtime. She ought to have something to eat, even though she didn't feel hungry. She saw a small group of people going into the wine bar and made to follow them, stopping abruptly as she remembered that it had been one of Zoë's favourite haunts. She couldn't go inside. What if...?

There was a coffee shop a little further up the street, and she made her way to it like a stranger in a foreign land, painfully and anxiously, alienated from the people surrounding her, the babble of their chatter a jumble of words that meant nothing to her.

'Alice... Alice!'

Stella gave an exasperated sigh as she had to call

Alice's name a third time before her friend finally turned round and saw her.

'Oh, heavens, what a day I'm having,' Stella complained as she hurried up to where Alice was standing motionless on the pavement. 'You wouldn't believe the way that Julie is behaving. She took Jack round to her mother's last night and then decided to spend the night there, if you please, without so much as a phone call to me, and then this morning… Well, if I was her mother I would have something to say to her about her manners, I can tell you, Alice. I mean, when I think of what I've done for her. And Richard is worse than useless. You really would think he'd be more supportive. Alice! Where are you going?' Stella protested, thoroughly affronted, as Alice walked off in the opposite direction without a word of explanation.

'Well, really!' she muttered crossly under her breath. But she hadn't got time to go running after Alice to demand an explanation. She had some shopping to do, and she had decided that it was time that both she and Richard lost a bit of weight and started taking more care of themselves. After all, if they were going to have an active toddler to run around after… So from now on Richard was going to accustom himself to eating much more healthily! He wouldn't like it, of course. Like all men he hated change, almost as much as he loved her pastries and puddings. Stella's face lit up as she anticipated making all Hughie's favourite foods for Jack when he was older.

She had spoken to her friend in social services again this morning and she had agreed that it would be far better for Jack to be adopted by a member of his own family rather than by strangers.

'If adoption is what his mother wants,' she had concluded.

'Of course it is,' Stella had assured her. 'She's said so all along!'

Happily making plans, Stella headed for the supermarket.

As soon as they had been given the news officially, Laura rang her father. He arrived just as the police car was driving away, swirling up the gravel in a cloud of dust in his haste. The ambulance and the fire engine had already left.

'Nicki? Joey?' he demanded, getting out of the car and hurrying towards Laura. 'Where are they?'

As he spoke he was looking in the direction of the house as though somehow he expected to see his wife and son come walking out of it towards him.

'It's all right, Dad,' Laura told him gently. 'They've taken them to the hospital.'

'I want to see them,' Kit announced immediately.

'I'll come with you,' Laura responded. She could have travelled to the hospital in the ambulance, but she had wanted to wait for her father.

On the other side of the gravel forecourt Oliver was comforting Maggie, rocking her in his arms, his face hollowed with shock and grief.

Dan watched them in silence.

Maggie had turned instinctively to him in the immediate aftermath of her shock, and as instinctively and as naturally as though they had never spent a day apart he had held her and mopped up her tears, telling her that she had done everything she could and more than anyone else could possibly have done, and she had leaned her head on his shoulder and sobbed in silent misery for the woman who had been her closest friend and who had shared so much of her life.

It had been Dan who had heard Oliver's car ap-

proaching and who had released her, going to the
other man to briefly update him, just as it had been
Dan who had taken Maggie's mobile from her and
rung Oliver's number in the first place to tell him what
was happening.

For a second they had locked glances measuring
one another, and Dan had felt a sharp, savage pang as
he'd recognised the challenge in the younger man's
eyes and the determination. It was his own fault that
he had lost Maggie and no one else's, he'd reminded
himself as he'd watched Oliver stride past him to
wrap her tightly in his arms.

On the way to the hospital Laura had to stop off at
the school to collect Zoë's sons. Her telephone calls
both to Zoë and to Alice had remained unanswered,
and although she tried to behave as naturally as she
could she could tell that both of them were infected by
her mood, especially George who demanded anxiously, 'Mum's all right, isn't she? She's not…she's not
poorly, is she?' he blurted out, casting an anxious look
at Kit as he did so.

Laura's heart went out to him as she recognised
what 'poorly' was his own word for. Poor little boy.
How many times had he been forced to witness his
mother's drunken confusion for him to know already,
at his age, that her behaviour had to be cloaked in se-
crecy?

'Everything's all right, George,' Laura told him as
cheerfully as she could. 'I'll have to drop you off at the
hospital, Dad,' she told Kit, 'and then come back after
I've taken the boys to their grandmother's. Zoë will
still be at work.'

When her father made no reply, Laura looked uncertainly at him. She knew how shocked he must be

feeling, how unable to take in properly as yet what had happened. Just as she had felt unable to believe it when the medical team had come to the house and told her bluntly, 'They're both alive—just. We're taking them to hospital, but it's going to be touch and go, especially for the little 'un...'

As Laura moved she heard and felt the crackle of the envelope she had picked up from the kitchen table and put in her pocket.

It was addressed to her father, and she told him about it now in a quiet undertone.

'It's for you so I haven't read it, naturally, but I thought... Well, I didn't know if the police would want...' She bit her lip, not wanting to put into words what she was thinking. The letter, quite plainly in Nicki's handwriting, had obviously been meant to be read in the event of her death...her suicide, and at some point the police were bound to want to see it, she suspected. Even if by some miracle both Nicki and Joey survived.

She shuddered violently, wondering what on earth could make a woman like Nicki do something so truly, unthinkably appalling. To attempt to take her own life was bad enough, but to kill the child she adored so much was truly beyond comprehension.

They had reached the hospital. Laura stopped the car and Kit got out.

'I'll be back as soon as I can,' Laura told him.

'Why have we had to come here? Has there been an accident?' William demanded eagerly, with the very young's unawareness of the true horror of what was going on.

'I'm going to take you both to your grandmother's,' Laura explained, without answering his question.

* * *

'Laura,' Alice exclaimed, automatically bending down to hug both her grandsons as they hurried into the house.

'I'm sorry about this,' Laura began, 'but—'

'We've been to the hospital,' William interrupted Laura excitedly, before hurrying into the house after his brother.

'You took the boys to the hospital?' Alice paled. 'Oh, I don't think you should have done that, Laura! Did Zoë ring you? The doctor told me that she had to stay in overnight…'

'Zoë?' Laura looked at her in bewilderment. 'I'm sorry, I don't understand.'

'You said that you went to the hospital,' Alice reminded her distractedly. 'Oh, Laura, I can't help thinking about that poor women Zoë ran into, and those children. Thank goodness none of them was hurt.'

Laura took a deep breath.

'Alice… I didn't go to the hospital to see Zoë. In fact, I thought that she was at work. You see…' She could hear her own voice starting to tremble. 'I actually went to drop Dad off there. There's been…' She hesitated for a second. As a close friend of her stepmother, Alice was bound to find out what had happened.

'I… Dad needed to be at the hospital… Something…something's happened. And, and Nicki and, and Joey… I had to collect the boys from school otherwise I would have stayed, and I was hoping that you could have them for now. I had no idea that Zoë…'

As she listened to her voice Alice realised that Laura knew about her daughter's drinking. She could hear it in the way she was talking. Taking a deep breath, Alice said as calmly as she could, 'Unfortunately Zoë had been drinking and was in no fit state to drive.'

Then she frowned, suddenly registering what Laura had said.

'Laura, what do you mean? Something's happened to Nicki and Joey?' she demanded anxiously.

Laura nodded.

'I can't say anything more right now, Alice... I'm sorry,' she whispered as tears filled her eyes. 'I have to get back to the hospital. I'm sorry about Zoë, too. Would you be able to have the boys tonight? Only I might have to stay with Dad depending on...' Unable to stop herself, she told her in an anguished voice, 'They said that it was going to be touch and go, especially for Joey...'

'Oh, Laura!' Suddenly she was in Alice's arms and Alice was hugging her, holding her as Laura had so many, many times longed to have someone do, offering her the maternal comfort she had craved so desperately and rejected so fiercely from Nicki.

'Nicki tried to kill herself and Joey,' Laura told her, unable to keep the appalling facts to herself any longer. She was, she recognised distantly, still unable to believe what had happened herself, and just listening to herself say the words made her feel as though she were playing a part in a bad movie.

'What?' Alice's face mirrored her own feelings. 'Oh, no! Oh, Laura. I'm so sorry! Oh, Laura... I wish I could come to the hospital with you...'

'No. The boys need you here,' Laura told her, sniffing back her tears.

Alice stood at the open door for a long time after Laura had driven away. The news she had given her had practically driven her own concerns out of her thoughts. Nicki... A cold shiver ran down Alice's spine. Maggie had told them that there was something wrong, but stupidly, selfishly, blindly, they had re-

fused to listen, believing that it was Maggie who had
the problem...Maggie who *was* the problem, Alice recognised guiltily.

Zoë was in hospital! Laura ached with pity for her
two small sons, and for Alice as well. She had seen
how hard it had been for the older woman to tell her
what had happened.

What was it that made a person so dependent on
something that could only destroy them? Laura wondered grimly. Modern thinking was that, especially
where alcohol was concerned, there was an inherited
vulnerability that preordained the addiction, in the
same way that some people were predisposed to suffer from certain types of disease.

Could a person be preordained to commit suicide...infanticide? Laura ached with anguish and
shock. She still could not believe that Nicki, who had
always appeared so strong, so together, could have
done such a thing.

Would have done such a thing, if she and Maggie
had not arrived at the house by chance. By chance,
or... But no, she wasn't going to start thinking along
those lines, Laura decided firmly. If there was a gov-
erning fate that oversaw human actions, then she preferred to remain unaware of it!

Maggie had been so brave. Laura couldn't bear to
think how she might have hurt herself and her baby,
breaking that window and trying to climb into the garage, never mind the potential damage from the exhaust fumes she must have breathed in.

Tears stung her eyes. A part of her had always envied Nicki whatever it was she had that commanded
that kind of friendship, created that kind of bond.

* * *

'Maggie, I do understand your feelings,' Oliver said soberly. 'But there really isn't any point in your staying here now. You heard what the doctors said. Why don't we go home and then we can ring in the morning and find out if Nicki and Joey are well enough to have visitors?'

'No,' Maggie repeated stubbornly. 'I'm staying here with her, Oliver. She needs me here. You have to understand...' She took a deep breath. 'Somehow all of us have failed her, let her down. If we hadn't, she would never... I've got to make it up to her, Oliver, let her know that she matters, that she's loved...'

'That's Kit's job,' Oliver objected.

'Yes,' Maggie agreed. 'But it's ours, mine as well. Especially mine!'

'Maggie, if you're going to try to take the responsibility for this on your shoulders, to blame yourself because of the baby...'

'No. I'm not going to do that,' Maggie replied firmly. 'But I *am* responsible for not following up my own instincts. I knew that something was wrong, that Nicki was not truly Nicki, but I refused to follow that instinct. Look, why don't you go home? I can ring you...'

'Is that what Dan would have done?' Oliver demanded.

Maggie stared at him.

'I'm sorry,' Oliver apologised immediately. 'It's just that, seeing him there...'

'He had called round to see Nicki,' Maggie told him quietly. 'They go back a long way. You have nothing to fear from Dan, Oliver,' she insisted. 'Dan and what we once shared together is a very important part of my life, my past...but it is *in* the past, whereas you and our baby are the most important part of my present and my future.'

'Oh, Maggie,' Oliver exclaimed gruffly, reaching for her and kissing her fiercely.

'Go home,' Maggie repeated. 'I promise you, I'll be fine... And besides, if anything should happen— which it won't because it's far too soon yet—I'm certainly in the right place,' she reminded him.

Alice was still standing in front of the open door ten minutes later when Stuart drove up.

As he got out of the car she studied him. He looked older, tired, smaller in some way.

She waited for him to reach her before she said, 'I've been trying to get in touch with you all day.'

'Have you? Must have had the damned mobile switched off,' he responded tersely.

'No, you didn't, Stuart,' Alice told him quietly. 'I couldn't reach you because your mobile is now inoperative. Why didn't you tell me that you'd lost your job?'

20

Stuart stared at her. This was his worst nightmare come true, Alice finding out before he was in a position to tell her that there was nothing to worry about and that he had found himself another job, a better job. Not the crap job he had managed to get by crawling on his belly from acquaintance to acquaintance, calling in favours until someone had reluctantly given him work. And what work. Flying for a newly set up cut-price delivery service, working inhumanly long shifts, on next to no pay, flying clapped-out planes, as well as doing his own paperwork and acting as a bloody delivery boy, with a dozen or more hungry newly qualified youngsters snapping at his heels, waiting for him to fall.

For a moment Alice thought that Stuart was actually going to turn round and walk away from her, but instead he rocked back on his heels and said thickly, 'Oh, God!'

'I thought you were having an affair… You were seen eating out with an attractive woman.'

The words hung between them, ludicrous in view of everything that was going on, Alice knew, but somehow she had not been able to stop herself from saying them.

'An affair?' Stuart stared at her. 'Are you crazy? An affair? Who the hell would want a failure like me? A

wreck like me, who can't even get it up any more—
God, Alice… The only woman I could have been seen
with would have been Arlette Salcombe, and she's the
one who had to break the news of my redundancy to
me.'

There was no mistaking the truth in his immediate
shocked denial, nor her own immediate surge of relief,
Alice acknowledged weakly.

'Stuart, let's go inside. There's something I've got to
tell you.'

'Zoë is what?' Stuart demanded angrily, raking his
hand through his hair as he glared at Alice. 'Oh, come
on, Alice, just because she has a drink and then
crashes the car that doesn't make her an alcoholic. For
God's sake, I had an uncle who was one, so I do know
what I'm talking about. My father was so ashamed of
him that in the end he simply refused to have anything to do with him. Died a raving lunatic!'

'An uncle? You never mentioned him to me.' Alice
frowned. To the best of her knowledge, Stuart's father
had been an only son.

'My father had forbidden us to mention his name.
Damned scrounger and a coward. Dad always said
that he only started drinking because he was too
damned afraid to act like a man during the war. He
used to turn up at the house, filthy and drunk, ranting
and raving that my father had ruined his life, claiming
that Dad had always been the favourite. My grandparents were as ashamed of him as Dad. And in fact I
think they were relieved when he died.'

'Oh, Stuart.' Alice bit her lip, instinctively feeling a
small pang of sympathy for the man who had obviously felt unloved and rejected by his family. 'The

doctor I saw at the surgery did tell me that alcoholism can be inherited.'

'Doctor, what bloody doctor?' Stuart stormed. 'For God's sake Alice it's a bloody good lawyer that Zoë needs, not some doctor!'

As she listened to Stuart rage and bluster Alice wondered if he realised how much his reaction gave away how afraid he was. Stuart had never been very good at dealing with the kind of crises his childhood had not programmed and prepared him to understand. They had always been her responsibility.

'Stuart might seem to be the strong one of your relationship, Alice,' Maggie had once told her forthrightly. 'But in reality you are much, much stronger than he is. And whenever there is a real crisis, it's you who has to deal with it, but you have been so brainwashed into putting Stuart onto a pedestal that you can't see that for yourself.'

She remembered that she had been rather cross with Maggie at the time, but nevertheless the words had stayed with her.

'Okay, I agree that Zoë liking a drink is not perhaps an ideal situation, but in all fairness, Alice, I have to say that the blame for that lies with you. You always were far too indulgent with her, and—'

'Zoë does not *like* a drink, Stuart,' Alice interrupted him firmly. 'She *needs* a drink.'

'Oh, now you're being dramatic,' Stuart blustered. 'Typical woman. And anyway, this is Ian's problem, not ours. Zoë is his wife now.'

'Zoë is his wife,' Alice agreed. 'And she is also our daughter, and the boys' mother, and the twins' sister! And according to the doctor the problem actually belongs to Zoë and not to any of us. We can help and support her if she asks for our help and support, but first she has to acknowledge that she needs them, and in order to do that she has to acknowledge that she has an alcohol addiction!'

'For God's sake, you sound like some bloody do-gooder, Alice. Like I have just said, if Zoë has had too much to drink then right now what she needs is a damn good talking-to from her husband, and an even better lawyer. Fortunately for her, Ian will have access to the best that money can buy.' He stopped speaking as he saw Alice shaking her head.

'What is it? The silly little fool hasn't gone and admitted to anything, has she?'

The temptation to tell him that she was far too much his daughter to do that was very hard for Alice to resist.

'There's a problem,' she told him instead. 'Zoë is refusing to tell Ian what has happened.' She gave a small sigh. 'Reading between the lines, it seems as though things aren't going very well between them at the moment.'

'Not tell him? Well, of course he'll have to be told. And if you had any sense, Alice, you'd have done that already instead of wasting time going to see some bloody medic. Obviously I'm going to have to ring him myself! God, as though I didn't already have enough to worry about. You realise that we're probably going to lose this place, don't you, if I don't get a decent job soon? I had to remortgage to pay for Zoë's university fees and the wedding!'

'You never said,' Alice protested in shock.

'No sense in making a fuss about it. At the time I thought I'd make a killing out of those shares I bought from Tom Bracegirdle.'

Alice frowned as she listened to him. Stuart had always had a tendency to be too trusting where his old

RAF chums were concerned, but she hadn't realised that he had lost so much that he had had to raise capital by remortgaging their home.

'Stuart, I really don't think we should interfere and ring Ian,' she warned, but Stuart was ignoring her.

Concerned as she was about Zoë, she felt an even more pressing urgency to be with Maggie and Stella. Right now they needed to be together, she recognised, for Nicki's sake and for their own.

The machinery of life hummed and buzzed in the hospital's intensive care unit. Joey and Nicki were in beds next to one another. Both were alive, but the specialist had made it plain that they had been rescued only just in time. They had been given drugs to combat the effect of the trauma they had experienced, and were deeply asleep.

Kit had gone to talk to the specialist about the events leading up to Nicki's shocking attempt to take the lives of herself and her son. Laura told Maggie that it seemed from what the specialist had already said that he suspected that Nicki had been suffering from undiagnosed depression.

'Dad told me that she's already had a couple of bouts of depression, and of course losing the baby must have—'

'What do you mean?' Maggie interrupted her, shocked. 'What baby?'

'Oh, Maggie, I'm sorry, I didn't realise you didn't know.' Laura looked uncomfortable. 'I just assumed... Nicki was pregnant—an accident—she and Dad had...words about it, more because Dad was in shock than anything else, but apparently a few days later Nicki lost the baby, and she blamed Dad for what happened.'

Nicki had been pregnant! And she hadn't known. Hadn't guessed. Hadn't cared enough to realise, because she had been too wrapped up in her concerns, Maggie reflected inwardly in anguished guilt.

'It seems from the letter that Nicki left for Dad that she had become obsessed by her fear that she would lose Joey too, and that she had to keep Joey safe. She'd decided that the world was too dangerous for him to be allowed to live in it. She thought that by killing herself and him she would be keeping him safe somehow.'

As they looked at one another Maggie unashamedly wept slow, sad tears for her friend who must have felt so lonely and alienated.

'If she's suffering from depression, at least they should be able to treat it, shouldn't they?' Laura asked Maggie anxiously.

'I should think so,' Maggie immediately comforted her.

'When I took the boys round to Alice's, she told me that Zoë is also here, in hospital,' Laura confided.

When Maggie frowned, she explained uncomfortably, 'I don't know whether or not you are aware of it, but Zoë is…has… She had too much to drink and drove the car,' she told Maggie simply. 'There was an accident, but fortunately no one was hurt. However…'

'If you're trying to find a tactful way of saying that Zoë has a drink problem, then let me put your mind at rest,' Maggie said quietly. 'All of us are aware that Zoë's drinking was getting out of hand. None of us discussed it in front of Alice. We didn't want to hurt or offend her. And I suppose, as well, we felt that we could be a little bit behind the times. Heavy drinking amongst young women wasn't really an issue for us when we were young.'

In normal circumstances she would have been on the phone to Nicki immediately, discussing what could be done to help Alice through such a bad time, Maggie acknowledged.

Laura, who had been sitting simply watching her young half-brother, went out to have a break, leaving Maggie between Nicki's and Joey's beds.

After a while, on the periphery of her senses Maggie was aware of a faint movement from Nicki, a breath of a sigh, no more. But immediately she reacted to it, reaching out for her hand and holding it in both of her own as she told her, 'Oh, Nicki, I am so sorry for not realising, sorry for not knowing, sorry for not listening better, but, most of all, sorry for not being the friend you deserved to have.

'You are so precious to so many people, Nicki, so very much loved by all of us. We've depended on you, Nicki, used your strength and given you very little in return. You've enriched our lives immeasurably, but we've been too selfishly engrossed in our own small concerns to see your need.'

Maggie tensed as Nicki's eyes suddenly opened.

'Joey,' she mouthed immediately.

Squeezing her hand reassuringly, Maggie moved so that Nicki could see across to the other bed.

'He's here with you, Nicki, and he's fine,' Maggie told her emotionally. 'You're both going to be fine.'

Almost immediately Nicki's eyes closed again. Swallowing hard, Maggie forced back her tears, glancing up as the door opened and the nurse came in followed by Kit.

'I'll sit with her now, Maggie,' Kit told her as the nurse started to check the monitors. 'I've talked to the medical authorities, and, although they can't be totally sure yet, they believe that Nicki did what she did because she was suffering very badly from depression,' he whispered to her emotionally. 'I blame myself. I should have realised… God, when I think how bloody callous I was. How damned selfish and uncaring…'

'You were under a lot of pressure, Kit,' Maggie reminded him softly. 'And when it comes to blame… We should have guessed that something was wrong!'

'The specialist says that as soon as Nicki is well enough, he's going to recommend that she receives appropriate treatment: drug therapy, counselling, that kind of thing.'

'We'll all do everything that we can. You know that,' Maggie promised him, bending down to kiss first Nicki and then Joey before turning to give Kit himself a brief hug.

Laura was walking back down the corridor as Maggie left the room.

'I've just been to see Zoë,' she told Maggie, shaking her head. 'She says that she's going to discharge herself and go home. She flatly refuses to accept that her drinking was in any way responsible for what happened. How are Nicki and Joey?'

Maggie smiled at her, thinking how much it would have meant to Nicki to know that Laura asked after her first.

'They're both going to be fine, and your father says the specialist has very high hopes that Nicki can be treated successfully for her depression.'

As she walked into the hospital foyer Maggie saw Dan walking towards her and for a moment her heart did a slow somersault that set her pulses racing.

'Maggie! I came to see how Nicki and Joey are.'

'They're fine. But I'm sure that Kit would welcome some male support,' Maggie told him. 'I'm just on my way home.'

'You're driving yourself? Is that wise?' Dan was frowning and Maggie knew instinctively that in another second he would insist that he should drive her.

'Oliver will come for me. I only have to telephone him,' she told him quickly, 'and besides, I'm only pregnant, Dan, not ill.'

The moment she had said it Maggie wished she had not. She could see from the expression in Dan's eyes just what effect her words had had on him.

'Oh, Dan!' she exclaimed remorsefully, reaching instinctively towards him. To her shock he stepped back from her, his face tight.

'Maggie. Don't,' he told her harshly.

'I can't bear it if you touch me,' he added simply, watching the colour come and go in her face as he did so. 'It may have taken me ten years to realise it, Maggie, but I know now that there is only one woman for me and that woman is you. You don't know how much I wish I could turn back time. How much I wish you were still mine. I don't have the right to speak to you like this, I know. You're in a new relationship now, a good relationship, I can see that. But I want you to know that if you ever need me…if you ever need anything, I'm here.'

Unable to speak, Maggie could only shake her head. Thank God Dan couldn't know how many nights after he had left she had lain awake aching to hear him say those words, aching just to have him there with her. Then the pain of loving him had been a pain she had thought would never ease, and for a part of her, somewhere deep, deep inside her, it never had. But that was her secret, her small, dark shadow that she was determined to carry alone, because there was no way she was going to allow that shadow to touch Oliver, who had given her so much. Oliver, who had given her the gift of his child. Oliver, who loved her so much!

'I have to go,' she told Dan huskily. 'Oliver will be worrying…'

As she started to walk away from him Dan was tempted to tell her that whilst Oliver might be worrying, he would have been here at her side. But knowing Maggie the way he did, he suspected that such a remark would have been unfair. She could be one hell of a stubborn and independent lady when she chose!

'Anyway, I've decided that I'm going to talk to Julie tonight about us adopting Jack,' Stella told Richard.

'Stella, I don't think that's a good idea right now,' Richard began warningly, breaking off as the telephone suddenly rang.

Since Stella was closest to it, she answered the call, her face suddenly draining of colour.

'Yes. Yes, I understand,' Richard heard her saying unsteadily, and then she was replacing the receiver and telling him, 'I've got to go to the hospital… That was Alice. It's Nicki… She's…' Unable to say any more, Stella put her hand to her mouth as her eyes flooded with tears. 'I've got to go, Rich!'

Alice and Stella arrived at the hospital just as Maggie was on the point of leaving.

'We had to come,' Alice told her.

Instantly they were holding one another, the three of them locked together in a silent, emotional embrace.

'How are they? How is…?' Stella demanded anxiously when she could speak.

'They're both going to be fine,' Maggie assured her. 'Nicki recovered consciousness whilst I was there. She spoke to me…' Fresh tears filled her eyes.

'Oh, Maggie, if only we'd listened to you,' Alice wept.

'No.' Stella stopped her quietly. 'You did listen, Alice. I was the one who refused to.' It had been on her conscience all the way to the hospital. 'I should never have doubted your judgement, and if I hadn't…'

'You mustn't think like that, Stella,' Maggie told her gently. 'The truth is that we've all been so preoccupied with our own lives that we've…'

'Neglected our friendship?' Alice supplied quietly for her. 'It's true,' she insisted when Maggie and Stella looked at her. 'I've been conscious of it myself. It's as though, somehow, somewhere, we've started to build up barriers between one another, to…' She paused and shook her head.

'Perhaps there's more to this modern myth that fifty is the new forty than we've been prepared to acknowledge,' Stella suggested.

When Maggie and Alice looked enquiringly at her, she went on slowly, trying to clarify her own thoughts as well as pick the right words to express her feelings.

'It used to be that forty was considered to be a certain watershed in life. Remember all those earnest, outdated magazine articles there used to be about not worrying if your husband suddenly hit forty and started wanting to wear jeans and listen to pop music? How we were all warned to be on our guard against wanting to decamp to Greece and find an unsuitable lover?' she added wryly. 'We all laughed about it when we actually did hit forty, didn't we? Because it just wasn't an issue for any of us. None of us felt remotely past it, or had any desire to prove anything to anyone. We were on the crest of a wave, weren't we? We were right there in the centre of everything. Forty was nothing, a breeze...we loved it and we laughed together about all those old horror stories!

'Well, I don't know about either of you, but for me fifty was different. Oh, yes, I know I never said anything...well, what was the point? We'd already gone through the forty high-water mark, so starting to panic and look back assessingly, critically at fifty seemed so...so un-me that I just didn't want to talk about what was happening to me. I didn't want to admit that I was suddenly beginning to question what my life had been about, what I had achieved...what I actually was. And I certainly didn't want to start saying that a part of me felt cheated, resentful, afraid. But...' Stella paused and looked at both of them. 'If I'm wrong then I apologise, but it seems to me that perhaps all of us have experienced...something...'

As Stella hesitated, waiting for their response, Alice looked at Maggie and then took a deep breath.

'I sat down on the day after my fiftieth birthday and hated the three of you so much. I hated being the baby, being, as I saw it, patronised by everyone. You all had your clear-cut identities, but I was just Stuart's wife, the children's mother. I had nothing of my own.'

She stopped and Maggie realised that both she and Stella were looking at her.

'I couldn't bear it that I didn't have a child,' Maggie admitted huskily. 'I thought that I was over that... I had my business, I had Oliver...but I so much envied the three of you the miracle of motherhood. And I felt so much less of a woman because I hadn't experienced it. I ached inside for the child I had never had, so badly... It was a physical pain, an emotional agony. And I felt too belittled by it to tell any of you. I didn't think you would understand... You all had children, after all.'

Silently they shared one another's confusion and pain. It was left to Alice to find a balm to put on their mutual wound.

'Sometimes,' she said shakily, 'in order to grow, we all have to break out of our own comfort zone.'

When Maggie and Stella looked at her, she shook her head and offered wryly, 'I read it in a magazine.'

To anyone else, the sight of three mature women standing in the hospital reception area, laughing until tears ran down their faces, might have seemed out of place. But to the three of them, their shared laughter was the most healing medicine there could be.

When Alice had collected herself enough to announce that she had to go, Stella waited until she had left before touching Maggie lightly on her arm and telling her gruffly, 'Maggie, that evening when you saw me in the car park…'

Immediately Maggie stopped her, shaking her head as she said firmly, 'Stella, I know that whatever had happened it couldn't possibly damage your integrity, or my friendship and love for you.'

'Oliver's here,' Stella told her, when she had regained her composure. 'And I must go too, Rich will be worrying.'

It was only as she walked towards Oliver that Maggie realised that she had not told Alice and Stella about the letters. But then, they didn't matter any more, she recognised. Nicki had been sick, suffering when she had sent them, and as such she must look at them as cries for help. And that was exactly what she intended to do!

21

Morosely, Zoë stared at the empty glass in front of her. She was alone in the house, having discharged herself from the hospital and got a taxi driver to bring her back home.

She frowned as she heard the front door open and then slam, turning round awkwardly in her chair as Ian strode angrily into the kitchen.

'So there you bloody are,' he gritted. 'They told me at the hospital that you'd left.'

Zoë could feel the familiar mixture of excitement and fear plunging her stomach like a lift crazily out of control.

'Who told you? Or can I guess? My cow of an interfering mother, I suppose.'

'Actually it was your pathetic "it's not my fault" father,' Ian told her. 'Your mother is worth a dozen of him.'

'Don't you speak about my father like that,' Zoë protested. 'Ian? Where are you going?' she demanded as he turned on his heel.

'I'm going upstairs to pack the kids' stuff and then I'm going to your mother's to collect them. I'm leaving you, Zoë, and I'm taking my kids with me.'

Zoë stared at him, too shocked to speak.

'You can't do that!' she protested, her whole body shaking. 'They're mine! You can't! Ian!'

She levered herself out of her chair, swaying unsteadily as she made her way towards him. As she reached him she put her hand on his arm but he pushed it away and stepped back from her so that she almost fell.

'Don't touch me,' he told her softly.

'You can't do this,' Zoë sobbed hysterically. 'And besides, you can't look after them.'

'I don't need to. That's why I pay Laura,' he told her sardonically.

'Laura! This isn't about the boys, is it?' Zoë hissed. 'It's her, Laura. You want to shag her, don't you?' She was screaming now, trying to claw at Ian's face as she staggered towards him, but he evaded her with contemptuous ease.

'Well, there's no way I'm going to let you shag anyone else but me, ever…' Zoë sobbed.

'You disgust me, do you know that?' Ian told her almost conversationally as he stood by the door. 'There's no way I am going to let my kids grow up like I did, with a drunk for a mother, never knowing—'

'I'm not a drunk!' Zoë screamed. 'I am not a drunk…'

But she was screaming into the empty silence of the kitchen as Ian took the stairs two at a time, ignoring her as he went into the boys' rooms and pulled open drawers and cupboards.

Zoë followed him, lurching drunkenly into the room, grabbing the door for support.

'Ian, please,' she implored him. 'I only drink because I love you and you aren't here and I need you… We are so good together… Come to bed with me now, and let me show you. We've always been so good together in bed, and you know it.'

'I don't want you, Zoë.'

'Yes, you do. You always want me!' She laughed, going up to him and sliding her hand down his body, pressing it into his groin as she took hold of him.

'Get off me!'

The force with which he pushed her away sent her reeling back against the door, to scream in furious disbelief, oblivious to the dark loathing in his eyes as he looked at her.

'You drunken bitch, don't you ever do that again,' he told her as he went past her, ignoring her screams and sobs.

Laura's mobile rang just as she reached the house, and at first she thought it was her father ringing, and tensed anxiously. They had agreed that she would return to his and Nicki's home and stay there for the time being—the hospital had warned them that, once they were well enough to be discharged, both Joey and Nicki would need looking after and Laura had said immediately that she wanted to do whatever she could to help. But then when she answered the call she heard Zoë's drunken ramblings.

'You aren't going to take Ian away from me, you bitch,' Zoë was screaming. 'He's mine!'

Already exhausted, the last thing Laura felt like doing was dealing with Zoë, but she made herself listen, and then calmly denied all of Zoë's hysterical accusations.

Ten minutes later her phone rang again. This time her caller was Ian himself. Politely but firmly Laura told him that she was unable to continue working for him, briefly explaining why.

She winced a little as she heard Ian swear.

'Fine. Then I'll just have to manage by myself, won't I?' he cursed her before hanging up abruptly.

* * *

'Julie…' Stella forced herself to smile as Julie walked into the kitchen. The last thing she wanted to do was to alienate Julie—she was Jack's mother, after all, and if she was to accept Stella's plan for Richard and herself to adopt their grandson, they would need—

'Where's Jack?' she asked her anxiously, realising that her grandson was missing. Nicki's suicide attempt had left her feeling shocked and off balance and somehow lacking in her normal self-confidence.

'I've left him with Mum,' Julie answered her. 'Her cousin's coming round and she wanted to show him to her.'

Proprietorially, Stella couldn't help feeling a little put out at the thought of anyone other than herself showing off her precious grandson, but she reminded herself that as soon as the adoption went through legally Jack would be all hers.

'Julie, I know you were planning to have Jack adopted,' she began, 'and—'

'I've changed my mind. I'm going to keep him.'

'Changed your mind?' It actually felt as though the blood in her veins had turned to ice as she reacted to Julie's announcement, Stella recognised distantly. Her heart was pounding. She felt sick with shock and disbelief, unable to function properly.

Julie couldn't possibly mean what she was saying… She couldn't… Frantically Stella shook her head.

'Julie, you can't possibly mean that,' she protested. 'You can't bring Jack up all by yourself. You're still only coming up for eighteen. You've got your education to finish, you—'

'I shan't be bringing him up by myself. Mum and Dad are going to help me. In fact…' Julie looked away from her and then looked back again, saying casually,

'Dad's totally besotted with him, and he and Mum are going to adopt him, and we're all going to move to Canada. Dad's been offered a new job there. He says it will be a fresh start for all of us. We've been to see the social services people and they're all in favour.' She stood up.

'Dad wants me to move back home. I was going to tell you and Richard this evening.'

'Julie, you can't do that,' Stella told her shakily, fighting to sound calm and in control. Her lips, her face, her whole body felt numb, and yet at the same time she felt as though she had been seized in a huge, tearing vice of intense pain. 'Hughie is Jack's father,' she reminded Julie sharply. 'And you can't simply arrange Jack's future without consulting him.'

'I have consulted him,' Julie told her, shocking her into silence. 'And he's okay about it. Anyway, it wouldn't really matter if he wasn't. Dad's looked into everything and Hughie doesn't have any legal rights where Jack is concerned.'

'Julie, you can't do this,' Stella protested again.

Julie gave her a stubborn look. 'Yes, I can,' she told Stella angrily. 'And you can't stop me. Just because Hughie is your son, that doesn't give you any rights over Jack! I'm fed up with listening to you criticising everything I do—Jack is my baby, not yours! Anyway, the midwife says that most of your ideas are hopelessly out of date now, and that I shouldn't pay any attention to you! I'm going upstairs to pack my stuff. Dad's coming round for me in half an hour.'

White-faced, Stella watched as Julie walked out of the kitchen. Nothing in her life had prepared her for the pain tearing relentlessly into her now. Nothing could anaesthetise her from it.

She had to bunch up her hand and hold it pressed

hard against her mouth to stop herself from giving voice to the primitive wail of grief rising in her throat.

This could not be happening. Julie could not take Jack away from her!

She was still sitting frozen in her chair an hour later when Richard came in. She had heard the clatter of Julie's feet on the stairs as she'd opened the door to her father. She had heard too his footsteps approaching the kitchen and then stopping. But now they had gone and the house was empty. It felt empty too.

Richard took one look at her face and sighed before going to fill the kettle.

'Julie's left—with Jack,' Stella told him emptily. 'Her parents are going to adopt him and take him to Canada.' Suddenly she was crying. Great, tearing, heaving sobs that shook her whole body. 'We can't let them take him, Richard. We've got to stop them.'

'We can't, Stella,' Richard told her quietly. 'Jack is Julie's son. We can't.'

'Rich, he's only a baby. I can't bear to go through the rest of my life without him… He's our grandson, a part of us…'

Richard sighed again as he took her in his arms. He had known that this was coming and had sensed that, when it came to it, Julie would not be able to give up her child.

'Stella, I do understand, but so must you. Jack is also Julie's parents' grandchild—and her son. She and Hughie aren't married. We have no legal claim on Jack, and even if we had…' He paused, his hand hovering awkwardly over her heaving shoulders. They had never been a particularly physical couple with one another, but her grief made him ache to be able to comfort her.

'It wouldn't be fair to Jack if we tried to pull him between all of us. I know how much you love him, Stella. Try to think of that love, and of how much you can love him best by allowing him to grow up in a safe, secure atmosphere without conflict…'

'I can't bear it!' Stella cried, her agony streaking her voice like blood from a wound. 'I can't bear to be without him, Rich, I just can't.'

Sighing, Richard held her.

'You must, Stella,' he told her. 'There is no other way.'

22

'Well, do you like it?' Maggie asked Oliver excitedly as she showed him the just-completed nursery. The decorators had finished three days ago, and since then the new carpet had been fitted, the curtains hung and the baby equipment and paraphernalia delivered and put in place.

It had been a miracle that they had found the house at all, really. Maggie had been on the point of giving up when the relocation agent had rung to say she wasn't sure whether it would suit them or not, but a small rectory had come onto the market, larger than they had asked for, older and, of course, rather more expensive.

Maggie had been reluctant to go and see it but Oliver had persuaded her, and the minute they had turned in through the gate set in its brick garden wall Maggie had known it was the house for them.

Fortunately, the previous owners had already done most of the heavy-duty restoration work, and they had been able to move in the moment the sale had gone through, but even prior to that Maggie had been busy organising decorators, choosing carpets and soft furnishings, nagging Oliver to go on furniture-hunting expeditions with her.

'Mmm...I like the colour,' Oliver acknowledged. 'But the walls look a bit...bare...'

Maggie gave him a wide smile. 'That's because you are going to paint a mural on them.'

'I am?'

'Yes! And it's going to be the mural of our love, Oliver, for each other and for…this…' she told him softly, patting her very obviously pregnant stomach.

It was late September and in over two weeks' time their baby was going to be delivered. Maggie wasn't sure which of them was the more wildly excited, her or Oliver!

'Mmm… I don't suppose you wanting me to paint this mural has anything to do with the fact that I'm due to see our most glamorous client today, has it?' Oliver teased Maggie as he drew her closer and kissed the tip of her nose.

'Certainly not,' she denied. 'Although, if you did decide not to go and stayed at home instead, it just so happens…'

'I can't, Maggie,' Oliver told her firmly. 'Look, you have a formidable reputation for being totally dedicated and professional, and it's got to be the same for me. Besides, I want to clear my desk so that I can have plenty of time off once our baby arrives.'

Kissing her a second time, a good deal more thoroughly and lingeringly, he finally released her, telling her, 'See you later. And remember, no overdoing things!'

'Don't worry, I shan't be,' Maggie assured him. 'I'm going to see Nicki later. It's so wonderful how much progress she's made! Laura was saying that the doctor is really pleased with the way she's responding to the treatment. She was so much more like the old Nicki when I saw her last week. She even apologised to me for what she said about me being pregnant, and she was giggling just like she used to when we were girls.

I still feel bad about not knowing about her baby, though. Laura says that it looks as though she isn't going to be prosecuted for—for Joey. Kit has been made his official guardian, and Nicki's specialist has confirmed that she simply wasn't responsible for her actions because of her mental condition.'

Oliver picked up his jacket. He had almost reached the front door when Maggie came hurrying down the stairs towards him.

'What is it?' he asked her.

'Nothing, just this,' she told him, cupping his face in her hands and kissing him with deep tenderness and love.

'You really are desperate to get me to do that mural, aren't you?' he murmured humorously when she had finally released him. As Maggie laughed he told her, 'I'll make a start on it this weekend, how's that?'

'You can't! Not this weekend.' Maggie shook her head. 'It's your birthday and I've got a surprise for you!'

The surprise was a full fifty-per-cent partnership in the business. She had had all the legal documents drawn up and was planning to present them to him over a special and intimate dinner.

'How are you feeling?'

Nicki smiled lovingly at Kit as he walked into the conservatory where she had been half reading some work and half admiring the vine, which was just beginning to turn from its summer green to the full richness of its autumn glory.

'Well enough to talk,' she told him, her smile deepening as he sat down beside her, taking hold of her hand as he did so. 'Maggie's coming round later.'

'Uh-huh, does that mean you want me to make myself scarce?'

Nicki laughed. 'As if! But we will be talking baby talk. Maggie says that she's terrified the baby will take one look at her and demand to go back! Oh, Kit, I am so very lucky,' she told him, suddenly serious. 'After what I did, I don't deserve to feel so…so loved and so cherished, so valued by you and…'

'Nicki, you do deserve it,' Kit told her firmly, moving closer to her. 'I should have realised that you weren't well, and, instead of behaving like a pigheaded, sulky child, I should have given you far more support and understanding.'

'Well, at least what happened has shown me how much you do love me,' Nicki whispered. 'And I did wonder…question…more than I sometimes wanted to admit to myself. I mean, we had agreed that it was better that we went our separate ways, and then there was that time, when you thought that there was a risk that I might be pregnant and so we got married, and it's always haunted me that it wasn't what you wanted. And then we had Joey, and money was tight…'

Kit lifted her hand to his lips and kissed it before telling her emotionally, 'First I was never wanting for us to go our separate ways! And second, when we made love that time and you told me that you were so convinced that things were over between us that you had stopped taking the pill, I was more than happy to seize the opportunity to do the manly thing and insist that we get married. And when we had Joey, I felt madly jealous because you seemed to love him more than you did me!'

Nicki shook her head.

'But it was my fault that we never talked, really

talked about any of this,' she admitted quietly. 'I was too busy, too afraid of confronting my own fears, too eager to hang onto the resentment I was building up inside myself as a safeguard to fall back on if you did leave me! But then when I became pregnant… It's all right,' she reassured him, lifting her hand to his face in a gesture of tenderness. '*I'm* all right now!'

'We could always try again,' Kit offered whimsically. 'Do a Maggie and Oliver!'

Nicki shook her head.

'No, if the pregnancy had gone full-term then that would have been one thing, but I hadn't planned or even wanted to conceive, and right now I want to focus on the people I already have in my life.' She took a deep breath.

'Kit, I've been thinking. Your business is doing much better now, I know, but I know you've thought about buying somewhere in Italy. Joey's growing up, and I suspect that Laura and Marcus could become a definite item—' Nicki laughed when she saw his startled look.

'Oh, Kit!' she exclaimed. 'You must have noticed how she's always the first to get to the door whenever he calls, and I know they've been out to dinner together at least half a dozen times.'

Kit looked bemused. Despite Nicki's amusement, it was news to him that his daughter was seeing Nicki's GP.

'Anyway,' Nicki continued, 'what I was thinking was that a place in Italy where we could spend time, especially in the winter, and where we can entertain the children and their partners and our grandchildren, would be a very good idea. I know it would mean you downscaling your business a bit, just when you'd started to build it up again,' she told him, 'but it would be such fun to have something…somewhere we can be together…just as us.'

'Fun? It would be sheer heaven,' Kit told her fervently. 'But never mind me downscaling, what about you?'

'Oh, that's already virtually sorted out,' she told him airily. 'I'm going to train Laura up as my second in command!'

'Is Dad around?'

'He's just gone upstairs,' Nicki told her stepdaughter, adding emotionally, 'Laura, have I told you how much it means to me that you and I have finally found one another? And not because it removes a problem from my life, but because what's happening between us now is immeasurably valuable to me. And so are you—not for what you've done, but for who you are!'

'I've just been to the garden centre,' Laura told her almost brusquely, but Nicki knew Laura too well now to mistake her abrupt *non sequitur* for any kind of negative or hostile emotion. After all it had been Laura more than anyone else, even Kit, who had fought for her to get better. Nicki had never mentioned it, but she had the clearest memory of lying in her hospital bed and hearing Laura say through gritted teeth, 'Don't you dare die on me, Nicki. I am not going to lose a second mother and you are not going to leave Joey! You *will* get better, Nicki. You have to. I can't cope with Dad and Joey's pain on my own. I need you!'

'Mmm? What did you buy? A pot plant for Marcus' flat?' she asked mock innocently.

Laura gave her a reproving look. 'No, as a matter of fact, it was a tree. I thought we might plant it together, all of us. You, Dad, Joey and me.'

Nicki looked at her, her heart slowing down to a heavy beat.

'Do you remember?' Laura asked her huskily. 'You bought one for me when…after… So that I could have my own special place to remember Mum.'

Nicki swallowed hard—and then held open her arms. 'Oh, Laura,' she whispered.

'I didn't understand then, but I do now,' Laura told her chokily. 'It's a special summer flowerer because the baby would have been born then.'

Alice saw Ian's Mercedes pull up outside from the landing window. Her stomach muscles tensed automatically.

Ian and Zoë were officially separated now, but, despite losing her sons and potentially her husband, not to mention her job, her driving licence and her self-esteem, Zoë was still refusing to accept that she had a problem.

Alice had suggested to her that it might be an idea if she were to return to live with them, but Zoë's response had been a stream of abusive language, and a flat refusal to move out of her house.

She was still living there, and unexpectedly Ian was still paying the bills, but Alice assumed that ultimately he was going to want to sell the property. George and William were living with their grandparents, Ian having arrived on the doorstep less than a week after he had taken the boys, announcing that he could no longer cope with them.

Alice reached the front door at the same time as Ian rang the bell. Opening the door, she eyed him uneasily. She wasn't going to fall into the trap of blaming him for Zoë's behaviour, but a part of her secretly believed that, though Zoë's marriage to him might not have precipitated her downfall, it had certainly accelerated it!

'Stuart at home?' Ian asked casually as he stepped into the hall.

'No, he isn't,' Alice replied. 'He's out on business.'

'Business?' Ian laughed unkindly. 'Oh, come on, Alice. Everyone knows that Stuart doesn't have any business to be out on any more. I hear you're putting the house up for sale, by the way.'

'It's too big for us now,' Alice replied calmly, but she knew that her face was burning with a mixture of anger and bruised pride.

Ian laughed again.

'I've just called round to tell you that I've decided to live full time in the States. I'm moving there at the end of the month.'

The casual way in which he delivered his news made Alice tense. 'Have you told Zoë about your plans?' she asked him.

'I haven't been to see her, if that's what you mean, but I have instructed my solicitor to start divorce proceedings. She'll probably be too drunk to read the letter, so I thought I'd better come round and tell you myself.'

'What…what about the boys?' Alice asked him.

Ian hesitated and then gave a brief shrug. 'They'd fare better with you. I've thought about this. We can make it legal, if you like. I'm quite prepared to pay you. After all, I know you need the money,' he told her insultingly. 'But I warn you, I don't intend to hand over money to Zoë to drink away, so if she tries—'

'Ian, they're your sons. And as for paying us…' Alice reminded him.

'Are they?' he interrupted. 'Oh, come on, Alice,' he added tauntingly as she looked at him in shock.

'Everyone knows how Zoë puts it about. She was renowned for it at university. She's a slut as well as a drunk… I never wanted to marry her. Did she tell you that? She blackmailed me into it. She even had the kids because she thought that after my own father's antics I'd never desert my kids. Well, she was wrong. I realise now I never wanted them in the first place. She had them, she can damn well keep them!'

Alice couldn't comprehend either his cruelty, or, more shockingly, his complete lack of any kind of emotional attachment to his children. She had never liked him, but this!

He was already walking away from her but he paused by the door, turning round to tell her insolently, 'Oh, by the way, I've put the house up for sale. It's in my name and, since the mortgage is so huge—lucky that I decided to increase it recently, isn't it? Lucky for me, that is. Anyway, you can tell Zoë, if she ever sobers up enough to ask, not to expect to get more than ten grand or so from the sale.'

'Who was that, Grandma?' George asked her a few minutes later, coming into the hall, followed by William.

'No one,' she told him, bending down to gather both her grandsons into her arms and holding them just as tightly as she could.

'When's Grandad coming home?' William asked her. Touchingly and unexpectedly, Stuart had thrown himself wholeheartedly into his role as a stand-in father. In fact, he was spending far more time with the boys than he had ever spent with any of his own children, insisting that Alice needed time to herself in these vital first weeks of her recently begun Open University course.

The catalyst of his redundancy had brought them

closer together than Alice had thought possible. And he had got a new job!

He had attended a school reunion where he had fallen into conversation with one of his ex-classmates, the finance director of a small and highly innovative charity that involved helping disadvantaged young people.

Initially Tom Fleming had merely asked Stuart to come along and talk to a group of boys about his work as a pilot, but things had developed from there and now Stuart had been offered a part-time, not particularly highly paid job working for the charity.

He had returned home from his initial talk such a very different man from the one who had left the house only hours before that Alice had been totally bemused. All he had been able to talk about had been the boys, and the wonderful work the charity did.

'My father would have loved getting involved in something like this,' Stuart had commented tellingly, and that night for the first time in weeks he had instigated sex, and maintained his erection.

Now it was as though he had discovered a completely new facet of his character. If Alice were honest, at first she had felt a little chagrined at this new compassionate, humbled, wanting-to-benefit-society Stuart. But now she was beginning to find that she was actually enjoying discovering this new man her husband was becoming! She could enjoy sharing his excitement and enthusiasm for what he was doing, just as he was sharing hers for her university course.

Alice had met both Tom Fleming and his wife, and had immediately liked them, and, although their lives were still naturally shadowed by Zoë's addiction and obvious unhappiness, Alice was beginning to feel that

suddenly she and Stuart were doing what she had
wanted them to do for so long—finally meeting as
equal partners.

The letter was there when Maggie came downstairs
from taking just one more delirious look at the deli-
ciousness of the nursery.

She picked it up abstractedly and then froze as she
turned it over and saw the jumbled mess of stuck-on
letters running crookedly across the front, spelling her
name.

She knew, of course she knew, but she still had to
open it.

Her hands shook so much that it took her several
seconds, and all the time the blood was drumming in
her veins and her heartbeat was racing.

Inside the envelope was a single sheet of folded paper. Shakily Maggie unfolded it, and read it.

'You think you're going to be safe, don't you? You
think that everything's going to be all right. Well it
isn't! Everything is going to be very, very horribly
wrong. And that's a promise!'

She was going to be sick.

Panting, Maggie only just made it to the downstairs
cloakroom, her head pounding now and her ungainly,
heavily pregnant body shaking violently. She could
feel the baby's agitated movements and immediately
placed her hands over it, trying to give it the reassurance she could not give herself.

She needed Oliver. This letter had not come from
Nicki! It could not have done! Which meant... Nauseously, Maggie knew that she did not want to think
about what it meant. Suddenly panicking in a way
that was totally alien to her, she went clumsily from
door to door and then window to window, making
sure they were all locked...that she was safe inside the

house and that no one could get in to harm her baby.

There was no reply from Oliver's mobile and when Maggie rang the office Kath told her that he was still out.

She couldn't go and see Nicki now. She just could not take the risk of leaving the house, Maggie decided. Picking up the phone, she dialled her friend's number.

Wretchedly Zoë stared at her reflection in the bathroom mirror. Her face looked thin, pinched, and somehow bloated at the same time, her skin an unhealthy sallow colour.

Ian was going to divorce her! Ian was trying to claim that he wasn't the boys' father! Somewhere inside her head she could hear her sons crying, as they had done when she had screamed and raged at her mother that it was her fault that Ian no longer wanted her. George had stood in front of her, his face red and wet with his tears, as he begged her, 'Please, Mummy, don't hurt Grandma!'

She needed a drink.

She was halfway down the stairs when she suddenly sat down, abruptly overwhelmed by disgust for herself. Reaching for her mobile, she flicked through the directory, her hands and then her whole body shaking violently.

'Mum,' she said shakily when Alice answered. 'You're right. I need help…' She started to cry. 'Please help me, Mum. Please help me.'

'Stella?' Richard questioned anxiously as he walked into the kitchen and saw Stella sitting motionless at the table. When she looked at him he saw the photograph of Jack on the table. Her eyes were full of tears.

The last few months had been unbearably painful for her, first Julie's bombshell, then Hughie's total refusal to do anything to stop her.

'Come on, Ma,' he had tried to coax her. 'You'll have other grandchildren.'

'Other grandchildren, yes,' Stella had agreed fiercely, 'but there can never be another Jack.'

She physically ached for her grandson, waking in the night imagining for a second that she could actually hear his cry; that her fears that she had lost him were simply a nightmare from which she had now woken. But of course the real nightmare was that he had gone!

'I've just been round to see Julie's parents,' Richard told her gently.

It tore at his heart to see the hope flickering in her eyes.

'Julie's changed her mind?' she demanded eagerly.

Regretfully Richard shook his head. 'No, nothing like that. I just thought we should have a talk about…things.' He frowned and cleared his throat, a small habit he had whenever his emotions were particularly stirred.

'Obviously their prime concern is for Julie and Jack and their futures, but Gerald and Lillian agreed that they could both appreciate our feelings, as Jack's other grandparents.'

Stella could hardly take in what he was saying. Gerald and Lillian? It was virtually unheard of in their relationship for Richard to take the lead, or make the decisions about anything, and yet here he was, telling her calmly and matter of factly that he had been to see Julie's parents—'Gerald and Lillian!'—and without so much as a word to her about his intentions.

'They further agreed,' he was continuing determinedly, 'that it is only natural that we should want to keep in touch with Jack and—'

Unable to stop herself, Stella made a small sound, somewhere between a moan of aching loss and a gasp of hope. Apart from pausing to frown at her, Richard made no comment, merely continuing with a formality that at any other time she would have immediately derided as being more appropriate to his role as a member of the bowling club committee than a form of address to his wife!

'And to that end, it has been agreed that certain channels of communication will be kept open between our two families to enable a…a free exchange of information, and to allow Jack to grow up knowing both sides of his family. In fact, Gerald even went so far as to suggest that it might be possible for some sort of semi-legal document to be drawn up—to protect Jack's interests, as it were, and to give him the right to make his own decisions with regard to his family, once he's old enough to do so. Until then…' He paused, and Stella felt her stomach muscles twist as the pain reached out and tightened its hold on her.

'Until then what?' she demanded urgently, her voice cracking with strain.

'Until then they, Julie and Lillian and Gerald, have agreed that you and I can remain in contact with Jack.'

'Remain in contact? When he's living in Canada and we are here in Britain?' Stella exclaimed bitterly.

'Stella, there is such a thing as air travel, you know,' Richard told her gently. 'And telephones and videos. And who knows, by the time Jack is talking we could be set up with a web cam so we can see each other via our computers.'

'Web cams? Air travel?' Stella could feel a bittersweet, dangerous hope rising up inside her. 'But you hate flying,' she reminded him unevenly.

'Yes,' he agreed simply. 'But you love Jack, and so do I. And what's more, I love you as well.'

Had she ever really been foolish enough to compare this man to Todd Fairbrother and find him wanting? Stella felt a huge well of moral indignation against her own stupidity rise up inside her to mingle with her earlier hope.

'Do you mean it?' she asked.

'Which bit?' Richard teased her, suddenly reminding her of the shy but sweet-natured man who had touched her heart so effectively when he had first courted her.

'Every bit,' Stella responded, and then somehow she was in his arms, laughing and crying at the same time as he held her and aimed a clumsy kiss in the direction of her mouth.

'Oh, by the way,' she could hear him mumbling as she held the side of his face and aimed her own kiss with much better accuracy, 'I almost forgot. Lillian and Gerald have asked us to go round before they leave. They want to take some photographs of us all together, do a video, that kind of thing, and it will give us all an opportunity to talk.'

'Oh, Richard,' Stella sobbed. 'You really are the most wonderful, wonderful man!'

Oliver sang under his breath to himself as he drove back towards the office. His meeting had gone well, and their client had confirmed her acceptance of his designs.

They had had a week of unexpectedly mild early autumn weather, and the leaves on the trees were only just on the turn. His route home took him down a long, straight, well-maintained road flanked by hedges and farmland, but Oliver resisted the temptation to increase his speed.

It happened totally unexpectedly, out of the blue. One minute the road was empty, and the next the woman was there, standing in front of his car, smiling at him.

Automatically he tried to avoid hitting her, even though he knew it was too late, turning the wheel of the car hard.

Two fields away, a farmer on a tractor watched in horror, unable to believe his eyes. He had seen the woman walk deliberately into the path of the oncoming car and he had seen, too, the driver's heroic and pitifully doomed attempt to avoid her.

From his vantage point on the hill above the road, he could see the tiny doll-like figure of the woman being thrown up in the air by the impact, and he could hear the sound of tearing metal and breaking glass as the car skidded off the road, and embedded itself in the ancient beech tree planted by his grandfather.

The young police officers who came to Maggie tried to be professional but stumbled betrayingly over their words. Maggie could see the shock in the eyes of the woman as she glanced at her belly.

'Where is he?' was all she could ask them, her mouth too dry to allow her to form any other words. Inside her Oliver's baby kicked furiously, as though refusing to accept what had happened.

'St Luke's. I… There… He has suffered serious head injuries,' the male officer told her, avoiding eye contact with her.

Serious head injuries. Maggie's gorge rose.

'I must go to him!' she said at once, oblivious to the look they were exchanging.

Half an hour later she was being escorted into Intensive Care by one of the nurses. Not the same one who had nursed Nicki and Joey, she noticed absently.

Just outside the ward the nurse stopped. 'The consultant neurologist wants to have a word with you before…before you go in,' she told her quietly.

The consultant was thin and aesthetic-looking, his expression grim.

'I'm sorry,' he told Maggie, 'but I have to say this. Oliver's injuries are such that, without the life-support machine he is on, he cannot survive. He's in a coma, and the extent of the brain damage he has suffered means…'

'Are you trying to tell me that he will be paralysed?' Maggie asked him tonelessly.

The consultant looked away from her and then back again.

'Mrs Rockford, I don't think you can have been listening to me. I appreciate that this is a most dreadful shock for you, and in your condition, but the truth is that Oliver is already, in every real sense of the word, dead. His heart, his breathing… Life, if you wish to call it that, is being pumped into him and through him by machines.'

'No,' Maggie protested stubbornly, her voice breaking. 'He's badly injured, I know. In a coma…' She stopped as she looked into the consultant's eyes, and the hope to which she had been clinging so desperately died abruptly. As abruptly as Oliver himself had died?

'I want to see him,' she insisted.

Consideringly, the consultant looked at her.

'I don't think…' he began, but Maggie overruled

him, turning towards the door very determinedly and pushing it open, leaving him to follow her. Oliver was in a different room from the one Nicki and Joey had been in. The nurse who had been checking the machinery was sensitive enough to walk out as Maggie went in.

Oliver's head had been bandaged. There were livid scratches on his face. His chest was bare, and all around him was a mass of tubes and attachments, evidence of man's clumsily inept attempts to mimic the wondrous workings of the human body.

Science could only do so much, Maggie recognised as she looked into the unseeing eyes of the man she loved. And yet it could also perform truly remarkable miracles, she reminded herself as she placed her hand on her body. The baby's movements seemed to mirror the heavy thud of her own heartbeat, which in turn matched the pulsing of the machine pumping 'life' into Oliver's inert body.

'In normal circumstances, he would have been pronounced dead at the scene of the accident,' the consultant told her quietly. 'But the paramedics thought they detected a heartbeat and so… However, it is my opinion that the life support equipment should be turned off.'

'No!' Maggie was surprised at the forcefulness of her own voice. 'No. Not yet,' she pleaded with the consultant, telling him jerkily, 'There is someone he needs to see…someone who needs to see him first. Please?' she begged when she saw him frown. 'Please…'

'I don't know…' The consultant was frowning and shaking his head.

'Please, just give me two days… Please…'

She had already decided what she had to do. Had

known, in fact, from the moment the police had brought her the news and explained to her how the accident had happened.

How pitilessly, appallingly ironic it was that she had feared for herself, when all the time it had been Oliver who had been in danger.

Maggie had no idea who the woman who had stepped out in front of Oliver was, but she did know that her act had been deliberate, and that it was in some way connected with the letters she had received. But she could not allow herself to waste time thinking about that—or her—now. There was something much more important she needed her energy for.

She rang the clinic from her mobile, standing outside the hospital and praying that her consultant would be there.

When he was, she gave a small mental prayer of thanks, quickly explaining to him what had happened and what she wanted to do.

'You want to have the baby delivered now? Advance the date by two weeks?'

'I'm thirty-seven weeks, nearly thirty-eight,' she reminded him, stumbling over the words. 'Is it possible…? Will it be safe for the baby? Only I want Oliver to…' Unable to speak for her emotions, she had to stop. But she couldn't cry yet, she told herself sternly. She had too much to do!

Whilst she waited for his reply, she automatically tensed her body against the aching pain that had been nagging at her all day, and which she had put down to her furious spurt of activity the previous day, putting the final touches to the nursery, filling its cupboard and drawers with the tiny clothes she had bought.

'It isn't quite that easy, Maggie,' she heard him saying slowly. 'An operating theatre would have to be made available, it would take me at least a couple of hours to get there, and then you'll need your surgeon and—'

'Please,' Maggie begged him. 'You said yourself when you saw me last week that the baby's head is engaged, and…' She stopped, gasping and recoiling from the sudden surge of pain that gripped her. She suddenly felt clammy and giddy, as though she was going to be sick. He had to agree. Oliver had to see his baby! He had to!

The pain receded, allowing her to exhale in relief, and then stand frozen with shock as she felt the sudden rush of fluid.

A passing nurse gave her a quick glance, and then stopped.

'It's all right,' she reassured Maggie with a smile. 'Your waters have broken, that's all. Well, at least it's happened in the right place. Are you having contractions? Oh, yes.' She answered her own question as Maggie's belly suddenly and very obviously tightened. 'Someone is getting impatient…'

Dizzily Maggie looked at her, and then at her own belly. She was still holding the telephone receiver, she realised.

'It looks like the decision has been made for us,' she told the consultant. 'I'm already in labour!'

She was whisked into the labour ward, and from there down to the theatre, even though she had pleaded with the obstetrician to be allowed to deliver the baby naturally. 'It's too much of a risk,' the doctor told her firmly.

Maggie was conscious throughout the whole procedure, her eyes brimming with tears when the obstetrician announced, 'Congratulations, Maggie, you have a beautiful, perfect, healthy baby girl,' as she placed her baby on Maggie's body.

A girl! Oliver had been wrong. It had been his daughter she had been carrying and not his son. And yet immediately Maggie felt a sharp, piercing thrill of joy and instant communion with her child as they looked into one another's eyes, and shared one another's pain. Kissing her, Maggie whispered heartbrokenly to her of their shared loss, and their shared unique gift of having been part of the life of so special a man, so special a love.

'But it's your right to know him, and to know just what a wonderful, special person he is, just as it's his right to know you!'

Somehow, without knowing how, Maggie knew that their child, Oliver's child, would know for all her life that her father had been with her when she had come into the world, and that that would hold her and boost her, keep her safe and give her strength whenever she should need it.

They had to push her in a wheelchair to Oliver's bed because of the Caesarean, the baby carefully wrapped in her arms.

Oliver was still surrounded by the paraphernalia of tubes and wires that were keeping him alive. The consultant neurologist looked on slightly disapprovingly.

'I...I want you to take everything away from him,' she told him huskily.

Holding Oliver's daughter, she watched as they did so. Her eyes blurred with tears as she asked for the wheelchair to be manoeuvred closer to the bed.

Once Oliver was free of everything, she laid their daughter tenderly in the curve of his arm, giving the nurse a grateful look as she realised what Maggie

wanted to do and lifted his arm to guide it round
the baby.

Without her having to say anything the medical
staff melted away, so that it was just the three of them.

'Here she is, Oliver,' Maggie whispered to him.
'Your daughter, and she is so like you. Look at her
nose. It is quite definitely yours,' she laughed. 'And
she's got your long, elegant bones. She's going to be
tall, lucky girl.

'Baby, this is your daddy,' she told her daughter.
'And he is the most wonderful man...' She stopped,
unable to go on, vaguely aware that one of the nurses
had returned and was discreetly taking some photographs.

Through the blur of her tears, she thought she saw
Oliver's eyelids flicker, felt the ripple of sensation as
he tried to move his arm, heard the softness of the
breath in his lungs as he breathed a kiss...as if somehow he knew...as if he could feel their presence...as
if, despite everything, the most elemental, special part
of him was there with them. And for Maggie, it was.

Handing her precious baby over to one of the
nurses, Maggie kept her vigil over Oliver until even
she knew that the coldness of his flesh beneath her
hand meant that he had truly gone.

And then she allowed herself to cry.

They were waiting for her in her private room on
the maternity ward, all of them, alerted to what had
happened by Marcus, who had chanced to hear the
news from a medical colleague.

Alice, her face tear-stained and puffy, Stella for once
without anything to say. And Nicki, holding Maggie
and Oliver's baby with the same fierce maternal pro-

tection and love with which she looked at Maggie herself as she was wheeled back into the room.

There was no need for words. No need for anything. Their presence was enough—their presence, Maggie recognised distantly, was everything.

Epilogue

Just over a year later

Alice reached the restaurant first. Stuart dropped her off. They had been to have lunch earlier with Tom and his wife, putting in place the final arrangements for the Christmas party that Stuart had masterminded for a group of underprivileged teenagers with whom he had become personally involved.

Tom had laughed when Stuart had initially suggested looking for sponsors to finance flying lessons for them, but Stuart had persisted and persevered, knocking on doors, until he'd had the support and the financing, and even retraining himself so that he could teach them.

They were closer now than they had ever been, happier than they had ever been in many ways, Alice acknowledged as she turned to wave to him before walking into the restaurant. He was going to go home and then pick up George and William from school later.

She didn't have to wait long for the others. Stella came in almost immediately, quickly followed by Nicki and Maggie.

'Laura said not to wait for them, as they may be a little bit delayed,' Nicki informed them.

'She's picking Zoë up, isn't she?' Alice checked.

Although Zoë had become an exemplary non-drinker after finishing her rehab and counselling courses, she was still banned from driving, a fact that she accepted with a firm cheerfulness and an open admission that she was lucky the only loss caused by her drink driving was that of her licence.

'Yes,' Nicki confirmed. 'She wanted to drop George and William's Christmas presents off. I don't think it will be very long before Laura and Marcus start their own family. If anything Marcus is even more broody than she is, and that's saying something!'

They all laughed.

'Well, with only a week to go to the wedding and two weeks to Christmas, we're lucky we were able to fit tonight in,' Stella said as they were shown to their table, a round one with ample seating for the six of them.

'What—miss out on our monthly get-together?' Nicki protested, shaking her head. 'No way. No way, ever, ever again.'

For a moment all four of them were silent, looking at one another, sharing in one another's thoughts and feelings without needing the clumsiness of words to communicate.

What Nicki had experienced through her depression had given her an insight and a depth that had allowed her finally to settle proudly and comfortably into her own personality—and it showed.

'That was a wonderful late summer break we all had at your villa, Nicki.' Stella smiled.

'Yes, Kit says we'll have to make it an annual event—and, talking of holidays, how was Canada?'

Before answering her, Stella looked round the table. The love and reassurance she could see in the faces of her friends gave her a warm feeling of security that was like curling into a thick blanket on a cold night.

'Canada was a bit like Jack.' Stella laughed. 'Exhilarating and totally exhausting. Neither of us could believe how much he'd grown, even though Lillian and Julie had both warned us. Which reminds me—you'll never guess what! Julie is thinking about coming back here to do her degree, and she asked Rich and me if she could possibly stay with us. She'll be bringing Jack with her, of course. We told her to think carefully about it and not rush into anything. But if she does decide to come back here, we'd love to have them both. Not that we won't be seeing plenty of them.' Stella beamed. 'Lillian and Gerald have invited us over in the spring, and Gerald was saying that they are planning to come over for a family wedding.'

'Talking of weddings, I've finally found an outfit for Laura and Marcus's,' Nicki announced. 'Well, at least, Laura found it. I was upstairs in the loft getting down the Christmas decorations when she rang.' She pulled a small face. 'I know it's sentimental, but I kept the ones that Jennifer used to use when Laura was little, and I seem to have kept every single one Kit and I have bought ever since. So Laura said the last time she was home that unless I went through them and cleared out all the old stuff, she was going to do it for me. Anyway, she was full of excitement because she'd thought she'd found exactly the right outfit for me and I had to drop everything and meet her in London straight away!'

They discussed wedding clothes for a little, then Maggie asked Alice warmly, 'How's Zoë?'

'She's fine,' Alice responded happily. 'I feel that she's finally beginning to put the past behind her. She and Ian are to divorce and she's really settled into the new house.'

'Zoë has certainly turned her life around,' Nicki approved.

'Yes,' Alice acknowledged. 'She's quite open about the fact that she will always have to consider herself an alcoholic, and she says that she will never drink again. Working for Nicki has made all the difference to her. It's given her a real sense of purpose and achievement. I can't tell you how grateful I am to you for giving her a job, Nicki,' she told Nicki appreciatively.

'There's no need for you to be,' Nicki responded with a smile before informing the others, 'I don't know why I didn't think of asking Zoë to work for me before. I know Maggie also thought of it once. Zoë's a natural—and as it happens it was Laura who suggested it. I must say, though, that I was impressed by their dedication when we were all in Italy, all those faxes to one another and splitting their time off so that one of them was here on hand all the time.

'I don't envy this generation, you know,' Nicki continued seriously. 'We worked hard but we had fun, we were pushing back barriers, exploring, and in some ways it didn't matter if we succeeded or failed, because we had nothing to measure up to other than our own dreams and ideals. Laura and Zoë's generation have so much pressure on them in so many different ways. Although I don't suppose we recognised it at the time, in many ways we were and indeed are a truly privileged generation.'

'How's Bella, Maggie?' Alice asked. She hadn't seen her god-daughter for over a week, and at Bella's age every day, never mind every week, brought amazing changes, especially to god-mamas as adoring and protective as Bella's were.

The vicar had commented that it was a little unusual for a baby to have three godmothers and no godfather, but he had accepted Maggie's decision.

'She's fine,' Maggie answered. 'We were worried that she might be starting with a cold the other day, but it was just a little sniffle.'

'No need to ask who's minding your baby.' Nicki grinned. They all laughed.

'Does Dan actually ever let her out of his sight?' Nicki teased. 'I have never seen a man so besotted…'

Maggie laughed with them.

She and Dan had remarried very quietly that summer. After the ceremony they had gone to Oliver's grave so that Maggie could place her flowers there, and Dan had tactfully left her alone for a little while.

In the shock of Oliver's death, her friends and Dan had gathered protectively around her to shield and love her.

Dan had driven her from the hospital with Bella, to the home she and Oliver had shared together for such a short time, and there she had found, waiting for her, three friends. And they had stayed there that night and for many, many nights after that, keeping a loving watch over her.

It had been discovered via the clinic that the woman who had caused the accident had been a patient there, and had a history of mental disturbance. The paranoid belief she had developed that Maggie had been given her non-existent eggs had stemmed from the fact that she had broken into the clinic and stolen some records, one of which had been Maggie's. For some reason, for which no one could find any real explanation, she seemed to have decided that Maggie had conceived the child that should have been hers.

It had become obvious to Maggie when the police had told her this that the woman must have been responsible for the poison pen letters.

Bella was the image of her father, and Dan adored her—as she did him. Initially Maggie had put up barriers between herself and Dan, but he had persisted patiently in persuading her to allow him to take them down, and the night she had finally accepted his proposal she had had the most wonderful and special dream about Oliver. In it he had been smiling at her as he'd told her how much he wanted her to be happy.

The truth was that she had never really stopped loving Dan, just as she would never, ever allow Oliver to become a forgotten part of Bella's life, or in any way excluded from it.

For Bella's first birthday, Dan had surprised her by presenting her with a photograph album for Bella, filled with dozens of photographs of Oliver, most of which she herself had never even seen.

The discovery that he had spent the months since Bella's birth painstakingly searching for them with just this very occasion in mind had shown Maggie just how much he loved and understood her.

This Christmas was going to be a very, very special one for them. They would be celebrating it at Draycotte Manor, having moved in there immediately after their wedding, and on Christmas Eve, when she and Dan unwrapped their presents to one another and toasted their love, they would be offering up a very special thank-you to Oliver for the gift he had given them both.

'Well, this is it, then,' Laura exclaimed as Zoë got into her car. 'We've made it, fully fledged, fully paid-up members of The Grown-Up Women's Club. Are we sad or what? Feels weird, doesn't it? Socialising with our mothers?'

'Weird but good.' Zoë grinned, adding, 'Do you think we can still claim junior league status and get them to pay?'

'What, now that we've both been made partners in the business?' Laura laughed, referring to the generous and totally unexpected Christmas present Nicki had given them both in the shape of partnerships only a few days earlier.

Picking up his precious, cherished stepdaughter, Dan carried her carefully upstairs to her nursery.

Holding her in his arms, he began to turn the pages of the photograph album he had balanced on his knee.

'And this is your daddy Oliver when he was at school,' he told her softly. He often looked through the album when Maggie wasn't there, so that he and Oliver could have a good old men's chin-wag together about women and life and football, and most of all of course about their wonderful, wonderful daughter. Not that he would ever have admitted as much to Maggie, much less told her how comforting he sometimes found it to open the album and feel that he had someone with whom to share the complex feelings and anxiety that fatherhood was bringing him. And someone, too, who understood and knew Maggie!

'So, won't be long until Christmas now, old chap,' he began, settling Bella firmly against his shoulder. 'Madam here is getting a sack full of stuff, which she will no doubt ignore in favour of the boxes containing it. I've put her name down for that season ticket that we talked about, by the way. I hope she isn't going to be like Maggie and natter on all the way through the game!

'And I hope you don't mind, but I've had a word with Stuart—you remember, Alice's husband—and there's going to be a special donation to this charity he's involved in, in your name. Know you don't like anything showy, but we thought it would be a cause you would like to be connected with. Those kids…'

Ten minutes later, when he quietly closed the door behind him and carried Bella back downstairs, a soft sigh of peacefulness whispered around the room as though somewhere, somehow, an acknowledgement had been made of love given and received.

PENNY JORDAN

66587	POWER PLAY	___ $5.99 U.S.	___ $6.99 CAN.
66515	THE PERFECT SINNER	___ $5.99 U.S.	___ $6.99 CAN.
66444	TO LOVE, HONOR		
	AND BETRAY	___ $5.99 U.S.	___ $6.99 CAN.
66414	A PERFECT FAMILY	___ $5.99 U.S.	___ $6.99 CAN.

(limited quantities available)

TOTAL AMOUNT	$_____
POSTAGE & HANDLING	$_____
($1.00 for one book; 50¢ for each additional)	
APPLICABLE TAXES*	$_____
<u>TOTAL PAYABLE</u>	$_____

(check or money order—please do not send cash)

To order, complete this form and send it, along with a check or money order for the total above, payable to MIRA Books, to: **In the U.S.:** 3010 Walden Avenue, P.O. Box 9077, Buffalo, NY 14269-9077; **In Canada:** P.O. Box 636, Fort Erie, Ontario L2A 5X3.

Name:_____

Address:_____ City:_____

State/Prov.:_____ Zip/Postal Code:_____

Account Number (if applicable):_____

075 CSAS

*New York residents remit applicable sales taxes.
Canadian residents remit applicable GST and provincial taxes.

MIRA®

Visit us at www.mirabooks.com

MPJ1203BL